OBSOLETE

Ghostmaker Book 3

Krista Walsh

Raven's Quill Press

Ottawa, ON

Raven's Quill Press

www.kristawalshauthor.com

Publisher's Note: This is a work of fiction. Names, characters, places, and incidents are a product of the author's imagination. Locales and public names are sometimes used for atmospheric purposes. Any resemblance to actual people, living or dead, or to businesses, companies, events, institutions, or locales is completely coincidental.

Cover Design © John Wenzel/Chris Reddie
Model: Karolina Roussakis

Obsolete / WALSH -- 1st ed.
Print ISBN: 978-1-9994923-8-0

To JY

Because you were who you were, I am who I
am, and this series is what it is

Chapter 1

Jet

"I HATE TOURISTS."

I kept my voice low, barely audible, but at my side, Gideon Leigh responded with a covert smile.

Madison Prince, her dark hair pulled high in a cheery ponytail that looped through the back of a white baseball cap, shot me a warning glance, but I didn't meet her eye.

The three of us were caught in a throng of photo-snapping hikers and history buffs. The morning was clear, the temperature already climbing, and people poured off the tour buses to get onto the grounds of the Mackenzie King Estate.

We stood by the back of the house, overlooking the gardens and tumbled ruins scattered across the property. Ruins that had been intentionally imported and left unfinished. Or so the story went.

Unfortunately, the story was interesting enough to lure

hundreds of people every day to check them out, even this early in the morning, making it impossible for us to access the area we needed without getting stuck behind a fascinated mob of snails.

I tugged on the hem of the T-shirt Madison had bought for me this morning. With Canada Day so close, the local dollar store was full to bursting with a bright array of patriotic garb, so it had been easy to replace the shirt I'd left in the department store change room during my escape from a syndicate heavy-hitter. At least this one was black instead of bright pink, which made me slightly less cranky.

Gideon somehow turned the shapeless blue cotton into a work of art. The T-shirt, a size too small, hugged his arms and stretched across his chest, and the group of women behind us and a few of the men in front of us had spent the better part of the last twenty minutes ogling him.

Even dressed as he was, however, he didn't fit in with the enthusiastic horde wandering the property. He came off as more of a reluctant tag-along, and I doubted I looked any more eager, which put the burden on Madison to keep up appearances.

I'd have to make it up to her later.

At the moment, I couldn't muster much more than the energy it took to stay standing.

My head throbbed. It had ached since I'd stumbled out of the labyrinth of tunnels running under the city of Ottawa, stunned by the revelation that my mentor, my colonel, Michael

Torrence, had betrayed his country—betrayed *me*—by aligning himself with the man who had murdered our department minister. The man who now served as our acting minister. Supernatural, Magical and Occult Affairs Canada had been compromised.

Since the attack a week ago that had killed ten of my twenty troops with a blast of the street drug called ghost, my world had grown smaller and smaller. Every layer of the conspiracy we'd peeled back had revealed a new double-cross. The people we'd once believed were responsible—the leaders of the country's largest supernatural crime syndicate—had turned out to be pawns, which left us face down in a growing pile of shit.

If we failed today to gain the support and resources to fight back, I worried about the future of our country. War between the mundane and supernatural, continued bioterrorism, and who knew what else. The leaders of this attempted coup weren't fucking around, and so far they'd successfully stayed five steps ahead of us.

I blamed my headache on the need to wrap my head around every new sucker punch. The rabbit hole kept getting deeper. More personal. I hadn't fully processed the hell we'd found ourselves in—though, really, I didn't have to understand it. I just had to stop it.

And now here I was, stuck under the hot summer sun, surrounded by people excited to be out of doors and taking in the glimpse of history that was the Estate. Every piercing laugh and childish shriek drove a spike through my right eye into my brain.

"Jet?"

Gideon's voice worked a soothing thread through my discomfort, and I realized I'd closed my eyes against the glare and noise. The lines around his dark stare were tight with concern, and I did my best to smile and reassure him I was fine.

"I hate crowds at the best of times," I said. "I really hate them today."

He grimaced and looked around. "I can't imagine why." At Madison's unimpressed grimace, he cleared his throat. "I mean, from a tourist perspective, the scenery is nice enough."

Madison chuckled and turned away, leading us across the grass towards the stone archway standing alone on the edge of a small wood. Lichen crawled over the carved pillars that stretched upwards into the lowest branches, and sunlight trickled through the thick leaves to create shadows over the grooves and planes. Through the archway was more of the same: trees and people.

"Don't let the photo finish fool you," I told him. "Everything you see here, everything you *think* you see, is so much older than the poster boards say it is. Mackenzie King thought he was in full control of his building plans, importing this stone, leaving these fake fragments of history all over the place."

I nodded towards another ruin segment across the garden, what looked like a bay window broken into five frames, missing only the stained glass to give the appearance of an old wall.

"*La fenêtre de la forêt.* Looks like a perfect place to snap a few photos with your friends, right?" Even as I spoke, a dozen high schoolers posed on the ledge, taking selfies and group shots. "Keep that in mind in a few minutes."

Madison nudged us into the long line in front of the archway, where even more groups waited to take photos or stand still in the dancing shadows to imagine the possibilities.

The young girl in me, the one who used to dress up in princess gowns and twirl in circles until I fell over, understood the appeal. The scene was right out of a medieval fantasy. Standing in that archway, it was easy to believe you were taking your first steps on some epic quest, or about to cross into someplace *other.*

Which was closer to the truth than most people realized.

"We'll have to get a photo of the three of us," Madison said, her voice pitched with an unfamiliar giddiness. She clapped her hands and gave a little hop, then smacked Gideon on the shoulder. "Come on, you can at least throw on a bit of a smile, can't you? We're here, it's beautiful. If we don't send Mum a picture, you *know* she'll be disappointed."

Gideon scowled and shoved his hands into his pockets. "Anything for you, *sis.*"

She turned to me. "And of course *you* have to be in it. You're part of the family now. Mum will want to put this photo on the mantel."

She gave me no time to answer before she prattled on about the sites she wanted to hit today. I was grateful I only had to listen, because my thoughts were a blurred mess over what awaited us when we took our turn in the archway.

The orderly queue moved group by group as the heat of the crowd pressed in on me.

Although Madison maintained a steady excitement in her tone, I recognized the freak-out happening behind her happy expression. She was the empath, but I wasn't without empathy.

It had been over a decade since she'd been here, and if our mission didn't go the way we wanted, she might never leave. The fact she wasn't hyperventilating or making a run for it was more than a little impressive.

"Have you been here before?" Gideon asked me.

I guessed he didn't mean the tourist side of things.

"A few times." We shuffled forward in the line. "The first time, I was still in diapers. My parents brought me."

Me between my mother and father. The memory was vague, foggy, more dream than reality. Had my mother really been as uncomfortable as I remember? My hand had been tight in my dad's, that much I knew for sure because I felt the pressure around my fingers as I stood here today, as though he were beside me right now. He'd been excited, crouching down and pointing everything out. Mom… I couldn't see her clearly. I thought I remembered her standing apart, looking around as though afraid someone was about to swoop in and devour her.

"I don't remember this, but Dad loves to tell me I cried the whole time," I said with a chuckle. "He presented me to the queen, and she took me in her arms and told me to stop. According to Dad, I did. Just like that. I couldn't look away from her. He says the only other time my eyes grew that wide was when I saw my cake on my second birthday. What I do remember is the most beautiful face I've ever seen. She still pops into my dreams from time to time. Sometimes calm, sometimes cold, but always perfect."

"That must have been quite an honour, being presented to the queen?"

"Yes and no. Yes that she held me, but not so much that we were there. It's parental choice, of course, but it's good politics for supernaturals to present their children at court. It shows respect for both sides of the wall. Confirmation that you agree to obey the rules laid down by the department and the realm."

I looked around to make sure no one was listening, but my voice was low enough—both to avoid detection and to prevent the extra noise from sparking my headache—that we hadn't attracted anyone's curiosity.

"Since then, I've come twice on business. Both times to meet with her advisers, never with Meril."

"Is it normal for there to be so much crossover between the court and the department?"

"It's not unusual. Bastien was a traditionalist, more inclined to keep the Shadow Council aware of any issues than some ministers have been, so we've seen a rise in diplomatic visits."

Gideon's brow furrowed, and I understood his confusion. The United States didn't have to deal with the wall. They could access the realm through designated doorways, but for the most part, all that awaited them on the other side were areas they chose to maintain. Markets, hideaways, isolated vacation spots. All official matters were dealt with in this world. One government, one plane of existence. Simpler in some ways, but less tidy in others.

"That's the side of Canadian supernatural culture many people don't know about," I said. "Lots of us turn our backs on the realm and rely on the protection of the perception filter and the resources the department offers. That's fine. We're entitled to that independence as part of the agreement made with the queen when SMOAC was founded, but it also means the court holds no obligation to help if you run into trouble."

"So it's an ultimatum? Swear allegiance to me or best of luck?"

"Not allegiance so much as leaving the door open. My loyalty is—" I stumbled, cleared my throat. "Despite everything, it remains to the department. If I ever had to choose between the two, I know the decision I'd make. But it's a matter of respect to report any unresolvable issues to the queen and her advisers. Especially if there's a possibility our people are in danger and SMOAC is not in a position to help them."

"In the hope she'll step in?"

"Hope isn't the word I'd use. If we were to ask her, it would be as an absolute, end-of-the-world last resort. Think of her as a kraken. If she rises from the depths, forget secrecy. The wall will shatter and the entire world will know that Canada, at least, has a face it keeps hidden. From there, it's a short jump to realizing every country is two-sided."

Gideon frowned and glanced at the archway as though expecting Meril to waltz through. "Would she take that risk? Doesn't she agree with the secrecy laws?"

I shrugged. "She does as far as it keeps her people safe. But if they're threatened? She won't hide on her throne." I paused, letting the weight of my meaning sink in. Depending on how our meeting turned out today, our lives as we knew them might change forever, and the us-against-them mentality we'd worked so hard to avoid would be inevitable.

"How long after that until we're hunted?" I wondered aloud, my worry a steady throb as my headache worsened. "Until we have to fight to protect ourselves, revealing more of what we're capable of? We might win in the end, but that's not a guarantee, and if we lost, what would the mundanes do without us? They have no idea how big a role we play in keeping them safe from evils they don't know exist."

A shudder ran through me, and I massaged the back of my neck as my muscles tensed.

"Are we sure this is our best bet?" Gideon asked, looking around us again. "I know Madison's been summoned, but couldn't we have found a way to put the queen off until we had something final to offer?"

"We would never have been able to keep Madi hidden, not now that Meril's deployed her Eyes. And it would be so much worse for us if we tried. Besides, Madi's right—going to the queen now makes us look good and gives Meril time to prepare for any eventuality. If we play this smart, and we're really lucky, the three of us get to walk out of here with a few extra resources."

"And if we're unlucky?"

I swallowed hard. "Then Madison will be bound to the Shadow Council, and you and I will have to make do with what we have. And brace ourselves for what happens if Gagnon wins."

Darkness cloaked the scale weighing our options, leaving me unable to guess which side we'd come down on. The queen's temper was notoriously unpredictable. It was the reason so many of our kind had opted to leave when the opening presented itself a hundred and fifty years ago. They'd wanted to escape her anger, her spies, her total control over every element of their lives.

My father had wanted to introduce me to this part of the world, to teach me how to show it the respect our history deserved, but when the Shadow Council had offered him a position at court, he'd refused, as much for my and my brother's sakes as for his and my mother's. It wasn't a life he felt any of his family should have to endure. Especially when my mundane mother and brother would have faced the brunt of supernatural prejudice.

The risk of being pulled back now was greatest for Madison, her being the queen's descendant and already having received a summons, but I had to be ready to trade my freedom as well if Meril commanded it. Gideon, being an American citizen, would be exempt, but who knew what she might demand of him instead.

"Maybe it would be better if you waited for us here," I said. Although I hated the idea of losing his steady presence at my side, it wasn't fair to lead him yet again into the unknown when the cost might be his freedom. "Meril doesn't give anything for nothing, not even in an emergency. I can't guarantee what we'll face once we're over there."

He caught my gaze, the deep brown of his eyes boring into me, drawing me in, lifting me out of myself.

"I told you I'm staying with you until this is over. Whatever she wants from me, I'll listen. If it's not something I want to give, I'll deal with it."

Sparks flew through my stomach, tightening the muscles down my legs and around my back. I wanted to touch him, to draw from his strength and courage as mine slipped away. My throat closed, and I looked away to gain control over myself.

What was wrong with me?

Before last week, I hadn't cried in years. So long ago, I

didn't remember what I'd cried about. Over the past couple of days, I couldn't stop the tears, unable to face a slight breeze without my emotions overwhelming me.

My sorrow over the loss of my team was bad enough, but Gideon… He'd triggered a whole slew of feelings I couldn't sort out, and the confusion was almost worse than the grief.

"Finally," Madison said. "Our turn. Come on." She grabbed our hands and dragged us towards the archway.

I had no idea if she'd overheard any of our conversation or if she'd been lost in her thoughts, but she acted as though we really were a trio out enjoying the day, to hell with anyone who tried to ruin it. I wished I knew what was going through her head, the true face behind the smile, but this was hardly the time to ask.

We crossed the grass, and as we got closer to the archway, vibrations hummed in the air and under my feet. Not anything the mundane would sense—not that they'd realize, anyway— but as clear to me as though a loud bass rumbled underground, radiating up through the soles of my boots. I clung to the air molecules whipping around my head and worked to settle them, but they wouldn't be tamed. My attempts spread the vibrations through the rest of my body, making the hairs on my arms and the back of my neck dance.

I let the air go, not wanting to put myself more off balance than I already was, and the sensation eased but didn't disappear.

"Whoa…" Gideon whispered as we climbed the steps to

the threshold of the archway.

"Smile for the camera!" Madison cried, and held her phone out in front of us. "Say *chlaid mo feanna!*"

I repeated the words, the lilting sounds tripping over my tongue as though the syllables came from somewhere outside me. They were clumsy, rough in my mouth, but as soon as they were out, a wave of power washed over me, and I shivered. The vibrations evolved into a smoother flow of magic, a stronger force than anything I experienced on the mundane side of the wall.

Gideon stumbled over the words, mumbled them so badly I worried he wouldn't trigger the spell, but as soon as he fell silent, he stiffened, and his gaze darted around as he sensed the change. The doorway was open. Easy as that.

And the people awaiting their turn in the archway hadn't noticed a thing.

Madison turned first, raised her chin, and squared her shoulders. She took a hesitant step forward, crossed through the archway opposite the way we'd come, and strode ahead until she passed out of sight.

I wondered what the mundanes in front of us thought of her disappearance, how their brains rationalized the impossible. The question occurred to me often, whenever the reality of our world flaunted itself in the innocence of theirs, but never more than when the sense of *other* was so overpowering.

From what my father had taught me about how the perception filter worked, their brains would hurry to create a logical memory, filling in the void where Madison should have been: stepping down from the archway and walking away. Still here on this field and finished with her photographs, on to the next site.

Whatever they believed, there was no surprise in anyone's eyes. No confusion or amazement.

As if nothing out of the ordinary had happened.

Letting their disinterest calm my anxiety, I followed Madison through the doorway, appreciating Gideon's closeness as we crossed the wall.

Into another world.

The differences were subtle at first—the same trees, the same grass. It was only when I looked more closely that I noticed the different species of plants and the vividness of the colours. The leaves were greener, the flowers a brighter hue than existed in our world. Everything touched by beauty and magic, their true natures, their best natures, visible to anyone who cared to see it.

To our left was the window of the forest, the stone wall around the window frames whole instead of in ruin, no longer freestanding on the edge of the garden but the exterior of a gatehouse. It was currently unoccupied, though it usually housed someone to greet high-ranking guests who arrived to request an audience with the queen.

Gideon spun in a slow circle, tilting his head back to take in the height of the trees and the clearness of the sky. "This is…"

He trailed off with a shake of his head.

"It's something, isn't it?" I said.

"That's one way of putting it. I don't think I could get any more specific."

Madison stopped a few metres ahead, waiting for us to catch up.

"So, where are we headed?" Gideon asked. "Everything looks… the same. Not the same, but the same."

Despite my stress over what came next, I couldn't help but laugh at his awe. His reaction was identical to my own the first time I'd come here in my capacity as a SMOAC captain.

Being here was like looking at the world in a funny mirror, one that distorted the image reflecting back at you, but in such tiny ways it took a while for your brain to catch up with reality.

Even now, I had trouble settling everything into place, but having expected it, I wasn't quite as disoriented.

"That way," Madison said, pointing left beyond the trees.

It was the same stretch of paths and field we would have followed on the other side of the wall. The same crowds, the same trees, the same sunshine. But over here, the crowds weren't tourists, they were residents going about their business, and more than a few of them would have drawn stunned gazes from the people snapping photos in the archway. Some had wings, some had four legs, some six—though still walking on two feet. Skin tones ranged from blue to grey to mottled green, and the eyes staring at us were white or gold or slitted through like a lizard's.

There were no perception filters here, no hiding. None of that was necessary. We knew who and what we were, so there was nothing to fear.

While millions of our kind had fled the queen's authoritarian rule, just as many had stayed behind for the freedom to be themselves. It was why the wall mattered, and another reason the consequences of it falling were so great.

Gideon looked down at himself and started. I followed his gaze to the layer of mist swirling around him, hugging close to his skin and following every slight movement he made.

"It's always there," I said, "even if it's not visible. Your magic is heightened in the realm, making the subtler parts of your ability easier to see. I bet dissolving would take you half the effort it usually does."

He raised his hands and watched the mist dance over his palms and around his wrists. In a smooth display, one hand disappeared, the mist keeping the shape of his fingers as he dragged them through the air. He rematerialized in the same sweep, still staring at his palm. "Huh." His attention shifted to my forehead, and surprise flickered through his gaze. "Your eye."

I brushed my fingers over the fine ridges of my third eye. "I know. The first time I came here as an adult and caught sight of myself in a mirror, I'm pretty sure I spent a good five minutes checking it out."

On the other side of the wall, my secondary ability looked

like nothing more than faint scarring in a somewhat eye-like shape, growing more noticeable when I used it. Here, there was nothing faint about the pale shimmering lines that stood out in sharp contrast to my skin, the definition of the eyelid, which I hadn't even known existed until I'd come here.

I closed my physical eyes and opened my third, chuckling at Gideon's audible reaction as the lid raised, the white iris and open pupil staring boldly at him. Even my ability to see the memories of the objects I came in contact with was enhanced, no longer vague shadows but blurred specifics, detailed with a fuzzy silver glow, like watching a scene from underwater as the light poured in. All around us moved figures from the last few minutes, all the various footwear and feet that had trampled this grass. A boring reveal in and of itself but hinting at the potential of what I would see if I rested my hand against the gatehouse wall and pressed back through time. A shame my priorities had never given me the opportunity to play.

Opening my other two eyes, I allowed the third to close and nodded towards Madison, who had once again outstripped us. "Wait until we get to court. I'm the least of the wonders here."

"I doubt that," he said, and the weight of his voice, the gentle certainty, the intensity in his eyes, dropped like pebbles in my heart and rippled out to the tips of my fingers.

Heat swirled under my skin, creeping upwards, and I turned away, unsure how to respond and embarrassed by my uncertainty.

What the hell was wrong with me? I wasn't some googly-eyed teenager, but he turned me into someone I didn't recognize. The way he'd looked at me after we'd spent the night together spun through my thoughts, tightening the pit of my stomach, and I pushed the memory away. If we came out of this—and that was a big if—there would be time to figure everything out, but for now I had to stay focused. Michael had called the queen's court a dragon's den, and while I disagreed with him about almost everything else, that much was true. All this sentiment messing up my head was a distraction that wouldn't serve me.

The future of our supernatural population was on the line. Getting justice for my team had to come before my hormonal urges.

Somewhere in the back of my mind, a voice cried out that having Gideon here to support me, an emotional buoy to keep me afloat in this tidal wave bearing down on us, was one of the few anchors for my courage, but that voice was all but drowned out by the steady ache in my head.

I quickened my step and caught up with Madison, who hadn't slowed to walk with us. I didn't want to guess why she'd given us space. If she was encouraging him, she and I would need to sit down and have a few words. She was supposed to be *my* friend, helping me get what *I* wanted, which was not, at this particular moment in time, Gideon, no matter what she thought she read from me. What I wanted was Lucien Gagnon's head under my boot, Mark O'Malley's balls in my grip, and Peter Dougall begging me to spare his life. And maybe, if it was possible, Michael to look me in the eye and tell me everything he'd said in the Labyrinth had been a horrible joke and he was still the man I'd looked up to all these years.

Gritting my teeth to steel my determination, I looked to Madison. "What's your plan to get in to see her?"

My question must have come out harsher than I'd intended, because she threw me a look from under the brim of her cap, and I stared into the trees to avoid her silent questions.

"I'd planned to walk in and request an audience," she said, not pushing the issue. "Ideally before anyone tips her off that we're here."

I was about to ask how anyone would recognize us when someone walked out of the forest. Their lizard eyes flicked my way as their tongue darted over their lips. The green tint of their skin blended into the grass until they passed in front of a tree, at which point it shifted into a dull, muted brown.

"I guess we do stand out."

"It's the T-shirts," Madison said. "I don't think these guys appreciate the whole Canada Day thing. Or the whole T-shirts thing."

I took in what the folks walking by us were wearing—some only in leaves, some in loose, flowing cotton, others in nothing at all. "I can't remember the last time I felt so overdressed."

"The more attention we attract, the faster we lose the upper hand, so let's make it to the throne room before anyone stops us to ask what we're doing here."

"Too late," Gideon grumbled.

I hadn't realized he'd fallen into step behind us, but when I glanced over my shoulder, I found him glaring at something to our right. I turned to look, and my heart leapt into my throat.

Four guards, clad in the green and brown of the royal house, approached us, swords drawn.

We stopped where we were, and I held back from drawing the air closer around me. We weren't here to fight.

"Halt," the head guard said, a captain by his stripes. A steel faceplate hid his features, the visor moulded into a raven's beak. "By order of the Blessed of the Realm, the Queen of Faerie, Her Majesty the Divine Ruler of the Magical Order of Calibne, Her Royal Highness Queen Meril, you are charged with breaking the tenth order of the supernatural mandate." The guards spread out, closing in on us from every direction. "I arrest you in the queen's name and sentence you to perish in the marsh jail."

Chapter 2

Madison

I WASN'T SURE if I was more amused or more furious.

I wanted to laugh, but equally strong was the urge to let Jet punch the man in the throat and kick him once he dropped.

"Is this change in the queen's hospitality a reflection of her loss of manners or a rise in poor counsel?" I asked, straightening my shoulders.

"How da—"

"Before you sentence us to anything, Captain, it would be in your best interest to bring us before Her Majesty. I believe she's expecting us."

The guard shifted his hold on his weapon and tightened his grip. "I will do nothing of the sort. You come here, dressed as you are, without a proper escort, and think you're entitled to make demands?"

Red spots danced in my vision. "The tenth order of the supernatural mandate you so boldly quoted states that no member of the court shall invite a mundane behind the wall without express permission from the queen. Unless you know something I don't, you'll find no one here is of mundane blood." My anger grew, and I blocked out the crowd forming around us, focused only on the incompetent, self-important twit in front of me. "I believe what you intended to say was that we broke the *fourteenth* order of the mandate, which states that no member of the court shall make use of the doorways to the realm when mundane eyes might pay witness. You *might* have a claim there, except for the twelfth exception, which states that such entrance *will* be permitted in the case of urgent business, and, I assure you, the business I bring to the queen's attention certainly falls under the category of *urgent*."

How I made it through all that without a tremor in either my hand or my voice was a miracle, but I earned quite a few nods of approval from the curious onlookers we'd collected.

I was never more grateful that my grandmother had made me learn the supernatural royal code from start to finish in my earliest studies, quizzing me on every order and condition on the long list.

"Knowledge of the system is never a waste of brainpower, *chailene*," she'd told me. "It can't hurt to learn it, and throwing it in someone's face can be incredibly satisfying."

She'd been right on both counts.

"While I'm pointing out the gaps in your training," I continued, "may I also say that if this is how you treat visitors to the court, with threats instead of welcome, then there has been a significant drop in standards since my last visit. I have to believe the queen knows nothing about it, because it has the makings of a diplomatic disaster."

Everything I said was true, but was the lack of proper etiquette a sign of failing leadership or evidence of rising tensions on this side of the wall? The discontent spreading through the protests and riots in our world about Meril's authority was worrisome enough, but if she lost control of her territory, our troubles would be so much greater.

My lecture didn't appear to sway the captain's opinions. I sensed his frustration that my performance had garnered enough interest to make his threat of the marsh jail empty. Word would spread quickly to the queen's inner circle if he tried to carry it out, which would not end well for him.

"If your business is so urgent, you can leave it with me," he said. "And if you turn around right now with no further fuss, I'll retract your sentence and pass your message on to the Shadow Council."

"No." I crossed my arms and made it clear there was no room for negotiation. "As a member of her court, I have a right to claim audience with the queen, which you know by the second order of the supernatural mandate."

I could have told him about the summons—informing him

of my relation to the crown would have him on his knees in obeisance in a heartbeat—but to do so would pass any small power I held back to Meril. If I was going to march into that throne room, it would be on my terms.

Behind his faceplate, the guard made a noise I guessed was a scoff. "Queen Meril is far too busy for an impromptu audience with othersiders. You'd stand a better chance if you left word with me and returned when you were properly summoned."

"Listen, asswipe," Jet said, and I cringed at her unleashed impatience. Her fatigue, pain, and fury swept over me in an acidic fizz, but I had no time to hold her back before she closed the distance between them. By her careful movement, she was conscious of the direction of his blade, but that didn't prevent her from drawing within a few inches of him. "If you don't take us to Meril immediately, Captain, me and my friends will spread the location of this doorway to every single blogger who has ever expressed a smidge of interest in the supernatural. Good luck dealing with the flocks who'll show up tomorrow to poke around."

Another surge of anger flared around me, this one from all four guards, and though they remained still, their superior looked ready to make his reaction physical. Gideon's pride and amusement tickled the fringes of my mind, but I worried his triumph was premature. The guard captain might not be able to throw us into an impenetrable black pit, but he *could* try to exile us from the realm. And I suspected he wouldn't hesitate, especially if he guessed how much our debate entertained the growing crowd.

"It wouldn't matter what you told them," he said, his tone smug. "They would never get through without the words, and if you shared *those*, you would certainly get your wish to see Her Majesty. You would see her long enough to receive the sentence of a slow and agonizing death for breaking the first order of the mandate. And *that* one—" he shot me a dirty glance "—I know is correct. Forget the marsh jail. The tortures that would rain down upon you would have you screeching for mercy."

In his arrogance, I found our way in. An ambitious man, he believed himself to hold a higher position in court than his current rank indicated. His desire for power and recognition flared like a beacon in the face of Jet's challenge, an easy mark for me to manipulate.

I chuckled and moved beside Jet, sliding the flat of his blade away with the back of my hand. "We wouldn't need to give them a way in. How do you suppose Her Majesty would react if her couriers weren't able to deliver her favourite oranges, the doorway blocked by nosy believers and determined skeptics? On whom do you think she would vent her wrath if she discovered you were the reason for the delay? Especially once she discovered the full impact of your obstruction. If you want to prove yourself worthy of her attention, I suggest you stand aside and allow us to deliver our message. If you do, then instead of being the cause of her fury, you would be helping to prevent a disaster beyond what our kind has seen since the wall was raised."

At the silence from behind his faceplate, I wrapped myself in confidence and stepped closer, lowering my voice so only he would hear me. "I can picture it now—Meril's gratitude, the appreciation of the entire court. Forget guard captain. You could be looking at a promotion to her private service. Or maybe a position within the Shadow Council. If it turns out our message isn't as important as we believe it to be, you can be the one who brought us forward to face justice. Either way, a win for you in front of the realm. Isn't that worth a few minutes out of your day?"

His aura trembled with uncertainty, but the possibility that I was right and glory awaited him for such little effort won out. He sheathed his sword and stepped back to give us some breathing room.

"If the matter is as critical as you say, the least we can do is escort you to Her Royal Highness's audience chamber forthwith."

I glanced at Gideon, and he nodded, impressed. Jet, however, stood pale-faced and shaking. A sheen of sweat coated her brow. I frowned in concern, but she caught my eye and shook her head in silent assurance that I shouldn't worry. I didn't believe her for a second but couldn't break our united front to pester her. We'd won our point with the captain and were about to get what we'd come for. As soon as we left our audience with Meril, I would make sure she got some rest. The temptation to crawl into her brain and force her to sleep nagged at me, but I ignored it. She was an adult, even if she behaved like a child avoiding bedtime.

I did wish I had a better understanding of what was wrong with her before we marched into the unknown, though. Tensions were high enough without her throwing any extra surprises my way. And I knew there was something wrong, no matter what she said.

From the time we'd found her in the Labyrinth, Jet's aura had changed, and continued to change. When I'd read her last night, I'd picked up on something I could only describe as hunger buried beneath her fear, heartbreak, and rage. I'd thought it might be a seed of vengeance, a waking desire to destroy the man who'd broken her trust, but now, twelve hours later, the hunger had grown, and it was like nothing I'd ever sensed before. If I hadn't been sure it was coming from Jet, I wouldn't have recognized it as part of her. It was so unfamiliar. So… alien.

As I read her now, I was alarmed to find it had begun to block her other emotions from detection, either spreading so far across her brain chemistry it blanketed everything else… or absorbing them into itself. I worried what it meant for her ability to see things clearly, but as long as she was here, putting one foot in front of the other, my only option was to watch and wait.

When she set off behind the guard, I followed, and Gideon fell into step beside me, his jaw set, his gaze hard. Was he wary of the guards, or did he also sense something off about our leader? At least I found comfort in the fact that, even if I wound up stuck here, Jet would have someone keeping an eye on her.

Our escort led us across the field towards the Abbey. In the mundane world, the scene appeared as a collection of unfinished ruins: a wall here, a few windows there, half-covered by long grass and worn down by years of people sitting, touching, climbing over the stone.

In the realm, the palace was a towering structure, the arches of the doors reaching as high as some of the treetops. The fleur-de-lys windows on both sides of the elongated entryway were unscreened and unshuttered, letting the bright uncovered sunlight spill across the white marble floor. Our boots thudded across the stone as we marched towards the far end of the audience chamber. The walls around the windows on both sides of the room were cloaked in tapestries and framed mirrors that made the space stretch into infinity.

A few faces popped into the mirrors of beings not in the room, species that existed on entirely different planes or were too far away to be here in person, and a few familiar folks waved at me. I nodded my acknowledgement but otherwise ignored the attention bearing down on us.

Our clothes were enough to draw eyes our way, and the royal escort had piqued even more interest, but I suspected the sizeable crowd was minuscule compared to what it would become once word spread about who I was.

The prodigal great-great granddaughter returned.

The woman who had sworn never to step foot in the Abbey again not only responding to a summons but asking for help to save a world she had already given up so much to protect.

Heat swept into my cheeks, and sheer willpower kept me from turning tail or throwing up all over the guard's livery.

My nerves stretched taut, braced for Meril's mental games and manipulations. She would manoeuvre this meeting to get what she wanted; my challenge would be to lay out the situation so our wants aligned. Doing so was my only key out of here.

Maybe we would be lucky and find her in one of her benevolent moods. She loved to play the generous benefactor, and I would happily face her condescension over her wrath.

The far end of the room came into view, most of the wall taken up by a window that reached from floor to ceiling, broken into three panels of stained glass that threw a kaleidoscope of jewel tones over the southern wall.

In front of the window, atop a dais, sat a carved wooden throne that looked as though someone had shaped it out of a growing tree, all twisting branches and worn knots. The queen was perched on the edge of the seat in a gown of dark green silk, the details in the skirt so defined and intricate I did a double-take to confirm it wasn't made up of a thousand leaves stitched together, each one veined and almost pulsing with life. A spatter of star-like diamonds splashed across her off-the-shoulder bodice. A yellow diamond the size of my fist rested against her collarbone on a fine silver chain.

When she'd visited my dreams and pulled me into her illusion, a meadow between worlds, her power had been dulled, relaxed. Here, the force of it prickled my skin. She was the forest incarnate, the epicentre of the magical flow that amplified our abilities. Standing in her presence, I picked up the emotions of every person in the room with such striking clarity that, if I tried, I could pinpoint who was feeling what without a moment's effort.

A gift that could be mine forever if I chose to stay. The thought was intoxicating. Beautiful. Tempting.

Dangerous.

It was why so many of our kind came from across the country to stand in Meril's shadow. If you had the opportunity to be the strongest, best version of yourself, wouldn't you be drawn to it as a moth to the flame?

Pity the odds of burning up were almost guaranteed.

It was part of why I fought so hard against coming here. I didn't want to be inundated by other people's emotions all the time. Not when it came at the expense of recognizing my own. But my feelings would no longer matter. Everything I sensed would be for the queen's benefit. My own needs, goals, dreams would be irrelevant.

Meril, the mother of the supernatural across this stretch of

North America. The queen who nurtured and scolded, praised and punished.

If anyone knew exactly what she was, they never spoke of it, and if she had ever revealed her true nature, the story had passed beyond memory. Nothing about her was certain. Not even her beautiful, perfect face. Theories abounded, of course. Demon, angel, goddess, the personification of magic—the possibilities were countless.

In the end, of course, it didn't matter. The myth she had built around herself had instilled the belief that to divest her of her throne would be to rupture the fabric of Canada's supernatural world.

Love her or hate her, we wouldn't survive without her.

For that reason, her royal guard comprised over three thousand soldiers, each of them the strongest, fastest, smartest of our kind on this side of the wall. Six of them stood by her throne, three on either side, lining the green strip of carpet that stretched down the centre of the floor and stopped a few metres in front of the dais.

Onto this carpet I now stepped, Jet and Gideon on either side of me, with our escort hanging back to create a barricade behind us. To protect us or take us in depending on the queen's response, but it made for a nice, formal presentation as we strode towards the throne.

Meril showed no reaction to my early, and willing, arrival, and the barriers around her mind were too strong for me to read her. Her face may as well have been carved from the same marble as the floor. Cold. Unmoving. Unreadable.

So different from the woman who'd visited my dreams.

I wished I knew which version of her was closer to the truth.

We stopped at the top of the carpet, and I bowed at the waist. I may have looked like a slob in my jeans and T-shirt, but etiquette had to be upheld.

When I straightened, I found Meril's inscrutable gaze fixed on me. It might have been a glower or simple curiosity, or it might have been joy at seeing me again, but since I couldn't be bothered to guess, I stared back, refusing to be intimidated.

"In darkness you were summoned, to secrecy sworn, yet you flaunt our mandates to cross a public doorway in high sun, Madison Prince, great-granddaughter of Clarissa who crossed the wall, blood of my blood."

It wasn't the most auspicious start, but I wouldn't let her cow me. Her melodious voice filled every corner of the room. No murmurs or whispers filled the silence as the final notes of her opening speech faded, no sneezes or throat clearings. Every person here, with more of them streaming in through the open doors, was riveted by the scene playing out. That was the power, the control, Meril held over her people.

I wanted to cough. Laugh. Dance a jig. Anything to break the spell that shrouded the Abbey. For now, however, I remained still and said nothing. It was better if she got this whole giving-me-crap thing out of her system. Then we could get to business.

"I know why you've come," she said, as though reading my mind—which she may well have. "For nearly two centuries, I have governed my court from this throne, safeguarding the realm and leaving the rest of my people to be led by your mundane prime minister." She spoke the title with a hint of a sneer that didn't cross fully into disgust. "Now trouble rises beyond the wall. My people are in danger, and those sworn to inform me of such a threat remain silent. Tell me, great-granddaughter of Clarissa, what right had you to withhold information from me?"

The challenge bore down on me. Depending on how we responded, we would be admitting that we didn't recognize her authority, that we knew we'd broken the rules, or that we'd failed to handle the issue ourselves.

A lose-lose discussion regardless of how we proceeded.

I'd spent most of the morning preparing for this confrontation, but Jet spoke before I could. "The situation was too serious for rash action. The department is no longer secure."

It took everything I had not to wince. What was she doing? We'd agreed I would do the talking, having the greatest understanding of how the court worked and what our best methods would be to gain the queen's support.

I stretched out my mind to test hers, and her frustration wrapped its scratching hands around my throat, the same impatience that had pushed her to take over with the guard captain. Whether it was her pain, her exhaustion, or her disinterest in playing the game of courtly intrigue, she'd opted to cut to the chase.

Anger burned in my chest, but there was no point in letting it grow. The only way we stood a chance now was if we stood together, which meant letting Jet take the lead and praying she didn't sink our cause before we made our position and request clear.

I returned my attention to Meril to observe her reaction and was shocked to note a crack in her marble veneer of control as her eyes narrowed the tiniest bit. Uncle Sercario had told me the queen was aware of the corruption in the department, but was it possible the full truth hadn't reached her? I wondered if our bringing the update to her directly would help or hinder my chances of getting home.

"Eight days ago," Jet began, "a criminal known as the Ghostmaker planted a chemical bomb in Ottawa's city centre. My squad was on the scene, having been ordered to shut down the leaders of a crime syndicate that has caused thousands of deaths, supernatural and mundane, over the years, most recently thanks to the distribution of the drug referred to as ghost. The intelligence we received was false and, as a result, half my team was killed in the blast."

Her throat bobbed, but her voice remained strong.

"I took it on myself to uncover the truth behind the attack, and my investigation has exposed a web so interwoven with the department that the threat to both sides of the wall is severe."

I questioned Jet's logic in being so forward. Making Meril work for details in exchange for reciprocal measures would have been my approach. Instead, she was revealing our whole hand, and I feared we would walk away with nothing.

While part of me wanted to tackle her to the ground to shut her up, I held still, teeth clenched, and allowed her to continue.

On my other side, Gideon looked as uncomfortable as I felt, and his gaze jumped around the room, searching for threats closer to home.

Jet took Meril through everything. The deaths of the informants who had first led Michael to order his squad into the high-rise, the syndicate moles in the department, the evidence in the documentation, the minister's murder, the proof against the deputy minister, and, finally, the connection to the head of SMOAC's special forces.

As Jet peeled away each layer of our mess, Meril's expression first opened in shock, then shut down and grew increasingly stoic. I tried to read her, but her emotions were as closed off as her face, as resistant as the stone wall behind her.

The rest of the room wasn't nearly as guarded.

Fear, shock, anger—the thickness of the crowd's negativity poured over me like hundreds of sharp pinpoints, each one pricking my vulnerable soul. I did my best to block them out, but there were too many individual barbs to tend off, and when

I closed in on myself to get rid of them, I lost all sense of Jet and Gideon. The emotional silence was too claustrophobic, a dense fog suffocating me.

So I relaxed my guard and tried to embrace the fear instead of avoiding it. This was why we had come, after all. Because it *was* terrifying. SMOAC was the stalwart fortress that protected our people on the other side of the wall. If it fell, it meant nothing was untouchable. It meant the wall itself would follow. It would have to. Meril couldn't leave her people stranded and unprotected while they suffered, their rights revoked and security threatened.

"So we come to you," Jet said, wrapping up our week from hell. "We have formed our resistance to defend the department, and we stand ready to fight. The reason for our delay in reporting to you was to determine the feasibility of our success. To present you with options for how to proceed instead of dropping only the problem at your feet."

She fell silent, and the vacuum of sound stole my breath. Even the hum of emotion evaporated as everyone awaited the queen's response. I felt nothing, heard nothing, and the void left me light-headed. I wished I had something sturdy to rest my hand on to keep my balance, but to show any sign of weakness would be to open myself up to the queen's manipulations, and standing this close to her, exhausted and afraid, I didn't know if I would be strong enough to resist.

I also fought the urge to applaud Jet's performance and

cursed myself for doubting her. Giving Meril all the details, showing her how hard we'd worked and how far we'd come on our own, demonstrated how crucial we were to the resolution of the issue. No one understood the threat better than we did, and no one stood as good a chance to end Lucien's plans before it was too late. The three of us, as a team. Ergo, she had to let me go.

Again, I reached my mind towards Meril, testing the barrier, expecting nothing, and to my amazement a trickle of rage slipped through her self-control.

The trickle grew, turning into a stream, and finally a river of fury. In the deluge, I expected her to heave herself out of her throne and pace the room, but if anything, she grew more still. The air around her seemed to crackle, the vibrations of an oncoming storm.

Although she didn't move, not even a blink, the reaction of the guards as they shifted on their feet, preparing to act, told me they sensed the change as well as I did.

After a few moments of excruciating suspense, Meril spoke to her seneschal through stiff lips. "Clear the hall. Leave the Eyes."

Her seneschal, an older woman who appeared as brown and wrinkled as an ancient tree, nodded and stepped to the middle of the audience chamber, stopping behind the guards who had escorted us here.

"Clear the hall," she said, projecting her voice so it filled every nook and cranny, every crack between the stone.

I wondered that her word would carry more weight than Meril's, but as the thought came to me, the desire to turn and walk out nearly overwhelmed me. When I looked down at my feet, I found they had moved without my knowledge, half-turning me towards the door. A quick look at Jet and Gideon showed them similarly affected, Gideon a full step backwards before he'd stopped, Jet half-twisted to face the exit. And the command hadn't even included us.

My changed perspective allowed me a view of the rest of the room as lines of people walked out of the Abbey in an orderly fashion, the glances over their shoulders giving away their reluctance to leave as their bodies gave them no choice.

I turned back to the queen once the only people remaining were her guards and a half-dozen people previously mixed into the crowd. The six strangers came to the front of the room, each taking place by a guard. Their skin was golden and their eyes were black. They each wore a simple brown tunic and soft, billowing brown trousers. Nothing particular about them, nothing conspicuous. Eyes as they appeared on this side of the wall. Nothing like my hoodie-wearing messenger from the other night.

For a full minute, the hall remained quiet, the queen apparently lost in thought, though her gaze bored into the three of us in turn. I didn't turn my head to check on the others, but I sensed the chill of Gideon's steeled stubbornness and the grittiness of Jet's exhausted resignation. We had made our move, the only one we had, and now we would see how the rest played out.

"I had no idea the situation was as dire as this," Meril said at last. "My Eyes have been accumulating information, bringing me what they knew, but—Sercario." The summons was quiet but may as well have been a bark for the speed with which my uncle reached the dais.

"Your Majesty."

I hadn't realized he was in the room, though I should have guessed he wouldn't be far once he heard I was here. Nan would expect him to report back if I couldn't.

He didn't look my way as he approached Meril's left side. His expression was impassive. No concern or fear that he'd messed up showed on his face, which amazed me. Considering everything he'd kept from her for my sake, he should have been shaking in his boots.

"Were you aware of these details?"

I expected him to lie and wondered how he'd fare, but instead, with the briefest flicker of his gaze in my direction, he said, "Yes, Your Majesty. Not these most recent updates, but my niece laid the matter before me the night before last. I immediately ordered more Eyes activated and put to use, and so far they've seen nothing to suggest any immediate threat to the wall."

A spark flashed in Meril's cold emerald eyes. "You neglected to make this report to the council."

"Your summons had been sent, Your Majesty," Serc said without batting an eyelash. "Any report I might have given would have been inferior to the information delivered by the source."

A risky call, but my uncle was no novice to the court. He'd served as judge, spy, and adviser for the Shadow Council for over forty years. He knew something about survival.

Meril glanced his way, then pinned her gaze on me. "Consider yourself fortunate you heeded my invitation, blood of my blood. More than your life would have paid the price."

My mouth went dry, but I held firm. I would not surrender to my shaking legs or turbulent stomach.

Finally, the queen closed her eyes and released a breath, for a heartbeat looking more human than I had ever seen her. Then she was stone again, her stare as hard as flint as she turned her attention to the room at large.

"For a hundred and fifty years, I have held my end of the agreement, and the prime minister, whoever it's been, has held theirs. If all you've said is true, then perhaps it's time to set new terms."

I froze, the air catching in my throat as I awaited her verdict. New terms would mean overthrowing everything we'd built. If she opted to shut down the department and reabsorb power over the country's supernatural population, more than a few groups would revolt, and depending on how she put down those rebellions, the results would be as catastrophic as anything Lucien and Michael had planned. They would just be better contained. It was the risk we had taken in coming here, but now that we stood on the precipice of her decision, I feared the result.

"Before I reach my judgement, I must see for myself." Although she sounded calmer, the vibrations emanating off her didn't lessen. "If true, these traitors have moved against me as well as against their department. They've signed their lives over to the marsh jail, as has anyone working with them." Her sharp eyes landed on Jet. "You'd best hope I find no evidence that your delay in coming to me has endangered us further, lest I deem you deserving of the same fate."

The blood rushed out of my face at the threat, but Jet held her stare unflinchingly. A minute passed, and, as though my friend had passed a test—for now—Meril nodded, set her hands on the armrests of her throne, and cast her attention over her Eyes.

"Pierce the wall."

As one, her spies fell into an eerie stillness, and their black eyes turned white.

Chapter 3

Gideon

Tʜᴇ ʀᴇᴀʟᴍ ᴡᴀѕ like nothing I'd ever seen before.

Sixteen years of wearing dozens of masks on dozens of missions as an agent of SilverGuard, a private supernatural security firm that dealt with all types of magical crises, and none of it had prepared me for what existed beyond the wall.

From the moment I'd mumbled that ancient password and stepped through the archway, it was like I'd walked onto a movie set. The kind of fantasy trash I used to watch and roll my eyes at because of how much they got wrong.

Now I realized I'd only thought it was wrong because I'd never seen the truth.

If a dragon swooped into the Abbey right now, I doubted I would be any more surprised than I was by the sight of these twelve Eyes turning into golden, white-stared statues.

Even they were insignificant compared to the woman sitting

on the tree-carved throne. I was pretty sure that if I stared at her for a thousand hours, I still wouldn't have her worked out. The details of her face, her clothes, her gestures—every single part of her was fascinating. Magic.

But as I stared in awe, my gaze fixated on the queen, my feet rooted to the carpet, part of me knew my fascination wasn't totally genuine. Somewhere in the back of my mind, the current of her control leashed my free will, the power of this place compelling me to pay homage, behave, obey. It was the same power that had forced everyone to march out of here like robots. I wasn't one of her subjects, and yet she'd managed to climb inside my head.

Acid burned the back of my throat as the awareness of her presence in my skull sank in. Carstairs had spent more than enough time screwing around with my brain; I wasn't about to let this stony bitch pick up where he'd left off.

I wrenched my will away from her influence, but her grip on my thoughts was tight, and the harder I pulled, the more a sense of loss took hold.

Illusion, I told myself. *Bullshit.*

I kept fighting, waging a silent mental battle, but quickly accepted it as a lost cause, the flow of the tide too strong.

Until, out of the corner of my eye, I saw Jet waver on her feet. As my concentration shifted, Meril's power snapped back into place, wrapped around my head like an uncomfortable helmet, but my worry for Jet overwhelmed my compulsion to gawk at Her Majesty. It anchored me to the present, to our reason for being here. Meril was a statue with a temper, sure, but she was the difference between our success and a big fat plunge into failure.

Jet had summarized our situation with military precision. No emotion, no elaboration. Fact after brutal fact. And somehow the facts made everything seem worse.

We weren't stuck in an overblown soap opera. This was real life, ground down to its deepest, darkest roots.

And it was taking a heavy toll on Jet. No one else might have noticed how she struggled to hold herself together, but I knew something was wrong. Something she didn't want to show, not even to Madison or me.

Yes, her mentor, her surrogate father, had recently admitted to killing her friends right before he'd shot her in the face, an incident that would throw anyone through the wringer, but there was something else. Something beyond the emotional. She'd been short with me, which wasn't strange, and with Madison, which was. She'd slept on the drive over here, and it had taken an effort to wake her up and help her out of the car. She hadn't regained any colour in her cheeks, and although she tried to hide it, the gentle way she moved, the way she occasionally squeezed her eyes shut, made it obvious she was in no small amount of pain.

Whatever had happened in the Labyrinth, the fallout was ongoing, and I was afraid of how far it would push her.

If I thought I could convince her to get checked out, maybe I would feel better, but I was more likely to convince this queen to dance a rumba. Hell, I was more likely to spontaneously learn what a rumba was.

So I would continue to keep my eye on her and help her bring this crisis to an end. Which, for now, meant playing nice with Meril.

I returned my attention to the twelve Eyes, but none of them had moved. I would have found the process boring if so much didn't ride on what they turned up. How much evidence did Meril need to lump Jet in with Michael and the others? Was she looking for a reason, or wielding the threat as leverage to force us to obey her commands?

If she laid a finger on Jet, I would fight, no matter how outnumbered or outpowered I was. There was no way in hell I would let her guards cart Jet off to some magical prison.

I glowered at the queen, but if she noticed, she didn't react. Up on her throne, she'd closed in on herself, her brow furrowed. Every once in a while, she twitched, or the furrow deepened, and I realized she was watching whatever her Eyes saw. Madison had talked about running into one of the queen's spies in the park. The dozen here had to be connected to the group on the other side of the wall, and Meril had hopped in on the conversation.

With that kind of communication system, she had the ability to peer at our side of the world with a single command.

Was that part of the agreement she'd made with the department? That she was allowed to spy on her people whenever she wanted without them being aware of it? If so, it struck me as more than a little sketchy.

I made a mental note to ask Madison later, but right now, the invasion of privacy ranked a lot lower on the importance scale than the answers she might dig up.

The wait stretched into forever, but the sun shining through the windows never moved, the shadows never shifted.

Finally, Meril opened her eyes. They glittered, sharp as emeralds, a green fire that burned deep.

"My people have confirmed enough of what you reported to convince me. Not only has your deputy minister broken a dozen or more orders of the mandate, but he's done so in such a crude way that I can't even respect his efforts." Her fingers curled around the wood under her palms. "These are people I have sat with. People with whom I have debated the division of labour between the realm and the other side. With every new government comes changes to the terms depending on their leaders' goals and ambitions. These people have lied to my face about their wishes for our people."

"So you know we mean what we say," Jet said, earning her a dark look from Meril's seneschal.

Meril regarded her with a narrowed gaze. "My Eyes aren't able to see everything, so the repercussions of your actions remain, for the time being, unknown. This plot of Lucien's is spread out across years, across the country, too sprawling to take in quickly. He buries his actions under the guise of legitimacy, which is why no one noticed sooner." She scowled. "I wouldn't be surprised if he delegated everything in such a way as to prevent me from seeing so I wouldn't step on him and squash him like the bug he is."

The air in the room grew thin, and I sucked in a deep breath to loosen my chest. How angry would she have to get to pull all the oxygen from my body and leave me an empty husk on the floor? A few hours ago, I would have laughed at the idea of anyone having that much power, but standing in Meril's presence, I suspected it was the least she was capable of.

Jet wavered on her feet again, and I held myself back from going to her. I didn't want to risk attracting attention to either of us. By telling the queen everything, Jet had taken on the role of spokesperson, and if she appeared too weak to stand on her own, Meril would never trust us to lead the charge on crushing Michael into the earth. We were here for support and resources, not to hand over responsibility to her people.

If she decided to take control, I doubted there would be much of a world to go back to.

Eventually, Meril's gaze landed on Madison. "What say you, blood of my blood? Do you believe it possible to put an end to their plans at this stage in their game?"

The weight in the room grew heavier as the tension between the two women stretched as taut as a guitar string. If I stood between them, I could probably strum a tune on it.

Madison lifted her chin and met the queen's eye. "I do, Your Majesty. Their position is strong, but we've gotten in their way at every turn, and if we've slowed them down at all, then we've revealed their weakness and can stop them for good. A small chance, perhaps, but one worth taking. I have people waiting on my side of the wall, ready to stand with us and fight if it comes to it."

My side, she'd said. Staking her claim. Meril's expression was too blank to know how she took the message, but there was no way she'd missed it.

"Pray it doesn't," the queen said. "Though the possibility of such a schism is very real. Lucien's full intentions may be hidden from me, but the sense of unrest and dissatisfaction in my people is present and growing. There is an… energy. An undercurrent travelling beneath every move, every reaction. Change is coming to our people, and the only element we can control is how this energy is channelled—whether it's directed into something productive, or whether it bursts and tears apart the foundations of our society."

She released a breath, and a glimmer of exhaustion touched her statuesque form before she pulled herself together. I didn't trust the display. Either she wanted to lull us into a false sense of security or sympathy to manipulate us further, or she was genuinely tired. Either way might mean we were screwed.

"We have worked so hard to find balance and keep our

people safe," she said. "We have fought for every inch we've gained. Now our progress is on the brink of being stripped away by some fool's petty desires." Her lip twitched with disdain, as though it offended her that a fellow supernatural would show such a mundane vice.

Jet pulled her shoulders back and stepped forward, moving past Madison. Madison's hand twitched towards her, then returned to her side.

"Will you help us, Your Majesty? Will you take a stand in this fight?"

My heart stopped. This wasn't part of the plan. Madison was supposed to handle the negotiation. Jet had already taken us by surprise in grabbing control and going the honesty route, but a straight-up ask with no guarantee of a fair return? That was leaving us open for a kick to the balls.

If I'd had to guess, I would have said her straightforwardness caught Meril off guard, too. She slipped so far as to blink before she composed herself and asked in turn, "Do you ask me to?"

Madison's breath hitched, and I appreciated the knife edge her question presented. Depending on how Jet answered, the future of the supernatural population would be affected. The burden of the decision had to rest heavily on her, but Jet didn't show it. She remained quiet, and I hoped she was debating her options.

"The wall needs to be protected," she said at last. "I refuse to believe everything we've worked for can be thrown aside so easily because of the ambitions of a few people. Not when so many of us continue to fight to maintain stability. I am prepared to press forward, to lead where I can, and to sacrifice whatever I have left to hold steady. All I need to know is whether you support our efforts."

Madison closed her eyes and relaxed, so I allowed my hands to fall slack at my sides, not having realized how much I'd tensed up.

It was like a storm had passed, the electricity in the air fading as the weight of power between the two women settled into an uneasy peace.

Meril nodded, and with her movement, everyone in the room shifted on their feet, as though having regained control of themselves. "In that case, you have it," she said. "My sanction to act, to gather reinforcements, to use whatever means necessary with my protection should you succeed in ending this coup. But know that you will be watched. If my counsellors deem your chances of success too poor, they will step in, and you will face official judgement for your handling of the situation. And should you fail, know that my protection may not extend so far as to save you from whatever sacrificial pyre your traitors have planned for you."

Jet's throat bobbed, but she showed no other sign that the queen's words terrified her. They scared the shit out of me. So far, we'd gotten what we'd come for, but there were too many mind games to know which way was up.

Meril looked to her seneschal and gave a small nod. The older woman turned on her heel and left the room through a door in the corner I hadn't noticed before.

"As long as you maintain leadership over the solution, the extent of my help remains limited," she said, "but I do have a few gifts to offer. While you work to resolve this matter, I give you access to my Eyes. You can place them as you need them, and they will keep you abreast of the key players' movements. With the right information, you should be able to plan your strategy. You also have my authority to bring in whatever groups you need. As I suspect you've already approached Sercario—" she shot the man a glance, and a lesser person would have withered "—I give him leave to work with you directly and provide the full extent of his forces."

"Thank you, Your Majesty," Madison said, and although she sounded grateful, her voice also held a note of uncertainty.

My throat tightened, and I clenched my hands at my sides. I'd been ready to fight for Jet's freedom and was no less prepared to fight for hers. The thought of leaving her in this bizarre house of mirrors, forced to do the bidding of a woman who mixed concern for her people with controlling them, threats with generosity, fury with compassion, turned my blood cold. How did anyone know where they stood with her? How would Madison, all gentle empathy and independent will, survive here?

But while nothing would have stopped me from championing Jet, I knew throwing my fists for Madison would serve no purpose. She was the queen's blood. She'd come here accepting it might be a one-way trip.

For all its wonders, I fucking hated this place.

Meril must have sensed Madison's apprehension as well, because the corner of her mouth quirked, the first hint she'd shown of a positive emotion since we'd arrived. "As for your summons, blood of my blood, you are aware of what it means."

Madison's eyes sparkled with unshed tears. "Yes, Your Majesty."

"You are aware it has been my wish for you to accept your place on my Shadow Council, and I believe the current turmoil presents a golden opportunity. You would be safer here, and I would benefit from your counsel as we navigate the conse-quences of whatever happens in the mundane realm."

Madison stiffened. "Yes, Your Majesty." Her voice was strained, not yet resigned but almost.

I caught the flash of panic in Jet's eyes and guessed she was having as much trouble staying quiet as I was.

"You, however, appear to have a different opinion on the matter," Meril said, and Sercario cast a warning glance in Madi-son's direction.

"I am ready to comply with Your will," Madison said, ever the diplomat, even if it sounded as though it cost her to say it.

Meril's lip twitched again, and I had no idea if it was a sign of irritation or amusement. "My *will* is to hear your true thoughts on the issue."

Madison swallowed, steeled her spine. "My true thoughts are that I would like to see this through on the other side. I've served the department for ten years, following in the footsteps of my family going back to Clarissa. I have lost friends in this fight. I wouldn't feel right leaving the battle to others while I stayed here. Your Majesty," she tacked on.

"I see," Meril said, and the pause that stretched out after those two tiny words was so clearly another manipulation I wished someone would swoop in and give the woman a smack. I continued to feel that way right up to the point when she said, "As it happens, I agree that you would best serve your people by remaining with Captain Dawson and planning our victory beyond the wall. Afterwards, we will have a conversation. One that is long overdue. You are the granddaughter of my progeny, a member of my family and of my court, and with that consideration, you have certain obligations you cannot deny because of some infantile desire to embrace the mundane world."

Her green eyes gleamed, the fire burning brighter, and I understood how lucky we were that our goals aligned so closely with hers. Madison had been right. If we'd led with any other priority than protecting the wall, we would have walked out of here—or not—with nothing. Even now, I wondered if we were out of the woods.

Every decision Meril made was based on whims and wishes. At any time, she might decide we posed more problem than solution. She might decide the best way to end this chaos would be to tear down the wall and destroy anyone who threatened her place on the throne. If she listened to the counsel of her advisers or Jet's recommendations, it was because she thought it was the wisest choice.

She might not feel that way ten minutes from now.

Meril held Madison's gaze until the door in the corner opened again and the seneschal returned carrying a carved wooden trunk by its two leather-covered handles. By the way her arms strained, the trunk wasn't light, but by its size—roughly four feet by three—I couldn't guess what it contained.

She set the trunk in front of the dais, and Jet knelt down to open it.

Three iron latches lined the side, and each one landed with a resounding thud.

When the third latch fell, Jet lifted the lid and exposed three weapons set into the velvet lining. The largest was a handgun, which surprised me. Practical gear in an impractical place. For Meril to have provided such a mundane solution was almost insulting, until Jet picked up one of the magazines tucked beside the gun and rolled a few bullets into her hand.

They weren't like any ammunition I'd ever seen. The casing looked normal except for a strip of luminescent blue that traced down from the point and circled the rim.

Jet ran her finger over it and snatched her hand away with a hiss.

"It might look like a normal weapon, but the ammunition isn't designed to kill but weaken," the seneschal explained, her voice rough and raspy, reminding me of tree bark. "Once the bullet makes impact, the serum is released into the bloodstream to seek out the supernatural markers and neutralize them."

My blood turned cold, and I curled my fingers against my sides to shake off the pins-and-needles sensation.

"It turns them mundane?" Jet asked, her thoughts having travelled the same paths mine had.

The queen bowed her head in a nod. "For a time. There are advantages to not immediately killing our enemies. This gives us the option of removing a threat without sacrificing a life, which is preferable for maintaining our numbers. But I trust you'll do whatever the situation requires, Captain."

Jet returned the ammunition to the magazine and returned the magazine to its slot in the velvet lining. Next she picked up the gun, which she handed to me to inspect, and turned her attention to the other items in the case: two knives with unremarkable three-inch blades. The handles were ebony, and when she pulled one from its sheath, she revealed a blade just as black. A streak of dark green lined the edge from the tip to the guard, where a small cartridge was tucked.

"Guns are loud," the seneschal said. "Given that our primary goal is usually not to draw attention but to eliminate a threat, this alternative should be of use. The serum built into these blades is a sedative. One nick of the skin, and the enemy will drop for up to three hours. On average, depending on species, of course."

Jet sheathed the blade and handed the knife to Madison, who took it as though she were afraid it would explode in her hands.

I tested the weight of the gun, aimed the barrel at the wall well away from the guards, and stared down its length, impressed if not surprised by the quality of the piece. Created by supernaturals for supernaturals, taking abilities and skin thickness into account. It was exactly what we needed, but would hardly be enough if Michael had a few on hand as well.

"Can you pick these up anywhere?" I asked.

Meril gave me a knowing look. "If anyone on the other side is armed with realm inventions, it would mean a traitor existed in my court. Anyone so foolish deserves whatever punishment I choose to mete out."

My skin prickled at the promise in her eyes. "Then hopefully you've given us the advantage," I said, preferring not to think about it too closely.

I was also wise enough to set aside any thought of bringing the weapon to SilverGuard as a prototype after we finished with it.

The queen's eyes narrowed. "Be warned, Mr. Leigh. From what I've seen through my Eyes, the enemy has advantages of their own. As it stands, they have the upper hand. Their pieces are well placed on the board, and they have been making moves unobstructed. We can't know how far they are into their game, but if they are risking my notice, it must mean they're close to their final manoeuvre. Everything I offer you will play its part, but whether its use brings success comes down to you."

Any relief or reassurance I might have felt evaporated, leaving the gun heavy in my grip and my hands cold. I knelt down and returned the weapon to its place in the trunk, and Madison bent beside me to replace the knife. Once all the weapons were safely encased, I flipped the lid closed and sealed it with the heavy clasps.

"Don't lose heart," Mcril said as I stood up. "You have already made moves they did not expect, forced their strategy into unplanned directions. Every shift of their intentions leaves room for gaps, and if you pay attention, you can create a wedge to push them further off balance."

As though her words were an incantation, while she spoke I saw it, the vision unfolding in front of me. The entire fight on a game board, the pieces aligned, the openings obvious. I saw how to navigate through it, a hop from square to square, the best moves to get in their way.

The whole layout in an instant, so visible that, if I started now, I could walk out of here and get this done within the hour.

As soon as she fell silent, the scene vanished into smoke, leaving me as directionless as I had been a minute ago.

Jet's eyes glistened with tears she hurried to blink away, and I suspected she'd experienced the same vision. If the glimmer and loss of certainty were frustrating for me, it had to be a million times worse for her. She needed to finish this. Not only for her team anymore, but for her. For the betrayal of her colonel, the breach of trust in everything she held close to her. She might claim she never got attached, but the past few days had taught me no one was immune to attachments, and now her claims were being tested.

Yet she was still here, still standing, still fighting, showing more courage than I'd believed anyone capable of. I might be uncertain about our next steps, but I had faith in her and would follow her into hell itself. I hoped our support would be enough to keep her going.

"If you succeed in preventing this war," Meril said, and she sounded like a different person from the heartless statue of a minute ago, her musical voice full of genuine feeling, "you will have my personal gratitude. We stand on the edge of disaster, and the resolution lies on you to avert it." She rose from her throne and approached Madison.

Madison tensed but didn't move as the queen took her hands. I braced for roughness, but the gesture was gentle, almost encouraging. "In stories, the dawn brings hope and safety. Today, darkness is your friend. Tread carefully, *chailene*. Stick close to the shadows and be friend to whispers so you might live and we may meet again."

She leaned forward, kissed her on the cheek, and a flash of green light blinded me to the room. I squeezed my eyes shut and lurched away from the glare that pierced my eyelids.

The light faded, a breeze picked up around me, and I eased my eyes open, testing my vision with a few slow blinks. Surprise morphed into confusion as I looked around.

Trees. Crumbled stone. People in mundane clothes walking around laughing, wearing bright smiles.

The queen had sent us back beyond the wall, leaving us under the hazy daylight in the dull green grass in the ruins of a half-finished abbey.

Chapter 4

⟷ ∾∾∾∾∾∾ ⟷

Jet

MADISON MADE THE executive decision to stop at a diner on the drive home. The throbbing ache in my head left me no interest in food, but I also wasn't in a rush to return to the safe house. Our haven had begun to feel like a prison as more of our allies turned out to be enemies.

The diner was a little tucked-away place off the highway. A dozen tables, bright with natural light, the servers all in white-and-orange uniforms, and ceramic roosters on every available surface. Corny, but I knew from experience they served some of the best pancakes in the area.

Shame I didn't have an appetite today considering it might be my last chance to enjoy them.

At this time of the afternoon, most of the tables were empty. Madison led us to a booth in the back corner, well away from the kitchen and anyone who might care to eavesdrop. A few of the servers shot us dirty looks for coming in so close to the end of their shift, but I doubted we'd be here long enough to keep them late. While food was important, we didn't have the luxury of dawdling.

I ordered a coffee and a piece of toast, ignoring Gideon's and Madison's concerned looks and grateful when they said nothing. Gideon ordered a platter with everything, and Madison stuck with her fruit and granola.

The coffee was mediocre but hot, and I wrapped my hands around the mug, a moan of relief escaping me as the heat soaked into my knuckles. The pain in my head had muted most of my other physical discomfort, but it returned now with a vengeance, as though I were made of sharp edges, each one digging into something else. I wanted a long, hot bath, or to sleep for three days straight. One was impossible, but maybe I could sneak in the bath while I put a strategy together. We could hold a meeting through the bathroom door.

We didn't talk while we waited for the food to arrive and, aside from a few attempts by Gideon to get me to eat a strip of bacon or a bite of pancake, remained silent until our plates were empty.

The others might have been lost in their worries or thoughts, but my head was full of static.

I tried to run through everything Meril had said and consider how best to use the weapons she'd given us. This was what I did—had done—for a living. As soon as I pulled my blade, I was usually able to shut out everything and let instinct and training take over. But as I'd stood in the Abbey, weapon in hand, all I'd been able to do was battle my nausea as the light shining through the stained glass windows stabbed me in the eyes.

After the server topped up our coffees and took our plates, I sank against the back of the booth and passed my hand over my face.

What was wrong with me? I was used to headaches after using my abilities, but they never lasted this long. And it was getting worse. Food and sleep hadn't touched it.

Tired, I told myself. *You're just tired. It will pass.*

It had to pass.

"Are you all right?" Madison finally asked. I was impressed she'd lasted this long.

"My head is so scattered I can't see straight," I said, hoping she wouldn't pry. "I'll be fine. Once this is over, I'll be fine."

"You've been off ever since…" She stopped, frowned, straightened her shoulders, and without giving me room to wriggle free, asked, "What do you think was in the powder Michael shot you with? I've tried to let it go because it was obvious you didn't want to talk about it, but you've been differ-ent since you got home. Felt different."

I scanned the diner hoping one of the staff was close enough to prevent me from answering, but for the moment, we were alone.

"I have no idea." I leaned forward to rest my elbows on the

table so I could massage my temples. "We know it wasn't ghost because I'm not dead. Other than that, I'm out of ideas. Could the drug have been diluted?"

I didn't want to think about this. I would have been happier to pay the bill, leave, and go home to take a nap. But Madison was right to push. We only had so much time left, and I needed to be at my best.

"It's possible." She picked at a chip at the base of her mug, a faint crease between her eyebrows. "They have the Ghostmaker at their disposal—what's to say they don't have him working on another version of the powder, something that takes out the positive effects and leaves the toxic reaction? High dose to kill, low dose to incapacitate?"

"If so, it's not very effective," Gideon said. "She stayed down for all of what? A minute? Enough time to make a move, maybe, but what's the point? Why not go for the kill? And if it's ghost, then why is it taking so long to leave her system? It's been over twelve hours."

"Exhaustion?" Madison guessed. "Stress? It's possible the drug *is* out of her system, but the symptoms are exacerbated by other factors."

"And if it's something else altogether?" He squeezed his right hand into such a tight fist his knuckles turned white, then he flexed his fingers and reached for his coffee. I wished I could say something to put him at ease—his worry doing nothing to settle mine—but I knew nothing but answers would stop him from spinning, and I had none to offer.

"Unfortunately, it doesn't matter," I said, and let my arms fall across the table as I sank against the back of the bench.

"What do you mean?" he asked, his brown eyes flashing fire as he turned to look at me. "Of course it matters."

"It doesn't, Gideon." I met his gaze squarely. "It could be ghost, it could be another drug, it could be bleach powder or flour or cocaine, but between the—" I scanned the diner again and dropped my voice. "Between the murder investigation, the manhunt, and our need to stay ahead of Michael and Gagnon, we have no access to any doctors or tests to figure it out. So as shit as it is, all I can do is suck it up because we don't have a lot of other options."

My spiel over, I closed my eyes, sagged into the cushion, and fought off a wave of defeat. If talking exhausted me this much, how would I have the energy for a full-out war?

It will pass, I repeated. *It has to pass.*

Either that or we had to move fast enough to kick their asses before whatever was kicking mine wiped me out.

A moment of silence followed my mini-rant, and when I opened my eyes, I found Gideon still staring at me, his lips pressed together against what I suspected was a string of curses and arguments. He dropped his gaze to his coffee and said, "We could always run."

Nothing else would have made me sit up so straight, my headache momentarily forgotten. "Excuse me?"

He lifted his hands. "I'm just saying, you say we're out of options, but we still have that one. It doesn't *have* to be on us. We could cross the border, get you to a hospital, let the queen deal with this however she wants to."

I gawked at him, too stunned to answer. He couldn't be serious. Just up and run?

"Let's say we did." His long fingers played with the handle of his mug, running up and down the ceramic, pausing over the cracks and a chip along the side. "For shits and giggles, let's say we went south. I could probably get you jobs with SilverGuard. The money is good, the work is interesting. We could work together to prepare my people for the backlash of whatever happens up here. Meril will do whatever she needs to do, or someone else will step up. Either way, we can steal some time to get our shit together before we have to face it."

I wanted to scream at him for suggesting I leave my country to its fate. I hadn't busted my ass this long to abandon my people now, and dumping the problem on someone else would earn me the label of traitor the department had already given me.

But fatigue had worn me down, and despite myself, the image he presented swept over me. Just as Meril's words had painted a vivid picture of our success, his idea played out through my imagination as a done deal. Run away, let someone else take on the fight, and if they failed, be ready to face battle with resources we would never have access to up here. Madison would be out of Meril's jurisdiction, and I could start a new life for myself, away from this one that had chewed me up and spit me out.

I was so tired. Even raising my coffee cup to my lips was a struggle. And somehow, in spite of my exhaustion, I expected myself to find the strength to stand against three of the most powerful men in the country? How? Why? So I could see their smug looks when they crushed me? Tore Gideon away from me again? Used Madison as a political catalyst?

I squeezed my eyes shut. How could anyone ask me to do that? Hadn't we done enough already? I had lost so much, and the odds that I would lose even more before the end were so great. So much greater than victory.

Madison had brought in Serc and Lilith. We could hand everything over to them and brace the rest of the world for what might spill across so many other national lines.

It was possible.

It would be so easy.

Only when the other two looked at me with questions in their eyes did I realize they were waiting for me to say something.

With a sigh, I took hold of my mug and spun it between my fingers. "Gagnon has already made an alliance with the syndicate, and O'Malley has connections of his own. We have no idea how many other groups are following their orders. On top of that, Michael has twenty thousand troops under his command spread across the country. What happens if he orders them home, or orders them to attack a few key spots under a false claim of security? He could shut down our supernatural defences and pave the way to an easy win. Even if we brought in everyone we know to stand against him, he would trample us. Hell, even if he only works with the troops he has on hand in the city, that's still a few thousand. What can we possibly do against that, even if Meril sent us home with her entire armoury?"

Silence descended on the table, and I bowed my head and sipped my coffee, hoping the caffeine would give me back some of my energy. It did nothing but curl my tongue and wriggle in my stomach, shooting acid up the back of my throat.

"I can't deny it's tempting," Madison said at last, and I raised my head to stare at her. "I'd be out of Meril's reach. No more watching over my shoulder for her to come after me, no more carrying the weight of a fragile department on my back."

Fear lurked behind her hazel eyes. To say we weren't terrified would be a pointless lie. To ignore the option of running would be a show of useless, even dangerous, bravado. The smart move would be to run. It was the only way we could be sure we'd survive—at least for a while longer.

Beneath my fear spawned a renewed fury. Fury that I should be in a place where I felt the need to run. Fury with myself that I would consider the possibility. Fury at Michael for making me doubt my abilities, and at Gagnon for making me question my loyalty to the department that had been my world for fourteen years. Above all, fury that they had turned against their people for their own ambition, no matter what benevolent lies they told themselves to help them sleep at night.

Michael said I was losing what was left of my team because of the decisions I'd made. Even if that was true, I would never win them back if I stopped fighting and ran away. No matter what they thought of me, I was still a wolf on the hunt, the leader of their pack, stalking my prey without doubt or indecision. That would never change as long as I drew breath.

I was no coward, and neither was Madison. We had made it this far, we had uncovered most of Gagnon's plan, and I would rather die fighting to uncover the rest than turn tail and make it easier for them to win. Because who else would go so far for SMOAC? Serc and Lilith might make a valiant effort, but their loyalty was to the queen. They would sacrifice the department before they let the wall collapse. Gagnon and Michael might escape, and to hell if I would stand by while they lay on a beach somewhere, sipping mojitos and drinking to their good fortune.

"I won't let them win," I said. "I need to look Michael in the eye before I take him down, and I *will* take him down."

Madison nodded. "The idea of getting out of dodge sounds great, but if I can walk away from a pint of double fudge cookie dough ice cream during budget season, I can stay here for this." She and I shared a smile, then hers vanished and her eyes hardened. "I can't watch my family's legacy burn to ashes. I've put my life into SMOAC, worked to make this country a better and safer place for my people. I won't throw that away to put off a fight we'll have to face eventually."

I turned to Gideon, expecting to find frustration or disappointment staring back at me, but saw only a satisfied gleam. The son of a bitch had known exactly what he was doing making his ridiculous suggestion. My determined rage had burned away my tiredness and overpowered my headache, and although the effects wouldn't last, the reprieve had helped me dredge up some of my waning strength.

It reminded me I still had strength to summon, and while any of it remained, I would hurl it in a hail of fire and brimstone at the people who thought they were too godlike to be touched—even if I burned myself up in the process.

Chapter 5

Gideon

I TOOK THE wheel after we left the diner. Madison's energy had given out somewhere between her granola and her second cup of coffee, and Jet looked ready to keel over. Of the three of us, I was most likely to get us to the apartment in one piece, but even that was dicey. My gaze went to Jet as often as it checked my mirrors, and every time I glanced her way, she looked worse. She sat with her head in her hand, her elbow against the window, her fingers massaging her forehead.

I'd hoped my comment about running would push her into action, but its effects had been short-lived.

"Did you know weapons like those existed?" I asked, trying to draw her out of her pain. The centre of her third eye looked red. From the massage?

"I knew Meril keeps a personal armoury," she mumbled, "but I had no idea the contents were so advanced. Now that

I've seen these, I wouldn't be surprised if they were muskets compared to what's hidden away."

"Her defences are extensive," Madison said from the back-seat. "She has a full team working on the next best thing, always with a goal of incapacitation over death."

"Why? I didn't think the population here was that small. Don't you guys sit somewhere around forty-seven million?"

"Something like that," Jet said, "but it isn't only a numbers game, is it? Our balance is fragile. We outnumber the mundane by such a small margin that if we were outed, it wouldn't take much for them to overpower us. Our supernatural advantages would give us a good head start, but mundane weapons on both sides would even the battlefield pretty quickly."

"Not to mention, the various supernatural factions are way too divided," Madison said. "Each group has their own loyalties, their own ideals and beliefs about fighting back. If it came to war, the mers would leave, the treekins would disappear into their trees. It doesn't benefit us to encourage in-fighting. Justice in the queen's court or in SMOAC's detainment centre is the preferred outcome."

Even as I listened with one ear, I shoved the information out the other. Had they forgotten who I was? SilverGuard would have happily spent millions working to get inside intel like this, and Madison and Jet had handed it to me on a leisurely drive home. If I were a good little spy, my next move would be to track down another pay phone to relay the details to Dark Wire.

If anyone else had told me, I wouldn't have hesitated to do exactly that, but like hell if I intended to betray the trust of people who had saved my life and who were putting everything on the line to prevent a wide-scale disaster. As far as I was concerned, I still had two more days of authorized independence from my firm. After that, regardless of where the situation stood, I would have to make my report, and would likely be ordered home, or risk my future as a security officer. Eventually, I would have to decide where my deeper loyalties lay, but until then, they were here in this car.

"So she's working on defences against supernaturals, but what about weapons against the mundane?" I asked.

Neither Jet nor Madison answered right away, but long after I gave up on getting a reply, Jet said, "I have no evidence she's working on anything."

"And I wouldn't know," Madison said. "I'm not that far in her confidence."

"But," Jet added, "it would be naive to assume she's unprepared."

They spoke as though they were uneasy about the possibility, especially Madison, but it only made sense for Meril to have defences lined up. Especially if the results of a war between supernatural and mundane were in doubt. Why not throw everything you had against your enemy? Secrecy would already have been lost, so survival would be the chief priority.

I hoped the queen wouldn't hesitate if the situation unravelled that far, but now that I'd met her, I had a hard time believing she'd hold back. She may have come off as a possessive, manipulative bitch, but she did seem to care about her people, and every country deserved that kind of leader. Someone who worked to ensure magic stayed grounded in their land's roots.

"How long has she sat the throne?" I asked.

"From the beginning," Madison said.

My eyebrows rose. "She's immortal?"

"No one knows," said Jet.

"But—"

Madison chuckled. "I know. She doesn't look a day over forty for all her years, but on that side of the wall, it's not as easy to know if someone is immortal or if they have the ability to manipulate time. And since no one can swear to the full extent of Meril's abilities…"

She trailed off and allowed me to infer the rest.

"So why is she queen? You don't know what she is or what she's capable of doing, but you've let her rule your people for who knows how long?"

It was Jet's turn to laugh, though hers was rough, as though she were half-asleep. "Your supernatural leader is voted in by democratic process, is he?"

I smirked. "I couldn't tell you. As far as I know, we don't have a Shadow Council. We have a few pockets beyond the wall, but for the most part, everything we do, we do on the surface, for all the world to see if they paid attention. I guess it makes sense. We have a president. They direct policy for everyone, supernatural and mundane. We're not like you crazy people who split your leadership between a democracy and some kind of bloodline fate."

"Clearly enough of us agree with you or we wouldn't need SMOAC," Madison said. "History is blurred after so much time, but according to most accounts, Meril was among the first supernaturals to exist. She claimed this land as hers and created the treekins and the fairies. Over time, she passed her bloodline down, and through evolution and cross-breeding, migration, and magic, the number of species grew. At first she ruled because she was the only one who understood what we are, so our people looked to her for guidance, but as the decades and centuries passed, she became our protector as well. There are some in her court who would fight to the death to maintain her place on the throne, many who would argue in favour of the status quo, and, so far, no one to challenge her."

"Who would want to?" Jet asked. "I don't envy her position. Especially in times like this where her wisest move is inaction. We might be in a shit spot, but at least I'm not stuck waiting for someone else to take care of it. I couldn't handle that."

"Obviously, or we wouldn't be here," said Madison, her voice touched with amusement.

I glanced at her in the rear-view mirror. She stared out the window as I turned into the downtown core.

"Do you think she'll force you to go back?" I asked.

In the reflection, Madison grimaced and met my gaze before I returned my attention to the road.

"I think she's strongly considering it. I've gained a reprieve, but you heard her. Today's audience was far from my last. After we've dealt with Lucien and the rest, there's a good chance I'll find myself leashed to the Shadow Council to fulfil my 'obligations.'"

"Would it be so different from what you do for SMOAC?"

"I suppose not on paper, but for me there's no comparison. Here, I can quit if I want to. I could decide tomorrow I want to give up my position, move to Prince Edward Island, and take up vlogging, and I would have the freedom to do it. If I'm recalled, I would lose that independence. I would be stuck in the role of adviser for the rest of my life." She paused. "And on that side of the wall, who knows how long that would be."

"Is that why your great-grandmother left?"

"Clarissa left because she saw the difference she could make for the people who crossed the wall. She heard stories of the hell they faced over here back then, forced into secrecy without the social resources they needed to thrive—or survive. If a supernatural gets sick, it's not like they can go to a mundane hospital or doctor. Any national or international conflict that came up, they were accused of cowardice if they didn't enlist, but how could they risk such close quarters or losing control over their abilities in the heat of battle? There were too many security issues, but they didn't want to return to the realm. So

Clarissa and a few others crossed over and fought for their rights. They busted their asses to build the department, formed a micro-cabinet, and convinced PM MacDonald to listen to what they had to say. He was reluctant to cede power, of course, but it didn't take long before he saw the wisdom of their offer. It took a huge chunk of the population off his hands and allowed him, mostly, to go back to forgetting we exist. So SMOAC was created. Off the books. Their own budget, their own rules, their own minister, and the only person who could veto them was the prime minister himself with the advice of a few trusted ministers. Why do you think he drank so much? So it's been ever since."

"Couldn't we go to the prime minister's people now, then? Tell them what Gagnon is up to? Get them to provide more resources?"

"And risk them panicking and turning the military on us to eliminate the potential threat?" Jet asked.

"Our situation has always been precarious," Madison said, "but the current mundane administration has put a lot of pressure on SMOAC, recommending budget cuts, suggesting we open our chain of approvals to include mundane central agencies. Jean-Luc was able to hold them back. He was calm, competent, and had a good enough grasp of their concerns to fend them off."

"With him gone and the deputy minister stirring up trou-ble, the PM might decide it would be easier to end the issue permanently," said Jet.

My skin prickled with the weight of their worries. We'd been so focused on how the queen would react to the news of SMOAC's corruption, I hadn't given a lot of thought to the mundane government's response. Rock, meet hard place. "That wouldn't happen, would it? How would they justify it?"

Jet glanced at me sidelong through squinted eyes. "It's politics, Gideon. They can twist anything to look like anything."

"But Meril would know."

"And what could she do? If she didn't want to make things worse, her only move would be to support the dismantling of SMOAC and open her doors to take in anyone lucky enough to get away before the mundanes turned on us. Then she would seal the wall, the terms would be broken, and Canada's supernaturals would no longer be a part of this world. As permanent as if we were all killed."

I couldn't wrap my head around it. The system we had in America wasn't perfect, but with everything supernatural existing on the same plane as the mundane, it meant we were all under the protection of a single organization. No one was at cross-purposes, and a move against one of us was a move against the country. End of story.

To have the prime minister and the queen fighting to maintain balance meant anyone in the middle stood a chance of falling through the cracks.

And yet it had the advantage of holding each side accountable, which was probably why more movement had been made in establishing protections and rights for their people than we enjoyed across the border.

No perfect system, just an ever-shifting pros and cons list and a hope that the people in charge would stick to their word and do the honourable thing, as much as any politician could— or would.

Madison's phone chirped, and at my next mirror check, her attention had returned out the window, her eyes glazed over, her phone tight in her hand.

Jet looked over her shoulder and, in a voice so low I almost missed it, said, "You should go home."

It took me a moment to be sure I'd heard her correctly. "What? Why?"

"I should have pushed for it sooner. We have Meril's okay to bring her people in. You should head back and warn your firm. If we don't win this, someone needs to prepare the rest of the world."

There was something in her tone that put me on edge. What was she doing? Trying to get rid of me? I'd noticed the way she'd pulled away from me at the Estate. She'd closed off from me just when I thought she was opening up. There had to be more going on than her pain and worry. I'd done my best to give her space and not push her to talk to me, but she still acted as though I were standing too close.

Really, she wasn't wrong. If my handler knew how much

I was working with her and how far I'd extended myself into another country's politics, I could kiss my job goodbye. Possibly even my freedom. Dark Wire had approved five days of free rein, but they'd laid down rules alongside that blank cheque, and I had broken pretty much every one of them. In part to save the world, sure—it sounded good on paper—but mostly for the woman sitting beside me. The same reason I'd almost lost my job the last time we'd worked together.

Idiot.

I knew all this.

The threat hung over my head of what waited for me if I went home with nothing but failure to show for my insubordination. Over the past few days, a solid knot of tension had formed in my stomach that I'd done my best to ignore.

But that knot would have to crawl up my throat and choke me to stop me from staying exactly where I was. When I'd suggested we run for cover across the border, I'd held only a sliver of hope they'd say yes. The rest of me had known they would never abandon their people, so I'd wanted to light a fire under their asses. As it stood, Jet didn't look like she could fight her way out of a paper bag, and she needed to be ready for so much worse than we'd faced so far. If she thought I was about to leave her behind, then she didn't know me at all.

I glanced at her. At first I thought she'd closed her eyes, her head resting on her hand with her face tilted towards me, but when the sunlight shone through the trees, it reflected off the thin slits of her irises half-hidden behind her thick lashes. The woman couldn't even open her eyes, and she thought she could do this alone?

"I'm not leaving," I said. "If you're fighting, I'm at your side."

"What about your job?" she asked, as though she'd read everywhere my thoughts had gone.

"To hell with my job." I tightened my fingers around the steering wheel. I hadn't told her about my five-day deadline or Dark Wire's rules. I still had forty-eight hours, and if I needed more, I would figure something out. "It's better for everyone if I help you clean up this mess before it migrates south. They'll see that when it's a done deal."

"So that's that?"

"That's that."

I waited for her to say more, but she leaned her head against the headrest and, this time, I guessed, actually closed her eyes. Not wanting to disturb her, hoping she would take the opportunity for a quick nap, I focused my attention on the final few turns back to the safe house on Somerset.

I had no idea where her feelings for me stood, or if they had changed at all in the past week, but to my growing frustration, I had to admit mine had.

If she was pushing me away for whatever reason, I would respect her wishes, but nothing would stop me from fighting to the ends of the earth to keep Jet safe.

Chapter 6

Madison

I WAS GRATEFUL the others left me alone for the rest of the drive back to the safe house. My head had been in a tailspin ever since my phone had pinged at me.

In the rush of going to see the queen and the adrenaline created by stepping across the wall, I'd forgotten about the text I'd sent last night. My goodbye message to Malcolm Bishop when I'd thought I would never see this side of the world again.

Looking back at my message now, I cringed, but what was I supposed to have said to the mundane I'd fallen for over years of conferences and coffee breaks and those few wonderful dates? I'd been as honest as I could have been, as firm as I could have been, and if he'd never heard from me again, it would have been enough.

Now that he'd answered?

A blush rose in my cheeks even as my heart ached that

although I was still here, our situation hadn't changed. If anything, it had become even more important that I cut ties with one of the most special men in my life.

WHAT DO YOU MEAN YOU MIGHT NOT BE BACK? he'd written. IS EVERYTHING ALL RIGHT?? I JUST SAW THE NEWS ABOUT YOUR MINISTER. TALK OF MURDER??? PLEASE ANSWER. I HATE THAT YOUR MESSAGE SOUNDED LIKE GOODBYE...

The sight of his name on my screen. The concern in every extra question mark. I spent the rest of the drive trying to pay attention to the conversation in the front seat and failing, lapsing into draft after draft of possible replies.

Colm knew about the murder.

Colm was worried about me.

What would he think if I told him I was on the run from the people who'd committed the crime?

Scenes played through my head of the discussions that might play out if I told him everything. In some, thanks to my romantic flights of fancy, he swept me into his arms, kissed me until I was dizzy, and swore he believed me. In most, he stared, stupefied, understandably uncertain how to react. In the rest, there was no discussion because I never replied to his message.

My heart wrestled uncomfortably in my chest, a ball of stress lodged beneath my diaphragm so it was impossible to take a full breath.

What the hell was I supposed to do?

Fortunately, I didn't have much time to suffer before

Gideon pulled into the parking lot behind our building and turned off the engine.

I shook myself out of my brooding and, with forced pep, said, "All right, let's get upstairs and start making phone calls. We have Meril's backing, which opens a few doors for us. I'll contact the Eyes I know about, and they can put us in touch with the others. They're probably expecting our call and might have a few ideas about where we should post them."

I kept talking as we rode the elevator to the third floor and as I let us into the apartment. I had to stay focused on the task at hand. Everything else was secondary.

The apartment was quiet, blissfully so, and in the light of day, the gory mess Gideon had left on the armchair—a mess I couldn't believe I hadn't noticed when I'd dragged my groggy behind out of bed yesterday evening—greeted us as a stark reminder of the dangers ahead. That he was still walking around, moving as though he hadn't been shot in the heart, astounded me. It also gave my hope a much-needed boost. If he could brush off a gunshot wound, maybe our chances of at least one of us surviving weren't so far outside the realm of possibility.

I made a note to throw a sheet over the chair. That much blood would draw attention if we brought it down to the dumpster, and I didn't want to have to look at it every time I came into the living room.

As soon as I was inside, I headed into the kitchen and

started the kettle for tea. It was an automatic response to being home, and only when the water started boiling did I appreciate how much I needed the time to slow my pulse.

Jet lay on the sofa, and her breathing grew steadier as the minutes stretched on. Gideon sat on the other side of the sectional, his attention unevenly split between her and the window.

"Is she asleep?" I asked.

He nodded and rose from his seat to join me in the kitchen.

"Do you think she's all right?" he asked, his voice quiet. "Can you sense anything from her? You said she felt different."

His brow furrowed and the corners of his mouth turned down. I flinched against the lash of his rising anger, sensed the shift in his brain chemistry as he struggled to rein it in, but as strong as his fury was, it was nothing compared to his concern.

I poured out two cups of tea and handed one to him. He accepted it readily, a marked difference from the last cup I'd forced on him, and breathed in the freshness of the herbs. His shoulders relaxed, and he sagged onto a stool at the island. I leaned on the surface across from him and wrapped my hands around my mug.

"There's something," I said. "I've tried to pinpoint what it is but can't get a grasp on it. It might be some kind of toxin or narcotic working its way out of her system, or it might be her drive to stop Michael and avenge her team. I've tried reaching out to redirect the chemicals it's releasing, but either it's stronger than I am or her resistance is too low to help me fight it. We can only—"

"Wait and see," he growled.

With one of the swords hanging over my head temporarily sheathed, I had the mental space to assess him more thoroughly. Stubble darkened his jawline, and his hair had lost its styled look, the thicker thatch on top sticking out at angles because of how often he'd run his fingers through it. His eyes were hard, the lines around his mouth harder. Even his hands were tight, the muscles straining as he clung to his mug. I worried for the ceramic's future if he didn't ease his grip.

"Do you love her?" I asked, blurting out the question without giving myself time to think about it.

For a second, I regretted my forwardness, but my embarrassment quickly passed, and I doubled down with a pointed stare. The answer was obvious to me, but I wanted him to admit it. With so many unknowns in front of us, we didn't have room for secrets and denials.

He raised his gaze to mine, the truth shining out in pained desperation, but he shook his head. "I don't do the whole love thing. What's the point? I'm never in the same place with the same name long enough to bother, and it asks for a lot more honesty and commitment than I'm able to give. Do I care about her? Absolutely. But love?"

He shrugged.

I didn't push it. As frustrating as it was to hear his excuses, maybe he was right. I thought of how devastated Jet had been when she'd discovered he'd lied to her about… well, pretty much everything. Playing her to gain classified intel. I couldn't in good faith push him to be honest with her now if he didn't think he could keep it up. I would be doing my best friend a disservice.

At the same time, my heart hurt that they were turning away from what could be. Especially right now, when the future looked so dark. Why couldn't anything be straightforward and easy? Why couldn't we pretend, just for now, that life was normal? No spies and soldiers, no Eyes or liars, no treason. Why couldn't they be two people who had found each other, found strength in each other, and used that strength to become the best versions of themselves?

A thought niggled at the back of my mind that their relationship wasn't the only one I was sad about. And a bit envious of. They knew where the other was coming from, knew their hang-ups and the stakes involved. What I wouldn't give for even that much openness. My phone burned a hole in my pocket, reminding me of all the possibilities that awaited me if I took a leap and accept the consequences.

I sipped my tea, swallowing my loathing for the unfairness of the universe.

There was no point wishing for things to be different, but all the same, I suffered the sting of resentment that I was stuck here, stranded in this complicated hell.

"I need to go for a walk," Gideon said, setting his half-empty mug on the counter. "Have a drink and a smoke somewhere Jet won't kill me, clear my head." He reached the apartment door, pulled it open, and paused before he left. "Call me if anything happens?"

"Of course."

"I won't be far."

Anxiety drifted off him like a bitter aftertaste, and when he cast a final glance at Jet, I wondered what he'd seen that I'd missed.

As soon as the door closed behind him, I took my tea and sank into the clean armchair by the window. From there, I watched him walk down the street and head around the corner, no doubt on his way to Mooney's.

Once he was out of view, I turned my attention to Jet. Even in sleep, her face was pinched with pain, and her skin was pale and slick with sweat. Her leg twitched, and a small whine squeaked through her lips. I considered waking her up, but she beat me to it, shooting up with a gasp, her hand flying to her chest as though she were afraid her heart was about to fly free.

I rushed to her side and rested my hand on her back. "It's all right. You're at the apartment. No one's here but me. You're okay."

I met her panicked gaze with what I hoped was a reassuring look, suspecting my skill in schooling my expression had vanished under all my stress and fear and uncertainty, and she soon dropped her hands to her knees. Her breathing slowed and awareness crept into her eyes.

"Must have had a nightmare," she said.

"No wonder. Considering everything, I'm surprised we aren't all screaming every hour of the day and night. Do you want some tea?"

She nodded, and I went to the kitchen to prepare another cup. I brought it to her, and as she inhaled the steam, the lines around her mouth softened.

I was about to stand up to return to my chair and give her some space when she tensed. "Where's Gideon?"

"He stepped out for a bit. Your headache has him worried, and I think sitting here not able to help was driving him to distraction."

Jet groaned and massaged her forehead. The skin beneath her fingertips was red, and I couldn't remember if it had been so bright before she'd rubbed it. Her third eye, the scar-like lines faint again now that we were on this side of the wall, stood out against the irritation.

"Could your third eye be causing some of your pain?" I asked. "You've used your abilities a lot this week."

"Probably. I kept it open the whole time I was in the Labyrinth, making sure no one followed me, that Michael hadn't brought anyone with him." The last part came out as barely more than a hiss, but with a sip of tea, she calmed down. "I'm exhausted, Madi. I'm trying so hard to hold it together, but I feel like I'm falling apart."

"So put some of the weight on us. You don't need to take everything on yourself, and I hope you feel you can trust us to carry some of the burden."

"Of course I trust you, but you shouldn't have to shoulder my responsibility."

"That's nonsense. We're in this together, remember?" I propped my feet on the edge of the coffee table. "If you don't share the load, you won't be able to keep up, and we need you."

Tears glinted in her eyes, and I floundered for what to say. She never cried. In all the years I'd known her, she'd shed tears three times. I'd watched this woman deal with a broken wrist, and her only complaint had been that she couldn't go back to work right away.

"I'm glad you're here," she said. "I'm really glad I got to you before Dougall's bomb went off."

"Me too."

She sipped her tea and rested her head on my shoulder. "Honestly. I don't know what I'd do without you. I'm glad you believed me, and that Meril didn't keep you. Without you, I'd be lost."

More terrifying than the tears was the sentiment. Bridget Dawson was far from an unfeeling woman, but her emotions ran deep, not something she expressed easily. Was this her fatigue and pain talking, or was there something more going on? The likelihood loomed over us that our days were numbered, but she couldn't let those thoughts get the better of her. I wouldn't let it happen.

"You're my rock, Jet. You have been for years. If you had come to me saying Jean-Luc was an alien from Venus, I probably would have given you the benefit of the doubt and looked into it. We wouldn't be here if it weren't for you. You were the only one to question, to dig into the truth when the official lines wouldn't. Without your persistence, Lucien might have already carried out his plans. Now we have a chance—small, sure, but a chance—to beat him."

"Too bad so many people had to die to shine the spotlight on him."

We shared a moment of silence for the fallen. Jet's team, the informants. Almost Gideon not once but twice. All crimes to lay at Lucien's door. More reasons to make him pay.

"Did you ever imagine this is where all our hard work would bring us?" She tilted her head to look up at me, and I brushed the hair out of her eyes.

"Never would have guessed it in a million years. I joined the public service thinking I'd be able to predict the rest of my life. The day-to-day would be different, the challenges would vary, but every evening, I'd go home congratulating myself on a job well done, have a glass of wine, and prepare for tomorrow. This is so far beyond my expectations that most of the time I can't believe I'm not dreaming."

Jet reached over and pinched my arm.

"Ow."

"Just checking."

"What about you? Did your training ever broach departmental implosion?"

She snorted. "Never. Now I have to wonder if it's because Michael's had this in the works since before I joined or because he's as surprised as I am by what he's done."

I hesitated before asking, "Do you think he buys into what he's saying? Does he really think he's acting for our benefit?"

She was quiet for a while, sipping her tea and staring into the blank television screen. "I like to think so. Somehow it makes his decisions a little less revolting, you know? If he means it, if his reasons are really so selfless, then I can accuse him of being misguided. But I only think that way when I remember what he meant to me. A big part of me—too big, maybe—isn't ready to cast him as a villain yet."

"I get it. I'm so sorry he's involved."

She gave a tired shrug. "Maybe it's not all that surprising, especially if he fell for his own excuses. Michael's devotion to the department is as strong, if not stronger, than mine. I don't think he would do anything to destroy it intentionally. Everything he's done has to be because he thinks SMOAC will be stronger for it. He's delusional, but I do think he believes it."

"Did he tell you what their goal actually is?"

"No. I asked him. He told me enough to make me realize he's insane, but not the details." She stopped, took another sip of tea, and when she spoke again, her voice was strained. "He says Eric knows. That he supports them."

I pressed a kiss into her hair and wished I could do more to put her fractured pieces back together. Not just her commander, but her lieutenant, too. Everyone she held closest betraying her. "Have you spoken to him since…"

Since he shot Gideon. The man was on a roll with breaking Jet's heart.

She shook her head. "What would I say? He would point out he'd already told me. That it shouldn't have come as a shock. But it did." Her voice cracked, but she pressed on. "All along, I thought he was too stubborn to see the truth, too willing to swallow whatever line our superiors fed him. But it's *Eric.* When he told me about FoSA, he sounded so sincere. I actually found myself wondering if we'd been wrong."

The Federation of Supernatural Affairs. A question mark in the middle of our trouble. I had searched for them across the internet and found nothing more than a brief company mandate. An international organization created to offer resources and services to supernaturals in any partner country. No other information online. What did they demand in exchange? Why hadn't Jean-Luc wanted to give them the time of day?

The questions nagged at me, but for now I set them aside. They weren't as important as the broken woman sitting beside me.

"But we weren't wrong, were we?" Jet continued. "Eric

knew what was happening, that Michael had sacrificed us for their cause, and he stood with him. I have nothing more to say to him." The waver in her voice hardened. "If they can justify their actions enough to keep them on this path, then I don't know either of them the way I thought I did."

"I'm more willing to believe Eric is sticking with Michael out of loyalty than because he agrees the sacrifices are necessary," I said. "He's a soldier first and foremost. It's why he never pushed to make it past lieutenant. He loves the fight but has always followed your lead. You were the independent thinker."

"More than Michael ever hoped I would be, obviously."

"Don't think that way. He was proud of you. I'm sure he still is." I didn't know what else to say. As far as I was concerned, the man was a monster, but he'd been there for Jet from the beginning. How could I hate the man who had moulded her into the captain who would now stand in his way?

I also wasn't sure how Jet would react to my badmouthing him, though my concern lessened when she said, "Not proud enough to not shoot me in the face."

"There is that." I studied her profile as she turned away from me, "I wish we knew what that powder was. You're right that we can't do anything about it yet, but I'd feel better if we knew what we were dealing with."

She bowed her head. "I guess I should be trying harder to figure it out, but with everything else—at least if he meant to kill me with it, he failed, right?" A sigh escaped her. "I wish

I could stop thinking about it. Stop replaying it. Maybe if I stopped seeing it every time I closed my eyes, I could pretend it never happened."

Her voice hitched at the end, and she turned her face farther away from me. There. I'd pushed as hard as I was willing to go for now. This was far from the end of the conversation, but we would pick it up when she was ready.

I gave her a moment to herself, then nudged her with my shoulder. "We're going to get there, Jet. You'll have your chance to call him out for what he's done. Trust me."

She cleared her throat, and when she turned back to me, there was a sly gleam in her eye that hid the emotional agony I sensed rolling off her in heavy, frothy waves. "Will you trust me enough to tell me about that text message you got in the car?"

I froze. I'd been ready for her to veer the subject down another path, but she'd steered us into oncoming traffic. Had my reaction to Colm's message been that obvious?

"It was the Muffin Man, wasn't it? You would have said something if it was anyone else." The corner of her lip curled at my surprise. "I might not be able to read your emotions, but I know you, Madi. Everyone has been so worried about me, but what about you? Is everything okay?"

I sighed, set down my tea, and drew out my phone. Sinking deeper into the couch cushions, I opened the app and handed the phone to Jet. I didn't need to read it again. My message and Colm's reply were imprinted in my mind.

"Shit," she said after she squinted her way through the exchange. "Word's gotten out about Bastien?"

"Hard to keep it quiet when he suddenly stops showing up to cabinet meetings."

Jet switched to the news app and scrolled through the national headlines. "There we are. Minister of Domestic Affairs and Trade found dead in his office. Sources report the cause of death to be the result of foul play. Details have yet to be released, but Deputy Minister Lucien Gagnon has announced a full investigation is in process. Yeah, well, of course he would. Shame they'll never find anything."

"Shame word got out at all," I said. "I pity our comms team for having to deal with the questions about to come their way."

"They'll shut the story down quickly. Even if Gagnon hadn't been behind Bastien's death, he'd want this off the front page as soon as possible. I guess the question will be who they'll pin the murder on."

Her eyes narrowed, and my worry surged. "You think they'll say it was us?"

"We'd be a good cover story, wouldn't we? A great way to get us out of their hair. Turn the public on us as well as our own people, and they'll have no trouble tracking us down. Gary won't say anything?"

"No. We're safe here as long as we keep our heads down and avoid the neighbours."

"Not a hardship." She leaned her head against the back of

the sofa. "What are you going to tell him?"

"Who?"

"The Muffin Man."

My face warmed. "I don't know. I guess I need to come up with a reply, don't I? I can't have him thinking I'm dead or hurt or involved somehow."

"You could tell him everything."

"What?" This coming from her, the complete opposite of what she'd said the last time we'd talked about him, shocked me so completely, I couldn't believe the words had come from her lips.

Jet shrugged. "Why not? You like him, don't you?"

"Yes, I do. Very much. Too much to drag him into this."

"You don't think he could handle it?"

"I—"

"The way I see it is this—either you think he can't handle it, in which case you're being cruel to both of you by dragging things out and letting him think there's anything between you beyond carrot muffins and lobby coffee, *or* you think he could, in which case you should suck it up and tell him you're a supernatural empath and the best chief of staff of a secret department the country has ever seen. He'll take it however he takes it, but at least he'll know."

"And if he freaks out?"

"Then he freaks out. Whether he comes around enough to accept the truth is on him, not you. Unless you think he'd blab?"

I considered it before shaking my head. "With all his experience overseas and in hospitals, I suspect the man's a professional secret-keeper at this point."

She turned to look at me, her eyes half-closed against the light spilling through the window. "Then what's holding you back?"

Fear. The answer came to me immediately, but I couldn't say it out loud, too embarrassed to admit it. What was I afraid of? Rejection? Wouldn't it be better to get it over with now instead of obsessing over what-ifs?

"I don't want to ruin his life. And I guess I'm not ready," I said at last.

Jet's smile widened, and she looped her fingers through mine. "I know what I said before, and to a point, my opinion hasn't changed. Mundanes don't always respond well to the blinders coming off. But the fact is I've been betrayed by more supernaturals than muns this week, so maybe magical ability is a crappy basis for whether we should put our faith in someone. Ready or not, we don't know how much time we have left. If it's a matter of regretting telling him or regretting not telling him, which can you live with? If something happens to you, would you want him to know the truth?"

She returned my phone, and I stared at his message for a while before opening the keyboard. Not quite as bad as it sounds, I wrote, but definitely in crisis mode. Will touch base soon.

A non-answer. A safe answer that left the door open without committing either way.

Jet watched me type, and the look she gave me when I hit send was too familiar. It was the same look I'd given Gideon only an hour ago when he'd walked out the door without admitting that the reason he refused to go home was because the thought of walking away from Jet was worse than what might happen if he stayed.

The three of us were ready to stand in the path of traitors and criminals and fight to the death to protect what we cared about, but not one of us could be honest enough to talk about our hearts.

Bunch of cowards.

Jet was right that I was running out of time. If Gagnon won or Meril stepped in to stop him, I would lose the opportunity to reveal everything to Colm on my terms. But right now he and I were Schrodinger's Relationship, real and not real, and in that paradox there was hope.

Before I made up my mind, I had to prepare myself to lose everything if I opened that box and the scales tipped the wrong way.

Chapter 7

Gideon

ONE DRINK BARELY took the edge off my uneasiness, and the second only made a small dent. By the third, I felt more in control of myself, and I opted to stop there. Four tended to push me too far onto the side of bad judgement, and I needed to keep my head. We were one misstep away from falling into the pits of hell, so I couldn't afford to be reckless.

Mooney's Pub was full tonight, the tables packed, the barstools taken, standing room only on the main floor.

Despite the crowds, the moment I'd walked through the door, the owner, Alyssa, had caught my eye, as though I sported some kind of homing beacon. She'd pulled an extra stool out beside the bar, glared at the guy who'd tried to take it, and for the next hour and a bit had kept my glass full. I was spinning the dregs of my last beer between my palms when she finally took advantage of a free minute to lean against the bartop across from me.

"How are things?" she asked, and although she sounded as cheery and professional as she did with anyone else in the room, the underlying question was loud and clear.

"Busy, and getting busier. Anything interesting happen while we've been gone?"

"A few new faces checking the place out, seeing if it's to their taste. They've come in the past two nights, but I don't think we're quite what they're looking for. They never stick around long."

"Out of towners?"

"Not my usual fare. First night was a rougher crowd, last night suits, but they don't smell like public service. They don't cause any trouble, though, so I have no complaints."

"New blood keeps things interesting. Good to learn how you could branch out. Did they give you any idea what they're hoping to find?"

"Nothing on the menu, but I wonder if they're waiting for some buddies of theirs. They pay particular attention to faces." She took my glass and replaced it with a half-pint.

"They stop by tonight?" I asked, accepting the drink.

"Not yet."

"Shame."

"Still early."

Maybe I would have to stick around a while longer to check them out. I wasn't in good enough shape right now to get rid of them by myself, but it would be smart to gain some insight into who Gagnon had sent after us.

"You on your own tonight?" Alyssa asked, scanning the room.

I raised my glass. "Needed some me time. Things have been a bit tense back at the homestead."

"My door is always open to you. And tonight, the drinks are on me." She knocked on the bar. "Be sure to pass my love along to the rest of the family."

She left me to serve her other patrons, and I nursed my half-pint as I watched the door. Every new person received my full attention. For every mundane who walked in, two supernaturals followed, creating an unusual balance for a public hangout. The mundanes had a faster turnover rate, too. They didn't look uncomfortable, but something about the vibe of the place must have made them less eager to stick around.

A few people drew my suspicion because of their sullen looks and the way they tucked themselves into shadowed corners, but when I caught Alyssa's eye, she shook her head. None of them.

The time passed with no sign of our new friends, and I was getting antsy to leave.

I'd been gone for over two hours, and it was high time I returned to the apartment. My desire to wake Jet up from her restless sleep and drag her to the hospital had been a big reason I'd left. Now that I'd settled my nerves with some liquid courage, I wanted to get back and see how she was holding up.

She'd consumed my life. I couldn't take a single step without weighing how it might affect her.

Madison's question echoed in my thoughts, hadn't stopped echoing since she'd asked it, despite my best attempts to drown it out.

Fuck, the woman is blunt.

Do you love her?

Love. The word was enough to make my stomach curl in on itself. I'd been honest with her. I didn't do *love*. Any thought of *love* had shrivelled in my heart when I was fourteen and my parents had made striking out on my own more appealing than staying at home. There had been no love under that roof.

Except from my brother, of course, but even my relationship with him was long-distance. I hadn't seen him in person since I was eighteen, a fresh recruit to SilverGuard and breaking off all prior connections to protect my professional anonymity. He'd given me a hug and a leather bracelet, and I carried both of them with me every day.

To think love might have come into my life over twenty years later was ridiculous. I wouldn't know where to begin with something like that.

Madison was a romantic, hoping for a happy ending. No wonder. A woman who spent her life drowning in other people's emotions, of course she'd prefer the good ones to the bad and do whatever was in her power to draw them out. Anything she might have read in me was wish fulfilment.

I drained the last of my beer and set the glass on the inside counter with the other dirty dishes, then reached into my pocket, pulled out my wallet, and threw a couple twenties on the counter. Alyssa might have covered the drinks, but it was only fair to leave a good tip. Her information was worth it, let alone the quality of the craft beer.

On my way to the door, I heard my name and turned to find her calling to me from a nearby table. "I think you dropped something behind you."

I spun around and found myself standing next to a table along the wall that had been claimed by two clean-cut fellas. Their dress shirts were starched and ironed, their shoes shined, their hair styled. Although Mooney's was far from a dive bar, my brief experience and Jet's description of the place fixed it as an end-of-day hangout for the supernatural public service. A place people went to wind down. These guys were as far from wound down as I was dressed up. They were also the most boring-looking people I'd ever seen. The sort I wouldn't have glanced twice at on the street.

Nice choice. Totally vanilla.

Following Alyssa's lead, I scanned the ground and ducked my head under their table. "Sorry, guys." I snaked my hand into my pocket as I stood back up. "Dropped my wallet."

"No problem," one of them said, and I swore I caught a hint of recognition, or at least suspicion, in his boring blue eyes.

I flashed a smile and wished them a good night, staying extra aware of my surroundings as I continued to the door.

As far as I knew, our enemies had no reason to think I was alive, so I had to be wrong about that guy recognizing me.

They could have seen photos.

I kicked myself for being so thoughtless. It would have been easy to pretend to pick up my wallet, sneak a glance at their faces, and move on without letting them get a good look at me. Instead, I'd practically introduced myself.

Had I royally fucked up, or was I in the clear to get back to the safe house and warn the others? If either of these men followed me, I might be able to hang on to them for a block or two before they blended in with the scenery, but I doubted I'd get them off my back before I reached the apartment.

Alyssa passed me once more before I left as she crossed to the next table. "Another outside," she murmured, running her fingers across the *Canada* printed on my T-shirt. "Denim jacket, black jeans, thick beard."

I touched my fingers to my forehead and winked at her, hoping anyone watching would take the exchange as a casual flirtation.

Outside, the tight crowd spilled across the patio, and I squeezed my way down the walkway. As I lit a smoke I had no intention of enjoying, I tilted my head to scan the area, trying to spot the person Alyssa had described, and found him leaning against the wall, a drink in his hand and his attention gliding over everyone in front of him through a pair of bright eyes—eerily, golden bright. Bright enough that I was amazed Gagnon had chosen him as his third when the other two were so easy to overlook.

The door opened again, and the Vanilla Twins stepped out, walking straight to Bright Eyes. One of them said something, and Bright Eyes looked my way to catch me staring.

I stuffed my lighter into my pocket and turned my feet down the sidewalk, as though my looking his way had been nothing but a coincidence.

Shit.

I snuck a quick glance over my shoulder when I turned the corner, and sure enough, he was only half a block behind me.

Picking up my pace wouldn't do anything except give away that I'd seen him, so I kept my steps slow, using storefront and restaurant windows to monitor my tail. He matched me step for step, and it took an effort not to turn around and confront him just to get the meeting over with. The only thing holding me back was the probability that a public scene would invite his friends to join us.

I should have gone somewhere other than Mooney's and avoided any chance of being seen, but in this unfamiliar town, with so many unfamiliar threats, I'd wanted something familiar. Alyssa had proved her loyalty to Jet, and I'd known I would be safe in her hands. Turned out I'd relied too heavily on my death to keep me under the radar.

At least it wasn't a total waste. Now we knew Gagnon had his people out searching for us. Both he and Michael would have known Jet and Madison were friends with Alyssa, so instead of wasting resources trying to track them, they were waiting for them to show up, staking out the likely spots. We'd have to double every measure we'd taken to keep our heads down if we wanted to stay ahead of them.

I'd fallen into their trap once, but if I played this smart, the guy behind me would never learn where we'd holed up.

Unless I led him there myself.

Even as I thought about turning right on Bank Street, away from the safe house, my feet took me left.

Bright Eyes was alone, with no sign the Vanilla Twins had tagged along. If I got him to the apartment, we could ambush him, maybe get some information out of him. Then we'd have a better idea of where to send the queen's Eyes—and where to go ourselves.

Crossing my fingers he wouldn't send a message to his buddies, and that I could move fast enough, I backtracked to the entrance of the apartment building and crossed through the lobby. As I waited for the elevator, I watched my golden-eyed friend peer through the glass door in my periphery, likely making sure I was alone. After a moment's hesitation, he came inside.

I accepted his nod of acknowledgement, noted the casual way he shoved his hands in his jeans pockets without concern, and appreciated how he stared at the elevator doors as though impatient for them to open. He was playing the neighbour. He had every right to be here because he, too, lived in the building. A role I had played many times in my career.

The doors opened, and I got in and hit the button for the third floor. I expected him to ask me to hit *2*, giving him an opportunity to take the last flight of stairs and catch me off guard, but he didn't bother.

"Isn't that a coincidence," I said, goading him. "You new here?"

"Nope, been here ten years or so," he said in a deep bass that was little more than a growl. "You?"

"Less than a week." What was the point in lying? He either knew or suspected who I was, and the whole point was to get him to follow. "Anything I should know that the landlord wouldn't mention? Faulty water pipes? Roaches? Chronic party animals?"

His only answer was a shake of his head as the doors opened.

"Have a good one," I said, and got out of the elevator with a jaunty whistle.

I wished I could have texted Madison to give her a heads-up that I was bringing company with me, but I hadn't wanted to do anything that might make my friend panic. I wanted him to think he held all the cards with no need for backup. So I hoped she and Jet were ready to move.

The door was locked when I reached it, so I pulled out the

key ring I'd forgotten to return to Madison, found the key to the apartment, and let myself in, not once looking behind me as I stepped inside.

One foot across the threshold, and Bright Eyes was on my back. He grabbed my wrist and twisted my arm, pressing it against my spine before shoving me into the kitchen island. Madison and Jet leapt off the couch with no time to do anything other than exclaim at the sudden chaos.

"Both of you, against the wall," Bright Eyes said.

I caught Jet's gaze, winked, and she obeyed his orders. Madison followed her lead, and Bright Eyes kicked the door shut behind him as he guided me farther into the room.

"I don't want any of you to move. Not a breath, not a twitch. I'm going to call my boss, and you three are going to come with us nice and quiet, or your friend here won't live to see dawn. Got it?"

He'd moved so smoothly, I hadn't noticed him set the knife against my side until he nudged the tip between my ribs, the blade piercing my T-shirt and scratching my skin. Nice to see him so confident.

With a breath, I dissolved into air, vaguely aware of him scrambling to regain his hold on me as I misted behind him, and solidified with my arm wrapped around his neck, my other hand holding on to his wrist to render the knife useless.

The bastard didn't give me an opportunity to say anything clever before he swung his heel into my leg. I avoided the blow, but my distraction allowed him to slip out of my grip and come at me. I ducked under his arm as he hurled a beefy fist towards my head and grabbed him around the waist to tackle him into the wall. He swung the knife into the space behind my shoulder blade, and I hissed through my teeth as I wrenched away. With his knife embedded in me, he was empty-handed, leaving Jet free to dart in. She grabbed him by the back of the neck, but her fingers slipped, her balance veering. The air in the room shifted as she summoned her ability, and with the added strength wrapped around her hands, she slammed his head against the island counter. Blood smeared across the granite, and Bright Eyes slumped to the floor.

I jerked the knife out of my back and tossed it onto the countertop with a grunt, sucking in deep breaths to clear the dark blobs from my vision.

"Is he dead?" Madison asked. She edged across the room towards us, her hand pressed to her chest.

"Do we care?" Jet asked, wiping her hands on her jeans. She stumbled as she straightened, and I raised an eyebrow, ready to ask if she was all right, but she shook her head to cut me off.

Anger and fear cut through me, spiked with adrenaline from our skirmish. No matter what she or Madison said, that powder was affecting her. An easy scuffle like that should have left her disappointed, not winded. For now, I let it go, but as soon as we dealt with the guy on the floor, there would be a conversation.

Pain from the stab wound radiated through my shoulder and down into my stomach. I misted from my left elbow up to my chest to knit together the torn flesh. When I brought myself back, blood stained my T-shirt—another one lost—but the wound itself was nothing more than an angry red gash I could deal with later.

I knelt down to check Bright Eyes's pulse. Nothing. "I had planned to question him about what his orders were, but that's fine. Either of you have the ability to speak to the recently deceased?"

Jet crouched beside me and rolled the body onto its back. The man's face had contorted in death, revealing a pair of sharp canines and a thickening beard that had spread down his neck and across his cheeks.

I sat back on my heel and rested my elbow on my bent knee. "What the hell? A shifter brought a knife to a fight?"

"It sounded like his orders were to bring us in alive, so I guess it was the only way to be sure he stayed in control," said Madison. "We're lucky Jet dropped him before he turned. I don't think a kitchen island would have done much to stop a fully formed were."

Was that why Jet had struggled? The man's shifter strength might have taken her by surprise. The possibility was reassuring, but I still planned to confront her.

"If we can't question him, we may as well go through his pockets," Jet said, turning her attention to his jacket.

Winded or not, she sounded a bit more energetic than she had this morning, and I hoped her nap had done some good. The tea on the table also suggested a secondary patch. If we survived the battle ahead, I would personally thank Madison's grandmother for helping us through it. Her magic potion didn't take away our problems, but it sure cleared my head enough to deal with them.

While Jet pawed through the guy's jacket, I worked on his jeans, checking his back pockets first and hitting the jackpot with his wallet.

"Bryan Letfield," I said. "Forty years old, Aries, licensed to drive but only if he's wearing prescription lenses—yeah, okay. Three credit cards, a gajillion membership cards, and a registered member of the Ottawa Curling Club." I looked from the card to him. "Really, Bryan?"

I tossed the wallet to Madison and checked Bryan's front pockets to make sure I didn't miss anything.

"Hey, don't knock curling," Jet said, moving to the jacket's chest pocket. "I'd love to see you get on the rink and try it."

"You'd have to get me drunk to consider it."

"That's the best way to play." Jet looked up at Madison and frowned. "What's wrong?"

I'd been so focused on searching the dead guy, I hadn't noticed that Madison had gone still. When I looked at her, I found her bracing herself on the island counter, Bryan's photo ID in her hand, her face pale.

Her gaze shifted from the heavily bearded man on the floor to the cleaner-cut man on the driver's licence, and she brushed her hair behind her ear with shaking fingers. "I recognize him. I've seen him around the office, going into meetings with Lucien. He was one of the project leads for some of our community efforts. That's how Lucien introduced him to me. But he wasn't. He was another lackey." She dropped onto the closest stool. "All this time, he was committing his crimes right under my nose. He brought this man into my office to introduce him, and I never saw through it. I never picked up anything that made me suspect him."

Jet rose to her feet and rested her hands on her friend's shoulders. "Stop it. This is not on you. You couldn't have known. They probably made a point of waving him in front of you. Michael told me Gagnon's big idea was to legitimize what they're doing. With everything out in plain sight, no one would think to question them."

I grabbed one of the mugs of tea from the coffee table, zapped it in the microwave, and brought it to Madison. She accepted it without looking and closed her eyes as she sipped it. A tear streaked down her cheek, but as she drew in a breath and let it out slowly, her nerves seemed to harden, and she set the mug on the counter.

"Thank you," she said. "I know I'm being silly. This is just so… infuriating. Insulting." She swallowed hard. "Embarrassing."

"It is," said Jet, "and that's why we'll make them eat every smug grin. Every clue they dropped thinking no one would notice, we're going to shove it down their throats so they know their arrogance was what ruined them. And it is going to be so fucking satisfying that nothing else in our lives will ever feel as good."

Her pep talk brought a smile to Madison's serious face, which faded as her attention fell once again to the dead man on the floor. "Then let's get to work."

Chapter 8

Jet

I KEPT AN eye on Madison as I finished going through Bryan's pockets. Her shock over learning how badly Lucien had fooled her had worn off a little, and in its place burned the steely ice of vengeance. An ice I recognized. The hard glint in her eyes was the same one Gideon wore when he talked about Carstairs and the same one I saw when I looked in the mirror.

Somehow, seeing it in Madison enraged me. She was the best of us, had done more for the department than most whole teams, and they had abused her trust. I would make them pay for it. Even if I didn't survive the fight, I would take the bastards down with me.

Gagnon thought he was so clever in leaving behind a paper trail, flaunting his lackeys in people's faces. At least Michael had enough sense remaining to understand how stupid it was. Yes, it might have helped their underhanded dealings go unnoticed as long as they had, but everything they'd rubbed in our faces would be what destroyed them.

Not in the mundane courts, maybe, but Meril was above the laws the department had set. The laws Gagnon believed himself to be skirting.

She wouldn't care about circumstantial evidence.

She would take what we brought her and crush him, and I hoped I'd be around to watch.

"Got his phone," Gideon said, jerking my thoughts back to the shifter corpse in front of me. He pulled the phone from Bryan's front pocket and tapped the screen. "Password protected. No facial recognition."

I held my hand out, and he dropped it into my palm. My aching head made it hard to see straight, but I managed to pry open my third eye to take in the recent history of plastic and electronics. The shadows were vague, and I had to exert more effort than I expected to get a clear image of a thumb sliding across the screen. This should have been easy, a quick glimpse, barely a moment's work, but I strained as though I were shifting a mountain.

Knife points lanced behind my eyes the harder I pushed, and bile bubbled up the back of my throat. I swallowed hard and focused on my breathing, not wanting to make any moves or sounds that would give my pain away. Gideon's and Madison's worry was bad enough already, almost suffocating, and I didn't need another cage closing in around me.

I replayed the image a few times to anchor the details into my memory, and when I mirrored my thumb to Bryan's movements, the lock screen vanished.

"Got it," I said, and Madison stepped closer to stare over my shoulders. "Let's see what you have to say, Mr. Letfield."

I started with his texts. His inbox was empty except for a single thread of messages, so we weren't dealing with his primary phone. A professional operation, then. Not some random supe Gagnon had enlisted off the street. That was fine. I didn't need to read the grocery list his wife sent him, just enough information to tell us where to go next.

The thread was from an unknown number he hadn't saved to his phone, and most of the messages were incoming. They'd started a year ago, mostly sharp, brief orders.

10:30 at the office. Bring documents.

Package ready for pickup. Deliver in hell.

"There's our connection to the syndicate," Madison said.

"How do you figure?" Gideon asked.

"Hell. Isn't Hell on Earth the name of O'Malley's new Kingston club?"

"I've always sucked at crossword puzzles."

"This also confirms my suspicions," she said. "The fact they're delivering packages to Kingston means the rumour is bogus. If O'Malley had moved production out there, they would be picking up, not dropping off."

I nodded, seeing her point. At least that was one loop tied

off. Not a useful loop, but one less bee buzzing in my ear.

I scrolled through the messages, moving towards the more recent ones. The orders remained brief, and Bryan rarely replied, once in a while requesting further instruction or confirming completion of a task.

As we reached the last couple of months, the number of messages increased, the instructions remaining vague but with a growing sense of urgency.

The tone of them also changed, becoming more abrupt and authoritative, as though someone else had taken over communications.

A message from last week chilled my blood and raised goosebumps on my arms.

Package delivered to GM. Monitor news.

"GM," I said. "Ghostmaker. And look at the date—that's the day before the de Lauer blast." My throat grew tight. "They were watching the whole time, wanting to see how people reacted."

"So we have it. Proof that Gagnon was involved in the explosion." Gideon brushed his thumb across his lip, his elbow resting on his bent knee where he knelt beside Letfield's corpse.

"And this one," I said, scrolling to a more recent message. "*The rock has been rolled. Prepare for next phase.* That's from the night Bastien was murdered. So much for thinking his death was unplanned."

"Everything is right here in front of us, but even if we had someone to bring it to, it wouldn't help much, would it?" said Madison. "We understand what it means, but there isn't enough detail to make it obvious to anyone else. Not enough to get us out from under a murder investigation, anyway. Too bad there's no hint of where we could go to get what we need."

"What about this?" I scrolled down another few messages. "*Pickup ready at HQ. 2300h.*"

As I read the text, my fingers went numb, the emptiness creeping up my arms to fill my chest, my stomach, my legs. My head felt light.

"O'Malley didn't send these texts," I said. "Or Gagnon. Michael did."

Gideon rested a hand on my back, his thumb running along the base of my neck in what would have been a comforting gesture under most circumstances. I held back from shrugging him off. "You're sure?"

I scrolled through the thread again from the time the tone changed. The to-the-point messages, the clear orders. I could have been scrolling through my own exchanges with the colonel. He didn't waste words in text. Said he hated typing with his thumbs. The brusqueness, the military twenty-four-hour clock…

"Positive. I guess he's been recruiting for more than my team. These are his soldiers—people ready and willing to carry out his commands without question or conscience."

I'm not going to throw up. I'm not going to throw up.

I rose to my feet and strode into the kitchen. After tossing the phone onto the counter, I turned on the cold water and splashed my face over the sink. The iciness brought me back to myself but did nothing for the pain in my head.

Why was I so upset? I already knew he was involved. I already knew he'd played a role in wiping out my pack. Somehow seeing the proof in print made it that much more real, and my heart broke all over again.

"What do you think he means by HQ?" Gideon asked, and I was more than a little grateful he'd chosen to focus on the text instead of my reaction to it. "Does Letfield have anything that might give us an idea of where it is?"

Madison grabbed the phone from the counter and poked around the other apps, but after a minute she shook her head. "There's nothing else here. No email, no call log, nothing. All communication came through that one stream of text."

"You have to give them credit for covering their tracks," he said.

I leaned my weight on the edge of the sink and bowed my head. Water dripped down my face and hit the stainless steel with a steady *plink, plink, plink.* I ignored all other noise in the room as I pushed through my headache to connect the dots.

Of course they had a headquarters somewhere. Gagnon had waved his operation in front of everyone, but he couldn't have carried out all his business in the office. He would have needed a place where his collaborators could meet and work safely. Somewhere O'Malley wouldn't attract interest from the authorities, somewhere Dougall could keep whatever supplies he needed to produce the ghost, because the search of his home had come up empty—or so we'd been told.

"If they're not going to be generous and leave their coordinates lying around for anyone to find, we'll have to work smarter," I said. "The information is somewhere, and I'm tired of waiting for it to come to us. Gagnon's office may be off limits, but there's nothing stopping us from paying a visit to his home."

Breaking and entering was not the act of the law-abiding people we claimed to be, but times were desperate. *I* was desperate. And I was ready to go to desperate measures.

Madison and Gideon exchanged a glance, and I waited for them to argue, but Gideon shrugged. "We've gone this far with you. Lead the way, Captain."

***

Madison reached out to Meril's Eyes, and while she made her phone calls, I went into my room to try a few stretches, hoping they would release the tension in my neck and loosen the vise around my skull. Five minutes in, the dizziness and nausea were so bad, I curled into a fetal position on the rug until I was sure I wouldn't pass out.

Eventually, I hauled my ass off the floor, dragged myself

into my leather jacket, and strapped one of Meril's knives to my belt. I didn't know what we might find at Gagnon's place, and I wanted to be prepared, ideally with something that would drop anyone we crossed without killing them. We already had one body to dispose of; I couldn't leave corpses littered around the deputy minister's house as well. The media would have a field day with the idea that someone was trying to burn the fictional Domestic Affairs and Trade Canada to the ground.

Only partly true.

More than that, Gagnon would have extra ammunition to hurl against us, and I wanted to give him as little solid ground to stand on as possible.

When I returned to the living room, Gideon was back in his regular attire of white T-shirt, black vest, black jeans. He was sitting on the couch, one foot on the coffee table, and was scrolling through his phone, reading the news headlines. As soon as he saw me, he put the phone away, but not before I spotted the reference to the ongoing investigation into Bastien's murder. That Gagnon hadn't hushed it up yet surprised me, and I wondered what his motives were.

One more way to destabilize everything? To keep everyone distracted from the greater crime? If the riots and protests across the country were part of his plan, then having an unsolved murder would fuel the fire.

I couldn't put my finger on how it was supposed to help them. To me, it reeked of self-sabotage.

Whatever the goal, I wouldn't find it in any news article, so I turned my back on Gideon and his phone and watched Madison pace the kitchen, her phone to her ear.

"You're sure?" she asked. "All right, keep us posted. As soon as it's clear, we want to know. Thanks, McGee." She hung up and pinched the bridge of her nose. "Lucien's at home, so we're not going anywhere yet. I stationed one of the Eyes in front of his house, and he'll call me when we're good to go. I hate to say it, but the only thing we can do until then is wait."

I knew it wasn't her fault, heard her regret at the delay, but despite what my rational brain told me was the smart move, all I wanted to do was throw something heavy across the room, march over to Gagnon's house, lock him in a closet, and get to work. For days, we'd played it safe, tiptoeing along boundaries, too afraid of setting off a chain of events we weren't ready to follow yet. I was tired of it. I wanted to act. Anything to get my mind off my pain.

"I doubt we'll have to wait long," Gideon said. I hadn't noticed him getting up off the couch, but suddenly he was beside me, standing with his thumbs hooked through his belt loops, fingers shoved in his pockets. "Things are picking up, and they're moving faster. Once Michael and Gagnon realize Bright Eyes is gone, they'll retrace his steps and reposition themselves without him. They'll know we're close. If they haven't already, the Vanilla Twins from the bar might realize the person who pretended to drop his wallet was in fact the dead guy known to be working with you, and they'll redouble their efforts to track us down before they get their asses kicked. We pushed them. They'll have to push back soon to prove they still hold the cards."

I couldn't help but smirk. "Bright Eyes and the Vanilla Twins? What are they, a seventies band?"

For a second, Gideon's seriousness melted into a teasing grin. "Yeah, I hear they perform at the local curling club."

I chuckled, but my amusement evaporated as the weight of his theory sank in. He was right, of course, and my pulse sang with the anticipation of this back-and-forth finally coming to a head.

"In the meantime, I suggest we sleep," said Madison. "We're exhausted, and I don't know how many chances we'll have to rest once the next play starts."

She grabbed a few documents from the table, and I didn't miss the way she slipped her phone underneath them. My thoughts drifted to our earlier conversation and the sorry excuse for a text message she'd sent Colm. Had he replied? Pushed harder for the truth? Part of me hoped he had, and that Madison worked up the nerve to tell him at least some of it. Two weeks ago I'd been iffy about her dinner dates with the mundane, though I hadn't said anything to shit on her parade, but now, considering what we faced... having someone to hold on to for support and courage was crucial. Something to hope for once all this was over. One of us deserved that much.

She disappeared into her room, leaving me and Gideon alone.

"She's right," he said, turning towards me. "You should hit the hay."

"I will. Eventually. First, I think I'll take a bath." The thought of closing myself in my room and lying sleepless in bed staring into the darkness nudged my anticipation into anxiety. If it weren't for the steady pounding in my head, I might have invited Gideon to join me, using his company to keep the monsters at bay, but if I couldn't handle a few stretches, I definitely wasn't up for anything more vigorous.

He pressed his lips together, his eyes full of questions, but said nothing. I left him to his worries, closed myself in the bathroom, and ran the water.

While I waited for the bath to fill, I pawed through every cabinet and drawer looking for painkillers, but there was not a single pill, lotion, or miracle drug to be found. Madison's contact had decked out the apartment with every convenience but had failed to consider we might come home battle sore.

Within a few minutes, the mirror had fogged up and steam danced through the air. I stripped down and stepped one foot into the water, the temperature so close to scalding it bit my skin with the same hot-cold burn as a sun-scorched patio or summer sand.

I relished any kind of pain that distracted me from the one in my head and lowered myself into the tub. The water climbed up my chin as I rested my feet on the edge next to the faucet.

Using my toe to close the tap, I leaned back and closed my eyes. I pictured my muscles relaxing, releasing their hold around my spine, my hips, my knees and elbows. My joints protested against the sudden change in temperature, but when they finally stopped fighting me, I sighed in relief. I hadn't realized how wound up the rest of my body had become over the past few hours.

I soaped up my arms and legs, though nothing touched the gross feeling that had followed me out of the Labyrinth, and when I was finally clean and loose, I sank against the back of the tub and closed my eyes.

The haze of sleepiness taunted me, but I pulled myself away from it. Drowning would not be a useful way to protect my country. I knew I should take Gideon's and Madison's advice and go to bed, but I wasn't ready to leave the warm hug of the water.

A knock at the door woke me enough to chase away the weights on my eyelids, and I called for whoever it was to come in.

I expected Madison to poke her head around the door to check how I was doing, but although I heard the door open and shivered against the draft of cool air from the hallway, no one spoke. I turned my head and swallowed a groan on seeing Gideon. He hesitated, his hand on the door as though waiting for me to order him out, but what was the point? Anything he wanted to say—probably more mother-henning—he'd find the time to say it. At least here I was comfortable.

When I resettled against the slope of the bath, he closed the door behind him and dropped onto the tiled floor to lean against the wall, stretching one leg out and drawing the other to his chest.

"I'm fine," I said, hoping to put off any of his fussing.

"Okay."

I waited for more, and when nothing else came, I looked at him more sharply. He was staring at his thumbs where his hands clasped his bent knee. A deep crease lined his brow, and his jaw worked as he ground his teeth.

If he'd come here to watch over me, his frustrated silence was a strange way to go about it. But maybe his being here had nothing to do with me. Maybe he didn't want to be alone. Maybe, like me, the thought of being stuck in a quiet room with nothing but thoughts and what-ifs was enough to drive him crazy.

"I've been thinking about the world beyond the wall," he said after a while.

The subject took me by surprise. "Oh?"

"The difference between that side and this one. I'm used to magic, you know? I deal with it every day in all its forms. I've chased it down, snuffed it out, helped to protect it. I thought I'd seen every possible variation of it. But what I saw this morning was… incredible."

I closed my eyes, and the memory of the queen's throne

room drifted behind my eyelids. "Every time I go, I tell myself I'm ready for it. I never am. Every time, I'm still that little girl in diapers, terrified of everything until the queen took me in her arms. The awe never really goes away."

He chuckled. "I keep trying to picture you in diapers, and I can't do it. In my mind, even Little Girl Jet comes equipped with a knife and a mean right hook."

I grinned. "Damn right." I opened my eyes and rolled my head against the back of the tub to look at him. "What about you? Were you always this much of a devil?"

His eyes grew bright with sinful humour, and sparks raced under my skin, warming me inside and out. "You know it."

The light of his smile faded, the lines around his eyes tightened, and he dropped his gaze to his bracelet. He looped his fingers under the black leather braid and wound it in a circle.

"I didn't really have much of a childhood," he said, and his sincerity caught me off guard. In all our time together in New York, back when he was pretending to be an FBI agent and lying to me about every detail of his life, he hadn't touched much on his past.

I immediately found myself on edge, braced for more lies, more stories woven to gain my sympathy and trust to get what he wanted from me. Despite everything we'd been through over the past week, that hint of distrust lingered in the back of my mind. An expectation that he would do something to confirm my worst opinion of him, to prove he was only out for himself.

I started to push it aside but stopped. It wouldn't be the worst idea to hang on to my skepticism. I'd believed Michael my entire career. Eric had been one of my best friends for just as long. They hadn't proved to be any more honest than Gideon had been. How was I supposed to know who to believe anymore?

Well, he could keep his stories. I turned away from him without encouraging more confidence, not in the mood to sift through the bullshit.

"I was the first supernatural in the family in generations," he said, despite my show of indifference. "My mom's great-grandfather or something was the last one. My mother didn't know what to make of me. She resented me for it, I think. Looking back, I guess I can't blame her. Not completely. How are you supposed to react when your infant boy turns to mist in your arms, and you spend an hour panicking that he'd dissolved for good? They found me naked in the laundry basket."

He let out a short laugh, the bitterness of it drawing my attention his way. He ran his fingers over the back of his neck and wiped the steam from his face with the crook of his arm.

"I can, however, blame her for being an absolute bitch the entire time I lived in that house," he went on. "She barely spoke to me, didn't bother to make me dinner or check on my homework. All that fell on Jared. My brother. He… well, he was the reason I didn't off myself at twelve years old."

"Is he a lot older than you?" I asked, unable to help myself.

There was a lot I expected him to lie about, but somehow I knew his brother wasn't one of them.

"Five years," he said. "So when I was fourteen, he should have been getting ready to head off to college, but he told me he wasn't going. He wouldn't leave me alone with our parents. I told him not to be stupid, that I was old enough to look after myself. He said I shouldn't have to. His guilt over leaving me behind would have held him back, and I couldn't let him do that. So I ran away."

He shrugged, as though his selflessness meant nothing. "I was on the streets for four years. Once in a while Jared found me, gave me some food and new clothes, offered to take me home with him, and every time, I disappeared again, swearing this time I would bury myself so deep he would never track me down. When I was sixteen, I finally succeeded. For two years, I was on my own. Then SilverGuard recruited me, and for the first and last time, I reached out to him."

He met my stare, emotion blazing behind his eyes like black fire. "They don't approve of relationships outside the organization. They have more control over us and are better able to maintain their secrecy if our loyalty is only to the firm."

The earnestness that had touched his words over the past couple days was back, as though he was desperate for me to understand what he couldn't bring himself to say. He couldn't apologize for how he'd acted in New York because there was nothing to apologize for—he'd been following orders. But there was regret, and he wanted me to know it. To know how much he hated that he'd pushed me away, and how much he was sacrificing to be here with me now.

I understood it all as though he'd dropped the thoughts directly into my head. Probably because, on some level, I'd known it all along. Because it was the same thing I would have done.

My reaction was such a jumbled mess, I didn't bother to sort through it.

Later. When all this was done, and my head stopped screaming at me, I would try to pick these knots apart, see where I stood when the ties that bound us together were unwrapped and sorted.

"Anyway," he said, drawing his other leg towards him and resting his arms on top of his knees, "I said my goodbyes, promised I would touch base when I could, and I haven't seen him since."

"You must miss him a lot."

"More than anything. He sent me a message about five years back telling me mom died. I could have received special dispensation to go to her funeral, but I didn't see the point."

He smiled, and his eyes lit up with an inner happiness, untouched by his hell of a life. "He went into social work. Earned his Ph.D. last year. He's written papers, been published and everything."

It was his look of deep, unwavering pride that washed away

any doubt I had that he was telling the truth. He wasn't messing with me, wasn't trying to manipulate me. This was him, a look into the centre of his soul for the first time since we'd met.

"I haven't spoken to my mother in years, either," I said, compelled by his show of honesty to bare something of myself. "She was jealous when it turned out I'd inherited my father's supernatural genes. She didn't want a daughter who had the ability to levitate or grab things off the top shelf in the kitchen without leaving the couch. She definitely didn't want a daughter who preferred jeans and karate to dolls and dresses."

"Sexist."

I laughed. "Right? My father obviously agrees with you, because he supported me in everything. He and my grand-mother trained me, taught me about our world, my abilities."

"Do they have the same?"

"A bit of control over the air—enough that Dad walked me through the basics—but his primary ability is strength. Plain old muscle power. Easier to hide, Mom says. Especially compared to my third eye."

"Yeah, but no one can see that. What does it look like to the mundanes? A birthmark?"

"A scar. Dad told people I fell off the swing as a kid. True enough, though I broke my arm, not my head. But the story didn't cut it for Mom. I don't think she understands how the perception filter works. She'd seen behind the curtain when she fell in love with my dad and he showed her the real world. She was amazed, fascinated, but also afraid. I think she saw it as a world she wanted to visit but also close the door on during her off-hours. So when the eye on my forehead turned out to be functional and the rest of my abilities showed up, she thought it would set our family apart from the rest of the neighbourhood."

I remembered how many hats she'd tried to make me wear to cover my third eye after it opened, never believing my father when he told her no one except one of our kind would recognize it for what it was.

Maybe that was why I hated hats so much now.

"My grandmother is the heart of our family, though," I said. "It's because of her I still have any family at all. I usually call her every Sunday, and I can only imagine what she's thinking since I missed this week. I'm surprised my father hasn't driven over from Alberta to make sure I'm all right."

"Will you reach out to them? Tell them what's happening?"

"Not a chance in hell. My dad worries enough about my job. I don't want to give him more reason to push me to quit."

"What does he want you to do?"

"Who knows? A desk job like Madison, probably."

"And your grandmother?"

"She wants me to be happy. She knows me sitting around doing paperwork would put people at the mercy of my temper, so she accepts the danger. But I do my best not to focus on it when we chat."

A spasm cut through my shoulder, and I winced as I shifted

in the water, hoping another position would ease the cramp.

Gideon slid across the floor behind me. I was about to sit up to see what he was doing when his hands—cool against my warm skin—settled on either side of my neck. His thumbs dug with gentle pressure into the flesh along my spine and deep into my shoulders, and I melted under his touch.

I'd experienced this particular pleasure in New York. Hours of sitting and waiting had left me tense and sore, and to pass the time, when we'd needed to pay attention to our surroundings so couldn't lose ourselves to other distractions, he'd worked the muscles in my back, learning exactly how much pressure to apply to what areas, what specific motions turned me to jelly.

Over two years, and he hadn't forgotten a single trick.

Although the headache remained, the tightness in my neck relaxed, and the looseness radiated downwards until I was nothing more than a puddle of butter in the water.

"You keep that up and I might float down the drain."

His low laugh rumbled close to my ear. "Float away, Jet Dawson. I'll catch you. You can always be sure of that."

Chapter 9

Jet

A KNOCK AT the door woke me up, and I needed a minute to piece together where I was.

I was in bed but didn't remember getting there, and by the arm draped around me, I wasn't alone. I twisted my already stiff neck to look over my shoulder and found Gideon lying beside me, on top of the covers, shirtless but still in his jeans.

A quick look down at myself.

I wore his T-shirt, bundled under the sheets.

Memories poured over me: Gideon helping me out of the bath, his arm tight around my waist so I wouldn't slip; my dripping body pressed against his as he wrapped the towel around me and patted my back and arms dry; me shivering as the change in temperature and my exhaustion caught up with me.

I remembered the way he removed his vest and peeled off his T-shirt to slide it over my head, my desire to kiss him despite my ever-present headache, to lose myself in the comfort he could give me… and the way his lips had brushed over my forehead before he'd picked me up and carried me to bed only to tuck me in and curl his body around mine.

I'd slept so well and so deeply that even my nightmares had left me alone, and on waking up, I'd forgotten what waited for us outside this room.

Why would someone wake me up when it was still so dark outside?

The bedside clock glowed a cheerful one in the morning, and it was an effort not to yell at the door for whoever it was to go away and leave me alone.

But if Gideon was beside me, that meant Madison was knocking, and if she was awake, that meant Gagnon had left his house.

"We're up," I mumbled, and Gideon groaned. He rolled onto his other side, and I thought he'd gone back to sleep, but by the time I dragged myself out of bed and pulled on my jeans, he was on his feet searching the wall for the light switch.

The sudden glare sliced through my skull, and I squeezed my eyes shut. This headache had to stop. I was one step away from chopping off my head altogether for a single moment of relief. The bath hadn't helped, sleep hadn't helped, Gideon's deft fingers hadn't helped—I was starting to think I'd been cursed.

I tugged Gideon's T-shirt over my head and tossed it to him, and in a smooth motion, he caught it and pulled it on. My clean clothes were on the chair beside the bed, so on my way to the door, I pulled on my black sports bra, my black shirt, and my leather jacket and was ready to go by the time I met Madison in the hallway.

"Lucien left about fifteen minutes ago," she said. "McGee is sitting on the house and will let me know if he comes back."

"Let's head out before he has that chance," I said.

I walked forward, but a sharp, stabbing pain drove a blade behind my third eye, and I stumbled into the wall. Gideon grabbed me before I fell, but I shook him off as soon as I regained my footing.

"Come on," I said, more harshly than I meant to, angrier at myself for stumbling than at them for fussing. *What the fuck is happening?*

I made it to the elevator under my own power and was soon in the backseat of the car where I could take a moment to myself. Gideon drove while Madison navigated, leaving me free to stare out the window and close my eyes against the ebb and flow of the streetlights as we headed up Bank Street into the Glebe.

It would have been nothing more than a twenty-five-minute walk to get there on foot, but I wouldn't have made it. Nausea bubbled in my guts, and I hugged my middle to try to get it under control. I worried how useful I would be on this mission. The others needed me to lead, to step into my role as captain and make sure we got in and out of the house without trouble, which meant I had to be at my best. At the moment, my best was on par with a drunk attempting parkour, but at the very least I couldn't be vomiting all over Gagnon's lawn.

As we turned onto a side street off Bank, a dark figure stepped into the road, drawing us to a stop. I reached for the knife at my side, but he crossed an arm over his chest, identifying himself as one of the queen's people, and Gideon pulled to the curb.

McGee met us on the sidewalk as we got out. In jeans and a July Talk tour T-shirt, he looked nothing like the golden-skinned, black-eyed spies in Meril's court. He could have been a guy in his 20s out for a late-night stroll if not for the white eyes. Good for us—far less likely to catch Gagnon's attention.

"Any sign of him?" Madison asked.

"Not since he left. He took the car and went off by himself. No one has been here since."

He pointed to the house across the street. It was one of the beautiful Glebe mini-mansions, with the sunroom on the eastern side of the house, balconies on both levels overlooking the front and back, and large windows in every direction. The kind of house you walked by as a kid and hoped you might own someday.

And the person who did own it was a lying, murdering traitor.

The world was unfair.

Then again, I didn't have to pay his property taxes.

I left Madison to issue a few last orders to McGee and made my way to the front door. Gideon kept watch as I picked the lock, and by the time I got the door open, Madison had joined us. The alarm sang its warning signal, not nearly as loud as it would be in a minute but still piercing. At any other time, I wouldn't have cared, but today, my head already screaming, the shrill beeps made my teeth hum. I set my hand on the security panel and swallowed my discomfort as I opened my third eye to learn the code.

Just like with Letfield's phone password, this should have been easy. Gagnon lived here, which meant he touched this alarm system multiple times every day to enable and disable it. The code should have been so imprinted on the number pad that all I needed was a quick glimpse.

All I got was static. Noise. Shadows fading in and out, never lingering long enough to show me the sequence. I sensed Madison's and Gideon's tension as the alarm tone picked up speed, increasing the odds of drawing the neighbours' attention, and inching closer, second by second, to alerting the police that someone had broken in. I tried harder to pierce the fog, and still the code escaped me.

Panic made me open my third eye wider, and it burned as though I'd opened my eyes in a chlorinated pool, but I finally caught a brief glimmer of a finger passing over the number pad. It wasn't entirely clear, but we were running out of time. Either I tried it or we lost our chance to snoop around. Making little more than a guess, I pressed each digit with a confidence that, I hoped, hid my uncertainty from the others.

The alarm fell silent, and I rested my forehead against the wall to keep my feet. I couldn't do this. In the state I was in, I was more of a liability than a help. At what point would my pain cause me to slip up and give us away or prevent our escape?

Cut it out, Dawson, I told myself, interrupting the spiralling path my brain had started down. *Focus. That's all you need to do. Focus.*

The others couldn't know. They couldn't fix me, and worrying about me would distract them and make them more likely to miss something or make mistakes.

I drew in a deep breath to steady myself and opened my third eye to take in the rest of the house, ready for the alarm to have summoned someone to check out what was going on. Everything was quiet. According to the gossip around the water cooler, Gagnon was a bachelor, and it didn't look like he shared this massive space with anyone but his ego.

A small blessing, and one I would gratefully accept.

We moved deeper into the house, past the living room on the left and the family room on the right. The kitchen sat at the back of the house with a gorgeous view of the spacious backyard, and as soon as we confirmed both were empty and held nothing of interest, we headed upstairs.

"My apartment could fit in here three times over," Gideon mumbled as we reached the second floor. "Who needs this much space without two-and-a-half kids and a pack of dogs?"

"People with secrets to hide," I said, and turned left at the top of the stairs.

Gideon came with me while Madison turned to the right. There were six rooms up here, four of which turned out to be bedrooms and one a bathroom. I ducked in there on my way to the next room and pawed through Gagnon's medicine cabinet. There were no suspicious prescriptions with his name on them, nothing that gave me any clue about where his headquarters were, but there was a bottle of ibuprofen, which I swiped on my way out. Considering the trouble this man had put us through, the least he could do was cover my pain relief.

I tapped two capsules into my palm and swallowed them dry.

"Good way to get ulcers," Gideon said.

"If it means getting rid of this headache, I'll welcome them." I slipped the bottle into my pocket.

Madison waited for us in the doorway of the last room.

The home office.

If the deputy minister didn't keep the information we needed in here, I was prepared to tear apart every dresser, end table, closet, and floorboard until we found it, but my gut told me we'd be lucky. From everything Madison had told me and everything I'd seen for myself, he was the perfect public servant. Obsessed with dotting every *T* and crossing every *I*. Everything in its proper place. He'd even filed his crime among the minister's papers, for Pete's sake. Somewhere in his private workspace would be an arrow pointing us in the right direction.

We couldn't turn on any lights, and I was leery of using my phone flashlight in case a next-door neighbour looked out their window. Fortunately, there was a streetlight right outside, and the orange glow offered enough illumination to help us navigate the room.

I gestured for Gideon to stay in the doorway and keep watch while Madison and I took charge of the search. Again we split up, Madison going for the desk while I took the filing cabinet. With my hands hidden in the deep drawers, I had fewer concerns about turning on my flashlight to read the neatly printed labels on each folder.

"Does Gagnon bring Erin home with him or something?" I wondered aloud, sparing a thought for his bitchy assistant. I tried to picture him sitting at his desk printing labels and couldn't do it. But what did I know? Maybe that was his way of relaxing after a stressful day of planning his next ghostbomb attack and brainstorming how to scam the government out of next year's budget to fund his personal project.

I flicked through the files one at a time, ignoring his tax documents and the receipts for his home updates, which took up almost an entire drawer. Because of course he was the type of person to maintain records for every renovation and upgrade he'd made to the house since the time of purchase ten years ago. He was a lover of paperwork. Michael had said so, and Michael had never given me a reason not to believe him. Never mind the important parts he'd chosen to leave out.

"Anything?" Madison asked behind me.

"Not yet. You?"

"Nothing except that he must have a lot of faith in his home security system. None of these drawers are locked. Unfortunately there's nothing in them but legal documents, a few postcards from family in BC, some bills he needs to pay, and a bottle of whiskey."

"Good brand?"

"Of course."

I reached out my hand, and Madison brought me the bottle. I twisted off the cap and took a swig. My mouth screwed up at the sharpness of the alcohol, but the warmth offered a much-needed boost as it slid down the back of my throat. Mouth moistened and nerves strengthened, I returned the bottle, and Madison passed it first to Gideon, then took a nip herself before she closed up the desk and joined me at the second filing cabinet.

We worked in silence for another few minutes until I landed on a file that made me pause.

"Interesting."

Madison peered over my shoulder, and I shone the flashlight beam across a folder marked *Insurance*. Inside was a policy for his house, which was assessed at a number I wouldn't have been able to afford if I'd saved up my salary for the past fourteen years. Behind that, though, was a second policy for a house on Main Street.

"What do you think?" I asked. "Parents' place?"

Madison quirked an eyebrow and gestured to the photograph printed at the top of the page. "Would a man like Lucien choose a place like this for his parents? If so, he's a pretty lousy son."

"Yeah, well, he's proved to be a pretty lousy deputy minister."

A decade or two ago, the house would have been a cozy, yellow-sided two-storey with white trim around the large picture window and a porch that extended from one end to the other. A small garden decorated the front lawn, simple and quaint. Time had done nothing for it. Faded and peeling paint marred the siding around the windows, and the screen door sat at an odd angle on its hinges. The garden was overrun with weeds that crept over the sides of the porch and up the wall, and based on the property value, I guessed it hadn't been updated in the past twenty years.

"Keeping his headquarters in the middle of a quiet residential neighbourhood?" Madison said with a shrug. "It fits."

"No one suspects the quiet neighbour of running drugs or attempting some kind of political coup."

Madison's phone went off, the chirp so much louder than usual in the creaky, empty silence of the house. She pulled it out of her pocket and checked the message.

"It's McGee. Someone's coming."

I snapped a photo of the address on the insurance policy, slammed the drawer shut, and rushed out of the room, Madison close on my heels.

Gideon fell into step beside me as I led the way to a bedroom at the back of the house. Downstairs, the front door opened and closed, and a rough voice floated up to us. "Alarm's been disabled."

"Show yourselves," a second man called.

Had Gagnon sent his people here to grab something he'd forgotten? To do a security scan? I'd failed to check if there were cameras around the house, and Gideon hadn't mentioned anything, but it was possible Gagnon had been watching us the whole time.

Dropped the ball again, Dawson. Get it together.

It was so hard to keep my thoughts in a row. All I knew was we had to get out of here and going by the front door was out of the question. Instead, I unlocked the door to the balcony and stepped into the cool night air.

"What are you doing?" Gideon hissed, taking my arm. "You're not up for this."

"I can handle it." I shook him off and stared over the edge of the balcony into the backyard. It was only a few metres. Easy enough to create a ramp down to the grass for me and Madison. Gideon could look after himself.

He clenched his teeth and glowered at me, but followed my lead and misted away. I lost sight of him until he reappeared behind a tree in the back corner of the lot, safe from view of whoever was inside but able to keep us in sight.

"Jet, are you sure?" Madison asked.

The hall light turned on upstairs, and my heart jumped into my throat. "We're out of time to consider anything else. Be ready to run, then get over the fence into the neighbour's yard. We can come around the side of the house and backtrack to the car."

I raised my hands and latched on to the air surrounding me, drawing it closer before I extended it outwards from the railing of the balcony to the ground below.

Madison looked ready to argue but held her tongue. She climbed over the railing and stretched out her arms to keep her balance as she found the invisible ramp. My body was trembling by the time she'd made it a quarter of the way down. It had been a few days since I'd pulled this same trick to get me and Gideon out of my apartment building, but I felt as weak as if it had been yesterday. I sensed patches widening along the ramp, the molecules pulling apart, and I squeezed my hands into fists, summoning the strength to keep them in place a bit longer. Madison had too far to fall, and I hadn't taken my first step.

She reached the halfway mark, and Gideon gestured for us to hurry. I didn't hear anything behind me, but I didn't waste time turning around to look. Accepting I wouldn't be able to hold on much longer, I climbed to the top of the railing and started down. The ground taunted me, and my head swam at the height. My grip on the ramp wavered, and I rushed to tighten it.

Sharp pain behind my eyes, a throbbing at the back of my skull, and now a pulsing in my temples that left spots in my vision.

One foot in front of the other. That's all it is.

If I hadn't told myself how to walk, I suspected I would have forgotten the motions. All my concentration was directed into not grabbing the sides of my head and squeezing it into pulp. Anything to relieve the agony.

The door to the balcony opened when I was halfway down. As the upstairs light cut through the darkness, my energy gave out and the ramp disappeared. Madison let out a squeak as she tumbled the rest of the way, and I dropped three metres into the grass. I landed on my arm, and it went numb from elbow to shoulder.

A shout sounded from somewhere, but for the life of me, I couldn't tell which way was up to get to my feet.

Madison reached me at the same time Gideon did, and they worked together to haul me up. Madison let me go to run ahead, but Gideon stayed with me, dragging me across the lawn and helping to hoist me over the fence, where Madison grabbed my waist to ease me down on the other side.

My head had cleared by the time I landed, and I was able to move on my own. We cut along the side of the house, through the gate, and into the front yard. Out in the open again for anyone looking out the window to see us, but the car was in view, so close. Halfway across, my attention leapt to Gagnon's front porch and the dark figure tearing down the steps.

He ran towards us, weapon drawn, his movements silent as he trampled the garden. I ducked and rolled out of the way as he fired. The shot barely made a noise, suppressed by the same equipment I'd trained with. The same equipment Michael swore would merit the highest punishment if he ever caught anyone using it outside official task force business.

Liar.

With a grunt, I lurched to my feet and threw myself at the figure. Meril's knife was in my hand, and I drew the blade along the back of his arm. His mouth opened in a silent scream, but before the sound made it through his lips, he crumpled onto the lawn.

Gideon reached my side as I sheathed the blade, and we dragged the man between us back to Gagnon's house. Madison opened the door, and with a few unnecessary bumps and jerks, we brought him inside.

"So much for avoiding the fight," I grumbled as she closed the door behind us. "We could have saved ourselves the effort of sneaking out."

Madison turned, and a shriek of terror escaped her throat as her eyes widened. I didn't need to look up to know what she'd seen.

Only by dropping my hold on Mr. Unconscious and shoving Madison to the side was I able to save her from the bullet that slammed into the door where her head had been. The second shot went wide. Gideon misted, and the body he'd taken hold of hit the floor with a thud, his head striking the marble tile with a sickening crack.

Gideon reappeared at the top of the stairs behind Number Two. A third shot fired, but its aim went wild as Gideon caught Gagnon's thug by the arm. Number Two threw an elbow into Gideon's chest, and he teetered into the wall.

I didn't stop to think before I flew up the staircase, throwing myself at the man as he raised his weapon to shoot again. I grabbed his arm, slammed it against the railing, and the shot careened into the chandelier. Crystal rained onto the floor in a rainbow of colour as the shards caught the glow of the streetlight through the window.

Madison threw her arms over her head to protect her face and dashed away from the slicing storm as I struck Number Two's arm against the banister again. He dropped the gun, and Madison ran to it and kicked it into the living room.

Gideon regained his footing, drew Meril's other blade into his hand, and plunged it into the guy's shoulder. Deeper than it had to be, but I wasn't about to give him shit for being over-zealous.

Number Two's pale eyes widened, his mouth formed into soundless questions, and he went slack against me. I stepped aside and let him fall onto the stairs.

My breathing was uneven, but the racing adrenaline had taken the edge off my pain and my arm moved without trouble. Gideon staggered on the step. I reached for him, but he waved me off.

"Bullet nicked my shoulder," he said. "I'll be fine in a minute. Let's take care of these two and get the hell out of here."

Madison stepped carefully over the shattered crystal and crouched next to the first man. She pressed her fingers into his neck and shook her head. "Only one to deal with. The second shot must have hit him." She frowned. "What a mess."

"What do we think?" Gideon asked, looking at Number Two where he lay sprawled on the stairs. "Leave him to wake up and report to Gagnon, or stop him from coming after us again? These are the Vanilla Twins from the bar. I'm not really interested in giving this one a third chance to track us down."

Madison crossed her arms. "You can't seriously be talking about killing him."

I understood her hesitation, but Gideon made a good point. "Gagnon obviously trusts him to do his dirty work. We take him out of the game, and he loses a key lackey."

Anger sparked in her eyes, and her nostrils flared.

"Come on, Madi," I said. "You knew this wouldn't be bloodless. He's taken so many of ours—he has to be prepared to lose a few of his. We'll be safer this way."

"We're better than he is." She marched over to the unconscious man behind me. "If we're so quick to stoop to his level, how are we the right people to bring the department back to what it was? Fortunately, we don't need to jump to death and destruction to get this one out of our hair."

She knelt beside him, and I moved closer to Gideon to give her space. With no explanation of what she intended, she rested her hand over his and closed her eyes. For a moment, nothing happened. And then the man twitched. He rolled onto his side and curled in on himself. Tears rolled down his cheeks, his body shuddered, and the unmistakable reek of urine filled the air. A low keening slipped from his throat, and he squeezed his eyes shut, drawing his knees closer to his chest to make himself as small as possible.

My stomach tightened as I realized what she'd done. She'd crawled into his brain and manipulated him into some kind of nightmare. I'd never seen her push someone so far.

Madison released her hold, stood up, and stared down at him. "There. I'll talk to McGee before we leave, and they can escort him across the wall to face Meril's justice. If we're lucky, he'll wake up ready to confess his crimes to anyone willing to listen. That is if his heart doesn't give out first."

She turned her back on him and started down the stairs. Gideon and I exchanged a glance before we followed.

I looked at my watch as we reached the bottom step. It was getting on two o'clock. Enough night left over to scope out the house on Main Street before the mundanes started waking up.

"Here." I held my phone out to Madison with the screen

open to the photo of the insurance policy. "We can plug the address into the GPS and drive over."

She took my phone without looking at it. "We should go home." Anger still simmered in her stare, no less intense for having won her point in not killing Gagnon's thug.

"Why?" I asked, too wired to work out for myself what might have bitten her in the ass. "We have the information we came for. What's the point of waiting? Gagnon's going to come home, find his chandelier busted, and realize we're onto him. What if he closes up shop or moves? He's working with O'Malley, remember? The king of cover-ups. If we give him the opportunity, we'll lose our chance. They'll have us chasing our tails to Kingston and back, just like last time."

"You really think you're up for breaking into another house tonight?" she asked. "Jet, you crashed. Your abilities gave out, and you fell, and you are damn lucky you didn't break your arm. You're not able to see straight, let alone do what it takes to save yourself if you run into trouble. What would you have done if Gideon and I hadn't reached you in time? If I hadn't warned you that guy was about to shoot?" Her volume rose, and her fingers curled around my phone, her knuckles straining with the tightness of her grip. "Stop trying to be a fucking hero and play this smart."

My restraint slipped as her anger grew, and I threw up my hands and marched towards the front door. "So you want me to do what, Madi? Go back to the safe house, put up my feet, catch a few Z's, and try again tomorrow? You think I'm going to feel better by then? My head is killing me, and it's not going to stop until I put a bullet between Gagnon's eyes, all right? I need to finish this. We could face a dozen extra guards if we wait until tomorrow, and then we'll only be in a worse position. Why not go now, take them by surprise, learn what we can, and get out? All I want is information."

We glared at each other across the foyer, Gideon wisely standing silent to the side, and finally Madison scowled.

"Fine," she said, "but if something happens to you, don't expect me to barge in and help. You might be putting our entire operation in danger, and I will not sacrifice myself and let us fail because of your arrogance."

She pulled the door open and strode across the street to talk with McGee. I stomped along behind her, hating that she might very well be right.

Gideon padded beside me without offering his opinion, though it was obvious by the way he stuck close to my side that he agreed with Madison.

But what choice did I have? My strength was fading with every passing hour, and I was terrified that if I didn't move soon, I wouldn't be able to move at all.

Chapter 10

Gideon

MADISON PLUGGED THE address for the Main Street house into her phone, and the automated voice navigated me across the canal.

If I thought I'd get away with turning the car around and heading back to the safe house, I would have done it in a heartbeat, but Jet sat right behind me, and I sensed her watching. One false move, and she would commandeer the car and drive us to the house herself, and right now the only thing that scared me more than Jet breaking into a criminal headquarters was the idea of her behind the wheel.

She hadn't spoken since we'd gotten into the car. Now and then she made a noise of discomfort, and more than once I heard the rattle of the ibuprofen bottle. Whatever was wrong with her, medication obviously wasn't a fix. She might refuse to consider that the pain was more than stress and fatigue, but I didn't share her denial. Her strength was flagging, every new effort taking more and more out of her, and I didn't know what to do.

Had Michael done this to her?

I didn't bother asking out loud—even if he had, what could we do about it if Jet wouldn't get checked out?—but I couldn't shake my fear that whatever was causing her pain was part of the colonel's plan.

To get her out of his way?

He'd shot her in the face, and the powder had been thick. It hadn't been ghost, and in our immediate relief about that, we hadn't stopped to consider it might be something worse.

"It's coming up on your left," Madison said gently, drawing my attention to the street.

I pulled over a few houses down from the one that matched the picture.

Focus.

I would be useless if I let myself be distracted. Jet's issues were beyond my control, but right here, right now, we might find the answers we needed. The sooner we got in and snooped around, the sooner I could try to persuade Jet to talk to a goddamned doctor.

As far as a supervillain's hideout went, the house was so far from my expectations I stifled the urge to laugh. Compared to Gagnon's place, his headquarters was a modest and comfortable family home surrounded by bungalows and compact two-storey houses. The neighbouring properties were tidy and well maintained, the gardens well kept, the porches wide, the lawns trimmed. The entire street was quiet. Not a single wild summer party to be heard.

"How did he do it?" Jet asked from the backseat. "Look at this place. You know in a couple hours, people are going to be everywhere, taking their kids out, going to work. How the *fuck* did he carry on with his business without anyone noticing?"

"Isn't this Canada?" I asked. "Maybe everyone noticed, and they were too polite to say anything."

"Fuck you."

Clearly her headache had stripped away her sense of humour.

I pressed my lips together to avoid pissing her off more. We had to work together to get inside and search the place, and we couldn't do that if she was biting my head off. My grey cells were tired and worn out, but I still needed them.

"What if we got the address wrong?" she wondered aloud after a few more minutes had passed. "What if his grand-mother lives here or something? What if it's his goddamned family home, and he's holding the insurance on it out of some warped nostalgia? We might be wasting our time."

"And we might not be," Madison said. "Let's give it a while, watch and see what happens. We know he's not home, and if he's not there, he's likely at his headquarters. If that's this place, we'll find out soon enough. What else would we be doing? Oh right. Sleeping."

She was obviously nursing some of the anger she'd shown back at Gagnon's house. I couldn't say I blamed her. The stress was getting to all of us, and she'd lasted longer than I would have expected before snapping.

Jet didn't answer, but the backseat creaked, and when I glanced in the rear-view mirror, I found her slumped down, her arms crossed, her face scrunched in a frustrated scowl.

I looked at Madison, who shrugged, and the three of us stared out the window.

The lights were off and the house was still, as quiet as most others on the block. The curtains in the front room were partially open, revealing a few pieces of furniture under the glow of the streetlights. In a few more hours, dawn would break, and Jet was right: the street wouldn't lend itself well to surveillance. Too many people would be out and about, and the last thing we needed were the mundane cops coming over to ask what we were up to.

Meril's final piece of advice rang in my ears. Darkness was our friend in this, not the coming dawn. If we didn't make our way inside within the next hour, we'd have no choice but to head back to the apartment and try again tomorrow.

"Screw this," Jet said as she opened the door and got out.

I rushed to join her, stepping into her path to block her mad rush across the street. "What are you doing?"

"I can't just sit here. We've been watching for twenty minutes, and nothing inside has moved. There's no one here.

So I say we go in and take a look around. It'll be pretty obvious if we're in the wrong place, right?"

I clenched my teeth to hold back the laundry list of reasons her logic was stupid. What if someone came downstairs? What if this was some poor old lady's house, and she stumbled on two strangers in her living room? There would be screaming, police, maybe some heavy *objet d'art* thrown at my head—it wouldn't end well for anyone.

"Why don't I go in," I suggested. "I can mist around, see what we're dealing with, and you can join me inside once I give the all-clear."

"And let you take the credit when you bring whatever you find to SilverGuard?" she asked, and stepped around me.

I flinched but tried not to let her bitterness get to me. My orders were to do exactly that—less so the taking credit part, but that came with the territory of completing a mission—so I could hardly hold it against her for throwing it in my face. I'd just thought we'd moved past it.

She's in pain, I reminded myself, though the excuse didn't do much to ease the sting.

I ducked my head through the driver's side window. "Wait here," I said to Madison. "Your friend has lost her mind."

"What else is new?" she asked, but her mouth was tight as she tracked Jet's journey towards the house. She offered me a nod of understanding, and I left her to keep watch as I jogged across the street to catch up with Jet.

She was already crouched beside the front door when I reached her, working her set of lockpicks. From what I saw, it should have been an easy lock to tackle—nothing more than an outdated tumbler—but her hands trembled, and when she dropped one of her picks, I gave up being patient.

My muscles were no less steady than her hands, reluctant to dissolve after days of exhaustion and forced healing, but I forced the issue and misted under the door, pulling myself back together on the other side. After a quick check to make sure the main floor was empty, I unlocked the door and opened it to a frowning Jet.

I raised an eyebrow, and she said nothing as she brushed past me into the house. Only as I turned to face the living room did I notice the alarm system on the wall, and a moment's fear clenched my heart.

But there was no sound, no light.

Unarmed.

I waited for a sense of relief to hit me, but it didn't come. Unarmed might mean someone had forgotten to set it, but it could also mean someone was home.

When I pointed the system out to Jet, she rested her hand on the wall and closed her eyes. Barely visible in the dim foyer, a film of sweat spread across her forehead, and when she opened her eyes again, her expression was disturbed.

"People have been in and out all day," she whispered. "I can't see who they are. Maybe the same people, maybe not. No movement in the past couple hours, but I don't think anyone's gone upstairs."

And I'd already cleared the main floor. So where the hell was everyone?

We'd have to take it slow and hope Jet's third eye wasn't so blinded by her headache that someone was able to take us by surprise.

She gestured for me to follow her, and what choice did I have but to obey? She would have gone on without me, and I couldn't let her go alone. Not when she struggled to walk in a straight line.

We passed through the living room, which revealed zero personal items—no photographs, no knickknacks, not even a book—then into the kitchen, which was equally empty of personality.

The more I poked around, the more I realized the scene was staged, set up so anyone peering through the windows believed someone lived here.

The discovery set aside most of my doubts that we'd found the right place, but if this was their headquarters, where did the magic happen?

Basement? I mouthed to Jet.

She rested her hand on the wall again and followed the hallway beyond the kitchen to a door tucked into the corner. She eased it open. No sound drifted up from the depths; no visible sign that anyone was here. I pulled my phone out of my pocket and turned on the flashlight, and the beam revealed nothing but shadows and a hint of concrete at the bottom of the stairs.

I really didn't want to go down there. The darkness was so deep, my light barely made a dent in it. Anything could be waiting for us. The odds of the alarm system at the door being the only security in place to protect the syndicate's goings-on were slim. There could be guards. Guard dogs. Booby traps.

Jet, apparently, didn't care. She started down the stairs with only a slight hesitation. Her footsteps were soft, making no noise against the wooden planks someone had nailed together and called a staircase. I didn't try copying her, my boots too heavy for that level of stealth.

I tapped her on the shoulder and handed her my phone so she could control the light, then focused on my cells and asked them nicely to work with me. It took more effort now than it had at the door, but I faded away and drifted past her.

She reached the bottom at the same time I materialized, but it took all of ten seconds to determine the basement was as empty as the rest of the house. No washer, no dryer. Just a lonely furnace in a sea of concrete and studs.

"God*damn* it," she said, and even though the only evidence that anyone had stepped foot in this house at any point since it was built were the few vague shadows Jet had seen at the door and a lack of dust anywhere, she kept her voice low. I would have done the same. Despite the emptiness, something about the room screamed *wrong*.

I walked to the far side and, with measured paces, scanned every inch of the walls and floor as Jet shone the flashlight over my path to guide my steps. The walls were intact, and the floor was flat. It was a basement. A standard, unfinished basement.

"I feel it, too," Jet said as I turned to walk back to her. "Something's off." She closed her eyes, her brow furrowed, but a moment later, she opened them again and shook her head. "Something's blocking me. Like there's an invisible shield around the room. I see the memory of people coming down the stairs, heading in that direction, and then they disappear."

I started in the direction she was pointing, but as I made my way along the wall, the toe of my boot slipped into a groove in the floor. I stumbled and slammed into the studs with an echo that made me freeze.

When we didn't hear anything after a full minute had passed, I loosened up again. Jet still frowned, but with an interested focus that told me her expression wasn't because of her headache. She'd directed the flashlight at the floor where I'd tripped. Where the floor dipped towards a drain that was only partially visible where it stuck out from under the wall.

"Well, that was a poor design choice," she said. "How would anyone expect half a drain to help in case of a flood? Think we're dealing with an incompetent builder?"

"Or a homeowner who feels very optimistic about their sewer backup coverage."

I crouched to get a closer look and spotted the slim gap

between the bottom of the wall and the ground, about half an inch wide. "This wall's not part of the original construction. Probably a recent addition, too. There's water damage on the floor, but none on the frame."

"And if someone felt it necessary to add a wall, then somewhere there has to be a door, right?"

She stepped forward with the flashlight. I moved with her, and together we inspected the studs and plywood inch by inch, testing every possible handhold and poking every likely panel.

In the far corner, near the front of the house, Jet stopped and wiggled one of the studs. "This one's loose."

She took hold of it and pulled, and we stepped back as a large section of the wall swung open to reveal a fully set up home office, complete with desk, three conference room chairs, and a table lamp that filled the space with a soft, warm glow.

"Bingo," she whispered, and I could have kissed her. I'd been ready to give up over the empty house, but this woman, even fighting what seemed to be the worst headache of her life, had seen through the cracks.

We slipped into the office, and I surveyed the room to make sure no one was about to pop out from behind the bookcase or anything so cliché, but it was empty. Which gave us a chance to take in the paperwork, which was everywhere. Scattered across the desk, sticking out of filing cabinets, piled up on chairs. If I had to guess, Gagnon had no hand in the upkeep of this office, and I hoped the mess made his eye twitch every time he came in.

A brief, superficial scan was all we needed to realize we'd stumbled onto the dragon hoard.

Bank statements, letters, instructions, maps. Everything we'd been searching for was here.

The bank statements alone, sitting out in the open on the desk, were damning. Michael Torrence, Lucien Gagnon, Peter Dougall, Mark O'Malley, four among half a dozen others, all with personal bank balances of over three hundred thousand dollars.

Jet handed me a contract between Gagnon and O'Malley for services and compensation, detailing the pickups and deliveries of ghost to be made and payment for each. I found Dougall's recipe for the drug, a complicated chemical break-down I didn't try to understand.

We worked in silence, handing papers back and forth, taking photos of everything. I wanted to cheer, to throw my arms around her to celebrate our victory. We had them, with more evidence than we needed to prove their treason. But my excitement was dampened by the sheer volume of information we had to sort through with no idea how much time we had.

A soft gasp made me turn around, and I found Jet standing frozen, her eyes glued to the letter in her hand. I inched closer, trying to read over her shoulder, but her fingers shook too badly for me to make out the words. As soon as she finished reading, she braced herself on the desk, and I took the letter from her to read it myself.

Deputy Minister Gagnon, it read. *We were most pleased to connect with you at the International Summit of the Magical and Occult this past June, and especially gladdened by your renewed interest in joining our organization.*

We understand that under past ministers, the leadership of Canada's supernatural groups has remained under the care of both Her Royal Majesty, Queen Meril, and Supernatural, Magical and Occult Affairs Canada.

While we have long believed your country would benefit from the resources our organization has to offer, previous ministries were not inclined to discuss the terms of such a transfer of responsibility.

The Federation of Supernatural Affairs governs the care of supernatural groups from different nationalities across each continent, with a current total of seventy-three partner-countries. This number grows annually, and with our continued success, we are able to offer more services and resources, including security, health care, and infrastructure, for a reasonable fee.

In return, the supernaturals under our purview have assisted us in our military efforts, medical research, and urban development, ensuring a strengthened global supernatural presence.

We would be proud to include Canada as one of our represented countries, and so remove the burden of such oversight from your mundane government.

If you wish to discuss the terms of the transfer, please contact…

I didn't bother to read the rest.

I couldn't believe what I'd already read.

Gagnon wanted to sell the country's supernatural rights. As though an entire population was something to be traded. Pawned off. To an organization that apparently had the goal of accumulating the rights—and manual labour?—of supernaturals across the world. By the sounds of it, they were succeeding.

It made sense that so many countries had jumped at the opportunity. Helping so many groups with such a wide range of abilities to blend into the mundane world was an expensive endeavour. It couldn't be easy to make promises for the safety, health, and prosperity of our kind when, at any moment, the truth might come out that we existed. And if it did, the government would be left holding the bag. It was a huge risk, and the fact that Madison's great-grandmother had convinced the prime minister it was a good idea was a testament to her stubbornness and skills of persuasion.

But to go so low as to betray your people in such a way… It was bullshit. Not even our shittiest president had tried to do something like that. Or if he had, he'd failed. Maybe he hadn't known this federation existed.

My blood boiled, and if I was angry, Jet had to be ready to erupt. I rested my hand on her shoulder, but she shrugged me off to search the rest of the desk.

The FoSA letterhead appeared on at least a dozen sheets of paper spread across the surface. She picked up another but didn't finish, throwing it down in disgust as she leaned her hip against the desk and glared into the bookcase.

Paul, the letter read.

Conditions are ideal for a change in this country. Leadership has grown lax, and there is a reluctance to admit the financial burden taxing our system.

In recent months, a national crime syndicate has released a drug that has taken the lives of hundreds of supernaturals and mundanes, and their reach is growing. These crimes, unchecked and unresolved by our government, are creating an unrest that is increasingly difficult to quell.

I'll be the first to admit a sense of disappointment and defeat that I don't see a way forward to help our people internally. I have worked closely with Minister Bastien to find a solution, but as far as I can see, allying ourselves with your federation is the best chance Canadian supernaturals have for a safe and successful future.

I would be most interested in discussing compensation and terms at your earliest convenience.

Lucien Gagnon

I had to read the letter twice for the finer points to sink in. The bastard was lying to everyone, even to the people he wanted to sell to. Did this federation know the truth, or were they as clueless as the subjects of Gagnon's twisted social experiment?

The rest of the letters were more of the same, breaking down terms and figures. The prime minister would forfeit all right to govern Canada's supernatural groups, and a sum of three billion dollars would be offered as part of the trade, to be split among the bank accounts listed.

Three billion dollars was all Gagnon believed his people were worth. I was glad Jet hadn't stumbled on that breakdown. She didn't need to know how little she was valued by the department she had devoted her career and half her life to.

No one needed that thrown in their face.

I leaned beside her on the desk and crossed my arms.

"So that's that," she said, her voice thick with grief. "If we don't stop them, all it means is a complete loss of autonomy for our supernatural population on the mundane plane. Meril would be forced to close herself off from this part of the world, and the chances are pretty good the States would feel the pressure of FoSA claiming North American soil."

"We won't let it happen." I turned around and set to work taking photographs of the letters when it became clear she couldn't bring herself to do it. Every letter got a picture of its own, same as the other evidence we'd already tagged, the files renamed to keep them organized. A clear record to save our skins and flay theirs.

"What's the point?" she asked.

"What do you mean? We have everything we need to nail these fuckers to the wall, and everything *I* need to avoid being crucified when I report to Dark Wire. This is the proof I came here to find—that ghost is on its way across the border. Just a hundred times worse than we figured."

"At least one of us is satisfied by this trip."

Her defeatist tone surprised me, and I shoved my phone

into my pocket. "You're not?"

"This is paperwork. More evidence confirming what we already know. They sold us out for money. Yeah, that's bullshit, but what is their plan? What is their next step? None of this tells us where to go or how to stop them. Has the deal been signed? Have we missed our shot? Even if we bag every sheet of paper, who do we take it to? The prime minister won't be able to step in. Hell, the folks in the PM's office might see it as a fantastic opportunity from a financial point of view. We need—"

Her eyes glazed over, and her fingers curled around the edge of the desk.

I stiffened, braced for danger. "Jet?"

She held up a hand to shut me up, but her expression didn't relax. "We must have passed through whatever was blocking my third eye. Someone's coming."

I spun around, hoping to find another way out, but there was only the one door, and someone was heading straight for it.

Chapter 11

Jet

I DON'T—THIS DOESN'T make sense."

I strained my third eye to get a clearer impression of the shadows I saw moving towards us, but all I gained was more pain and confusion. Panic gripped me as my ability to dip into the memories of objects and spaces slipped. The mirror was foggy, and no matter what I tried, I couldn't clear it.

A shiver ran down my spine, and goosebumps tugged my skin under my jacket. I felt open and vulnerable and braced myself for shit to fly.

"What's going on?" Gideon asked.

"They're coming closer, but by the movement of their memories, they should be right here. Where I'm standing. I—"

As I pressed the heels of my palms against my temples, voices reached us from… somewhere.

Gideon stepped away from me and spun in a circle, trying

to figure out where they were coming from, but what was there to find? We were alone in the room. But the voices were getting louder, as though they were rising from the depths.

I scanned the room for myself, and the bottom of my jacket caught on the FoSA letters. As the papers drifted to the floor, Gideon bent to pick them up, and something made him pause. My vision blurred as I focused on the darkness under the desk, trying to see what he did, and I squeezed my eyes shut to block out the dizziness that came with the effort. When I opened my eyes again, I spotted what had grabbed his attention: a deep crack in the floor, a seam leading under the desk.

Gideon set the papers on the desktop above him and ran his fingers over the gap, tracing the line to where it met another one, and then another, forming a perfect metre-by-metre rectangle in the kneehole.

The voices were coming from below, and they'd almost reached us.

"Oh shit," he whispered.

He jumped to his feet, gripped my arm, and pulled me into the corner of the room. My reaction times were slow, too slow to find my own hiding place, so I squeezed myself against Gideon behind the armchair and hoped the shadow of the bookcase in a room lit only by a desk lamp would be enough to keep us hidden.

The trapdoor flipped open, and more light streamed into the room from the space below.

"The prime minister is coming off like a total jackass," a man was saying. A familiar voice. Peter Dougall. "The protests are getting worse, and the media's babbling about nothing. They have no idea what's happening, and it shows. Another riot in Moncton. One by one, the provinces are crumbling."

He sounded excited, like a hyper kid who'd been stuck inside too long. Anger bubbled inside me, and I clenched my hands to keep from flying at him.

All thought of moving, fighting, breathing disappeared as Michael came into view behind him, and I was grateful Gideon was holding me steady. If not for his gentle squeeze around my bicep, I might have toppled over in shock.

Why did my heart keep breaking at each new proof of Michael's treason? He had admitted his involvement to my face, and yet some twisted part of my brain was determined to hang on to the foolish idea that he was acting, wanting to protect me. *Yeah, Jet, it's me. I'm the big bad—wink, wink—so go on and get the hell away from this before you get hurt.*

I had to accept I wasn't twelve years old, where all stories finished with a happy ending. He was climbing out of a mysterious subbasement in a hidden room behind a secret door in a house specifically designed to go unnoticed, accompanied by the man hired by a crime boss to create a lethal street drug. I'd read the letters, seen the bank statements. There could be no redemption. No revelation that made me proud to call him my colonel again. He'd killed my troops.

At least now I had a full understanding of what he'd meant about only having the good of our kind at heart. He'd bought into this federation as the solution our country needed. From the day I'd met him, he'd complained about the clunkiness of the department. We never had enough money to ensure our safety and development. It was always a fight with the minister or the prime minister. How many rants had I sat through about Bastien's useless diplomacy and the prime minister's ignorance?

As far as he was concerned, selling us out probably sounded like the perfect option. Privatize the supernatural. Commercialize magic. It was despicable. The deepest betrayal of our kind, and in his mind, he was doing us a favour.

The son of a bitch was lucky I wasn't up to a fight right now, or he wouldn't have made it out of this room.

All these thoughts flitted through my head before he stepped off the ladder and straightened up.

"About damn time," he said to Dougall.

"Now we need the mundie cops to react, the more violent the better. Then the provinces will be ready to accept whatever fix Gagnon suggests."

The Ghostmaker oozed cunning and sleaze, and I wondered how I'd missed it the first time we'd met. Had he really been that good at hiding the truth, or had I been too ready to underestimate him because of his baggy clothes and hunched shoulders? Regardless, I kicked myself for not having seen it. I could have taken him down before the situation went further than the de Lauer blast. He never would have gotten his hands on Madison, Eric would never have shot Gideon.

And we'd still be in the dark about Gagnon's plan.

A harsh reality, but true. Dougall's path of destruction had been our clearest trail of breadcrumbs. He was their greatest weapon, but also their greatest weakness, and we'd exploited him. *He's been good for something, at least.*

"Yeah, well, Lucien better make his move fast," Michael said as he reached the door. "He wasn't in the PM's good books when Bastien kicked it, and he hasn't done much to secure his position since. It's a real shame Bastien sniffed us out. We'd be in better shape if he was still around."

"How can you say that? We would have been stuck dragging our feet. Now we're making progress."

They stepped into the empty basement, and panic wrapped around my chest that we'd left some trace of our visit upstairs. An open door that was supposed to be closed? Had I moved anything?

"It would have been better to hide behind him like we planned until we exposed him as a useless piece of shit," Michael said. "Everyone's looking at us too closely now. Lucien better start licking the PM's boots or act soon, because if a new minister steps in, we'll lose every inch we've gained."

The door closed behind them, drowning out the rest of their conversation.

I sagged against the wall.

And looked at the open trapdoor.

"Jet, no," Gideon hissed in my ear.

His intensity made me hesitate. He was right. We'd already tested our luck tonight. One man was dead, and another guy's mind might have snapped with terror. I felt close enough to death myself. It would be smarter to take what we'd learned and go home. With what we'd discovered here, we had options. If we were careful about how we positioned ourselves, we could go to the prime minister and work with him to take Gagnon down, or we could go to Meril. Either direction put our people's freedom on the line, but so did delay. The prime minister might think the deal with FoSA was a brilliant solution; the queen might believe her only choice was to dissolve the department and reabsorb us into the realm; and if Gagnon got his way...

Another option was to go after Michael and Dougall. They were alone upstairs. We could deal with them tonight and take Michael's troops and Dougall's drugs out of the equation. Gagnon would have a fun time carrying out his plan without military support or his chemical distraction.

But that would mean facing Michael again, and I wasn't ready. Not yet. In my current state, he would have the advantage, and I couldn't expect Gideon to defend me. Especially when we didn't know what surprises Dougall might have up his sleeve.

A loud click echoed through the room, and the trapdoor started to close, obviously on some kind of timer. I hadn't seen any handle or number pad anywhere. Was it an entrance or only an exit? Dangerous or not, I couldn't take the chance we were about to lose our opportunity to find out what lay beneath us.

I tugged my arm out of Gideon's grasp and dove across the floor. My fingers slid into the gap before the door closed, and I pried it open wide enough to slide through.

I glanced at Gideon to see if he was coming. He rolled his gaze to the ceiling but hurried over to me, just as I'd known he would. He'd never been one to miss out on a stupid idea.

The lights were on, but I heard no voices, and though I picked up memories of people walking around, none of them lingered this close to the ladder, disappearing farther down the corridor. Trying my best to keep my third eye open a sliver, I set my foot on the top rung of the ladder and climbed down.

The distance was a full storey, if not more, and when I dropped the final foot and turned towards the corridor, my boots may as well have grown roots deep into the cement. I'd expected a subbasement. A few rooms, maybe, where the meetings were held, the files kept. I hadn't prepared myself for a fully formed underworld. Doors lined both sides of a hallway that stretched well out of view. A full subterranean headquarters, all hiding beneath a quaint family home.

Extending who knows how far.

The hallway branched in a few directions, and I tried to imagine how many other exits might be hiding in how many other homes or storefronts. No doubt these tunnels linked to the Labyrinth, which was why Michael had asked me to meet him there. If I'd listened to him and accepted his job offer, he would have led me here and revealed this secret city. The whole operation.

I started forward, but Gideon's fingers closed around my hand.

"I want to see how far the tunnel goes," I whispered.

"Madison's waiting for us. She's going to worry if we're not back soon."

I held up my free hand, fingers splayed. *Five minutes.*

His jaw worked as he ground his teeth, but he followed me down the hallway. At each doorway, I opened my third eye wider to make sure the room was empty before easing the door open, and by the third door I understood we weren't dealing only with paperwork and rendezvous points.

The first clue was the reek that wafted out of some of the rooms—sometimes sulphuric, sometimes something more rancid, and sometimes sweet. I followed the source of the sulphur to a full laboratory, and although I didn't detect anyone nearby, some kind of chemical process was in the works. By the plastic-wrapped bricks on the table against the wall, I had a pretty good idea what it was.

I gestured for Gideon to look into the room, and his eyes widened as he reached the same conclusion. Their ghost lab. No wonder we'd never been able to find it in all our months of searching. All those community centre raids, all those dealers taken down… and all that time, our deputy minister had been housing and financing the source.

The desire to smash the equipment nearly overwhelmed me. We could land a huge blow against them here, tonight, and the destruction would be more than a little satisfying.

But too many people might be drawn by the noise, and if Lucien kept the ghost lab here, what else hid behind these doors? Michael's troops? More bombs? We couldn't take the chance that one minor strike against them would mean the end of the road for us.

We'd found all we would tonight. The longer we stayed, the more my third eye blurred, and I was too nervous to stick around if I lost the ability to detect any approaching threat. Gideon and I would return to Madison, and she could take us to Serc and Lilith. Once we knew what numbers we had on our side, we could form a plan to storm this place and burn it out. Confiscate the paperwork, destroy the lab, make it impossible for Gagnon to recover his losses before we dragged his ass over the wall and dumped him in front of Meril's throne. With a bright, shiny bow taped to his head.

I waved at Gideon to pull his attention away from the photos he was taking and pointed back the way we'd come. The corridor was still empty, but when my shoulder brushed against the wall, my third eye picked up shadows moving towards us. Before I considered the fact that we were already on our way out and company didn't matter, habit kicked in and I opened my third eye wider to get a better idea of how much time we had.

A pain sharper than anything I'd felt all day tore through my skull, scraping across my brain and blanketing my vision with bright, flashing lights. I was only aware I'd collapsed when my knees struck concrete, and Gideon threw his arm around my chest to stop me from falling flat on my face.

I must have cried out when I landed, because he clamped a hand over my mouth, and I leaned into him as I squeezed my eyes shut. I was going to be sick, black out. Even though I knew I had nowhere to go, that everything I wanted to escape was inside my head, I squirmed in Gideon's hold, unable to stay still.

From somewhere down the hallway, I heard the click of footsteps on the concrete floor. Two sets, getting closer.

They drew to a stop, and through my screaming agony, I heard a chuckle.

"Well, well," Lucien Gagnon said, "I never thought you two would come straight to my door."

My stomach dropped, and horror left me numb to everything except the stabbing in my head.

I'd fucked up. Should have listened to the others, accepted my weakness. We'd been found and were trapped with no way out, unable to fight even if I thought we stood a chance.

We'd been so close.

We had answers. Had proof. Had the start of a plan.

Part of me screamed at the unfairness that we'd come so far only to fail now.

But as the sharp pain grew into a raging fire behind my eyes, all thought of Michael, of FoSA, even of Gideon fell away under my prayer for a final release.

Chapter 12

Madison

ITAPPED MY fingers on the windowsill and glowered at the dark stillness of the house.

Once more, I'd been left behind. Left to stand watch while others took the risks. As though they thought I couldn't handle myself. That I was too precious.

Sure, I looked like a defenceless woman with no skills to serve in a fight, and sure, I hated using the full extent of my abilities unless absolutely necessary, but I was capable of so much more than I appeared to be. I didn't need to be protected because of my warped connection to the queen.

I would probably be able to save both Jet's and Gideon's asses in a pinch, as well.

Next time, I would put up more of a fight to accompany them, but with no idea what was happening inside, I didn't want to stumble in when following them might put us all in danger.

I would be their lookout, even though they'd been inside for twenty minutes with no reassurance they were all right. I'd watched them pass in front of the picture window over fifteen minutes ago, and there had been no movement since.

For all I knew, the house had eaten them and I was on my own.

I'd give them another ten minutes, and if they hadn't contacted me by then, I'd… reassess my position.

With a groan, I dropped my head against the headrest and beat my palms against the steering wheel. As soon as Gideon had left, I'd moved into the driver's seat, wanting a better view of the house and to make sure I was able to hit the gas and go if they came out in a hurry. At least as a getaway driver I could be useful.

I regretted that my last words to Jet before she'd gone inside had been in anger, but she'd pushed me too far to hold back. For over twenty-four hours, I'd watched her wilt away, growing paler, less coordinated, less coherent with every turn of the clock, and instead of listening to me and getting some rest, she'd dug her heels in.

I hadn't been able to stay quiet any longer.

Now I wondered if I should have. I'd known my speaking up wouldn't change anything. Part of me had hoped my outburst would shock her into reason, but of course her anger and determination were greater motivations than my feelings.

Now she'd disappeared into the unknown, leaving me to sit

here and pray we'd have time later to set things right between us.

My phone buzzed where it lay on the passenger seat.

I stole a glance at the screen to make sure it wasn't Jet or Gideon, then ignored it.

Colm.

Again.

Fourth message tonight, and I hadn't answered any of them. I told myself it was because I needed to stay focused on the house, be ready to move at a moment's notice, but I didn't believe me for a second. In truth, I had no idea what to say to him.

Some uniforms came to my apartment tonight asking about you. Are you okay???

Who the hell are these people? They asked all kinds of weird questions. I told them I don't know anything. I don't care about any of it, I just want to make sure you're all right. Please call me.

Madison, will you please call me? I'm worried sick.

His concern coiled around my heart, as soft as warm blankets, as sharp as thorns. Tears pricked the corners of my eyes, and I blinked them away. I didn't deserve to cry. I was hurting him by keeping my distance, but it was nothing to the pain he might face if I brought him closer.

With each new message, I told myself I wouldn't read it, but despite myself, I picked up my phone.

I should take the hint and leave you alone, but I can't. Not yet. First you say goodbye, then you say it's not that

SERIOUS, NOW THESE QUESTIONS? I CAN'T WALK AWAY UNTIL I KNOW YOU'RE OKAY.

This time, a tear dripped over my cheek before I could rationalize it away, and I wiped my face with the back of my hand.

In a perfect world, I'd reply with some inane chatter. *Let's get together next week, and I'll fill you in on the absolute madness that is my life right now.* We'd meet, have a few laughs, maybe I'd finally untangle my jumble of feelings for him.

Instead, I did my best to put him out of my mind while I waited for my friends to finish breaking into my acting-boss's house to learn how he was involved in my previous boss's murder and the attempted destruction of our country.

How did I end up here?

It was far from the first time I'd asked myself the question and suspected it wouldn't be the last.

My mental flurry was close to spinning me into a tornado of anxiety when a light turned on inside the house. I leaned in so quickly to see what I could make out, I decked my head against the window and was still rubbing my forehead when a figure stepped into view in the living room.

My mouth went dry.

The studied slouch, the loose-hanging shirt, the baggy jeans.

Peter Dougall.

The man who had tied me to a chair and strapped a ghostbomb to my lap. If Jet hadn't shown up when she did—and sorted out her priorities in quick measure—I wouldn't be here stressing over text messages. I'd be in the morgue with my brain half-melted out of my skull.

He stood by the window, laughing about something, looking as though he didn't have a care in the world, and I wanted to crawl inside his head and warp his emotions until he shrieked for his demon of a mother. Too bad he'd proved to be immune to my ability. I would have to settle for strangling the bastard.

When a second person stepped beside him, I tightened my fingers around the steering wheel. From this distance I couldn't make out his face, but his bearing made him easy to identify. Shoulders back, spine straight, hands by his sides. Michael and the Ghostmaker together in the house Lucien had set up as his headquarters.

But if they were on the main floor…

Jet, where the hell are you?

I tried not to imagine the worst. What if these two men were relaxed and laughing because the people chasing them were no longer a problem? I opened my mind to read their emotions, but they were guarded by metal and glass and distance. There was stress in the air, terror, but I suspected it was all mine.

And the only thing I could do was wait.

Chapter 13

Gideon

A CHOKING RAGE kept me from replying to the smug bastard standing over us.

Jet struggled against me, refusing or unable to fall still, and I crouched over her, protecting her from herself as much as from the two men who had discovered us.

I'd never seen Lucien Gagnon up close before, but I assumed it was him by the suit and the fact he was wearing a tie at two o'clock in the morning. In my opinion, he wasn't much to look at, with narrow shoulders, a weak jaw, and the physique of someone who hit the squash court a couple times a month and once in a while skipped the steak for a salad. Tailored suit, well pressed, clean-shaven, and oily-haired. His vibrant blue eyes were sharp as knives, and I guessed that if he had the ability to shoot daggers out of them, he would have by now.

The man beside him, on the other hand, was very familiar,

and I had to fight not to recoil at the sight of him.

After all, how do you forget the person who climbed inside your body and plucked every individual nerve like a harp string? Carstairs, the man Jet's lieutenant had turned me over to, who had strung me up from the ceiling and tortured me in ways that haunted me waking and sleeping so many days later.

To see him standing here, looking eager to get his hands on me again, made me curl tighter around Jet. He wouldn't get near either of us. I wouldn't give him that satisfaction. But if I didn't want to kill us to get out of his reach, I'd have to come up with a better plan. Quickly.

"Gideon Leigh," Gagnon said. "They told me you were dead."

"Sorry to disappoint."

He chuckled. "On the contrary, we're happy to invite our American neighbours to join our venture. Do you like what you've seen so far?" He shoved his hands in his pockets and surveyed his personal kingdom. "Not bad for a few years' work. You know about the ghost, and Michael told me he gave away the details of our military forces." He smirked. "But I don't suppose he went into detail about the side projects our Ghostmaker has been working on, hmm?"

Arrogance gave his Quebecois accent a slick, sleazy drawl that burned my blood and filled me with the urge to launch myself at him. At the moment, I didn't care if Dougall had created robots to spray the entire city with ghost, I just wanted to drive my fist into this guy's face.

More footsteps echoed behind me, closing us in on both sides and removing our last path of escape.

"Honestly, I'm impressed by how quickly it acted," Gagnon continued, looking at Jet, and in a breath the heat in my veins was gone, extinguished by a vat of ice water that ran down my spine. I didn't even thaw out when he laughed. How quickly what had acted? Did he know what Michael had shot her with?

"No, I suppose he wouldn't have said anything, would he? He thought the results would be long, drawn-out, slow to affect her in any real way. He'd be horrified to learn what he's done to his protegée. Has she been in a great deal of discomfort, or has she been a good little soldier and hidden it from you?"

"What did he do to her?" I asked through clenched teeth. I was willing to let him blather on about anything else, but if he knew what was wrong with Jet, he was going to tell me. I wasn't beyond setting her down and forcing the issue if I had to.

"We call it an earthworm. A parasite that migrates through the eyes or nose and burrows into the brain. Still in beta stage, I'm afraid, so the full effects aren't yet known. In most of our trials, it took days for symptoms to show, but Captain Dawson's third eye must have offered it a direct route. Unfortunate for her. From what I understand, the experience is quite unpleasant. Excruciating, even. Sensory disruptions, physical pain, confusion, paralysis. A heavy impact with very little effort on our part, which is perfect when one needs to collect information from a subject. She could have spared herself and taken the beating, but she had to fight back, and now she'll wither away."

My mouth went dry and my brain filled with static. I couldn't look away from him, hoping to catch some hint that he was fucking with me.

"It starts with a headache, but soon she'll lose coordination, impulse control—that could be fun to watch—and that's only the beginning."

His words wriggled in my ears, burrowing as deeply as his goddamn earthworm. They travelled down my spine, numbing everything as they went, until they reached my lungs. Suddenly I couldn't draw breath. Panic wrapped its fingers around my heart, set my pulse racing, and I clung tighter to Jet. She moaned and her eyelids fluttered, but she didn't open her eyes to look at me. She didn't respond to anything Gagnon was saying, and I didn't know if it was a blessing she couldn't hear him or if it meant she was too far gone to understand him.

"She'll deteriorate until she gives up and begs someone to kill her—unable to do it herself—or until her body does it for her." He shook his head. "I would love to observe how she changes, but it would be kinder to our dear colonel if we put her out of her misery. Wouldn't you agree, Mr. Leigh?"

Time had run out. Jet had gone slack in my arms, so I was on my own. There was no way in hell I could fight our way free.

"I suppose I should thank you for bringing her to us. With her corpse in our possession, we can use her as the perfect scapegoat for Bastien's murder, the attacks, and the trouble in the department. You've bought us so much time."

He wavered behind the red haze filling my vision. "There's no point. We have Meril's protection. She knows everything. The minute you announce Jet is dead, the queen will destroy you."

Gagnon laughed. "No one will believe her. The majority of supernaturals on this side of the wall have swallowed my propaganda. They think her authority is outdated and destructive. She can try to sway them as much as she likes, but they won't listen. What's the term these days? 'Fake news.'" He grinned and turned to Carstairs. "Take care of her, will you? Make it quick, as a favour to the colonel. Do what you want with the spy."

He turned and walked away, not even willing to watch his orders being carried out. The worst kind of coward.

Carstairs turned his sick grin on me and aimed his gun at Jet. Of course that's how he'd start breaking me down, by making me watch while he stole her away.

I closed my eyes to block him out. He didn't matter. What he didn't understand was that if he killed Jet, nothing would ever matter again. He would lose his hooks in me and may as well shoot me here and now for all the enjoyment he'd get from stringing me up for another round of Guess the Agony.

But we weren't dead yet. We still had a chance—a very, very slim chance. The exits were blocked, guarded. I could summon strength I didn't know I had and still not make it to the ladder only so many feet away.

Not in physical form, anyway.

I clasped Jet against me, doing my best to remove any space between us. My breath evened out as I homed in on my individual cells and branched into hers. Time slowed, every thump of her heart morphing into a drumbeat. A death march, maybe, but the rhythm of my pulse helped me find hers, and I squeezed her tighter until I couldn't separate whose heartbeat was whose. This had to work. I had to find a way. My cells were ready to fall apart and dissolve into mist, but I held myself together, desperate to tear down the barrier that remained between her body and mine.

I'm not leaving you here, Jet. Come on.

All my life I'd worked on strengthening my ability, learning how to disappear in a blink, taking my clothing, weapons, possessions with me. Never had I attempted to dematerialize with another human being, and I honestly didn't know if I could.

But if ever there was a time to try, if ever I believed I could connect with someone on that intimate a level, it was with the woman in my arms. I was terrified about what would happen if I succeeded—so much might go wrong—but I couldn't afford to think about what would happen if I failed. There was no other option but to try. I'd spent my life detaching myself from everyone. New names, new cover stories, never staying anywhere long enough to call it home. Jet was my exception.

Ever since I'd crossed the border, she had been my motivation for every move, every decision. Not even Carstairs had gotten inside my head the way she had. This woman was all over me. We were all over each other, inside each other, and if that were the case, then I could reach her. There had to be a way.

Somewhere beyond us, words were exchanged, but whoever it was and whatever they were saying slipped around me, never breaking my concentration.

Despair—the sense of time flowing, each second taking us closer to the end, stripping away my chance to save us—tore at me, and I threw myself deeper into the feel of Jet's skin under my fingers, the softness of her hair, the curve of her body.

Deeper.

The shallowness of her breath, the flutter of her heartbeat.

Deeper.

The rush of blood in her veins, the contraction and release of every artery. I was inside her, flowing through her, with her.

The room faded, the threat hovering over us a vague afterthought. Finally, I found her—the trace of her that existed deeper than skin and muscle and blood. She resisted me at first, her genetic makeup sliding away from my attempt at absorption, and if she'd been conscious, she might have succeeded. As it was, I was only just able to wrap myself around her, inside and out, and, with a strength greater than I believed possible of myself, pull her apart.

A shot rang out, but by the time the bullet reached her, we were gone.

Chapter 14

Gideon

I'D TOLD JET the truth when I'd said the first time I misted was in my mother's arms. I'd travelled across a room before I knew how to crawl.

I just didn't remember it.

The way my mother used to talk about me, I did it all the time. She found me in the dryer, on shelving units, one time inside the kitchen wall, and according to my brother, I'd thought it was the best thing ever, even if I had no idea what the hell I was doing.

The first time I *remember* breaking my body down into individual particles was in kindergarten. I was playing with one of my favourite toys—one of those sandbox dump trucks—and a bigger kid wanted it. In my memory he loomed over me, but then, at five years old, most of the world did. My chest still tightened at the imagined threat, my innocent fear when he raised a hand to hit me, the sudden lightness when my body dissolved.

It was the first time I'd vanished by choice. A conscious effort to mist away.

My terror at having disappeared—that's what seared the memory into my head and made the details stand out as though it had happened yesterday. No longer the buzz of dread that comes in the face of physical harm, but something much more visceral. The horror of being lost.

A five-year-old kid, broken into a million pieces, trapped in the air with no sense of grounding but still aware of existing. I had no lungs, no heartbeat, none of the physical signs I later came to associate with panic, but it was there all the same, not in one central cerebral region but split across every atom, every microscopic cell freaking out with silent screams and a certainty that I would never see my brother, my friends, or my toys again.

Later I learned I was gone for over an hour. The teacher didn't believe the other kid's story, of course. Obviously I couldn't have *disappeared.* They thought I'd run off, and my mother was ready to agree with them when they called her, finding it easier to lie than to explain the truth. The staff scoured the school, the playground, every nook and cranny I might have squeezed into.

They found me huddled beneath the cloakroom bench, naked, drenched in sweat, and shaking so badly I threw up all over the teacher's back when she picked me up, wrapped me in her sweater, and carried me to my mother's waiting car.

I had never experienced that kind of terror, that intense dissociation, from using my ability since.

Not until today, as I balanced myself and Jet on the edge of extinction to get us out of that headquarters.

Too much was happening. Too much for me to focus on. The strangeness of carrying an extra set of organic cells made it impossible to direct my attention to our surroundings, and more than once I ended up stuck against a wall, needing to rely on the drifting air currents to guide me through the hairline cracks in the concrete and drywall, up the stairs, and out an open window in what I guessed was the kitchen.

I'd hoped that once we were outside, I'd feel more comfortable, but if anything, I was more afraid. My grip on Jet was shaky, loose enough not to absorb her into myself even as I scrambled to avoid losing a single particle of her being.

If I could have left the parasite in her brain behind, I wouldn't have hesitated, but I had no idea what I was looking for or what else I might release if I tried. More important was getting her back in one piece. It had taken me years to figure out how to get my clothes to materialize without giant patches missing, and I didn't have the leisure of practice time with Jet.

In this form, my thoughts were sporadic, fleeting. Consciousness without structure, an awareness of direction and movement, of obstruction and my own existence. The effort of stretching myself beyond those limits made it a challenge to stay incorporeal, and more than once, parts of me began to reform.

The first time, I decked the point of my elbow against a bush somewhere in the front yard. The second time, I nearly lost my hold on Jet as I struggled to gain control of my wavering self.

I had no sense of Jet's consciousness—and no way of communicating with her. Fear sparked from particle to particle. What if I'd made a huge mistake? What if I couldn't bring her back? What if I did, but I'd left some part of her behind or accidentally scrambled a woman who was never meant to be anything but whole?

But what other choice had there been? Save myself and let Carstairs gloat as she died in front of him? I would rather have killed her myself. Maybe I had.

So now we floated in this world without top or bottom, woven together in a way that should have been impossible. One bundled collection of atoms dancing around each other, bound solely by my determination and unwillingness to let her go.

Somewhere out there was safety, and time and patience would get us there.

Panic would achieve nothing.

I couldn't be that five-year-old boy again.

Anger sparked beneath my fear. We'd found each other in the darkness despite our mutual stupidity and stubbornness, and if we could do that, then I could find our way out of this.

I anchored myself to the desire of seeing her face again and tripled my focus on the world around me, resolved—desperate—to bring us back.

The fringes of my consciousness brushed against something solid, and I spread out to take in the shape and makeup of the obstacle. Wisps of me dipped into a gap in the wall. Another door? A house across the street? No, too many cracks. Too many doors.

Car.

Window down. Someone waiting?

Madison.

Wrapping myself more tightly around Jet, I poured through the window, brushed against the person in the front seat, and spilled into the back.

I started to pull myself together but snagged on a fragment of matter I didn't recognize. The pieces of Jet that had intertwined with mine. Without knowing how I'd done it, I'd broken her apart, and now I had no idea how to put her back together.

Vibrations of panic took hold of me again, the tiny cells of my being dancing at a frequency that made it impossible to find structure. The more I vibrated, the less I was able to differentiate between Jet and myself, until there was no differentiation. We were one person, and I didn't know how to separate us.

But I wasn't about to bring myself back if I couldn't take her with me, so until I figured it out, the two of us would remain here, trapped, but trapped in each other. If nothing else, there was that.

A sense of not-me drifted along my awareness, and I latched on to it, learned its shape and feel. It sparked against my consciousness, each contact between us shooting energy into me like flashes of lightning.

With each new flash, more of my fear faded into fascination, and I set about collecting every speck that triggered the electrical reaction, gathering them, piecing them together, splitting what was me from what was not-me until two distinct presences took shape. Mine came together with the natural ease of practice and ability, but the closer I studied, the more I recognized Jet's makeup, the uniqueness that made her Bridget Dawson on such an invisible, cellular level I would never be able to unsee the complex beauty that was her, so much more intricate than anyone else would ever know.

As soon as I learned her signature, pulling her back became as easy as forming the bracelet around my wrist or the blade at my hip, and with one last burst of effort, we materialized in the backseat, my solid arms around her solid frame.

Her solid and unconscious frame.

"Get us out here," I said to Madison, who'd twisted around in her seat to stare at us. "Get us the fuck out of here before they barge through that door and start shooting."

Chapter 15

Madison

I STARTED THE car and pulled into the street, doing my best not to stomp on the gas. Speed would get us away from the house faster, but it would also draw attention. At this hour of the morning, any traffic was conspicuous, but tearing through a residential neighbourhood would be as subtle as installing a giant neon arrow on the roof of the car, pointed downwards, with a flashing sign that read *Fugitives Here*.

My hands trembled against the steering wheel, and I watched the rear-view more than the road to make sure we weren't being followed, but when I turned onto Main Street without any obvious tail, I began to relax.

I could not say the same for Gideon.

"Can't you go any faster?" he demanded, and not for the first time.

His fear coated the back of my throat like sour slime. From

the moment he'd materialized in the backseat with Jet in his lap, I hadn't been able to get my bearings.

"They shot a parasite into her brain," he said as he tried to shake Jet awake. Beyond a faint murmur on his first attempts, she hadn't made a single movement or sound, which had done nothing to settle his state of mind. "A fucking parasite, and it's eating her brain, and how the fuck are we supposed to help her?"

He wasn't shouting but was only a few decibels short of it, and in the closed-in car, the noise battered my eardrums, filled my head with his panic, which left me incapable of forming thoughts of my own.

"What the hell am I doing here? I don't know anyone, I don't know what I'm doing. I'm not even supposed to be here." He barely took a breath before throwing himself into another stream-of-consciousness tirade. "Hell, I don't know *you*. I'm trusting you because Jet does, but for all I know, you're as greedy as the rest of them. Could even be part of this deal they're making. Do you know what they're planning, Madison? Do you know why all this is happening? They're selling you out. Selling you *off*. Say goodbye to Canadian supernatural culture and hello to some corporation based out of who knows where that's snapping up countries like some kind of collectible set and putting the people to work. You didn't see what's down there. Full laboratories, hundreds of packages of ghost ready for distribution, and who knows how many bombs ready to be planted. We were right about the riots. Everything they did was to stir up shit in the public eye. They're building themselves up for the final play. And while they're busy preparing that, your friend is literally having her brain eaten because her mentor—a man she trusted with her life—*shot her in the face with a fucking parasite.*"

"Shut up for a minute and let me think, all right?" I snapped, my restraint slipping.

Did he think I wasn't terrified for Jet? The sight of her, white as death and barely breathing in the backseat, was enough to make me burst into tears if I gave myself half a second to consider what it meant. But if he was losing his head, I had to hold on to mine and come up with some kind of solution.

The first step was to get far away from that headquarters.

"We won't be able to help her if they track us down," I said.

"So where can we go? We need help, and we need it fast. Jet won't last much longer, and I'll be damned if she's not going to survive to kick a serious amount of ass. We can't give up. We can't let them win."

"And we won't," I said, "but if we make moves without a solid plan, the odds of us doing anything useful are next to non-existent."

I was grateful he didn't ask me what that solid plan might be, because as I drove towards downtown, I had no clue. Worse, I couldn't mute the part of my brain screaming at me that Jet's life was secondary to whatever massacre Lucien was organizing. Gideon's report had filled me with a cold dread that settled deep in my gut. Whole laboratories? How much chaos would they create if they unleashed their inventory? How would their plans change now that they'd found us there? Would they speed things up to prevent us from blocking their next move?

Gideon wasn't wrong, either. I was driving away from their headquarters, but where the hell were we supposed to go? Who could we trust with what they'd found? If Meril caught wind of this deal, she would be over here in the blink of an eye to crush the operation, the headquarters, and anyone remotely involved. No chance to save Jet. Secret blown. War started.

Bile crept up the back of my throat at the idea of letting Jet die. And in such a way. That Michael could have done something like this to her was unthinkable. It would have been one thing to kill her and get her out of the way, but what purpose did this slow death serve? Revenge?

Distraction.

The answer slapped me across the face, and I slammed my hand against the steering wheel and wrenched the car to the side of the road. If we focused on saving Jet, we gave them what they wanted, the same thing they would have gotten if they'd killed her tonight: extra time and us off their backs. They saw us as a minor threat—and they weren't wrong with three against an army—but enough of a hindrance to want us out of the way. Why else would Lucien tell Gideon what Michael had done?

"They want us to focus on her," I said.

"Then they'll get what they want. There is no other option."

"Is that what she'd want? To survive only to discover she's lost her job, her department, her *freedom*?"

"I think she'd want to survive. Period."

"Gideon—"

"No. You do whatever the fuck you feel you have to, but if you think I'll let her slip away from me without doing everything possible to save her, then your fancy mind abilities aren't worth shit."

I ground my teeth and glared at the empty road ahead. Of course he would make an impossible decision even more impossible. Of course he would try to turn me into the villain because I was attempting to come at this objectively, the way any good negotiator would.

The obvious answer stood in front of me, an obstinate brick wall. Jet was my best friend. She had taken us this far, and I would be devastated if I didn't try to bring her back, but we were talking about the futures of millions of beings. How could we prioritize her life when the rest of our people were about to be turned over to an international organization like cattle?

I hadn't spent the better part of my career negotiating trade deals only to be traded myself.

Especially not for the financial gain of someone I had trusted.

This wasn't the time for sentiment. Lucien had obviously lost any of his in this cold, logical bid for wealth.

"Didn't you tell Meril you'd made connections?" Gideon asked. "Didn't you say you had full armies awaiting orders? Call them. Send them after Gagnon. They can clear out the headquarters while we figure out how to get this thing out of Jet's head."

I caught my lower lip between my teeth and worried it as I scanned the street, searching for anyone watching us, any cars pulling up behind us.

"What do you suggest?" I asked. "That we send our last-resort resources into what could very well be a trap? That we dump the entire responsibility of stopping the FoSA deal onto other people's shoulders, to hell with the consequences? Serc, Lilith—they both report to Meril. Calling them in now would risk everything we've worked to avoid."

"How far do you think we'll get without Jet? If we can't—*until* we bring her back, we're out of moves anyway."

I choked on my anger. Goddammit, he was right. Without Jet, we would have my documentation and Gideon's field expertise, but he would be on his own, without backup, and there was only so far paperwork would get us without someone to show it to. With Jet, we could formulate a plan. Stay on the defensive, push them back.

Without her, we were out of options.

"We'll need time to mobilize our allies," I said, doing my best to ignore the pulsing pressure behind my right eye. "That's if they agree to help us. Lilith warned me her people wouldn't take the front lines, and I don't know how much danger Serc is willing to bear. We'd be asking them to go against their wishes and take the lead on this."

"That's on them, then, isn't it," he snapped. He took a deep breath, and the maelstrom of his emotions evened out, just as intense but steadier. "If we can get Jet back on her feet, we can keep control of the situation. Put your people on standby. Let them know they might need to act on something huge. Keep the Eyes on our key players twenty-four-seven so we're ready to act if they do. But if Gagnon thinks Jet is down and we've been scared off, they might get overconfident. They might make mistakes and give us an opening we'd never get if we tried to go after them while they're expecting us."

I caught his gaze in the rear-view mirror, and his dark eyes burned like coal. Every word he spoke battled the arguments in my head, and I wished he didn't sound so logical. With Serc and Lilith ready to go at a phone call, with every resource we had on high alert, we could try to save Jet without sacrificing the greater mission.

I prayed I wasn't giving in to empty wishes.

Nan, why did you never prepare me for this?

A sharp ache shot up my palm into my wrist, and I loosened my grip around the steering wheel.

My thoughts whipped around so quickly I couldn't pin them down, but at least now I had a next step. As long as I kept putting one foot in front of the other, I would get through this.

Scrambling to figure out what the hell I was going to say, I grabbed my phone from the passenger seat and scrolled my call log to the number of the queen's Eye posted outside Lucien's house.

He answered after the third ring. "McGee."

"It's Madison. We found the headquarters, and it's bad. Worse than we feared."

"Have you informed Sercario?"

I squeezed my eyes shut. "Not yet. I'll brief him shortly, but an immediate forward manoeuvre wouldn't be to our advantage."

"Understood."

"We need more watchers on this." I gave him the address of the headquarters. "On this location and on every person who comes out of it. The deputy minister, Colonel Michael Torrence, Peter Dougall. Anyone you recognize, we want tailed."

"I'll see to it right away."

I swallowed. "And McGee..." I hesitated. Asking for his help with Jet would reveal the order of my priorities, and Meril wouldn't respond well to them once she found out. It would be one more strike for her to hold over my head during the conversation she said was coming.

To hell with it. What was another excuse for her to bring me back?

"Captain Dawson has been injured. If we don't seek medical help for her straight away—" I opened my eyes and, when

I found Gideon staring at me in the mirror, avoided the brutal truth and said "—we are royally screwed."

There was silence on the line, and my chest tightened. I shivered under the hum of disapproval. My focus was misdirected. I should have reported to Serc first. I was wasting precious time. I heard it all in everything he didn't say.

"I can't help you," he said at last, and at least he had the decency to sound regretful. "It's not in my power to act outside the orders of my queen, and she's given no command beyond serving as your eyes in this world." He cleared his throat. "Even if I had the freedom to assist you, there's little I could do. What supernatural power is there to be trusted in this world? If you return to the Estate and pass through the wall, someone on the other side might—"

"No," I said. "We don't have time for that. Thank you, McGee, I understand your position. Let me know when the Eyes are in place."

I ended the call and bowed my head.

Thankfully, Gideon said nothing, though I felt his eyes on me. Even more accusing were the emotions rolling off him. Impatience, frustration, anger, worry, fear. Not a single positive vibe among them.

I did my best to raise a barrier around my mind to block him out. Anything to save myself from the raw force of his pain.

How was I supposed to break it to him how little hope we had? McGee was right—even if we took Jet to one of the three supernatural clinics in the city, what could they do for her without word getting back to Lucien or Michael? The Peaview was her best shot, but that would mean walking onto enemy soil.

While the medical ward behind the wall was established with the best equipment, it would take us at least forty-five minutes to get there, not to mention however many delays we might face on the other side dealing with the queen's people. We would also be open to Meril's intrusion.

Our isolation weighed on me, closed in on me, prevented me from seeing any way out. Throughout my career, I'd prided myself on the relationships I'd fostered, and here I was, unable to think of a single person to call.

Except one.

The air caught in my throat, and the tips of my fingers went numb.

McGee had said there were no *supernatural* resources at our disposal, but what about mundane ones? We couldn't walk into the ER and expect anyone to be able to help, but maybe there was a way around the usual formal channels.

Colm.

In a heartbeat, every argument I'd ever had for and against revealing myself to him rose and faded, guided by the racing priorities of reason and emotion. Neither approach, neither side of the debate, struck me as better than the other. Did my feelings for him make me think he was exactly what we needed, or was it a rational choice? Did I trust him with the truth of our world—with Jet's life—with our secret?

And if I did trust him, was I ready to put his life in danger? Dragging him into this—now, especially—would put him as directly in Lucien's sights as we were. It would mean one more person to keep safe.

If he doesn't run out of the room screaming first.

If he believed me at all.

A groan sounded behind me, and I turned around to look at Jet. Gideon cradled her in his arms, his hold as gentle as it was secure. She sat with her head draped on his shoulder, her arms slack at her sides. Since they'd materialized, her face had been smooth, but now her brow was furrowed, and her back arched as a jolt of pain passed through her. She jerked again, her arms flailed, and in a heartbeat, she lapsed into a full seizure.

"Madison." My name came out as a plea through Gideon's clenched teeth as he held Jet on her side, the muscles in his arms straining to maintain his grip on her.

We were out of time and out of options. No matter what the consequences were for my future with the man I'd kept at arm's-length for so many years, he was our best shot at saving the woman dying in the backseat.

My hand trembled as I reached for my phone.

This is stupid. There has to be a better way.

Between the time it took to find Colm's number and bring the phone to my ear, I racked my brain trying to come up with another solution, one that wouldn't risk shredding the bound-aries of my life into a million tiny pieces.

The phone rang, and only on the fourth ring did I look at the clock. It was almost four in the morning. Not only was I about to tear down the perception filter and destroy Colm's worldview, but I was going to wake him up at an ungodly hour to do it.

But when he answered, he sounded as awake as if I'd called him at four in the afternoon.

"Madison, thank Christ," he said. "Where are you? What's going on? Do you know what people are saying about you? Those men I messaged you about, they want to know if you had something to do with your minister's *murder*. I'm supposed to call them if I hear from you, can you believe that?"

I drew in a slow breath, grateful I didn't have to block his emotions over the phone and amazed the only note in his voice was one of concern. No accusation, no anger. Just worry on my behalf.

It warmed me even as it made me that much more reluctant to do what I was about to do.

The marching clock, however, pushed me to say, "Colm, it's okay. I promise, I will explain everything." Had I really just said that? *Madison, what are you doing?* "But first… I need your help."

Silence stretched down the line, and I held my breath. What would I do if he said no? He would be well within his rights.

Hell, he would be smart to deny me. But where would that leave us? Leave Jet? He was the only hope she had.

"What do you need?" he asked, and I swallowed the sob that threatened to rise from my chest. I hadn't done anything to deserve this man in my life.

"My friend is sick. I can't take her to the ER. There's no one else I can trust, and something is literally eating her brain."

I was babbling. Nerves and fear and desperation had wiped out my ability to be coherent, and I was one nudge away from hysterics. Only Gideon's presence behind me, his emotions matching mine, kept me stable. One of us had to stay strong.

Eventually it would be my turn to crumble.

"Madison, I—" He sighed, and I pictured him pinching the bridge of his nose, a posture he took whenever the day got to be too much for him. "I'm not a surgeon anymore. There's really nothing I can—"

"Please." I didn't want him to finish his sentence. If he didn't say it, it wasn't true. "Jet will die if we don't help her, and she can't. There's—there's too much to get into over the phone, but she needs to survive this."

"I don't understand what's going on."

Despite everything, I laughed. "Neither do I, Colm, believe me. All I know for sure is that I need you."

Another stretch of silence. Another excruciating, eternal pause. My pulse throbbed in my ears, my hand was slick on the gearshift, and I was certain that if he said no, my heart would explode. I couldn't keep spinning in circles, slamming into walls at every step. I couldn't keep running only to have Lucien half a step behind me every time I paused for breath.

For the past three years, Colm had been my lifeline to what was normal. If that lifeline snapped tonight, I would be set adrift.

"All right," he said, and I bowed my head as tears pooled in my eyes. "I'll call in a few favours and see what I can do."

Chapter 16

Madison

ON THE WAY to the hospital, I called first Serc and then Lilith. Neither of them sounded thrilled at the idea of raiding a house in the middle of a quiet neighbourhood, potentially setting off the largest ghost explosion the world had ever seen, but they also didn't refuse.

"You know Meril will have no choice but to take a stand if we go in," was Serc's only warning.

"I know. But the alternative is to let Gagnon sign off on this deal, and to me that would be a million times worse."

Lilith, at least, sounded eager for the fight, her fae blood warming at the possibility of battle. "We'll be ready when you call. From what you've told me, it'd be satisfying to rip that fed's arms off and feed them to his lackeys."

Feeling better if not completely at ease, I found a parking spot outside the Civic Hospital emergency bay and held the car door open as Gideon edged out with Jet draped over his arms.

Her lips moved in an unintelligible murmur and every once in a while her leg twitched, but those were the only signs she gave that she was still with us. My hopes that she would come out of this okay were stretched thin.

"You're sure we can trust this guy?" Gideon asked as we crossed the lawn to the hospital's side door.

"Yes."

"Who is he? Or what? A healer? A demon with nimble fingers and x-ray vision?"

"He's a mundane."

Gideon drew to a halt, his face slack. "Excuse me?"

I propped my hands on my hips and stared him down. "Mundane. Non-magical."

"You're bringing some random Joe off the street to deal with this? How the hell can he help?"

"He was a military surgeon," I snapped. "Helping people is kind of his thing. He also knows how to keep a secret, which counts for a lot right now. It's more than we can expect from most supernaturals we know."

"If this goes bad—"

"Then I have more to worry about than you do."

He glared at me, and I glared back. My blood pressure spiked, and it was a challenge to hold my temper in check. He had no idea how much I was putting on the line here. Possibly the loss of two of my most important people instead of one.

"You asked me to call someone I trust. Colm is our option, Gideon. Our *one* option. Are you going to stand here being a prejudiced ass because he's a mundane, or are you going to accept the help he's offering and follow me? Take your time answering. It's only Jet's life in the balance."

My anger surged at his hesitation, but beneath my flaring emotions, I detected no anger from him. His front was a mask for the dread that cloaked him like a shroud. He knew as well as I did that if this didn't work, Jet was lost to us, and in the face of that finality, he'd frozen, too afraid to move forward.

I knew it, understood it even, but it didn't prevent me from lashing my frustrations out at him.

Fortunately, he didn't test my patience much longer. With a violent jerk of his head, he gestured for me to lead the way, and I spun on my heel and pushed through the door.

Colm had called me back ten minutes after I'd hung up with him. By some miracle, he'd wrangled us an emergency MRI he promised would never happen on paper. Fake names for all involved, with the results conveniently misplaced before they were filed. I'd driven straight here, and now crossed my fingers everything would go as smoothly as we needed it to.

The knots in my stomach writhed, snake-like, as we followed the directions Colm had given me over the phone to help us avoid the busier wards. As we walked, keeping a pace that rivalled that of even the most experienced nurses, Gideon snagged a wheelchair propped against the wall and lowered Jet into it.

His face was flushed, his breathing ragged, and I suspected his fatigue had less to do with carrying her and more to do with how he'd gotten them out of the subbasement and into the car. I hadn't pressed him on the subject, but after what he'd done, his feelings towards Jet had changed again. They were deeper, grown past the familiar warmth of love into something vast and far-reaching. Nothing superficial. More like the blood-deep, mind-deep connection I sensed between the few telepathic couples I'd met over the years.

His hands wouldn't settle on the handles of the chair, every few seconds smoothing Jet's hair or touching her shoulder. To prove to himself she was there? I prayed Colm was able to save her, because not only would we be dead in the water against Gagnon, but I didn't know what would happen to Gideon if he lost her.

Colm met us outside the diagnostics wing, and my heart leapt into my throat at the sight of him. Somewhere he'd gotten his hands on a white lab coat, and it fitted him so perfectly, so naturally, I doubted I would ever again picture him without one and not think something was missing. Beneath the coat, he wore a dark green shirt and a pair of jeans, and despite everything, my mouth watered.

Though his reaction to Jet's condition cut the buzz of my desire short.

"Jesus," he muttered, and passed a hand over his mouth before pushing open the doors and guiding us through. "This way. End of the hall, turn left."

Gideon didn't waste time, his grip turning lethal around the handles, knuckles white and popping.

Colm fell into step beside me.

"Thank you," I said. "I have no way to tell you how much this means to me."

"Don't thank me yet," he said. "You told me her situation was critical, but I didn't expect—" He cut himself off. "We'll have to wait to see how much I can do."

There was a hint of greyness around his lips, though he worked hard not to show how shaken he was.

Too bad for him I picked up every trace of it. The waves of confusion, worry, even fear. I longed to know what thoughts were going through his head, but now wasn't the time to ask. If I pried, he would have questions of his own, and nothing I said would make him feel better about the situation. If Lucien had told Gideon the truth about what was killing Jet, Colm's eyes would be opened soon enough.

A parasite.

The bastards.

I swallowed the acidic hatred creeping up the back of my throat and followed Colm through the door. The bright lights in the room were harsh after the pre-dawn darkness outside. Gideon was already pacing the vinyl floor, never straying too far from where Jet sat in her chair. Her head leaned to the side, and I guessed he had positioned her so she would be more comfortable.

"Can we get a move on?" he demanded as we came in. "Please?"

"We'll need to get her changed," Colm said as he approached Jet and took hold of her shoulders, bracing her neck against his arm. I detected no reaction to Gideon's tone either internally or externally, as though he'd grown immune to the rudeness of a patient's loved ones over the course of his practice.

He was a professional. A man who had travelled to the most heartbreaking regions of the world to offer aid in high-stakes, high-stress conditions. He would find a way to cope with everything he was about to learn. Or so I told myself over and over, hoping I would eventually believe it.

"Why?" Gideon crossed his arms, his narrowed eyes full of suspicion.

Colm huffed out the faintest of breaths. "The MRI is a giant magnet. Anything metallic, from the button on her jeans to a watch or a hairpin, could take out the equipment or burn her. Either way, a hefty price to pay. Madison, can you help me?"

"I'll do it," Gideon said, stepping in front of me. I wasn't offended. From all I picked up from him, I expected his possessiveness, though if the attitude kept up, I wouldn't hesitate to smack him down.

"Let's get her on the table first," Colm said. "It'll be easier to manoeuvre her."

Gideon took hold of Jet's legs, and together they lifted her out of the chair and stretched her out on the lowered table, her head towards the machine. I stood by and accepted her jacket, T-shirt, bra, and jeans as the two men worked together to change her into a plain blue hospital gown. Both men moved with gentle consideration, Colm from years of experience and Gideon as though he were afraid to break her.

My hands shook with exhaustion. I eyed the metal-and-vinyl chair in the corner but wasn't ready yet to sit down. Instead, I tried to distract myself by watching Colm as he fitted a pair of headphones over Jet's ears and hit a few buttons on the side of the machine. A helmet slid over her head, and Gideon stepped forward, his body tense, almost vibrating.

"What is that? What are you doing?" He looked from Jet to the machine to Colm, as though debating whether he should tackle him to the floor.

I squeezed my hands at my sides, ready to step in, but Colm kept working. "It's part of the camera," he said. "The process is loud, and the headphones in the helmet will protect her hearing. The cameras will get her brain from all angles and give us an idea of what we're looking at. She's fine. This is all procedure."

"Gideon, why don't you come away?" I suggested, stretching my hand out to him. "Let Colm run his tests."

"No," he said, not looking at me. "I promised I wouldn't leave her side, and I won't." His jaw flexed, his challenge loud, daring anyone to try to make him break his word.

His emotions were as intense as his voice. He didn't trust Colm enough to leave Jet alone with him, but stronger than his distrust was the worry that if he left, he would never see her alive again.

"You don't need to leave," Colm said, as calm as he'd been from the start. "Family's allowed to stay."

The veneer of Gideon's mask cracked. His throat bobbed, and I sensed the effort it took for him to cling to his stubborn anger. The act broke my heart. He looked so lost, and the weight of his concern stripped away my resentment that had grown towards him over the past few hours. I dropped into the chair, exhaustion winning over my worry, as though my frustration with Gideon had fuelled my movements since we'd left Main Street.

One more blow against us amid the thousands of others we'd faced this week.

I prayed this blow wouldn't end in tragedy. We were here. We were doing what needed to be done. I would hold on to my last hope that we still had a few rolls of the dice to play.

"I'm going to start the test. It'll be loud, and it may take a while." Colm glanced my way. "I'll be in this room over here watching to see what the camera picks up. You can stay with her or you can come with me and watch through the window."

Gideon acted like he hadn't heard him. His attention was fixed on Jet, his hand tight around hers.

"Madison?" Colm turned to me. "Will you join me, or did

you want to stay here as well?"

I stared up at him. His dark eyes were full of questions, circled with bruises from stress and a lack of sleep. To go into that room with him would mean offering some of those explanations I'd promised, but not to go would be an act of ingratitude so glaring I would be ashamed of myself. He had put his faith in me in arranging this test and keeping everyone else out of the room without even a lie on my part to justify our actions. To repay him with a rejection would be the end of any confidence between us. The end of any relationship I might hope to have with him.

That might happen anyway.

A consequence I would have to accept.

I steeled my nerves, rose onto unsteady legs, and followed him into the next room.

He left the overhead lights off, much to my relief, and through the glass, the MRI machine flickered.

"I should tell you that, depending on what's wrong with her, I might not be able to do everything myself," Colm warned as soon as he closed the door and we were alone. He looked through the window at Gideon, who stood as still as a stone guardian next to Jet, and I understood his concerns. So far, our dear Mr. Leigh had not shown a deep well of patience when it came to Jet's well-being. "Typically, a radiologist performs these tests. With nurses, a whole professional team. I have enough basic knowledge to tell you if it's something obvious, but…"

"I wouldn't worry about that." I wanted more than anything to put him at ease, but if I had to settle for putting him on his guard so the next hour didn't shock him out of his sanity, so be it. "If it's what we think it is, obvious won't be a problem."

He frowned. "What do you think it is?"

I exhaled sharply. This was it. The moment of truth. He pulled out one of the chairs at the desk for me, took the other for himself, and turned his back to switch on the monitors and get everything ready.

If I had any doubt I cared about this man, it vanished there and then. His impatience for answers was as glaring as his lab coat was white, but even so, he was giving me time to compose myself and figure out how to begin.

In that moment, I wanted to tell him everything. Start to finish. Every single detail of my life.

Maybe someday, when time allowed, if he was still interested, I would, but for now I would limit myself to why we were here, and why, from here on out, he needed to be incredibly careful about who he spent time with and what he said.

I pulled the chair a little farther away from him to give him space, and to create a buffer between me and his radiating emotions, and lowered myself into the seat. It took a bit of shifting to get comfortable, and by the time I finished, the first image splices were coming up on the screen.

"This world…" I started, then stopped and cleared my throat.

I had never done this before. All my life, the necessity of secrecy had been my guiding force. My career revolved around reinforcing and protecting our people from the mundane, strengthening the divide between us so we could move safely and seamlessly in a world no longer designed for our kind. To reveal that secret willingly—intentionally—went against my character and my nature, and I didn't know where to start. I definitely didn't know how to make the truth sound plausible and not like something he'd watch on TV. There was nothing for me to do but talk and hope the words came to me as I went along.

He spun his chair around to face me when I fell silent, and I clasped my hands in my lap, forcing myself to meet his gaze when what I really wanted was for one of us to turn the other way.

"This world is not what you think it is," I tried again. His frown deepened, and I winced. There was no way he would believe me. He'd think I was making fun of him. Or that I was crazy.

My heart raced, leaving me with shallow breaths, as, without giving myself time to think, I reached out and rested my hand over his. His skin was soft and warm. How many times had I imagined him touching me, these hands running over my face, my body? It hurt to wonder if this slight contact might be the last I had with him.

We were off to a shaky start. The emotions running through

him coated my tongue with an acrid smokiness. The only warm and gentle feelings were buried deep beneath a snow pile of fear and confusion, and I braced myself for even that faint light to be snuffed out in another minute.

"You're afraid," I said, pushing the words through my tight throat. "Not of me, I don't think, but of what I might be about to tell you. You're also a bit angry, and I suspect that is directed at me. Maybe not angry. More frustrated. And it's a long-standing frustration, one you've harboured and buried but have never been able to get rid of. As I'm talking to you, you're getting… irritated." The effort of continuing grew increasingly difficult. Why was I torturing myself like this? I should have ripped off the bandage. So much better than tracking that fading warmth.

"What are you trying to tell me?" he asked, pulling away. I curled my empty hand into my lap to hide the burning sting of losing his touch. "That you're some kind of psychic?"

Definitely sliding into angry now, the tight hold he'd had on it slipping. As though his emotions were fingers clinging to the side of a mountain, the grip of each one slowly peeling back. If I pushed him too hard, moved too quickly, he would fall. Slower was better, no matter how much harder it was for me.

"Not a psychic," I said. "An empath." A small, dry smile tugged at my lips. "I wish I had something more impressive to show you. Jet can manipulate air molecules, letting her levitate or bring down a building. She can also read the memories of anything she touches. You can probably see her third eye on the scan."

I nodded to the monitors behind him, but Colm didn't turn around. He crossed his arms and stared at me, expression stoic, so I kept talking. I didn't want to leave space for him to call bullshit.

"Gideon can dematerialize into smoke, limb by limb or all at once. My minister, the one who died, had perfect night vision. Some of us can create lightning, know if you're lying, turn into wolves. It's wild and impossible, but every word is true."

Colm pressed his lips together, and I leaned forward to rest my elbows on my knees. Now that I'd revealed the hardest part, the rest was simple fact. Easier. Manageable.

"I don't work for Domestic Affairs and Trade. That department doesn't exist. It's a cover for Supernatural, Magical and Occult Affairs. Our offices are on the top storeys of our building, numbers you wouldn't see in the elevator unless you knew they were there. You could look up at the building from the outside and fully believe it stops on the seventeenth floor. You're not supposed to see it. Your mind is not capable of seeing it. The supernatural, the paranormal, they're as real as anything on these computer screens, but no one without magic in their blood is aware of it. Until their eyes are opened to reality."

I sensed his uncertainty now. It was written as much in the faint furrowing of his brow and the tuck of the corner of his mouth as it was in his brain chemistry.

"I don't judge you for thinking I'm lying," I said, "or wondering if the woman you've shared coffee and the occasional dinner with for four years is completely off her rocker. Unlike Santa Claus, the only way to believe it is to see it. Hiding the truth is what perception filters are meant for. The truth is the supernatural and the mundane are on the brink of war, and hardly anyone—on either side—knows it. We have a traitor in our department trying to tear apart the peace that has existed for almost two hundred years. They shot Jet, and whatever they shot her with is eating into her brain, and that's the least of what they've done so far. If we don't stop them, the perception filter is going to explode, and the world is going to see what lies beneath the surface."

I sucked in a breath. There. Everything on the table. And by Colm's expression, I might have lost him a few points back.

I didn't care. My confession was out, and I felt giddy. Incredulous of what I'd done. Proud, anxious, sympathetic.

With a bit more effort, I calmed my nerves enough to add, "All I ask is that you wait to form an opinion about what I've said. The evidence will back me up, and once it does, once you see… well. Red pill, blue pill—it'll be up to you."

His gaze bored into mine, and in the deluge of feelings pouring off him, I couldn't guess at what might be going through his head. Was he hoping I was lying, that my insane story was some attempt to keep him at a distance? By the faint trace of longing that stood out from the confusion, at least part of him wanted my story to be true, though I couldn't guess why.

Before I broke down and begged him to say something, I spotted a white splotch on the monitor over his shoulder, a blemish on Jet's brain that even my untrained eye couldn't fail to recognize at this angle.

The evidence I'd promised had arrived just in time.

I nodded again at the screen, and he swivelled his chair to look.

The muscles in his back tensed, and his shoulders crept towards his ears, a defensive motion as his body closed in on itself to protect his vitals.

"What the hell is that?" he asked as he leaned forward.

I rose from my chair to stand behind him and get a better look myself. Though I stood close, I was careful not to touch him—not only to avoid absorbing any of his emotions, but also to allow him whatever space he needed to process what he'd just heard and the truth that lay before him.

Because on the screen, nestled about half an inch into Jet's frontal lobe, was a bright spot, long and tapered. Like a worm.

"Dear God," he whispered.

He turned to face me, his complexion bloodless and his eyes wide. In his stare was his acceptance of everything I'd said. The weight of the world had dropped onto his shoulders as the veil that existed between what he believed and what was real fell away.

I waited for him to run screaming, to order me to get away from him. I searched for disgust or horror on his face, some sign that this revelation had ripped whatever connection we had in half and left it in tatters on the floor.

And although he said nothing, although he turned away from me to stare once more at the screen, I worried what else Lucien's conspiracy had stolen from me.

Chapter 17

Gideon

JET'S FIRM LEG was too still under my hand. Colder than it should have been. Lifeless.

The noise of the MRI machine was loud enough to drown out my thoughts, but not enough to jolt her back to consciousness. Only an occasional twitch of her muscles let me know she hadn't died on the table.

Every minute drove me closer to insanity. Carstairs may as well have taken me again, because this torture equalled anything he might have thought up.

Finally, what felt like hours later, the cameras stopped.

I didn't wait for Madison's mundane to come to me. As soon as the test was over, I flew across the room and wrenched the door open.

"Did you see it? Is it in there? Can you get it out?"

The man looked more stunned than my questions deserved,

as though I'd come in and punched him in the gut instead of asked him to do his goddamned job. Did he think we were here for a fun night out? Able to waste time dawdling over possible diagnoses? The woman on the table was dying, and we were here to prevent it. End of story. Whatever motivation he had to stretch this out, which was hard to miss from the way he'd eyed Madison since we got here, he wouldn't get his way.

"I—I don't…" he said.

The restraint on my remaining patience snapped. "Don't look at me, look at the screen and tell me what you see."

"Gideon, cut it out," Madison said as she stepped between us. "Colm is doing us a favour, and you acting like an asshole won't bring Jet back any faster." She looked at Colm over her shoulder. "What do you think? Any idea what we're dealing with?"

"It's…" His attention slid to the screen, the stunned expression still on his face, and I realized it hadn't been my barging in that had surprised him but whatever the cameras had picked up. "What the hell is it? It looks like a—a tapeworm or something. And it's moving. Burrowing."

I glared at Madison until she stepped out of my way, and we both stood behind Colm to look at the white speck that had made itself at home in Jet's brain.

"Gagnon was telling the truth." I'd hoped he was lying. I'd hoped he was spinning a story so we would rush to the hospital and get out of his hair for a few hours, wasting our time to learn she'd pushed herself too hard and needed some sleep and a good meal. I'd been half-right. He'd wanted us out of his way. The half I'd gotten wrong made me want to punch a hole through the wall. "It's a goddamned parasite."

"But how—" Colm asked.

"They shot it into her face." My jaw ached with the effort of explaining, my teeth clenched together so tightly I couldn't unhinge them. "She was an easy mark. The fucker crawled in through her third eye."

"Third eye…" Colm murmured with a shake of his head.

Had Madison told him nothing while they'd been alone in here? We didn't have time to ease him into the fact his entire worldview was a lie. I used my knee to spin his chair around so he faced me. "Can you get it out of her?"

I phrased it as a question out of respect for Madison, but by the way his pupils dilated and he pulled his shoulders back to make himself look bigger, he understood I wasn't making a request.

A moment later, he licked his lips and relaxed his defensive posture. As though he'd dismissed whatever threat I posed to him. In a calm, measured voice, he said, "I'm not a neurosurgeon. If I dig around in her head, I'm as likely to kill her as that parasite is."

"Then what the fuck was the point in coming here?" I demanded, and my hands longed to grab hold of his collar and throw him into the wall. The only thing holding me back was the knowledge, faint and nearly overpowered as it was, that he was the only resource we had to help us save Jet. But I imagined myself doing it. Slamming him backwards again and again until there was a Colm-sized hole in the plaster. My vision swam red, my breaths came quick, and a sharp pain shot up my arms as my fingernails dug into my palms.

Two dark eyes stared back at me, braced, unsure what I was going to do.

Smart. I wasn't sure myself.

"Gideon."

A cool hand rested on my arm, but I burned too hot to let it soothe me.

"We proved something we already knew," I said, squeezing my fists that much tighter, refusing to look away from this mundane, savouring his expression as fear bled into his eyes, because goddamn if I was going to be the only one terrified. "He builds up hope that he can help her, and now he's saying we stand no fucking chance?"

"How about you take a breath, and together we can figure out what to do next."

She sounded so calm. How the *fuck* did she sound so calm? My life was falling apart, and she was strolling through the daisies.

The fingers on my arm slid to the back of my hand, and my blood cooled so quickly my head reeled. I staggered backwards and dropped into an empty chair. My hands shook. My whole body trembled. Madison kept her hand on me, and as my mind cleared, I realized she'd wound herself through my head and leashed my emotions, stifling them. Choking them. They were still there, swirling below the surface—my terror, my rage—but distant, giving me space to see things her way.

Another wave of anger, this one directed at her, threatened to bubble up, but it was just as trapped under the net she'd draped over me, and her grip on my hand was too tight to shake off without getting violent.

Colm's gaze moved from me to Madison. His body was tensed, ready to protect itself, but he didn't appear nearly as afraid as I would have expected a mundane to be in this situation. Even in the heat of my fury, I had to give him credit: whatever else was true about him, he had guts.

"So what can we do?" Madison asked him, not giving him an opening to engage with me. I was sure that given the opportunity he would have punched me in the face. Maybe I would have deserved it, but I would have gone at him twice as hard.

He ran a hand over his short hair, and his gaze darted through the window to where Jet lay on the table. I followed the path of his attention, already feeling I'd been away from her too long. The hospital gown made her look so much more fragile than she was. I needed her fighting. She wouldn't have let me get away with treating this guy like shit, but she wouldn't have used Madison's gentle gift to put me in my place. She would have wrestled me into an armlock and pinned me until I calmed down.

I needed her to be all right.

"I don't understand anything that's happening," Colm said, and I heard his effort to stay cool. "I don't—you tell me these things, Madi. Magic. Monsters. This woman shot by some supernatural parasite bullet. I can't—" He exhaled slowly and rubbed his jaw. As he stared through the glass, his back straightened and the wildness in his eyes ebbed. "I might not have the skills to get that thing out of her, but I know someone who does."

"Who?" I asked in a rough grumble, my emotions, my exhaustion, fighting to free themselves from Madison's cage.

"A buddy I studied with and later served with. He's a good man, and the best neurosurgeon I know. He's handled some impossible cases and seen more strange things in a human brain than you could imagine—or not. If anyone can get in there with any chance of cutting that thing out safely, it's him."

"You trust him?" Madison asked, and I understood the layers of her question. Trust him not only to save Jet, but to handle—and keep—our secret. The blinders had dropped from Colm's eyes. Only he could say if his friend was up for the same awakening.

"With my life," he said.

"What about his?" she pushed, her hazel eyes serious, showing no sign of coddling. "You know what's at stake for anyone involved with us. Would this man die for you? Because that's what it might come to."

Colm hesitated, and his throat flexed with a hard swallow. His gaze locked on hers with an expression I recognized too well—without her, he would drown under the wave of his mental chaos. Finally, though, he nodded. "I believe he would."

As the clock on the wall ticked by, none of us said anything, Colm and I waiting for Madison's answer and her focus drifting into the middle distance, no doubt laying out every possible implication, variable, and consequence.

My impatience writhed under her hold. What was there to consider? What other options needed to be weighed? The potential cost of one mundane life for the sake of saving Jet's? It was nothing more than basic math. Of course it was worth it. Ten people's lives would be worth getting her back. What was taking her so long?

Madison's hand left mine, and a moment's panic flittered through me that without her support I would lose my shit again, but she'd also freed me to call her out on her delay.

Before I opened my mouth, however, she shifted her attention through the window, and I realized what was going through her head. She wasn't debating the risks to Colm's friend—or if she was, she wasn't stuck on them. She was coming to terms with the fact that his life mattered less right now than the woman in the other room. Jet was our leader. We might find a way to take Gagnon down without her, but we'd be losing one of our greatest advantages, and at this point a single disadvantage could lose us the war. A heavy truth, but one she had to face.

"All right," she said at last. "You make your phone calls, and I'll draw up the paperwork."

Chapter 18

Gideon

IT TOOK LESS than an hour to get Jet into surgery. Colm had needed to bring in more people than Madison would have liked, but I didn't care.

Whatever it took.

While we'd waited for his surgeon buddy, the anesthesiologist, and the nurse to arrive, Madison had made use of one of the computer terminals to draw up a standard confidentiality agreement. Nothing that happened here tonight was to leave the operating room. Any hint the mundanes had spoken about us to anyone after they left here, and the full weight of the federal government would come crashing down on their heads.

It was as much for their safety as ours, but I wondered how hard it would be for them to keep their mouths shut. It wasn't every day you plucked a live parasite out of someone's head while avoiding the extra nerve bundles branching out from their third eye.

I paced the length of the waiting room for the fourteenth—twentieth, thousandth—time. The clock ticked towards seven-thirty in the morning. The three of us were the only people in the cramped space, the hallways empty, muted voices rising and falling with the shift change. If there were any other emergency surgeries happening right now, they were being kept as well under wraps as ours was.

As I crossed the length of the room again, I passed Madison, who spoke quietly into her phone to arrange for a new safe house in case our apartment had been found by someone other than Bright Eyes.

Colm was staring intently at the wall as though hoping the plaster and public health posters would help him make sense of everything he'd learned in the past few hours. It had to be tough wrapping his head around the fact that magic existed, demons were real, and this might very well be his last night on earth. As it stood, I was impressed he hadn't run for the door yet, or suffered a complete psychological collapse, though by the grey pallor around his lips, I didn't think he was too far from doing either.

It was a lot to take in, and part of me, a small part, felt sorry for the guy.

My sympathy wouldn't last long if Jet didn't survive this surgery, but if all went well, maybe I'd find it in me to cut the man some slack. For Madison's sake, it would be great if I didn't have to threaten major bodily harm.

The rage that had filled me earlier lingered under my skin, ready to flare up at a single breath of bad news. I did my best to suppress it, to cling to the net Madison had dropped over me. Anger would not help Jet. Fury would not save her life. Her future was out of my control. I'd done the best I could.

No matter how often I repeated these platitudes to myself, the prickle of heat in my blood ebbed and flowed, and with every minute that passed, the closer I came to turning on Colm and demanding to know why he wasn't in the operating room helping. Why was he out here with us, waiting, pretending our situation mattered to him, instead of assisting his war buddy in dragging Jet back from the brink of death?

Not his job. Not his problem.

Deep down, I knew his sitting here wasn't my issue.

He could have been wrist-deep in Jet's head, and I'd still be annoyed with him. For no other reason than because he was a mun who'd involved himself in our lives. Not one of us. Lesser. Exactly how I'd come to see most people with no extra skills or strengths or abilities. They were easy targets when things went wrong.

But I couldn't deny his refusal to back down, not to mention his lack of fear in the face of my growling, had earned a degree of my respect, and I used it as an anchor to keep my cool.

What I needed was a distraction. Something to get my mind off the ticking clock.

As I turned around for another pass across the room, a news story playing silently on the television mounted in the corner caught my attention. More protests and more violence, now in Edmonton and Saskatoon.

A cut to the prime minister, Canadian flags waving in the background, with the closed captioning reporting that the cause of the protests remained unclear, the messaging changing from one region to another. Dental care, jobs in the oil industry, conservation efforts.

"Hey," I said to Colm. He jerked out of his brooding and cast me a wary glance. Fair. We hadn't exactly gotten off on the best footing. I jerked my head towards the television. "What do you see on those signs?"

He pushed himself out of his seat to stand next to me and get a better look at the screen.

As focused as I'd been on getting him to help us, I hadn't noticed the difference in our sizes, but now that the red haze over my vision had cleared, I was almost glad I hadn't exchanged punches with him. Although he stood an inch or two shorter than me, his shoulders were wider, his chest thicker. Ex-military or not, this was a person who kept up at the gym. Even mundane, Colm would have given me a good fight.

Physically, anyway.

Mentally, I wondered if I'd just sent what remained of his sanity out the window. He squinted at the TV, blinked, passed a hand over his eyes.

"All part of the adjustment period," I said. "For the first little while, you'll see double, but eventually the only thing in front of you will be the truth unless you make an effort to ignore it."

I clapped my hand on his shoulder, and he flinched.

"What do the signs really say?" he asked. "How can my brain read *Toil for Oil* at the same time it sees *Protect our Supernatural Rights*? Does it actually say both?"

"No," Madison said from across the room. Her usually smooth voice carried a few rough edges, and she reached for the cup of watery hospital tea on the table beside her. "It's all about context. A few signs are advocating for the oil industry, enough for mundane eyes to see them and apply the message across the entire event. The rest is your brain playing tricks. Making you see what you expect to see."

Colm shook his head and looked again at the screen. "I don't know what to think," he said. "I mean, I know our brains fill in a lot of gaps, but this—this is extreme. This isn't telling ourselves stories to patch up our memories or fill in missing details, this is our senses *lying* to us."

His voice wobbled, and I watched him closely. Was he about to lose it? I gave a tentative nudge to test the waters. "Nothing is more skilled at self-defence than the human brain. The truth risks the mundane mind snapping like a twig."

He grunted. "You're telling me. I'm questioning if maybe I did fall asleep last night. Maybe there were no men in black at my door, and I'm not here right now. All this time, I've been fast asleep on my couch, trying to explain to myself why…"

His gaze flicked towards Madison as he fell quiet. A pink flush touched her cheeks, which she did her best to hide behind another sip of tea, and Colm shifted his weight on his feet.

I didn't bother asking either of them to fill me in. They obviously had a history, and it was none of my business. Even if I wanted to be curious, I had too much on my mind to care about someone else's problems. My attempt at distracting myself had done nothing to keep my mind off Jet, so I turned my attention back to the TV.

The prime minister was still on the screen, and the closed captioning spun out some ridiculous story about a social media movement. All the answers were vague and brief, and the result was that everyone involved looked incompetent. With the minister dead, the prime minister's office had to rely on Gagnon to provide information and advice. Unfortunately, they had no idea he was fuelling the fights, a traitor to his people who benefited by feeding bullshit to the media. Disinformation to sow discord, and the rioters were eating it up.

"Do they do these sorts of supernatural-related press conferences often?" Colm asked, and there was an underlying tone to his question I couldn't make out.

"Often enough," I said. "Not that I watch much Canadian news."

He shook his head. "You know when you're working on

a jigsaw puzzle, and the surface you're working on is the same colour as part of the image, so you don't realize right away that anything is missing… That's what this feels like. The cover-up is so clean, you don't notice it until you do, and then certain things fall into place, and you can't believe you never saw it before. All the pieces in the world I shrugged at, they were gaps in the picture. This is what was missing."

Awe? Fear? The look in his eyes ran a gamut of emotions I was sure Madison identified the moment they arose but I could only guess at. The guy's mind was probably a kaleidoscope of feeling, and the only thing to do was let him spin and figure out on his own where he wanted to land.

The scene cut to a news anchor standing in front of a shouting crowd, talking about how the protests were being put down, sometimes violently, and tensions were rising between authorities and the public.

The anger I'd worked hard to wrestle down flared again, this time not directed towards the mundane at my side.

These idiots.

Everything was going the way Gagnon intended. Nothing we'd done had slowed them down. If anything, we'd boosted their confidence. If the only people onto them were two public servants and a foreign spy, they had nothing to worry about. I pictured them laughing over the bottle of whiskey in Gagnon's desk. Michael celebrating the termination of his best soldier, Gagnon chuckling over the fact he'd fooled the minister's chief of staff. Maybe Dougall and O'Malley were with them, toasting the golden path Gagnon had paved for them to spread the Death's Head Syndicate wherever they wanted.

They had reason to be smug. We'd been stupid and put our faith in people who hadn't deserved it. Never again. Once Jet made it out of here, we would wipe the smiles off their faces.

And Jet would make it out. Gods help the bunch of them if she didn't. They thought they'd won? Legally we might never prove anything against them, but if she didn't pull through, the last thing these bastards would see tonight would be my face hovering over them as I drove my knife through their hearts. Damn the consequences to myself, they wouldn't outlive her for long.

"Hey," Colm said, his turn to pull me out of my spiralling. I whirled around to face him and found his attention trained on my shoulder. I glanced down. Blood had soaked through my T-shirt. Pain twinged through my back, and I remembered the knife-wielding shifter with the weird love of brooms and rocks. I thought I'd patched myself up, but in the rush of everything else we'd faced tonight, I must have missed a seam or two.

"Why don't we get you cleaned up," he offered.

I stiffened. Respect for his courage or not, I wasn't about to tolerate pity from a mundane. "I'm fine."

He raised an eyebrow. "Yeah? Spontaneous healing one of your superpowers?"

I opened my mouth to tell him it was, but the smartass

answer withered on my tongue. I was too damn tired to spend the rest of the night dematerializing half my back. If I wanted to be in fighting form when Jet woke up, conserving my energy was the smartest route, and it wasn't like I could get a good angle to stitch the wound by myself. At least with a surgeon, I'd be in good hands.

"Let's do it your way, then," I said.

"You'll be all right alone for a few minutes?" Colm asked Madison.

She sat with her head propped on her hand, her eyelids half-closed as she replied with a sleepy nod.

"Here," he said, and pulled off his lab coat. "In case you get cold or need a pillow or something."

Even half-asleep, she smiled at him with enough warmth to send a streak of envy through my chest. Whatever these two had going on, there was no world of hurt lying in the past, no bitter feelings they had to wade through. If they survived what was coming, if Madison didn't care that Colm was a mun and he didn't care that she wasn't, they could take the leap and see what happened.

I wondered if the same could be said for me and Jet.

I caught myself. *Drop it. Grudges or not, survival or not, Jet is not in your cards.*

Hardening my heart to the reality of my circumstances, I followed Colm down the hall to an exam room.

"Shirt off, rest can stay on," he said.

"I'd hope. I'm not in the mood to get freaky with you, big guy."

I pulled off my vest and tugged my shirt over my head. The muscles in my shoulder pulled, screamed, and it took an extra grunt of effort to get the T-shirt off. Thankfully, Madison's boy toy didn't offer to help.

"You've got quite the array of tears and gashes on you. What happened?" he asked as he snapped on a pair of gloves behind me.

"Got stabbed," I said, focusing on the most recent assault. He didn't need to know my entire life story when only one of my injuries was bleeding.

"Bar fight?"

"Home invasion."

"Huh."

He didn't warn me before spraying something into the wound. I bit my lip to prevent any sound from coming out but couldn't prevent the full-body twitch as a sharp, hot pain shot across my back.

"Just cleaning it out," he said, and I swore there was a smirk in his voice. The bastard had enjoyed that.

In response, I snorted a laugh and my smidge of respect widened by a few extra particles. Hard to look down on a mundane who would voluntarily risk pissing off a supe to prove he could hurt him if he wanted to.

His point proved, Colm's skills took over, and something

warm and almost soothing, though still incredibly uncomfortable, replaced the disinfectant. Letfield had known what he was doing with his blade.

"This sort of thing normal for you?" Colm asked.

I started to shrug, but pain cut the gesture short. "Depends on the case."

"So what are you exactly? Some kind of… superhero?"

He sounded skeptical, and I didn't hold back a laugh. "Fuck no. No one could call me a hero." These days, I was more likely to have the word "rebel" taped to my back. "I work for a private security firm in New York."

"So you're here as…"

"A spy, basically." The guy had learned so much already, I didn't see the point in being discreet. Who was he going to tell?

"Huh."

I glanced over my shoulder and caught his blank expression. "It's like you're catching a preview of a bad thriller movie, isn't it?"

"Something like that. Still not sure how to make heads or tails of it. Or what the hell I'm supposed to do now that I'm in the loop. Do I pretend I'm not? Is someone going to kill me if I tell people what I've seen?"

"Probably not, but you may as well save your breath. No mundane would believe you. Would you have believed it if some rando on the street had told you what those protest signs said?"

"I would have assumed they were drunk. Or insane."

"All very low danger levels for us, so I don't see you being important enough to silence."

Another poke at my back, another flinch from me, but this time Colm apologized before continuing. That one hadn't been intentional, just a sign of unsteady nerves. As calm as he appeared to be, the good doctor was probably shitting his pants right now, and who could blame him? A few hours ago, he'd thought his life was confined to a neat little box with everything in its proper place. Magic was something he read about on weekends or lost himself in at the movie theatre. He obviously hadn't known about Madison. And if I was right about there being something between them, the last thing I wanted to do was push him over the edge and make him run screaming. Regardless of what I thought about her involvement with a mundane, I didn't want to do anything that might hurt her. She deserved better than that.

"It's not always like this," I said. "Just your luck, you're getting introduced to it at its worst. Worse than I've ever seen it. But if we win, you'll get to see some of the good parts, too."

A stretch of silence as he pressed something against my shoulder, then he said, "I'll bear that in mind."

"And Madison," I continued, though I suspected I should have stopped there, "she's the best choice to walk you through it. Smart as a whip. Always knows the right thing to say. Seriously. That's kind of her ability."

"So she mentioned."

Nope, I'd wigged him out again. *Dammit, Gideon, shut the hell up.*

It was too bad for Madison she'd been caught up in this. We wouldn't have made it far without her, but she'd had to make so many sacrifices. I hoped they were worth it.

"What about you?" Colm asked. "Madison said you can… disappear?"

Beneath his uneasiness was a strong note of curiosity, and I latched on to it. Curiosity was good. Curiosity meant a desire to learn more, and maybe, if introduced slowly enough, the courage to accept it. It was possible Madison hadn't lost him yet.

"I don't go invisible or anything." I held my hand at eye level and allowed the cells to fall away, my hand turning into mist that drifted in a cloud until I pulled myself back together.

When the only reaction I got was more silence, I looked over my shoulder and found Colm staring with his eyes wide and his mouth open. He caught my gaze, snapped his mouth shut, and nodded. "That's pretty wicked. Not a bad skill for a spy."

"It's got me out of more scrapes than I can count."

"And your friend Jet she can really see into the past?"

At the mention of the woman hovering on the edge of death, my throat closed. Why was it that him calling her my *friend* bothered me so much?

Because we're not friends.

Was that true?

We'd slept together, fought together, made each other

miserable. But she was also one of the few people in the world I trusted. If that didn't qualify her as a friend, what would?

Or was the real problem that I wanted so much more from her than friendship?

It took more than one clearing of my throat to tear my thoughts out of that loop and say, "Recent past." Once the first words were out, the rest came more easily. "She's not a seer or anything. She picks up shadows—she calls them memories. Reflections, interactions with objects and spaces around her going back over a few hours."

"And the levitating?"

"Truth. Not like flying, though. More like creating lifts out of the air."

The last time she did it, it nearly killed her.

I pinched the bridge of my nose and squeezed my eyes shut. What did it mean that we hadn't heard anything yet? What if, despite our rushing around, we were too late? What if that parasite had done all the damage it needed to, and even if they got it out, she was too far gone to bring her back?

In spite of myself, I imagined my life without Jet in it. No one to compete with on the other side of the border. No one to watch and lie to myself about why I was watching. No one to argue with in that way she had that drove me up the fucking wall and made me want to throttle her even as it made me want to wrap my arms around her and kiss her.

I hadn't seen her in two years—in the grand scheme of our

lives I hardly knew her—but she was part of me in a way no one else was, and without her, there would be a void in my life I would never be able to fill.

Gods, Jet. Make it through this.

A gentle hand rested on my uninjured shoulder, and only then did I realize I'd spoken the last part aloud. Colm didn't say anything, and other than his show of support made no sign he'd heard me. Some reassurance would have been nice, some comment about how she was in the best hands even if I didn't trust that would be enough, but he offered nothing.

It was hard not to read into his silence.

I forced my attention back to his treatment of my shoulder, and when I noticed him reaching for the sutures, I waved him off.

"Don't bother," I said.

"It'll open again if we don't seal it."

"In a few more hours, after a bit of sleep, I can pull myself back together. Seriously, man, thanks, but it's not necessary."

Colm shrugged but took me at my word and set to work with some bandaging, wrapping gauze under my armpit and over my shoulder to hold the padding in place.

We returned to the waiting room different men, neither of us quite as ready or eager to tear the other's throat out, and by the curve of Madison's eyebrow as she raised herself from her makeshift bed, she recognized it.

I winked at her, then resumed my worried pacing.

Colm had just sat down beside her and I'd just begun my second pass when the surgeon walked in. Colm and Madison rose to their feet, but I reached him first. He stood a few inches taller than me, but the paleness of his face, his wide blue eyes, and shaking hands made him look small enough I worried I'd lose sight of him if I didn't pin him down.

"How is she?"

"I've never done anything like that before," he said, dazed. "The anesthesiologist fainted—outright collapsed on the floor—when we got that worm out. And it was beautiful. The most perfect creature I've ever seen. I think it's dead, unfortunately, but—"

"How. Is. Jet?" I asked again.

Madison's hand returned to my arm, but this time there was no numbness, no cooling of my temper. She wasn't trying to manipulate me, only to remind me this mundane was on our side. Fine, as long as he remembered Jet was his patient, not the parasite.

He gave himself a shake, and his gaze cleared as it met mine. "She made it through the surgery."

He said it as though it were a miracle, but the real shock was that my legs didn't give out.

"We won't know the full extent of the damage until she wakes up—and you need to be prepared that she might not— but she seemed to be—" a crease formed between his brows, and more blood leached out of his face "—healing as she went?

Impossible, I know, but there's no other way to describe it."

He looked to Colm, who shrugged and shook his head, then to Madison, who offered a supportive smile.

"Anyway, I guess it's not the weirdest thing I've seen today," he continued when he accepted he wouldn't receive either confirmation or denial. "She's still asleep, but you should be able to see her soon."

"Thank you, Billy," Colm said, and fist-bumped his shoulder. "I know this is a weird one. I'm grateful you came."

Billy cast all of us a glance before he headed to the door. "The strangest case in my career, and I can't even talk about it," he mumbled to himself as he walked out.

The door closed behind him, and I dropped into the nearest seat.

Jet was alive.

Despite the doctor's shaky confidence and less-than-subtle warning that she wasn't out of danger, there was no doubt in my mind: she had faced the worst Michael had thrown at her and would rise again to fight harder.

She had stepped back from Death's door. I had to believe nothing would stop her now.

Chapter 19

Madison

IF I'D THOUGHT waiting for Jet to get out of surgery was awful, it was nothing compared to waiting to see her.

Gideon wouldn't sit down, and even I, with all my skills in soothing other people's emotions, had a hard time staying still. There was nothing on my phone to keep me busy, and I was too nervous about Colm's reaction to what I'd revealed to think of any safe topic of conversation. The television in the corner had switched away from the news at least, but the show that replaced it—some kind of fishing documentary? Who designed this torture?—failed to hold my attention.

For the better part of an hour, my only form of distraction was wondering what state Jet would be in once we were allowed to visit her. Would she be awake? Lucid? I worried what we would do if she'd suffered any permanent cognitive damage. Michael's strike against us would be complete, and I hoped he'd be happy. That he could live with the knowledge he'd destroyed his protegée. The wolf he'd raised from a pup.

Can't think like that. Only good. Imagine throwing the lot of them at Meril's feet.

Jet jumping out of bed, ready to lead our way to victory.

Tracking down Michael.

Throwing an air-wrapped punch right into his traitorous face.

I played the fantasy through my mind a few times, each loop bringing me a deeper sense of satisfaction.

If anyone could fight through this and come out swinging, it was Jet. I couldn't underestimate her. Not after everything else we'd survived.

When the nurse finally sought us out, Gideon froze, and I was immediately on my feet at his side. He reached blindly for my hand, and I squeezed his fingers, doing my best to stay out of his head and leave his emotions to himself.

"We've moved her to a private room," the nurse replied to our silent questions.

From the cloud of uncertainty and agitation that surrounded her, I would have expected a tremor in her voice, but she spoke matter-of-factly, as though digging a supernatural parasite out of someone's brain was an everyday event. I made a note to catch her name before I left the hospital. She'd been introduced to the true state of the world, and we might have need of her in the days to come.

"If you'd like to follow me, I'll take you to her."

"Is she awake?" Gideon asked, hope glinting around him like fireflies, too bright for me to ignore.

"Not yet," she said, dousing the brightness too soon. "But her vitals are strong, which is a good sign. Now we wait."

We followed her out of the hated waiting room and down the hall towards the elevator. It was a silent, awkward parade. Gideon disappeared into his thoughts and worries, Colm was mentally trapped between concern and curiosity, and the nurse had no idea what to make of us. I wished I could say something to put her at ease, but what ease was there to find?

The elevator pinged, and she led us down another long hallway towards a room at the end. Someone had written the name *Murray* on the whiteboard outside the door, and I thanked Colm for his good thinking. Fake names, fake reports, fake everything. Let the surgical team bill for their time for a procedure that never happened on a patient who never existed.

With luck, the lies would keep everyone involved off Lucien's radar.

Under the patient name was the name of the nurse in charge. Rita. Unlike everything else on the board, I suspected she'd used her real name to keep things organized for the other day-shift nurses.

I tucked the information away for later and turned my attention to the room.

Rita left us to enter alone, and Gideon lengthened his

stride to reach Jet's bedside in the space of a heartbeat. He dropped into a ratty vinyl armchair that looked only slightly more comfortable than the ones we'd endured in the waiting room and took her hand.

He spared us no glance, no word, as though he'd forgotten we were here with him. As though, as far as he was concerned, Colm and I no longer existed.

I didn't blame him. Jet looked so pale and weak that I couldn't tear my eyes away from her.

Where was my captain? My unbreakable, bull-headed veteran?

The woman in this bed, her head thickly bandaged so her third eye was hidden from view, the pale blue hospital gown washing out her already bloodless features, was far from indestructible.

If Michael saw her now…

Anger warmed my blood and washed away the smidge of pity that had risen for her former commander. If Michael were here to see her, I would grab the cheap vase off the bedside table and smash it over his head. Let *him* be the one lying vulnerable in a hospital somewhere. Better yet, leave him untreated. Throw him in a dumpster to rot as he'd done with so many people who had put their lives in his hands.

The machine beside the bed beeped in a reassuring rhythm, and I hinged my hopes on the sound. As long as those beeps remained steady, Jet would find her way back. Worry wouldn't help her.

Neither would sitting around waiting. Much as I didn't want to leave, there was so much that needed to be done. Gideon had made it clear he wasn't going anywhere and had no thought for anyone else. Staying here with him would only get in his way, and Colm needed answers. He'd been patient long enough.

"Gideon?"

He didn't show any sign he'd heard me, so I tried again. "I'm going to go clear out the apartment and get us settled in the new place, all right?"

Still nothing.

"I'll text you when I have the address so you'll know where to go if you want to freshen up and get some rest."

I waited another beat.

"You'll call us when she wakes up?" I refused to let him leave this question unanswered. While I understood his desire to be alone with her, I wouldn't let him be so selfish as to keep her all to himself once she opened her eyes. He wasn't the only person who loved her. "Gideon?"

At last, his gaze flicked my way before resting again on Jet. "I will. I promise."

Wishing I could do more to help him and accepting the only cure for what ailed him was time and a miracle, I gestured for Colm to follow me, and when we reached the door, Gideon called after us, barely loud enough to be heard over the beeping machines. "Thank you."

His gratitude wrapped around me like a comforting blanket, and I snuggled into it. "Try to get some sleep, okay? She'll probably be out for a while yet."

He replied with an absent-minded nod, but I doubted he'd listen—if he'd even registered what I'd said. His vigil continued, as dedicated as it had been since her collapse.

I left him to it, and Colm closed the door behind me, leaving us alone in the hallway.

My heart raced and my palms grew clammy. As long as I'd had Jet and Gideon to think about, I'd been able to put my personal concerns aside, but now that we'd done as much as we could for Jet, and Gideon was on his own, there was nothing left for me to do but face the consequences of my decisions.

After years of having his questions avoided, days of waiting for his texts to be answered, and hours of being kept in suspense, how would Colm respond? I'd opened his mind to the truth. He'd done what he'd promised he would.

Would he run now that his help was no longer needed? What would I do if he did? Chase after him? Let him go?

I brushed my hands over my thighs to hide the trembling as he escorted me to the elevator. He hit the button, and every moment while we waited for it to arrive passed in agonizing silence. I did my best not to read him, wanting to respect his privacy until he made his desires clear, but despite my best efforts, I sensed a resistance that hadn't existed before tonight. Without asking him, I didn't know if it was a conscious choice or his brain protecting him from the full impact of losing the insulation of the perception filter, but on some level, he was fighting the truth. Fighting me.

I tried not to let it hurt.

"So," he said once we stepped into the elevator, and while I was beyond relieved he'd been the one to start the conversation, my stomach clenched over where it might lead. "What's next? Do I go home and wait for you to decide when you're ready to tell me more?"

He spoke without anger, without resentment, but I detected both all the same, as thick and sludgy as molasses. His dark eyes were tight, his jaw stiff with an effort to keep his frustration hidden. Not anger. *Annoyance.* At the thought that I was going to disappear again and leave him in the dark?

A thrill ran through me, my racing heart tripping into a patter. He wanted to know more. Not running. Not yet. Whatever his psyche was trying to protect him from, he was willing to explore it further before he made up his mind, and for that level of trust, as microscopic as it might be, I was more grateful than I could express. I felt like dancing, like throwing my arms around his neck and smothering his face in kisses.

I settled for asking, "How would you feel about helping me move? I could use an extra hand, and you can ask me anything you want."

He jerked his head back in surprise, and the muscles around his mouth relaxed. "Whatever you need."

This time, I didn't hold back my smile as the depth of his answer barged through the remaining walls around my heart. This man had been there when I'd needed him, broken rules, risked his career and reputation for a woman he'd just discovered he hardly knew at all, and he was still here.

He was my personal gift from the universe, and now that I fully appreciated it, now that I'd dragged him into our fight, I would do anything, risk anything, to keep him safe.

Chapter 20

Madison

DESPITE MY OFFER to answer questions, we didn't talk much on the drive to the apartment. Instead, Colm paid rapt attention to the CBC news, and I guessed he was listening for more between-the-lines details.

Although most of the items were standard mundane affairs, one or two held subtle language twists that meant something different to those who listened for it. There was nothing sensational, nothing more interesting than heat wave warnings for the frost fairies and a few minor crimes of public supernatural exposure, but fascinating enough for anyone new to our world. He missed most of them, but every once in a while, his shoulders tensed, his face went slack, and I picked up on the increasingly familiar mix of apprehension and awe spilling off him.

As long as he remained silent, I respected his choice and did the same, but I longed to learn what he thought about it all.

The news switched to a show about a local bookstore, and Colm sat back in his seat, chewing on his bottom lip. My patience to hear his voice ran out, and while I intended to keep my promise to let him start the important conversation on his terms, I couldn't help but ask, "Did you get an opportunity to talk to your surgeon friend about Jet's condition? I know it's not possible to say for sure, but do you think she'll pull through?"

I hated leaving the question open to a negative, but we couldn't stick our heads in the sand. If she died, we would have many hard realities to face, so it was best to steel myself to them now.

"It depends on how much brain matter the parasite consumed," he said, shaking himself out of his stupor. "There might be changes to her personality, to her ability to function. I'm not saying you should give up hope, but I don't want you to be surprised if she wakes up different from the woman she was."

I gritted my teeth but forced a smile. "Considering how often she's changed within the past week, I wonder if I'd notice another shift. As long as she hangs on to her stubbornness, we'll be all right."

Colm ran his tongue over his bottom lip, followed by his top lip as he bit down on something he was about to say. I waited, and eventually he asked, "What Billy said, is it possible? That she was healing as he operated on her?"

I pulled into the parking lot behind the safe house and relaxed into my seat. "I wouldn't say she has any actual healing ability, but all of us have… well, our systems work differently than yours do. Resilience is perhaps the best word for it. Even those of us with less impressive abilities have hardy immune systems."

"I hope you don't include yourself in the category of 'less impressive.'" He said it with such intensity, my cheeks flushed, and I tried to cover my fluster with a dry laugh.

"Compared to Jet's ability to move heavy objects across a room, you don't think extreme empathy is a little dull?"

"Not a bit."

I shot him a glance, trying to catch him in a lie, but his features were soft, relaxed, inviting. Although I scolded myself for being rude and selfish, I opened my mind to his emotions and, for a moment, thought I might cry. The effort he was making to accept his new reality astounded me—an act of heroism as far as I was concerned. At no point had I expected his transition through the perception filter to be smooth or painless, but I hoped he would tell me if there was any way I could make it easier.

Unable to come up with the words to express myself clearly, I settled for a smile and nodded towards the apartment building. "Come on, I'll give you the tour."

We got out of the car, and Colm slowed to a halt as he stared at the moulded archway over the front doors. He hesitated, looked down the alley at the other buildings, then back.

"This… this is a condemned building," he said. "The whole

time I've lived in Ottawa, this place has been papered windows and scaffolding."

I said nothing, keeping my distance while he took it in. The swirl of confusion around his head buffeted me, and in the shimmer of illusion that overlaid reality, I saw what he'd always seen: the piles of gravel, the crater of a foundation, the lie created by the perception filter.

"None of it was real?" He turned to look at me, his eyes brimming with the need to understand, to land on solid ground.

I shook my head and did my best to stay practical. He was a public servant. He understood practical. "The mundanes in the city know this building is awaiting restoration, so that's how they see it."

He frowned. "What about tourists? Anyone driving through town?"

"Who knows? They might see it for what it is, but let's say they point it out to a local. That local laughs, says the building has always been an eyesore, and suddenly it is. The lovely corner building must have been somewhere else, because obviously this place is a crumbling trash heap."

Colm swallowed and, in a shaking voice, said, "Incredible."

I sensed his brief flare of panic, an internal battle as he fought against his cracking worldview. "Want to see inside?"

His nod was unsure, but he extended his hand towards the door. "After you."

I let us into the building and led the way up the wide

staircase to the apartment. When I opened the door, I found the place spotless. Bryan's body was gone, as was the bloody armchair in the corner. Gary's people had worked wonders. At least I wouldn't have to explain the mess to Colm. Yet. Baby steps.

"I'll take my room and Jet's if you want to do Gideon's?" I said. "First door on the left."

He hesitated and, half-laughing, asked, "I'm not going to run across any monsters under the bed, am I? Literal skeletons in the closet that will devour my soul?"

I offered my best reassuring smile. "Unlikely. I haven't heard any bumps in the night to warn me of unwanted houseguests."

"That's something, at least."

Even so, he looked wary as he pushed open the door to Gideon's room and stepped inside. I waited until I was sure he didn't stumble on anything horrifying, then went into Jet's room across the hall.

One of the perks of being on the run was we'd had no time to accumulate anything. One duffle bag for Jet, another for me, and I was back in the dining room to clean up the paperwork we'd left stacked on the table.

"What's all this?" Colm asked as he helped me stuff it into my satchel, keeping the piles as organized as possible.

"Proof that our department is selling out a portion of the Canadian population for a few billion dollars." Once we had hard copies of the photos Gideon had taken at Gagnon's headquarters, the evidence would be damning. Not that we could do anything with it until we had our dear deputy minister in custody.

He blinked. "Oh, is that all?"

I smirked. "I hate to tell you, but that's just the beginning."

A last pass through the apartment confirmed all trace of us was gone. I left the keys on the island for Gary's people, and we returned to the car. The new address waited for me in a text message from Gary, and in the bright, late-morning sunshine, I drove across the bridge towards the University of Ottawa campus.

"You're going to try blending in with the students?" Colm asked as he stared out the window.

"I don't think I appreciate your skepticism," I said, shooting him an amused glance. "But no. I couldn't handle being so close to the dorms. My university days are far behind me, I'm afraid."

I drove past the campus and continued to the residential side streets until we pulled up in front of a two-storey Victorian with a heritage sign in the window. Like the safe house on Somerset, this house had earned a reputation of being a financial black hole. Its heritage status meant no one could tear it down, but the city wasn't willing to put in the money to restore it. Or so they said. So it remained boarded up, with graffitied windows, a wild, overgrown lawn, and a sagging roof.

To my eyes, however, it was a beautifully renovated single

family home, and we'd lucked out that it was available.

I watched Colm for his reaction as he stared through the windshield. So far, every step of the way, he'd been cautious in his acknowledgement of what he saw, sticking with doubt until his senses confirmed that the new version of events was more accurate than the belief he'd always held. With every reveal, his transition from incredulity to tentative acceptance had gotten smoother, faster, and as we faced another critical shift in his perceptions, I was curious to measure how far he'd come.

To my surprise, I witnessed no shock. No awe. His brow remained furrowed in confusion, his stare intent on the house. "I don't get it. I'm assuming you're not suggesting you'll sleep in a hovel, so this is another illusion, isn't it?" he said, and I understood why he hadn't reacted to the perceptual shift.

"It is. Nothing you're seeing about this place is real."

"So why could I see through the filter around the apartment so easily while this place still looks like a shithole?"

"I don't know. If I had to guess, it's a matter of familiarity. You didn't notice the change to the Somerset building until I pulled around back, an area you'd never seen before. Your mind had no set memory to fill in the gap, and because you're aware of the truth now, it didn't feel the need to make up something new. Here, what you're seeing is what you've always seen. It might take time for the perception filter to fade completely."

I bit down on a grin. Never had I imagined I would have so much fun peeling away the layers of the world for this man.

"Look again and try to see. Remember the kind of world you live in. Remember that secrets are everywhere."

He squeezed his eyes shut, and when he opened them, his frustration morphed into shock.

"I can't believe this. Seriously. I cannot believe it. This house… it's supposed to be a crumbling piece of junk. How is it possible none of what I saw is actually here? The details were so clear. Right down to the rubble."

A frosty anxiety crested over him, and his trembling hands fumbled with his seatbelt. I rested my fingers over his and navigated the path through his emotions until I found the source of the fear and picked it apart, preventing it from overwhelming him. His breathing slowed, and he turned towards me with a lingering hint of panic in his eyes.

I caught his gaze with mine, anchoring him to the here and now. "All that stuff at the hospital, all the negative stuff you've seen so far, that's the exception. This —" I gestured to the house, to the intact windows and the recently overhauled roof "—is the magic. The beauty of the divide between your world and mine."

He frowned. "Did you use your empath thing on me? I *felt* my adrenaline drop."

Heat filled my cheeks, and I dropped my eyes as I let go of his hand. "I'm so sorry. I should have asked first. I won't sneak up on you like that again."

"No," he said, "it's fine. It helped. Thank you. That was

amazing, just… unexpected."

I looked up to read his expression, and when the lines on his face remained tight, my heart lurched with regret and trepidation. "Am I moving too quickly with all this? Did you want me to drop you off at your place? You can call me when you've had a bit of time."

His throat bobbed with a hard swallow, and he licked his dry lips. "No, I'm okay. Thanks. This just—I think it's going to be a while before I can take anything for granted."

"I won't rush you. Ask questions, explore. This is the rest of your life." I hesitated before adding, "If you want it to be."

I kept my stare averted as I clasped my hands in my lap, too afraid of what I might find staring back at me. Overcome with a wish of being out of the car and in the open air, I took the keys and stepped outside. Colm followed my lead and grabbed the three bags from the trunk while I got my computer bag and satchel from the backseat, and together we walked around the house to the back door.

Gary's people had left the keys in the mailbox, so I let us in, and even I was impressed by the sight that awaited us. Polished hardwood flooring, all bright maple, and large windows that cast light into every corner of the main floor. A narrow set of stairs across from the door led to the second storey, with the living room to the right and the kitchen and dining rooms beyond and to the left. A door tucked under the stairs led to the basement.

"You guys spare no expense," Colm said as he toured the living room, poking his nose into the fireplace and testing the light switches. As I'd suspected, having something practical to focus on settled the wild current of his nerves, and I was equally grateful for the distraction.

"This isn't the department's money," I said, hauling my satchel into the dining room. "This is all me. Years of planning and preparation thanks to a grandmother who considers a healthy amount of paranoia to be the best defence."

"Wise woman."

"She would agree."

I pulled the documents out of my bag and arranged the piles on the dining table in the same order we'd had them in the apartment. Lucien's guilt screamed at me from every page, the reminder of his betrayal, his treason. The paperwork had served its purpose, but I preferred to keep it visible. I needed to see it—the overview not only of what we were up against, but a reminder of my ignorance. I had chosen to take Colm into my confidence, and I would continue to do so until he gave me reason not to… but that didn't mean I wouldn't watch him closely. Our people had called on him, asked questions about me. He said he'd told them nothing, but was that true, or had his willingness to help us, to listen to me, to stick around, been a strategy to learn more and report back?

I didn't think so, but I'd made too many mistakes to discount the possibility altogether.

I looked up and caught him watching me. "Tea?" I asked.

***

By the time the two mugs of my grandmother's tea were empty on the dining room table, Colm had settled into a somewhat comfortable groove as I filled him in on the various elements of our situation, my reason for postponing our dinner date, and why government agents had shown up at his door.

He held up better than I would have expected given his reactions to the other revelations of the day, and I suspected having the briefing notes in front of him—something tangible, recognizable—had delivered a dose of reality to the unbelievable. Most mundanes had an easier time putting faith in what was familiar to them, and nothing was more familiar to a public servant than a well-crafted proposal signed by a federal minister. Even if his signature had been forged.

"What about the letters Jet and Gideon found at the headquarters?" he asked, shuffling through the documentation on the table. "Do you have copies of those?"

"According to Gideon, he took photos of everything they found, but he hasn't sent them over yet. We have it, though. Everything we need to out them."

"Then why don't you?"

"Politics," I said, and wished I were joking. "We currently have no minister, and our stand-in is the person trying to ruin us. Who will the prime minister believe—Lucien with his years of service under Jean-Luc, or the people on the wanted poster for the man's murder?"

"But you have the paperwork."

"Which he could easily explain away or deny or even destroy by the time we came forward. And even if we did show someone, what could the prime minister's office do with the information? Take down an entire department—an entire population—of supernatural beings? How? Violence? There would be too many casualties on both sides." I curled my fingers on the table. "There's also the possibility they'd agree with the deputy and see FoSA as a great solution. No more budget for the monsters."

Colm rested his hand over mine, the warmth of his palm travelling up my arm to loosen the tightness in my neck. Through the contact, I picked up his receding fear and a strengthening resolve. "I wouldn't stand by and let that happen, and I'm sure a lot of other people wouldn't if they knew. But if you're right, what will you do?"

"I don't know." Tears pricked the corners of my eyes. Not even Nan's tea had helped take the edge off my exhaustion, terror, and uncertainty. It smoothed the sharpness, but the heaviness of our situation pressed down on my shoulders, crushing my chest.

"What happens if they win?" he asked.

I met his eye and found the worry in my heart reflected in his gaze. "I don't know."

The possibilities varied. There was a slight chance every-thing worked out for the best. We might end up with resources we'd never enjoyed before, a full range of services to support our eclectic population. But how could any organization main-tain the same standard of care across so many countries in so many reaches of the world? More likely, expenses would rise, and we'd be forced deeper into hiding, owing more and more to the powers that be until we'd lost our freedoms.

At that point, it would be better to cross the wall, but how long would Meril leave the doorway open after her agreement with the prime minister ended?

It wasn't a future I wanted to test.

"The streets are going to run red no matter what we do," I said. "The only difference will be whether it's with our blood or theirs."

His fingers tightened around mine. "Then we come up with a plan. We fight."

My heart skipped a beat. "We?"

He didn't flinch. "We."

"Colm…"

I picked up the mugs and brought them into the kitchen. He didn't know what he was saying, what he was offering.

He followed me, and as soon as I'd set the mugs on the counter, he turned me towards him and took my hands in his. His palms were warm and callused, and mine tingled under the contact. His eyes burned, dark as coal, lacking any of the self-doubt or idealist shine I might have expected to find.

"Maybe I'm rushing into this whole thing and it's going to hit me like a two-by-four once I've had time to think it over, but from where I'm standing right now, I don't see any other way forward. Yes, I'm confused, and more than a little terrified, but this isn't the first time I've felt that way. I was a soldier and a surgeon, stuck in situations that made me question all kinds of things, but I've always done my best to stand up for what's right. I'm making my choice, Madison—right here, right now—to believe what you're telling me. I may not be able to sense emotions like you do, and I'm aware this might be the hardest, scariest, most bizarre fight I will ever sign up for, but I won't walk away now that I know what's at stake."

"You've been through this before," I said. "You know there's a good chance you won't walk out the other end." I pulled one hand free and worked up my courage to rest it against his cheek. A thin layer of stubble brushed along the heel of my palm. He must have skipped shaving in his rush to get to the hospital. In his rush to help me. "This isn't your fight. I am so grateful for all you've done and all you want to do, but you should go home. You should go to work and carry on with your life. Once this is over, no matter how it ends, not much will have changed for you. You would be safe."

"Everything would change if I lost you."

My breath, my heartbeat, all logical thought stopped.

He stroked his thumb across the palm still caught in his

hand. "When those men came to my door asking questions—when you stopped showing up at work or answering my texts—I was afraid something had happened to take you away from me. I understood your work was top secret. Every time I asked about it, you evaded. It didn't matter. All I cared about was that whatever trouble you were in might mean we never got our dinner." The corner of his mouth quirked upwards, but the expression didn't erase the concern in his eyes. "I was afraid I'd never be able to tell you how much I love our chats. How every time I catch sight of you in the lobby, my entire day brightens. How much spending time with you makes all the bureaucratic bullshit I face every day worth it."

His smile widened, and this time it softened all the hard lines around his mouth. "There was always something about you that was unlike anyone I'd ever met, and now I guess I know what it is. Maybe it should scare me, but all it does is make me want to learn more. Find out what makes you tick. The fact is, I have been in love with you since we shared our first carrot muffin." His smile vanished. "So if these bastards are threatening to steal that from me, then this is as much my fight as it is yours. I'm not helpless. I might not have knives built into my hands or the ability to blow things up with my mind, but I can help. Let me stay with you."

I couldn't allow it.

I also couldn't deny him.

It was like my brain had short-circuited. He kept saying

all these wonderful, kind, incredible things, and the more he spoke, the less capable I became of responding. More touching than his words was the depth of his emotions, growing more intense, radiating more widely off him until they filled the room from wall to wall. Feelings that I—for all my skill—had never detected in him. Feelings he'd suppressed, denied, now thrown open to envelop me, and the beauty, the perfection of them left me reeling. It was everything I'd spent my life searching for and basking in with other people, the positive emotions that drowned out the negative. And here they were, directed at me.

My throat closed, and I wished he could pick up half of what I was feeling. But he didn't share my ability. Either I told him or I found some other way to show him.

Not giving myself time to think or second-guess what I was doing, I rose onto my tiptoes and brushed my lips over his. Careful, hesitant. Not how I ever dreamed our first kiss would be.

I'd imagined us outside a restaurant after a fabulous meal.

Along the canal as we walked hand-in-hand through a beautiful sunset glow.

In every daydream, we were happy, at peace, excited to see where things led.

Not desperate and conflicted, the weight of the future bearing down on us.

He tensed. I pulled back, my cheeks burning. "I'm sorry, I—"

He slipped his arm around me and pulled me closer, cutting

me off with a kiss that turned my stomach upside down. Lips as soft as velvet consumed me, the molten heat of his tongue rushing through my blood.

All thought slipped away as instinct took over. I abandoned his kiss to trail my lips along his jaw, tasting his skin. One of my hands found its way to the back of his neck, drawing him closer against me, while the other teased the hem of his sweater, exploring the hard muscles of his stomach.

None of this was how I'd imagined it, either. I'd never been a first-kiss-to-bedroom woman. But then, I'd never been with a man like Colm. Never felt so safe. So certain.

I drew my fingers out from under his sweater, grabbed his hand, and brought it to the neckline of my blouse. I needed to make sure we were on the same page, but words had escaped me.

Fortunately, he understood what I needed without me uttering a syllable. His fingers slid over my chest, undoing the buttons of my shirt until it hung open between us. I circled my arms around his neck, and he picked me up as though I weighed nothing. With my legs wrapped around his waist, he carried me to the stairs.

The longer I held contact with him, the more powerful his emotions became. Love, passion, awe… and a desire so strong it left me drunk. How was it possible I'd never noticed the ocean of feeling within him? And how was it possible I was able to read him better than anyone else I'd ever met? Better than Jet, better than my family?

When I pulled away to look into his eyes, I found myself staring into a well of awareness, and any doubts I had about where we were going or what I felt for him washed away.

The reason I read him so clearly was that he wanted me to.

He was projecting his emotions, not hiding them. There were no walls between us, no barriers. Everything I sensed was as pure and voluntary as if he were standing on a rooftop shouting it into the sky. Never in my life had I experienced so much honesty. So much emotional vulnerability.

We made it up the stairs and into the first bedroom we found. I had no eye for the decor, the layout, the view. There was only this man, now beneath me, now on top as he peeled off his shirt. My fingers and lips explored the hills and valleys of his muscles, and his strong arms stayed around me, guarding me from anything that might keep us apart.

I slid my arms out of my shirtsleeves and tugged down my pants, hating every article of clothing that separated us, and by the time he slid inside me, I'd never been more ready to accept him. In so many ways, he was my perfect fit.

With every stroke of his body, his desire heightened, and mine responded. I didn't know what belonged to him or what was mine, and for the first time, the confusion didn't frighten me. At no point could I consider this *want* one-sided. My need was as great—if not greater—and I gave myself to the ebb and flow of his passion. His hand stole between us, cupping my breast, sliding lower, sneaking between my legs. I shifted, giving him deeper access, wanting to be as full of him physically as I was emotionally. For right now—for as long as this lasted—I wanted to forget Madison Prince and all her troubles. There was only this, only Colm, and as my passion crested, everything else disappeared.

Chapter 21

Gideon

THE LINE ON the heart monitor followed the same steady pattern it had for the past three hours.

Was it supposed to change if she was close to waking up? What did it mean if everything stayed the same?

My attention shifted between the monitor and Jet's face. I'd covered her with an extra blanket, hoping that by hiding her stillness, bulking her up under more layers, I would stop seeing her as vulnerable. Broken.

Only her hand remained out from under the covers, and I hadn't let go of it since I'd settled into the stiff armchair beside her bed. Every hour I squeezed her fingers, and every hour I'd been disappointed when she didn't squeeze back.

The nurse had come in a few times to check things over and make sure I didn't need anything, but she hadn't been able to answer my question of when Jet would open her eyes. By her last visit, I was pretty sure I'd annoyed the crap out of her, but that wouldn't stop me from asking again the next time she came in. She was welcome to call me out for being impatient, but what else could I do?

I'd tried to sleep, as Madison had suggested. With Jet's hand in mine, I'd kicked off my boots and put my feet up on the bed to try to find a comfortable angle in the world's most uncomfortable chair, but every thirty seconds I thought I heard her make a noise, or move, or the pattern of the heart monitor change, so after fifteen minutes I gave it up as a lost cause.

"I don't know what you're waiting for," I said as I bent over to kiss the back of her hand. "For us to do all the heavy lifting so you get to wake up and have the world put to rights? Not very soldierly of you, Captain."

The door opened, and I looked up expecting to see the nurse again. Instead, Colm's surgeon buddy walked into the room. His face was white, his lips whiter, and the sight of his fear sent a whirlpool of dread foaming through my stomach with the anticipation of bad news. Had he found something else on one of Jet's scans? Learned more about what the parasite had done to her? Come here to unleash some fresh new hell?

Before I drove myself crazy, I cut off my spiralling thoughts and asked, "What's wrong?"

The doctor—what was his name? Billy?—pulled up a chair on the opposite side of the bed and dropped into it. Without answering me, he reached for the remote control and turned on the small TV hooked up in the corner of the room.

Jet's face stared down at us. Alongside mine and Madison's. Wanted for questioning in connection with the dead minister.

"They're saying your captain snapped after losing her team," he said, not taking his eyes off the screen. "That she tracked down the man who planted the bomb and beat him to death, might be involved in five other murders around the city connected to the attack, and stabbed the minister."

My blood ran cold. Every single murder connected to Gagnon's plan had been laid at Jet's door. We'd known they would try to pin the minister on her, but Weldon as well? The informants? She had to be Canada's Number One Most Wanted, and here she was, lying unconscious and unable to protect herself.

I faced Billy, staring at him until he caved to the pressure and met my gaze.

"What are you going to do?" I asked.

If he said he had no choice but to call the police, I was ready to wrestle him into the bathroom and lock the door. It would be loud and messy and wouldn't help our cause, but there was no way I would let Jet wind up in Michael's clutches while the media cheered him on for capturing the rogue soldier. I'd have to get her out of here without endangering her recovery, but I would do it.

"Nothing," he said, taking me by surprise and interrupting my hastily formed exit plans. He passed a hand over his face. "I just thought you should know."

I watched the flicker in his eyes, the flex of his jaw. Were these the signs of a liar or a nervous mundane who'd found himself helping three possible murderers? Years of experience had taught me what to look for, but they'd also taught me intentions mattered more than thoughts.

"Why?" I asked.

Billy puffed out a breath and stood up. His white lab coat caught around his legs as he pushed his chair back with his calves. For a while he didn't say anything, busying himself with unwrapping the bandages around Jet's head.

"Because I owe Colm my life, and he told me to keep my mouth shut," he said. "He thinks you had nothing to do with the murders, that you're on the right side of whatever this is, and there's no one whose judgement I trust more than his."

As closely as I watched his answer, I detected no trace of a lie. "What about the nurse? The anesthesiologist?"

He chuckled. "I think you and your friend put the fear of God into them. They won't say anything. Besides…"

He started when he pulled away the last layer of gauze to reveal that the incision he'd created only a few hours before was nothing more than a stitched red streak along Jet's hairline. With shaking fingers he checked the healing wound, reached for the sterile gauze beside the bed, and stopped. I didn't question him. There was no point wasting supplies.

"How can this be real?" he asked, more to himself than

to me. "How has a genetic makeup like hers not been tested? Think of the good her blood cells could do if we cracked the code of what makes her heal so quickly?"

"And possibly kill millions of people in the process," I said in a tone that left no room for argument. This doctor wouldn't be the first person to consider the benefits of using supernaturals to mundane advantage, but every one of those people had met an untimely end. And so had all the people they'd tested their theories on. Supernatural blood was not a miracle drug.

Billy shook his head, and the glow drained out of his eyes.

"I don't know what I pulled out of her brain, but I spent an hour dissecting it, pulling it to pieces, and it's still moving. It's like nothing I've ever seen. Whatever it is, are there more of them?"

"Yes."

Based on what Gagnon had told me, Jet wasn't the first guinea pig for their new weapon. He and his twisted cronies probably had buckets of writhing worms lying around their headquarters.

I hoped I'd get an opportunity to shove a handful down their throats before we turned them over to Meril.

Billy shuddered. "And the person who… shot her with it is still out there?"

"Yes."

He raised his eyes to meet mine. "And there's a chance that, before long, more of your kind will need help, isn't there?"

I held his stare. "Yes."

He swallowed and, after a moment, reached into his pocket. "Then I'm not going anywhere. Here's my direct number if Colm isn't around to call me. Whatever you people are, whatever you need, if I can help prevent anyone else from suffering what Captain Dawson might have suffered, you can count on me. I won't breathe a word."

I nodded, the closest I could manage to a thank you.

I'd assumed we'd tapped the last of our resources. Madison's uncle and the warrior woman. Meril's weapons. All the help we'd drummed up so far had been reluctant, tied with strings, and supernatural.

I never would have imagined we'd find another ally here in this mundane hospital.

My doubt remained over whether it would make a difference.

"When you're ready to leave, I suggest you use the freight elevator around the corner from the supply room," Billy said. "Fewer eyes."

He waited for me to say something, but I had no response in me. He was doing his duty, just as I was doing mine. Any gratitude I felt, I was in no state of mind to express it. He could perform all the surgeries he wanted on the people we brought to him, but what good would it do if the fallen didn't get back on their feet?

Jet's chest rose and fell, the line on the heart monitor keeping in time. The same steady pattern. No change.

Billy finally accepted the only reply he would get to his grand gesture was silence, and he rose from the chair and started for the door.

"Hey, doc," I called.

He stopped, turned around. "Yes?"

All my attention remained on Jet. "When is she going to wake up?"

Chapter 22

Madison

WHAT ABOUT WEREWOLVES?"

Colm hooked his fingers through mine, and I shifted so my head rested on his shoulder. We both lay on our backs, one of his hands splayed lazily across my stomach. I hadn't thought I could feel so relaxed with the rest of my life falling apart, but the oxytocin dripping through my veins was doing its job. If Colm's earlier desire had made me drunk, his current state, combined with mine, left me pleasantly, hazily high.

"Shifters are real," I said. "Not too many around here because of the vampire politics, but there's a pack that calls Algonquin Park home. A few others throughout the country."

"Wait—vampires are real?"

"They are, but they keep to themselves. Whole different hierarchy."

"Huh. Aliens?"

I laughed. "If they've ever touched down, they didn't inform us."

He took a moment to let the information sit.

So far, I'd left the speed of these revelations in his control, not volunteering anything that didn't fall in line with his questions but not holding back when he asked. It was the only way I'd come up with to tackle the conversation that didn't overload him. A person could only handle so much reality at once, mundane or supernatural.

"What is *your* hierarchy, then?" he asked after a while. "For non-vampire supernaturals, I mean. Are there different species or just different abilities?"

"A little of both. There are the human-looking supernaturals who might walk by you a hundred times a day and you would never know it unless you knew what to look for. They have telltale signs if your mind is open to them—markings on their faces, extra limbs sometimes. Tails. Forked tongues. We come in all shapes and sizes, but the more extreme the differences, the less we mingle with the mundane world."

"Where else would you go?"

"Wherever we want. Even for us, it's a free country. The tree-minded folk— -the wood sprites, the treekins, the giants— head to the forests and mountains. The water species—naiads, mermaids, selkies—prefer the rivers and lakes. Some creatures are so small they exist anywhere without notice. Gnomes and pixies build their lives in gardens, for example."

"For real?"

"Oh yeah, that part is accurate enough. Just don't try to get cozy with them—they bite."

"And all this is hereditary?"

"So the research suggests, but there's a lot we don't know. If a supernatural and a mundane have a child together, the odds are fifty-fifty they'll show some supernatural ability or physical trait. Even if no ability presents itself, the child will see the true world, unlike a child born to two mundane parents where the chances of being born without a perception filter are incredibly slim."

"That's got to suck if siblings are involved, if one of them is born with abilities and the other isn't?"

"Ask Jet. She's hardly spoken to her brother in years. I don't think he appreciates the cost of being what we are."

Colm kissed the backs of my fingers. "What about you?"

I tilted my head to look at him. "What about me?"

"Any jealous members in your family?"

"Not a one. I'm one of the rare full breeds."

"You're kidding me." He pulled away, and I raised an eyebrow as I rolled onto my side.

"Is that so hard to believe?"

"No, I just…" He looked down at himself. "Will I have to fight off your father or something for seducing you away from your kind?"

I grinned. "I don't think he'll find that necessary, though it's good to be prepared. As it happens, his father is mundane."

Colm's expression pinched with confusion. "Then…"

As much fun as it was messing with his understanding of genetics, I chose to satisfy his curiosity. "I'm descended from the queen of our territory, so the blood runs thick down the maternal line. With only one generation of mundanes in the family tree, I'm about as close as it gets to pure supernatural on this side of the wall."

Colm blinked. "A queen."

"Yep. Meril is one of the original magic workers. It's because of her any of us live here at all."

"You said queen of this territory. There are others? How have the mundanes—we—never heard of you?"

"You have, though, haven't you? All those fairy tales, mythologies. They're not based on nothing."

"Sure," he said, his brow furrowing. "But I mean facts. Certainties."

I shrugged. "Because when the first non-magical people traipsed into our corner of the world, we hid. Our queen, Meril, created an invisible wall to divide the country, separating the supernatural realm from the mundane world. The realm still exists in its untouched perfection on a separate plane. Here but not here, almost like one world overlaid on another." I saw I was losing him and opted to save that line of explanation for another time. "We were lucky she acted when she did. We wouldn't have survived without her."

The furrow on Colm's brow deepened, and I brushed my

fingertips over the skin to smooth it out. He caught my hand and planted a kiss on the inside of my wrist. Through our touch, I picked up a glimmer of his discomfort—not strong enough to call it apprehension, but something I'd said had unsettled him.

"What's wrong?"

"You said you're descended from this queen?"

I hesitated before confirming. "She's my great-great-grand-mother."

His eyes widened, and he pulled back again to get a better angle on me. "Are you saying I'm lying naked next to supernatural royalty?"

Laughing, I ran my fingers over his bare chest. "Trust me, if I start singing and dancing with the forest creatures, it'll be because of your performance, not any princess gene. On this side of the unseen wall, I'm just a government employee who enjoys carbs and long soaks in the bath."

I caught his lips with mine, and my heart raced as his fingertips traced patterns up and down my back.

"Seriously, though," he said when he pulled away. "Is that an issue?"

"No," I assured him. "Meril and I aren't… close."

Was now a good time to tell him we might be a good deal closer in another few days? Probably, but I couldn't bring myself to ruin the moment with tomorrow's troubles. Today's were enough.

When he remained quiet, I searched his face, doing my best to leave his emotions to himself. "Is something else bothering you? Something about Meril?"

"No. Yes? Maybe?" He didn't continue right away, putting his thoughts together. "I have to wonder why you aren't all in this realm place. Why spend your life on this side of the world with all its issues and threats to your safety?"

"Why put mundanes in danger, you mean?" I asked, reading between his words.

"No, I didn't mean—" he rushed to say.

I held up a hand to cut him off and reassure him he hadn't offended me. "You're not wrong. Many of our kind prey on yours. They're watched to make sure they don't lose control and our secret isn't revealed, but it happens. The tragedies in the Ottawa River—people reaching into the water and getting grabbed by seaweed—that's the mermaids having fun, hunting their dinner. It's not something we condone, but like all things in nature, there's hunter and there's prey."

"I guess I'm used to being higher on the food chain," he said, attempting to hide his flash of fear under a light tone.

I grinned. "It's not that much of a shift. Most of us find mundanes too fatty."

He laughed, and the tear ebbed under a warm glow of joy.

"To be honest, you're safer with us on this side of the wall, despite the few species who see you as food. If Meril forced us to return to the realm, especially after all this time, there would be a rebellion, which would mean an even greater threat to your world and ours. So she gave us the choice. Some of our kind are here because they enjoy the challenge of weaving magic into a non-magical world, some because they couldn't find their place in the queen's court, and others, like me and Jet, because we want to do what we can to make the world better on both sides."

I paused, unsure whether to let him in on the other half of the truth, but in the end landed on yes. It was better he learn the worst up front. It was the only way he could be sure he'd made the right decision.

"There's also the fact that Meril's authority is limited to her borders, which more or less follow the mundane Canadian lines. Leadership differs across regions. Some territories have a monarch, others a council, others, like the United States, have mundane and supernatural bundled together under a head of state. It means there are different rules and different legalities depending on where you go. Yes, some supernaturals in Canada pose a threat to the mundanes, but if Meril pulled us across the wall, our absence would leave you open to the threat of supernaturals from other regions. Our presence provides a degree of security."

Colm pressed his palm against mine, and his discomfort morphed, still there but focused elsewhere.

"Your ability…" he said. "You never turn it off?"

"I can't. It's as much ingrained in who I am as the colour of my eyes." I curled my fingers through his, trapping him.

"Before today, I've never used it on you, if that's what you're wondering. Aside from some superficial dips into your aura, the first time I touched your mind was to read you in that hospital room and to calm you down in the car." I dropped my gaze to the line of his chin, the stubble darker after the passing hours, filling out along his jawline. "It's a big part of what held me back from getting close to you. I struggle sometimes to untangle emotions, so it was hard to tell if the attraction and desire I sensed were mine as well as yours."

He released his hand from my hold and brushed his fingers across my cheek, guiding my eyes to his. "Are you sure now?"

My face flushed as I remembered the heat that had carried us away. The aftermath of it still rippled through every limb, every cell. And it was all mine, a wholly physical reaction without room for anyone else's pleasure. "Without a doubt."

Colm's fingers slid over my waist to rest on my hip, and he pulled himself closer, the length of him pressed against me.

"This world you've described, the complexity of it, your people have kept it going in secret for almost two hundred years. The arrogance of these people to think they have a right to destroy it for their personal gain."

The sudden twist in conversation to the threat hanging over us was an unpleasant wake-up call, but I respected Colm all the more for giving the problem such serious consideration. Though I wished we could have had a few more minutes to ourselves.

"I like to imagine Lucien didn't make the first move," I said. "That FoSA reached out to him and not the other way around. Call it rose-tinted glasses, but he's always been one of our loudest advocates for funding, for progress, for support. He's always worked to help us thrive in a fast-changing world."

"Until he stood to make money by selling you out."

"Until that, yes."

The truth hurt. So much else had happened since we'd discovered Lucien's treachery, but beneath my shock and humiliation was such deep disappointment I almost believed I might forgive the man if he changed his mind right now and refused the deal. He'd been such a big part of my life and my career that it pained me to think about going forward without his competent leadership.

Then again, if I'd followed his lead, I'd be joining him on the beach, wearing a million-dollar bathing suit while my family, my friends, all the people I'd helped as a public servant poured money into this organization to maintain their basic needs. Not to mention being conscripted to fight in who knew what battles or to work who knew what jobs.

Privatizing the supernatural.

How could they do it?

My stomach twisted, and I tucked my head under Colm's chin, wrapping myself around him to fight off the waking nightmares creeping up on me from every angle.

"I haven't been able to make sense of anything since the

first attack," I said, working to keep my voice from breaking as tears pricked my eyes. "That was the point when everything I've worked for came crashing down. Then we lost all those informants—people we'd relied on for years—our minister… Jean-Luc fought for everything that mattered. My father must be devastated, and it hasn't been safe for me to call him. They were best friends for over four decades."

"I'm sorry you've had to face all this with so little support." He kissed the top of my head. "I wish I could have been here for you weeks ago."

I held him tighter. "You're here now." I hoped he understood how deep my gratitude ran, even if I never found the words to express it.

He stroked his fingers through my hair. "I'm also amazed at how far the three of you have come by yourselves. Not everyone could have done that."

I gave a very unladylike snort. "I can't exactly say it's gone *well*. We've learned a lot, but we've made so many mistakes. Now that Lucien found Gideon and Jet in his headquarters, now that they know Gideon is alive and we're still digging, who knows how much we've rushed their timeline. Our snooping gained us a pile of information we can't use yet and might have shot us squarely in the foot."

"Why is it only their timeline that can speed up? Isn't there something you can do to close in on them? Can't the queen do something?"

"You know how I said having supernaturals on this side of the wall helps keep the mundanes safe?"

"Yes…"

"That's only because of the balance of power. If Meril steps in, a quiet resolution is impossible. Especially considering how high in the department this treason goes. She would crush them. Loudly. As much to ensure she stamped out the problem as to send a message to anyone who thought to follow in their footsteps. And the repercussions…"

"One of those shots heard around the world moments?"

"Exactly. Keeping her at bay has been as great a priority for us as finding out what Lucien is up to. It's like trying to hold back a tidal wave while working to put out a wildfire. One would solve the other, but at too great a cost."

Again he tightened his arms around me, and I sank deeper into the strength and comfort he offered.

"You must have some resources left. Other groups who can help."

I nodded against his chest. "We have a few on standby. Their numbers aren't big, and I don't know how best to use them. Jet is our strategist, and she's…"

I stopped, not wanting to lose myself to tears.

"You can't send these groups to the headquarters?"

"By now, Lucien has probably cleared everything out except a few ghostbombs." I wiped my eyes with the back of my hand. "Even if he hasn't, I'm not prepared to sacrifice our few allies for a stepping stone. Destroying their base of operations would be a blow, but it wouldn't stop them. I need to be smart about this, save our hammer for the keystone. If we fail before then, it will mean a war that spreads across the wall. Across the border."

"So a mass manoeuvre won't work yet, but what about something on a smaller scale?"

"The smaller scale is what you see. What more can the three of us do?"

"First, there are four of us now," he reminded me with a tap under my chin. "But let's play hypothetical. If you had a team you could lead, where would you start?"

"I'm not..."

"Don't tell me you're not a planner. I saw the way you organized those documents—you know how to prioritize your efforts. Where would you go first?"

"I'd want to keep our movements quiet," I said, starting slow, picking my thoughts one at a time. "Pen them in without them noticing. Cut Lucien, Michael, and O'Malley off from each other to block communication and prevent collaboration. They'd find their way around us, but in the meantime, I'd take Dougall out of the picture. He's their greatest weapon. As soon as we dealt with him, we could work on closing ranks around the rest. Stamp out each fire individually instead of attempting to spray down the entire blaze at once."

"What if they didn't give you a chance to separate them?"

"Then…" I waded through the possibilities. "I suppose it would be better to squeeze them in together. Instead of cutting them off from each other, draw them in and cut them off from their resources. Their power lies in their numbers and their planning, but if they don't have access to their soldiers or the ability to set their plans in motion, they're just four people. Just like we are."

For the first time in a week, the situation lay in front of me, unshadowed by personal doubts and fears. I saw the people involved as pieces on a game board, movable avatars I could shift around as needed.

The vision evaporated within moments.

"But again, we don't have the people to get it done. It's impossible for us to do it alone, and Serc and Lilith won't accept that level of risk for a mid-game assault. They've made it clear they prefer to be endgame only. Nothing that might draw unwanted attention their way. Or require too much approval from the throne."

"So we take them off the board until we have a better idea," Colm said. He went quiet for a while, his thumb tapping the seconds against my shoulder blade. Eventually, he asked, "How many of Jet's troops survived?"

I frowned, thinking. "Ten. Nine died at the blast site, and she lost another in hospital."

"Where are they now?"

"They remained loyal to the department. To Michael. They

think she's lost her mind, turned traitor."

His thumb paused in his rhythm. "With all due respect, if that's the case, she must be an awful captain."

I tensed, fighting an instinctive prickle of indignation. "Not at all. Her squad—her JetPack—adores her. Or at least, they did. They would have followed her into the mouth of hell if she'd asked them."

Every principle I had told me to fly off at him for talking about things he knew nothing about, but I clung to my last thread of rational thinking that he wouldn't have said it without a reason.

Colm shifted both of us so we sat up against the pillows. There was a brightness in his eyes that hadn't been there a moment ago, and a spark of excitement passed from him to me.

"If that's true, I guarantee they would follow her still. Unquestionably. I've had my share of commanding officers, and if any of them called me up today and asked me to hop on a plane, I would. Without question. They might respect their current commander, but a good captain creates a bond that is damn near impossible to break. What happened to her unit— the shared loss, the lack of answers—would have strengthened it, not cut it. If they haven't reached out, if they're not clamouring to help her, something's not right. Who's leading them now?"

I scrambled to catch up with where his thoughts had gone. "Eric, probably. Her lieutenant."

"All of them?"

I wanted to stop him, tell him he was travelling down the wrong path, but it was too late. Hope had ignited in my chest, and the more I thought about it, the more the embers burned. Why hadn't we tried calling in Jet's pack? Because Michael had told her they'd turned on her, lost faith in her leadership.

But of course Michael would have said that. Anything to isolate his captain, get her on his side.

Trembling with the possibility, my hope feeding off Colm's, I leaned over to grab my laptop… only to remember that in our hurry to get to the bedroom, I'd left all my bags downstairs. Reluctantly I scrambled into my underwear, pulled on my shirt, and rolled out of bed, not checking to see if Colm followed me before I rushed downstairs. I grabbed my laptop bag and took it into the living room, dropping onto the couch as I booted it up.

Colm joined me a minute later, doing up the button on his jeans.

The boot-up icon taunted me, ticking its way in slow little circles before finally bringing me to my desktop.

"IT blocked most of my access, but I downloaded a few files before they shut me out. I think one of them was the personnel records. It'll be out of date, but it should at least tell us where things stood a few days ago."

I brought up the records and scrolled through until I reached the section for military personnel. Ten names were stamped deceased, and my heart ached for their loss. Even if

Colm was right, would any of the remaining ten be willing to jump back into the fight?

We can ask.

"All right, here are the survivors. Based on this—" I clicked through each name, mentally noting their status and commanding officer "—five are serving under Eric." I recognized most of the names. Jet had talked about all of them. Three of the five, Adam, Katie, and Xander, were newer recruits, the ones she called her pups, the troops eager to get their hands dirty, impatient but focused. The other two, Ray and Marc-André, were among those she called her wolves.

I scrolled through the other four, and these names stood out even brighter. Zeke, Jason, Sara, and Luvy. Jet's dream team, the heart of her pack. "These guys stayed on leave."

Colm shook his head. "Unless they're still injured, they wouldn't choose to sit around rehashing everything that went wrong before the attack. If I had to guess, they smelled something was up when Jet was removed from active duty and didn't want to go back until things were resolved. These are your troops."

With shaking hands I reached for my cell phone. "Let's pray you're right."

Chapter 23

Gideon

THREE MORE HOURS of the same steady beep. I'd memorized the timing and tensed at every irregularity. My ass was numb, my eyelids were sagging, and every minute was a recurring hell loop of waiting and expectation.

"You're awake, aren't you."

I said it as a statement, needing it to be true.

Jet didn't move, didn't react. My imagination and wishful thinking had added a bit of colour to her cheeks, but I knew it wasn't real. These hospital lights would have made it impossible for anyone to look healthy. I probably looked like a ghoul, a cursed soul drawn from the grave to walk the earth for eternity. That was how I felt, anyway.

"You're lying there with your eyes closed, holding yourself still, paying me back for New York. That's what this is. Revenge. Well, you've succeeded. The son of a bitch who strung me up in that cell, stabbed me, cut me, whipped me, screwed around with my nervous system? That was nothing. This—" I jabbed my finger into the armrest of the chair. "This is the real torture, Jet. You've won. So come on and wake *up*."

My phone vibrated in my pocket, and I jumped to my feet, my heart in my throat. After so many hours of undisturbed silence, I'd apparently turned into a jittery scaredy-cat who screamed at shadows.

"Your fault," I said to Jet as I pulled my phone free. Madison's number danced on the screen, and I fought through a sea of reluctance to answer it. She would want an update, and I hated having to tell her there was no change.

Not wanting to disturb Jet, I walked over to the window. "Everything okay at the new place?" I asked in greeting.

"Perfect, actually. When this is over, I'm selling my condo and moving in."

"The neighbourhood will be lucky to have you."

"You have your own bathroom."

"Well, all right, then, roomie, I'll update my visa. Think I can get away with saying I'm a student?"

The banter was easier than anything else we had to say, but when it died, it died hard, leaving a thick emptiness interrupted only by the damned heart monitor. I was ready to pick it up and chuck it through the glass.

"I wanted to give you a heads up that, thanks to Colin, we're working on a new plan. Something that might give us an unexpected edge."

"Edges are good. Sharp?"

"Lethal."

"Excellent."

The lack of details about said plan told me it was far from a sure thing, but what did that matter? Gambles and crossed fingers were my bread and butter. At least this time it wasn't me dealing the cards, so there was less chance of it biting me in the ass. Let Madison make the bet—I would wait to find out whether we'd hit the jackpot.

"How are things there?" she asked, as I'd known she would.

"No change."

Not in Jet, not in that stupid beeping monitor. Even the nurse had given us a break and left us alone for over an hour.

"You know she's fighting, Gideon. Whatever it looks like, if there's anything left of Bridget Dawson in that skull, she's clawing tooth and nail to come back to you."

I didn't miss her choice of words but didn't respond to them. The coiling sensation they created in my stomach was nothing I wanted to read into—built hopes I didn't want raised. When she came back, it would be to tear Michael's heart out, and that had to be good enough.

"Good luck with your plan."

"I'll check in again soon."

I hung up and slid my phone into my pocket. The chair, my new friend, invited me to return to my place, but my nerves crawled with bugs and my legs refused to stay still. I paced the length of the room, and when that satisfied the bugs, I did another lap. On each pass, I poked my nose into something—the supply cupboard, the bathroom, the end table—anything to keep my mind focused on useless details for a few seconds at a time. If my brain wouldn't let me sleep, I would take a different kind of break from staring at my Sleeping Beauty—my version of the fairy tale who, if I tried to kiss her awake, would grab me by the balls and twist until I dropped to the floor.

Maybe it would be worth the pain if it woke her up.

I stopped at the window again and stared out over the city. Golden sunset streaked the fields and trees across the busy street. Another day over. Another day of waiting. What had Lucien and Michael done today? They'd likely cleared out their headquarters, or at least booby-trapped the place to prevent us from slipping back in unannounced. There hadn't been any more attacks on the news beyond the continued riots, no revelations announced, so they hadn't made leaps and bounds on the plan to close their deal.

Were they waiting, just as I was? I hoped they were suffering with whatever delays they faced, that I was a model of patience compared to their current state. Call me petty, but I was in no mood to wish them the best.

"We'll be the ones laughing in the end, Jet. That's what we do. We work as a team to bring down the bad guys. We did it in New York, and we'll do it here."

I glanced across the room to check her reaction, and all I got was another beep of the heart monitor. Stoic bastard.

Even the spatter of distant stars, visible now that the sunset had shifted into a deep shade of red, held more warmth and empathy than that beep.

"I've been thinking a lot about New York over the last few weeks," I said to Jet's reflection in the window. "Pretty much from the moment I was ordered to come up here to follow the ghost trail. Not that I didn't think of you a lot before then," I added over my shoulder, "but knowing we might cross paths again… it put some things into perspective. It made me remember how much fun I had on that job. Partnering with someone who knew what they were doing. Someone who worked with me to come up with ideas. Someone who challenged me, argued with me. How long did it take us to come up with our own code? Three days? Entire conversations with gestures and looks. I don't know about you, but to me that kind of connection doesn't happen every day. Like we synced on a whole other level. Some folks stay married for sixty years and don't have that kind of communication. Maybe it was our training, but I've never had that with anyone else. Honestly, I think the time we spent on the streets was even more fun than the time we spent in bed, and that—that's saying something."

I cleared my throat and shoved my hands into my pockets. What was I doing? Spilling my soul to a woman who couldn't hear me?

Thank fuck. I'd hate for her to listen to all this sentimental bullshit.

Despite my self-disdain, I couldn't stop myself. The sound of my voice was better than whatever the nattering in my head had to say, and somehow it felt good to get these words *out*. Hopefully once I did, they would stop yelling at me every time I tried to sleep.

"I guess what I'm saying is I'm sorry I lied to you. I'm sorry I pushed you away when all I wanted was more of you. More time. More… everything. Instead I went and fucked up whatever chance I had. To be fair, how the hell was I supposed to know, Jet?"

I whirled around, walked back to the chair, and rested my hands on the back of it, too filled with frenetic energy to sit. "How was I supposed to know you would turn out to be so… you?" A gesture at her very being, impossible to pare down to any one trait or feature.

"By the time I realized you were someone I could *trust* —a word I haven't used in over a decade, by the way—the case was almost wrapped up and you were ready to go home. You never did give me credit for breaking every protocol in the book by telling you who I was. I didn't have to do it. I *shouldn't* have done it. I was suspended three weeks without pay while the firm performed a full investigation to make sure I hadn't committed a massive security breach."

My fingers found their way to the top of my head, passed over the short sides of my hair to the too-long thatch on top. I needed a haircut. Needed to get my life back together.

"In the end they decided I wasn't a traitor, just stupid, and stuck me on rookie missions for two years. This was my first chance to prove myself, and here I am—again—almost overdue for my check-in, hiding information, risking my firm's reputation. Basically, I'm costing myself a job."

The chair's siren call finally tempted me, and I threw myself into the uncomfortable seat, dragging it as close to the bed as I could wedge it.

"And you know what? It's worth it. It's fucking worth it. *You* are fucking worth it. I may be a liar and an asshole, Bridget Dawson, but I am a liar and an asshole who is head over heels in love with you, so you'll have to fucking deal with the fact that I'm not going anywhere. Not until this is over and not until I'm sure you're able to give me shit the way only you can."

The flood of words I hadn't known were coming ran out, leaving me lighter, satisfied. My mouth was dry, my throat was tight, and goddamn if my eyes weren't stinging with tears I refused to shed.

I half-rose from my chair and pressed a kiss against Jet's third eye, the cause of all our current troubles.

"So toughen up, soldier," I whispered. "Fight this and come back to me. There's still so much to do before we're done."

Chapter 24

Jet

CONSCIOUSNESS DRIFTED TOWARDS me as slowly and leisurely as a run of syrup, heavy and sweet.

Awareness began around my lungs, the in-and-out of air, the rise and fall of my chest, and my concentration was so caught up on that one action that, for a moment, I forgot how to breathe. Only when my attention shifted to my thumping heartbeat did my automatic function kick back in.

Heart, lungs. Check, check.

My mind stopped there. Everything else was too cloudy, too distant. The rest of my body might as well have been floating on a cloud, lost to gravity for all the control I had over my arms and legs. I couldn't wrangle my thoughts in any one direction, and my mouth felt as though someone had glued it shut. Somewhere, far in the deep recesses of my rational brain, I knew I should be panicking, but the reasons weren't clear, and

I couldn't find the energy to work myself up.

I drifted for a while, wrestling with my thoughts to do something other than grow mould. Where was I? The last thing I remembered—the vague snippets of emotions and events reaching me through a faded video—was Gideon. Fear on his face. Hovering over me. Voices beyond him, a quiet murmur. Cement walls, cold floor. All of me cold.

A shiver ran through me, and I latched on to it, holding it by the tail to drag me further into wakefulness. The panic I'd sensed waited for me, and I did my best to ignore it. First, I had to figure out what was wrong with me. My toes tingled, and I wiggled them. They moved, which was more than I'd been capable of who knew how long ago. At least I still had toes.

I tried to dig up the memory of what had brought me here, but it snaked away, so I didn't push it. Easier to wiggle my toes and find out what else I was able to move.

Fingers?

Those worked, too, though controlling them took effort and devoured most of my strength.

Blackness wavered in front of me, then again the world came back, little by little.

Smells reached me, clawing their way into my nose to tickle my senses. Alcohol. Detergent. Somehow familiar, but not in a good way. More memories tumbled over themselves trying to get my attention, and I landed on one of me at six years old, on the ground, my arm lying at an awkward angle. Swing set.

Broken.

Hospital, then. That explained the smell and the floatiness, but what had I broken?

My lurking panic pounced, filled me up, sent my system into an erratic spin of racing heartbeat and rapid breaths. Somewhere, a beeping noise poked my eardrums, getting faster and louder.

Hospital. Means I'm alive. Means I'm safe.

Did it?

Had I been injured? Again the memories, but this time none of them settled, scurrying away like cockroaches running from the light.

I slid my tongue against my teeth, tried to swallow, but my mouth was too dry.

My eyelids were heavy, crusty. I reminded them who was in charge and wrestled them open. Just a crack at first, unable to widen them more than that as the bright, sterile hospital lights streamed through my eyelashes. I tried to turn my head away from the glare, but large movements were beyond my ability, and I only twitched against my too-soft pillow.

The second attempt to open my eyes was a little easier as my retinas adjusted to the light, and I was able to take in the room. A private room, thank god, with stars and a bright moon popping in for a visit through the window. A mounted television in the corner, the screen off. The artwork on the walls wasn't half-bad for a hospital room, though I couldn't for the life of me tell what the paintings were supposed to be.

To my right was a chair, a privacy curtain, and a door—the chair currently empty, the curtain open, and the door closed. To my left, the window and… Gideon.

He sat in a low armchair, slunk down with his hands clasped across his stomach and his head tilted to rest against the wing closest to the window, angled to face me. His eyes were closed, his long eyelashes brushing his cheeks as his fingers and legs twitched with dreams.

At the sight of him, more flashes tumbled through my head. Michael, a gunshot, an agonizing throb in my head… getting worse… so bad I couldn't see.

I reached out with my third eye, and pain swept through me, a sharp stab that made me cry out. All numbness and distance were forgotten as my hands flew to my head to stop my brain from squeezing through my forehead. No physical pain at the contact, but a piercing pressure through my skull.

Worst of all, my extra sight was blank. No shadows of Gideon or anyone else in the hospital, no memories rising from the objects nearby. The blankets were silent, the pillow, the mattress, as though they were brand new, created seconds before someone stuffed them around me.

Never had I felt so isolated, so claustrophobic, the immediacy of the room squeezing me, cutting me off from everything except the oppressive present.

"It's all right, Jet. I'm here, you're okay."

Gideon's voice, soft and soothing, worked through the rocking in my head. His warm hand touched my shoulder, stroked my back as he eased me up and pulled me towards him. His solid chest beneath my cheek. His heartbeat a steady rhythm to counter my racing pulse.

"What—" I tried to ask, but everything was too dry, and the sound came out as little more than a croak.

Gideon left my side, and the world opened where he'd been—too big but closing in on me at the same time. I couldn't catch my breath, couldn't stop the room from spinning. My stomach revolted, but Gideon was back again with a metal pan and a glass of water. I retched into the pan, bringing up nothing, and wrapped my shaking fingers around the glass.

Why can't I see? What happened to me? What did they do?

"You're all right," he murmured, and his hand returned to my back, his gentle fingers tracing patterns between my shoulder blades.

Eventually, my breathing slowed, and I took a few sips of water without bringing it back up. My throat stung at the iciness, but it was a pain I could handle. Anything was better than the now-subsiding throb in the middle of my forehead.

"What happened?" I finally managed to ask. "My third eye. I can't—"

"Why don't you lie back down?" he suggested, and I mustered my best glare, though I was sure it didn't carry the weight it usually did. Still, it worked. He sighed and found a seat on the bed next to me. He clasped and unclasped his fingers in his lap, his gaze sliding from his hands to mine, which were wrapped tightly around my blue plastic cup.

"When Michael shot you—" His brow creased as his eyes flicked up to meet mine. "You remember that?"

I nodded, careful not to move too quickly in case it set the room spinning again.

"The white powder he shot you with, turns out it contained a parasite. A tiny son of a bitch that crawled through your third eye and…" His throat bobbed and his jaw worked. I didn't rush him. If whatever this parasite had done made him squeamish, I wasn't sure I wanted to hear it. "It was eating into your brain. Burrowing into your frontal cortex."

My stomach turned again, but this time I breathed through the nausea. A parasite eating away at my third eye. Blinding my ability. Permanently?

Vomit burned the back of my throat, and I heaved bile and water into the metal pan.

The idea that my life would always be this suffocating gripped me, made me frantic. How would I cope? At the moment, I didn't think it was possible. I would lose my mind.

Michael had done this to me?

"If he wanted to get rid of me, he should have used a bullet," I said, and Gideon replied with a wry half-smile.

"He'll wish he had," he said. "Madison called her mundane sweetie pie—"

"Colm?" I interrupted, the shock jolting me from the edges of my mental haze.

"The one and only. He ran some tests, called in some favours, got you into surgery, and here we are. You got to take a nice, long nap while the rest of us suffered crappy chairs and hospital coffee."

Now that I saw his face more clearly, the circles under his eyes stood out in sharp contrast against his paleness. I wondered if he'd had much sleep since I'd lost consciousness.

Since I lost...

I stiffened. "How long was I out?"

He didn't bother to check the clock, which increased my worry. A look at the clock would have meant hours, but to not check...

"About a full day," he said. "All things considered, not bad. You've got to love this Canadian health care system."

How could he be so calm? A whole *day*? I grabbed his arm. "What about Gagnon? What about the headquarters?"

More memories. The lab, so much ghost ready to go out.

"Did you tell anyone?" I asked. "Has anyone moved in on them? What are you doing sitting here while they're still out there?"

"Jet."

His dark, exhausted stare bored into mine, and I pressed my lips together. He was about to spew off some bullshit about needing to take care of me, but couldn't he see how low a priority I was compared to saving the rest of the country?

"We haven't been twiddling our thumbs," he said, "but we didn't want to risk running in without a plan. Meryl's spies have been tailing everyone involved, and Madison's at the new safe house working on some mystery idea. So far, there's no sign of movement from any of the key players, so you have time to rest and regain your strength."

Rest.

The word triggered my fatigue, the heaviness in my arms and legs. The rush of adrenaline had drained me, and though my terror over losing the use of my third eye pricked me like a million thorns, I couldn't find the strength to react, so it lay stifled under a blanket of lethargy.

Guilt stirred beneath my fear. Here I was, losing my shit over my ruined ability when I should be grateful it was all I'd lost. So many people had stepped in to help me, people who didn't know me, and thanks to them, I was still here to the fight. Maybe not right away, maybe not in the same way I had before Michael's betrayal, but functional. Thanks to them, I was alive.

Tears stung my eyes. I held them back, but my usual restraint was gone, making the struggle near impossible. Gideon pulled the plastic cup from my hands, set it on the side table, and wrapped his arms around me. He said nothing, but he didn't have to. His warmth, his strength, replaced the shield I'd dropped somewhere between blacking out and waking up, and I absorbed his courage to keep my emotions at bay.

I couldn't even pinpoint what I wanted to cry about. Everything in the past twenty-four hours had happened without my knowledge. Retroactive fear? Waste of time. Guilt? Grief? Waste of tears. Resting while I had the chance would serve a greater purpose than losing my head to irrational feelings.

Anger at myself, at my vulnerability, at my openness in front of the man I'd tried so hard to distance myself from, steeled me against the threatening breakdown, and though a few tears escaped me, I pulled away from Gideon and wiped my eyes.

"Goddammit," I said. "What the hell did they take out of my head? A parasite or my ability to control myself?"

He chuckled and brushed a loose strand of hair behind my ear. From there, his fingers travelled over my shoulder, down my arm to my hand, then jumped to my leg, then to his lap, then back to my hand. As though he couldn't not touch me.

"You don't have to with me," he said. "Control yourself, I mean." His cheeks flushed, and the muscles in his jaw flexed as he clenched his teeth. I stared at him, not sure what to say or how to react. He cleared his throat and tried again. "I just mean, I won't judge you. All things considered, I think you're entitled to a tear or two. You have a hole in your brain."

I narrowed my eyes, wondering what he hadn't told me. I thought he'd delivered the bad news up front, but the way he was acting... was there more shit on the horizon? The Gideon Leigh I knew was never this awkward, never so determined to hide his discomfort behind horrible jokes. Why wasn't he making fun of me? Mercilessly tormenting me over the fact I'd collapsed in his arms?

Collapsed...

"How did we get out of their headquarters?" I asked.

I remembered Gagnon standing over us in the subbasement, remembered hearing voices, though I couldn't make out what they said. Someone had pointed a gun at us. We'd been boxed in with no exit.

How were either of us here?

To my amazement, Gideon's cheeks flushed a darker shade of red. He cleared his throat again and became very intent on rearranging everything on the bedside table.

"I misted us out."

My stomach dropped, and my jaw followed. "You what? But you—I didn't think—"

He shrugged. "Neither did I. I figured it out."

Suspicion danced in my heart. "Just like that?"

"I'll admit it took a while to bring us back, but I found our way in the end."

He'd risked his life to get me out of there.

I didn't care how hard he tried to deny how huge this was, the effort it must have taken to dissolve us both, not to mention put me back together... no wonder he looked like he'd been dragged under a bus for over a dozen blocks, Ottawa potholes included. Why had he done it? He should have run. I'd told him not to give them another chance to kill him. I'd ordered him to look after himself.

"Gideon—"

He flinched away from my outstretched hand and strode to the window, keeping his back to me. "What else was I supposed to do? Leave you there? With Carstairs so eager to get back to work? After Gagnon told me what they'd done to you? I did what I had to do."

"You could have saved yourself. Gone to Madison, raised the alarm and charged."

A spark of anger burned through me, waking every last sleepy cell. Not only had he once again put himself in danger for me, but he wouldn't even acknowledge how brave and self-less he'd been. Where was my bragging, arrogant Gideon who would have demanded credit? In his place was this man who wouldn't look me in the eye.

I wouldn't let it stand.

I wouldn't let him brush this off as if it meant nothing.

"You didn't risk death, you risked not existing. Stuck in a mist, aware of everything, and never able to interact with it? You might have trapped yourself in an eternity of *nothing*."

"And I would do it again tomorrow if I had to," he said, spinning around to face me.

Fire burned in his eyes, and his hands trembled. Mine weren't any more stable.

And to hell if more tears didn't rise to blur my vision. Son of a bitch, I was an emotional wreck.

In three steps, Gideon crossed the room and reclaimed his place on the bed.

"I mean it," he said, his voice softer but no less intense. "I would have pushed even harder, gone to any lengths to get you out of there. I will never leave you behind."

My heart fluttered in my chest, and damned if the beeping machine beside me didn't give me away, revealing to the room that Gideon Leigh made my pulse race.

"Thank you." It was nothing compared to how I felt or what I wanted to say, but it was the best I could do, the most my current state of mind and body would allow.

He seemed to understand my meaning, though. The fire in his eyes burned brighter, warm enough to dim the glaring hospital lights, and he pressed a kiss into the palm of my hand. "Anything for you."

Why were those words enough to shatter the last of my resolve? The fear of losing my life, my future, was gone, replaced by the terror of losing whatever it was that had made Gideon put himself on the line for me. I didn't want to keep fighting. Didn't want to go back into the unknown, just the three of us, and have him be torn away from me again.

My lungs ached with the depth of my sobs, and Gideon bundled me against him. He guided me to my pillow, his arms tight around me, and nudged me over to make room for himself. His hand returned to my back, that space between my shoulder blades where contact somehow made everything better. His kisses in my hair, his words of comfort in my ear as I cried out everything I'd held back since this whole mess started.

I hated how broken I felt, but with Gideon, my grief poured out without guilt or shame. He'd confessed his moment of weakness, the moment that had pushed him to give up everything to save me. Somehow it seemed only fair to show him I was as weak as he was. It put us back on equal footing, which was what I needed to feel strong.

With his arms tight around me and the heart monitor beeping in the background, I found my way through the storm of tears into a calm ocean of sleep.

Chapter 25

Jet

WHEN I AWOKE again, my brain ran through its standard wake-up check, piecing together the details about where I was, why I was here, and what I needed to do today. The same emotions that had struck me last night returned in a series of rolling waves, each one ebbing as the next one flowed, and in the end, my courage went out with the tide, leaving a beached sense of fear.

I wasn't afraid of the greater situation—here, in this hospital bed, I was as safe as I was going to get—but terrified that when I opened my eyes and started my day, the walls Gideon and I had lowered between us last night would be back in place. Not only on his side, but on mine as well. If they were, I didn't know if I was brave enough to break them down again.

And never in a million years would I have guessed how much I wanted them to stay down. I'd spent most of my life avoiding that sort of deep connection with anyone I wasn't one hundred per cent sure I could rely on. Not to mention anyone I wasn't one hundred per cent sure could rely on me.

Gideon had taken me by surprise with his willingness to open up, revealing as much of himself as he had, and no one could have been more surprised than I was that I'd been able to return the sentiment.

But that had been last night, and I was well aware that any life changes that happened during the witching hour often retreated into self-preservation come dawn.

When I opened my eyes, however, Gideon was still beside me, his solid frame tucked against mine, his arm a guard around me. His eyelashes flickered, as though even in sleep he sensed me watching him, and when he woke up, he graced me with a warm smile that set my fears at ease.

His lips brushed across my third eye. "Morning," he mumbled. "How are you feeling?"

He sounded as comfortable as if last night had been ten years ago, any distance between us far in the past. There were no walls, no barriers. As if there never had been. Whatever we'd gone through last night, we'd hit a turning point, and I never wanted to look back.

"Like I've been shot in the face and had a parasite eating my brain," I said.

"Rough night." He gave me a sleepy wink, and I mustered a smile in return.

In truth, I felt a lot better now than when I'd first woken from the dead. Carefully, slowly, I tested my third eye and could have cried when I detected faint shadows moving around the bed. *Grabbing supplies. Tapping the buttons on the monitor.*

The sharp pain that shot through my skull made the effort less than a total success, but at least it wasn't the same white-hot agony as before. Progress. I had no idea when or if I would get the full use of my second sight back, but the world felt a little larger this morning. As for the rest, I would have to accept my new reality regardless of how much it hurt. To force the issue would only distract me from our actual problems.

The door opened, and a nurse walked in. She started in surprise—on finding me awake, or maybe on finding me awake with a man in my bed—and broke out in a smile as she approached.

"Well, isn't this a nice surprise. Dr. Millbourn didn't think you'd be up so soon. But then, nothing about your condition has been standard."

Gideon squeezed my hand as he rolled out of bed to give her room to check me over. I would have preferred he stay close but supposed it was for the best we got back to normal. We had work to do, and lying comfortably with him wouldn't motivate me to turn my thoughts to the threat hanging over our heads as soon as we walked out the door.

"What do you think?" the nurse asked. "Up for a shower? Maybe some breakfast?"

At the mention of a shower, my scalp itched, and I looked at Gideon.

"I'll go grab a coffee." He leaned over to kiss the top of my head. "Give you a chance to rehumanize."

I squeezed his hand, overwhelmed with fear at the idea of him leaving, and he smiled and squeezed just as hard.

"I'll be back in ten," he said, and I heard the unspoken promise.

Nodding, I let him go. He kissed me again before he left, and something in my chest relaxed when I caught him hesitating by the door, as though he were as reluctant to leave as I was for him to go.

As soon as he was out of sight, however, the bathroom situation became much more urgent, and I realized he was right: rehumanizing myself sounded amazing.

The nurse—Rita, who looked as though she were running on caffeine, determination, and a few kips in the breakroom—helped me to the bathroom and stayed close as I shuffled from toilet to sink to shower. The hot water was blissful, but not nearly as refreshing as brushing my teeth.

Feeling more alive, I stumbled back to bed, where a less-than-appealing breakfast waited for me. Rita made sure I ate every bite, checked my vitals, let out a few curious mumbles, and just as she finished, Gideon returned, leading a beaming Madison and a wary Colm behind him.

"Look what I found wandering the hallway," Gideon said as

he dropped into the armchair and drew it close to my bedside. I expected him to take my hand, but he leaned back and twined his fingers over his stomach.

Not quite where we were last night, then, but I accepted the change. I wouldn't have wanted to invite Madison's questioning looks, either. By the quirk of her eyebrow as she glanced between us, I guessed she'd already figured some of it out without the physical display.

"I didn't think we'd find you awake," she said. "*Someone* was supposed to call me."

"*Someone* was asleep," said Gideon. "Besides, everyone could use some happy surprises this morning."

Did I imagine the look between Madison and Colm? Knowing smiles hidden under their attempt at seriousness? What had they been up to while Gideon and I enjoyed our heart to heart?

I stared Madison down with my silent questions, noted the flush in her cheeks and the way her gaze dropped, and couldn't help but grin myself. At least a few rays of happiness existed in the middle of this shitstorm.

"How are you feeling?" she asked, taking the chair opposite Gideon.

"I wish everyone would stop asking me that," I said. "It makes me feel like an invalid. I'm not. I'm fine."

"To be fair, you had a parasite working its way into your brain," said Colm as he shifted to stand behind her. "I think you're entitled to a bit of whining."

I didn't know Colm well. At all, in fact. Only what Madison had told me. But here he was, facing the worst of our side of the world, looking as comfortable as if he'd never lived behind the perception filter. For all my doubts about Madison's relationship with a mundane, if she had to fall for one, she'd chosen well.

"All right," I said. "Fine. I have a headache and my third eye is temporarily out of order." I noted Madison's look of concern and squared my jaw. "I said temporarily. I'm not considering the alternative. But that's not important right now, is it? We've got a big bad bureaucrat running a weapons operation out of his basement, all our connections are dead, hiding, or would prefer not to get involved, and if we don't shut down the FoSA deal, every supernatural in the country will be barcoded or micro-chipped and owe fealty to some money-grabbing organization. How's that? Did I sum up our situation nicely?"

I hadn't intended to run off on a depressed spiel, but as soon as I started, the heaps of problems facing us overpowered me. By the shock on everyone's faces, they also hadn't expected a tirade. My full night's sleep had helped bring me back to baseline, but obviously my current baseline was shakier than my usual calm-in-a-crisis self. I wondered how many sleeps it would take to level me out.

After a moment's pause, while we sorted through our various thoughts on the subject, Madison reached for my hand. "I know it seems like the world is against us, but we're not alone."

"No?" I asked. "Did Serc and Lilith change their minds and agree to march with us, or are they still on standby, ready as a last resort? What chance do we have, Madison? We're three people. Three people against a government no one else knows is corrupt."

I expected her to have some motivational speech ready for me, one I was willing to hear, but her expression turned from reassuring to smug.

"That's not exactly true," she said.

She looked to Colm, and he, with a sneaky smile all his own, moved to the door.

What had they done? Had Madison talked Serc into fighting with us? I understood her uncle's reservations, and he was right that there would be consequences if the queen's soldiers took front-line positions on this side of the wall, but what else would make these two look so proud?

For all my guesses, all my suspicions, nothing could have prepared me for the sight of my team walking into the room. Goosebumps broke out over my skin, the hairs rising on my arms, across my scalp. More burning tears tickled my eyes.

Zeke led the way, followed by Jason and Sara. Luvy came in next with Adam, Katie, and Ray. Seven faces I never thought I'd see again. Faces I especially never expected to see in my hospital room, showing their support despite everything that had happened in the past week.

"I don't understand," I said, or tried to.

Madison's smile grew. "It's the perk of asking the advice of a military vet." She looped her fingers through Colm's where they rested on her shoulder. "He suggested we reach out."

Zeke shook his freshly shaved head. "All this time you were kicking ass and taking names, and you didn't call us in? I'm hurt, PL."

He pressed his hand to his chest, but the gladness in his eyes belied his exaggerated sulk.

His dark skin was flush with colour, a nice change from the deathly pallor the last time I'd seen him. New scars flecked his right cheek and the right side of his neck, and his fingers twitched in an involuntary movement against his chest, but he looked as strong as ever.

Same with Luvy, her smile bright and eyes glowing, and Ray, who must have cowed to peer pressure and cut his horrible hair after he left the hospital.

The last time I'd seen any of them, they'd just woken up after the de Lauer attack, brought to the brink of death by the ghost in the air and saved by stubbornness and luck.

As for the other four, they'd seen everything I had during that attack, heard the same horrors. They knew what the department, the news, their commanding officers said about me, and yet here they were, looking happy to see me.

It meant more to me than I could express that they'd answered Madison's call, but I couldn't ask them to stand with me. "It's so great to see you guys, but—"

Sara propped her hands on her hips. "We're not leaving."

"But—" I tried again, and Ray shook his head.

"Madison and Colm caught us up," he said. "We know that everything we've been told about what happened in the de Lauer basement is a lie, and we're not about to stand down while there are traitors in our ranks."

"The risk—your *careers*." What would it take to make them see that fighting with me would earn them more than a slap on the wrist if we failed? Even a win would come at a cost.

Jason crossed his hairy arms and bared a set of elongating teeth. "What careers do we have if Torrence and Gagnon stay in power? We'd be taking orders from traitors, and I didn't sign up for that crap. From the moment I found that note on the ground, I knew something didn't smell right. There's too much shit being stirred up and not enough flushing from the people in power. The reek of fear in the air—not just from the protesters, but from people who claim to know what they're doing—is enough to set my teeth on edge. So when Madison called and filled in the blanks, you're damn right I picked my side. I've already talked to my pack—my other pack—and the shifters are ready to fight with you, Captain."

The shifters. My heart swelled. There was only so much they'd be able to do in the light of day, but used strategically, they'd deal a lot of damage.

Ray, his wide chest stretching the seams of his T-shirt, stuffed his hands in his pockets. "We know what the colonel did and what he hopes to do. Most of us didn't want to believe it at first. I'm sorry, PL. We should have had more faith in you."

I shook my head, unable to speak. I didn't want their apologies. What use were they? They were here, and that was all the faith I needed.

"Me, Ray, and a few others returned to work as soon as we could under Eric's leadership," Adam said, "and I'll admit, Zeke had to work hard to convince me I was defending the wrong side." He lowered his gaze. "Xander and Marc-André are sticking close to Eric. I hate to say we weren't sure they wouldn't rat us out, but…" He shrugged, and the others averted their gazes, shame and disappointment etched into their features. I understood. It hurt that doubt had created cracks between us, but there would be no healing them until the truth was revealed.

"But it's business as usual at the office," he continued. "Monitoring the protests, tracking down O'Malley's people—everything we would have expected to do under your command."

Katie frowned. "I wouldn't say things are *normal*, though. From the moment I went back, everything's been too… easy O'Malley's thugs are always where we're told they'll be, and when has that ever happened? But only his lower-ranking hires. And the decisions the colonel's making—I don't know. He sent us out to gather information about the protestors, like *they* were the ones doing something wrong, and I don't know if I'm crazy or what, but it struck me that he was targeting people with interests on the other side of the wall. Loyalists."

Ray nodded. "I noticed that, too. He had us pull a few of them in. I don't think I've ever seen the detainment centre so full. He keeps saying we're keeping the peace, swearing up and down we're closing in on the Ghostmaker, but none of it sat right with me."

"So when Zeke called us," Katie said with shrug, "there was only one option. We met in the breakroom this morning to talk it out and left as soon as we could. We refuse to follow anyone's orders until the right people are back in control."

Luvy nodded. "We stand with you, PL."

"Guys," I said, curling my fingers around the blankets to help keep my emotions in check, "that's desertion. You could get brought up on charges. It's why I kept you out of it in the first place. You've seen the news. You know they've turned me into the villain here. I don't want that to be you."

Sara's blue eyes flashed with fury and sparks danced across her fingertips. Colm noticed, started to step away, then held steady.

"Our colonel betrayed us and our lieutenant is too married to duty to see it," she said. "What charges could they lay on us that wouldn't be a mockery of honour and regulation? You are our captain, and we'll follow you. Whatever it takes to set things right."

The others nodded, solidifying their stance, and I could only sit, throat closed, eyes burning. This was my crew, my pack. The team that had gotten me through the hardest times. Now they were here for me again, ignoring every lie Michael had told about me, every attempt Eric had made to convince them their cause was just. It broke my heart Eric hadn't joined them. That the man I'd trained with, slept with, mourned with, believed I'd lost my mind and was a traitor to my principles, but I couldn't afford to regret him. As Sara said, his dedication to duty was too strong to crack.

Always had been, now that I thought about it. Michael had praised my ability to question everything and come to my own conclusions. I'd never followed orders because my superior officer told me to, I'd followed them because they'd made sense. Because they'd fit my moral code. As soon as that stopped, I'd stopped. Which was why Eric was both the better and worse asset for Michael's treason. In him, the colonel had an unfailing lackey, but he would never lead his troops the way I did.

That Zeke and the others had given up so much for me was proof of his short-sightedness. Like me, they followed logic and reason, and because of that, we stood a chance against Michael's confidence in his people's devotion.

Eleven was still a small number compared to the army Michael commanded, but it was more than the three we'd been yesterday.

They stood staring at me, expectation in their eyes, waiting for… something, but I was lost. I had no orders to give, no praise to offer. All I had was the truth, weak and sentimental as it was.

"We'll be going up against people we've served with, people we care about," I said. "We'll have to go in low, in a way that doesn't attract media attention. There will be ghostbombs, brain-eating parasites, and who knows what other nightmares. There is a very good chance we won't all make it out. As your captain, I'm giving you permission to walk away. Consider your families, consider everything you might leave behind. If you believe the sacrifice is worth it, then we work together. Our department is rotting from the inside, but I believe that as a pack we can save it. We can fight for what matters."

As I spoke, my team transformed, drawing their shoulders back and lifting their chins. Motivation shone in their eyes. And in their rising courage, my own strengthened. The bed was suddenly too low, too degrading. I needed to move.

I looked at Colm, who, to my amazement, looked as inspired as my team. His eyes were bright and his chest was puffed out, as though he stood at attention. Once a soldier…

I met his gaze and nodded at the door. "Will you help me get out of here?"

Chapter 26

Gideon

COLM DIDN'T WANT Jet to leave, that was obvious. As soon as she made her request, he fussed over her, checking her vitals, her temperature, questioning her ability to walk on her own.

Jet pushed back with the full force of her iron will.

"I'm grateful for all you and your team have done, but there's nothing more mundane medicine can do for me," she argued. "For everything else, it'll either get better or it won't."

I couldn't argue with her. Madison's grand reveal had done more to shed the rest of her low spirits than any words of mine might have. With me, she'd been safe to collapse, but in front of her troops, she was Captain Jet Dawson, leader of her JetPack, capable of overcoming the worst injuries.

I wondered if Madison liked chocolate, or fruit baskets, or mini muffins. I owed her big time.

Colm and I led her team out of the room while Madison helped her get dressed. The soldiers left to grab anything they needed from home and would rendezvous at the safe house, and Colm went to track down Billy to sign the discharge papers, so soon enough I was alone with my thoughts.

Feeling more optimistic than I had in days.

Jet had been so sure her squad had turned against her, it had never occurred to me to push her to contact them. It had taken a mundane to prove her wrong. In less than twenty-four hours, Colm had secured us well in his debt.

When he returned, Billy was with him. The surgeon made no attempt to convince Jet to stay, but I watched him perform the same checks as Colm had, as though searching for an excuse to keep her.

When he found nothing, he stepped back, shoved his hands in his pockets, and did his best—and a piss-poor job it was—to hide his amazement.

"I told Mr. Leigh, but I'll tell you as well," he said, "I'm on standby. Whatever's happening, whatever help you need, call me. Rita and I will be available."

"While I hope we won't need to take you up on the offer, I appreciate it," Jet said. She shook his hand, and when she let go, Billy stared at his fingers as though expecting some of her supernatural to have rubbed off.

He shook himself out of his wonder to exchange an elaborate handshake with Colm, and Madison, Jet, and I left them to their goodbyes.

"Are you sure you don't want the chair?" Madison nodded at the wheelchair waiting outside the door, and Jet scowled.

"No chance in hell. If I can't rely on my feet, how can I lead my troops?"

I clamped my jaw shut to stop myself from spouting any words that might sound like pity. That's not what she wanted, even if she was pushing herself harder than she needed to.

"Jet..." The sadness in Madison's eyes was everything I was working so hard not to show. "You don't have—"

"I do," Jet said, her tone forceful.

The two women stared each other down until Madison nodded and started down the hallway towards the freight elevator. Colm joined us a moment later, catching up to Madison, and the two of them leaned their heads in, exchanging words and looks that gave away how they'd spent their evening. I stayed close to Jet in case she needed support, but step by slow step, we made it to the elevator, then to the car, and eventually to the new safe house.

The place was significantly bigger than the apartment on Somerset, which was a bonus considering we had eight extra hands on deck. As they arrived, Jet's wolves divided the bedrooms between them, and it somehow went without saying that Jet and I would be sharing. I raised an eyebrow at Madison, but she didn't acknowledge me beyond a knowing smile.

Whatever. Her already understanding that things had

changed between us meant we could avoid the awkward conversation. I'd leave everything Jet and I had shared in that hospital room to Jet's discretion, to tell her what she wanted. Frustrated as I was by my inability to stay detached, I had no regrets and no shame in anything I'd said. If ever I was going to fall, there was no better woman to fall for. Watching Jet control the fort from the head of the dining table later that afternoon was the single sexiest scene I'd ever witnessed, and I was happy to sit on my barstool in the corner and watch her.

She commanded her troops with ease, taking suggestions, listening to concerns. Her weakness and fatigue were obvious in the shake of her hands and the circles under her eyes, but although I remained on alert, ready to bully her into resting if she showed any signs of fading, she gave me no cause to pull her aside. She acknowledged her limitations openly and relied on Zeke and Sara to walk her through issues she didn't see clearly. Which they did without judgement or doubt in her ability to lead them.

I'd had a preview of her skill in New York, but this was the first time I'd seen her among the team she'd hand-picked and worked with throughout her career. Her pack. I'd never been prouder of her. Or more turned on, if I was being honest.

Detail by detail, she and Madison had taken us through the past week, from the moment the ghostbomb had gone off in the de Lauer building, to the dead informants, the minister's death, my near-death times two, and Michael's betrayal. They'd laid out the evidence, bringing everyone onto the same page so any doubts or questions could be cleared up from the outset.

When the conversation turned to our next steps, the afternoon was closing in on two o'clock, and as far as I was concerned, even after listening to the entire story again, I had no clue what our ultimate play might be.

"I think our smartest move would be to attack their HQ head-on," Zeke said.

I'd sketched out what I remembered of the subbasement's layout and operations, and the drawings lay spread across the table.

"We could get in there and destroy it," he continued. "They would lose their defences, their negotiating tools."

"What if it isn't their only HQ?" Luvy asked. "Or what if they expect us to do exactly that?"

"I agree," Jet said. "We'd be moving on enemy territory, their high ground. The advantage would be all theirs. We have to assume Dougall will have laid the same trap for us under that house as he did at the high-rise."

"So what do we do instead?" Jason asked. "Wait for them to make another move and hope we catch them in the act? Risk more casualties if we don't stop them in time?"

He scratched at the hefty stubble on his chin with fingernails as thick and long as my dead grandfather's. This had to be the shifter, the butt of the JetPack in-joke. I made a note to avoid those claws if he got too pissed off.

Jet shook her head. "No, we can't afford to wait, either. Even if we did, we would face the same problem. They might suspect I'm out of commission, but Michael's not an idiot. Whatever they do next, he'll keep me in the equation to cover their bases. Maybe we'd have a better chance of taking them off guard, but they'll have staked out their location before they attack. No, we need to get them on neutral ground. Away from civilians. Somewhere we can manoeuvre them, offset their strengths with some of our own."

"Where did you have in mind?" Madison asked. She and Colm stood against the wall, leaving the table for Jet and her troops so she could preside over her military court.

Jet released a groan of frustration and dropped her head into her hands, her fingers massaging around her third eye. I worried she was flagging but held my tongue. Nothing I said would stop her now that she'd started. Blood could spill out of her ears, but she would work until she solved this puzzle.

For myself, I had no brilliant suggestions to make. The parking garage under the old train station came to mind, but I had a sentimental attachment to the place. My blood stained the concrete.

As a defensive position, though, it wouldn't pass muster. There were too many exits, too many chances for civilians to walk in.

"The SMOAC subbasement?" I offered. "You'd be limited in space, but we can cover the exits. It's as close to neutral territory as you're going to get."

Jet looked up, her gaze clouded in thought. "You might have something there. We'd have an easy time moving around in small numbers, and it would force them to limit their reinforcements." Then her brow furrowed, and she shook her head. "No, too exposed. We have a murder charge hanging over our heads, remember? Wherever we go, we have to make sure we won't be caught by any official authority, even if they're not involved with Gagnon. No one would believe our side of the story. Remember what Meril said? If we fail, her protection disappears, but as long as we come out ahead, we can control the narrative with her support. If we let them own the board and drag this into the public eye, we're looking at murder charges at best, treason, at worst. Either way, it's the inside of a cell for a long time—if Gagnon doesn't have us killed first."

A shudder ran down my spine at the idea of being locked away again. My nerves fizzled, and my muscles burned with an icy fire as the memory of Carstairs's grinning face taunted me.

I rubbed the back of my neck with one hand and buried my fingernails into my other palm, grounding myself in the here and now. He wasn't here. He would never get me again, and if the opportunity presented itself to give back everything I'd gotten, I wouldn't hesitate.

Everyone in the room jumped as Jet slammed her hand on the table.

"I've got it," she said. "The answer is obvious. We get them into the Labyrinth."

I frowned as I pictured the underground hub with its seven tunnels branching off in every direction across the city. Hardly an easy-to-control location. "Are you sure?"

I might as well have nominated her for a death sacrifice from the way her pack turned as one to glare at me.

"I worry about the number of access points," I said, undaunted by their glowers. "There's no way we can cover all the tunnels and keep a low profile. They'd know they were walking into a trap."

Jet's tired face broke into a sly smile. "Exactly."

Now everyone's attention jumped to her, bombarding her with unasked questions.

"They'll suspect a trap anyway. The minute I pick up the phone and ask for the meet, they'll know I'm not dead and am still working against them. They'll plan for an easy slaughter and think my suggestion of the Labyrinth is stupid, proof that their parasite screwed up my head for good. They'll think they can direct the encounter."

"But in reality..." I led, unsure where she was going.

"We pull a double-bluff."

I could almost see the wheels spinning as she thought through her plan. She reached for a blank sheet of paper and a pencil from the middle of the table and sketched out the channels of the Labyrinth. Considering the number of tunnels, there was no way she'd be able to outline the entire place, but before much time had passed, she'd drawn a rough map from the hub.

"There are seven exits from the centre," she said. "Six on the bottom, one up these stairs. They have no reason to think there's more than three of us, so they'll expect to have full access to at least six of them."

"Where do you want us?" Zeke asked.

"Everywhere," said Jet. "You, my beloved JetPack, are our secret weapon. All these tunnels are connected at various points, and we're going to take advantage of every crossroad. We let them come in from wherever they want, let them get as close as they want, and we close them off. Michael's too smart to come without backup—he'll want to crush us before we put up much of a fight. We'll overestimate his numbers to play it safe, and if we lay this out well enough, we can flank them."

Ray frowned. "If they bring ghostbombs with them, containing the powder will be impossible."

Jet's gaze hardened, and a moment of silence passed over the room. While it lasted, I felt closed off from the discussion. Every person sitting around the table had witnessed the devastation of that first bomb. So many friends who should have been here weren't because of it. No doubt the thought of facing that level of destruction again had them shitting themselves, but none of them faltered.

They had to know their odds of walking out of this were slim, and yet, to look at their faces, none of them cared. It didn't matter that Gagnon had ghost, parasites, numbers—who knew what else. Jet's team was ready for losses if it meant avenging their fallen and ending this threat.

"For what it's worth," I said, crossing my arms, "the probability of them bringing a ghostbomb to the fight is low. There's too great a risk of being hit themselves. Especially somewhere like the Labyrinth with its crap ventilation."

Jet nodded, acknowledging the point. "We should still be prepared. Gas masks aren't readily available, but we can make do with what we have. If you cover your faces, it might cut down the dosage at the very least."

A small hope, but something.

"We have our other resources as well," Madison said. "Sercario and Lilith don't want to be on the front lines? Fine, we don't need them anymore. Their people can guard the perimeter, stake out the various access points on street level, surround the headquarters. We'll close in on the tunnels, and they can prevent anyone from getting away."

Jet's wolfish smile widened. "Michael thinks he knows me so well, and he'll drive himself crazy trying to figure out what my plan is, but there's no way he'll see this coming. They'll go in expecting a fight. We'll bring them an ambush."

"How will you convince them to meet you?" I asked, daring her team's anger a second time. Someone needed to ask the hard questions, and if my role for Jet was to play devil's advocate, I wouldn't back down. The more holes we poked into the plan now, the fewer there would be when we marched. "Michael will come for the chance to see you again—he'll want to know how you survived the parasite and Carstairs's bullet—but how do we guarantee the whole gang will show up? Gagnon, Dougall, O'Malley. We need to take down all four or risk the others running."

Jet nodded. "You're right. To a point. O'Malley won't show up because he has no stake in this part of the game. We might lose him, but without Gagnon's support, he'll be forced to crawl back under his rock and lick his lost fortune. He's not the real game. Dougall's the one we want, and if Michael's prepared for a battle, he'll make sure the Ghostmaker is by his side. That drug is the greatest weapon he has."

She paled, her skin taking on a greyish hue, and swallowed hard. I resisted the urge to go to her, knowing she wouldn't appreciate the attention. She needed to stay strong, and that sort of strength could only come on her own. I hated it, but I accepted it.

"We also need to be prepared for him to bring the rest of our pack," she said through stiff lips. "He'll think I won't attack him if they're close. I refuse to believe they know everything about what's happening, and if they don't, he'll hide behind his rank and reputation."

Zeke rested his hand over hers, and a flare of jealousy burned through me for no other reason than that he sat close enough to offer the comfort I wanted to give.

She cleared her throat and pulled her shoulders back. "We know it, so we can brace ourselves and deal with it when the time comes. The way I see it, all we need is Michael and Dougall. If we take them down, it will leave Gagnon without military reinforcements. He'll lose his fuse to spur on the riots, and he can't do it on his own without revealing his hand. Dougall is also the lynchpin between Gagnon and O'Malley. If O'Malley can't lend him his Ghostmaker, what else does he have except a few thugs? Gagnon will cut ties before the connection goes public. It could buy us time to go after them once we take care of Michael. So that's it. That's my plan. Unless anyone sees any other options or issues?"

She looked at each of us in turn, her gaze lingering longest on me. Was she hoping I had more questions? A better idea? If so, I had to disappoint her. It was a horrible plan, one that would leave us crammed underground with too many openings for Michael to overtake us, but it was the best shot we had. Anywhere else would leave too much leeway for the fight to spill onto the streets, and the last thing we needed was for the mundane media to get wind of it.

I wished we had more time for her to rest. Her movements were still so stiff, her pain so visible. A million times better than how she'd looked last night, but far from her peak. I worried about her going up against Michael but clung to my faith in her. Delay would only swing the odds further in his favour. Moving now, even as weak as she was, gave us the greatest potential of success. So I offered a subtle nod of support, a promise that I would stand beside her in this as in all things.

"The way I see it," Zeke said, "they've got everything on their side. The weapons, the public support, and the soldiers. On our side, we've got a small window to take them by surprise." It sounded grim when he put it like that, but no one argued with his point. Instead of looking defeated, however, he shrugged. "If we tried to figure out every single angle before we went in, we'd never make a move. Let's take what we have and run with it."

My blood cooled at the small smile that curled the corner of Jet's mouth. "I had the same thought before we walked into the de Lauer building. Look how well that turned out."

"Yeah, well, this time we're all thinking it," Jason growled, "and we all agree the risk is worth it."

Sara raised her hand above the table and sent sparks flying over her fingers. "They can throw whatever they want at us. This time, we'll be ready for any surprises they throw our way."

More nods circulated around the table, and when no one else spoke against the plan, Jet rested her palms flat against the tabletop. "All right, then. I guess there's nothing left to do but get started."

She pulled her phone out of her pocket and set it on the table. No one said a word as she dialled Michael's number and put the call on speaker. I imagined what the colonel's reaction would be if he knew who sat around her right now. If he knew his hold over his troops had slipped another notch. He might have the numbers, but this was Jet's squad. We stood a better chance now than we ever had.

The realization poured steel down my spine, and I found myself shaking with anticipation as Jet waited for her commander to answer the phone.

"Hello?"

"Hello, Colonel."

"Jet Dawson." Michael's deep surprise filled the room. Did he worry he was receiving a call from beyond the grave? "I never thought I'd hear from you again."

"What can I say—I don't go down easy."

I don't know what I'd expected from her. The shake of anger? Grief? There was nothing but iron, not even a trace of the fatigue that had been written on her face a moment ago.

Michael chuckled. "Don't I know it. What can I do for you?"

"I want to meet."

"Again? That didn't go so well for you last time."

And just like that, Jet's strength faltered, broke. She bowed her head, hunched her shoulders, and I rose from my seat to go to her. We'd moved too soon. She should at least have had a good night's sleep before arranging the meet.

"These weapons you have, Dougall, the earthworm, the troops—my troops," she said. "I could fight against you until the last of my strength gave out, but there's no way in hell I'd win, is there?"

Such defeat in her voice.

Then she looked up at me and winked.

My pride grew, and I resettled on my stool. Once again, I'd underestimated her. The exhaustion was real, twisted to feign weakness. Not pushing herself, but adopting the role she knew would play best with her former mentor.

"I've seen your base of operations," she continued. "Found the letters from FoSA. I read what they're offering, seen the money that comes with it. It's… given me cause to reconsider."

There was no way Michael would fall for her ruse once he had time to think about it, but all we needed was his agreement to meet, and she'd landed on the best possible way to guarantee it: showing interest in joining him.

"When you said you were doing this for the betterment of our kind, you meant it," she said.

"I did." Goddamn he sounded sincere. He genuinely believed it. "I know it might not look like it, but I swear I wouldn't be doing this if I didn't think it was the right decision. We're fading, Jet. Generation after generation, our numbers are getting smaller, growing weaker. This is our chance to hang on to what we are. To grow our power and abilities until we stand equal with our mundane enemy instead of beneath them. To get Meril off our backs so we can be free of her yoke."

"I don't—" She passed a hand over her face, and I didn't like the way her fingers trembled. That wasn't part of the show. "I want to give you a chance to explain your view of things. I'm ready to be convinced."

A moment of silence on the line before Michael said, "I'm glad to hear it, kid. You know there's always a place for you by my side."

I hated his heartfelt relief, so deep I had to wonder if she'd sold her change of conscience better than it seemed from my seat across the room. Unfortunately, none of Michael's actions up to now suggested he was gullible. He might wish for Jet to see things his way, he might even hope she was being honest with him, but while he relied on the unquestioning devotion of others to further his ambitions, I doubted he suffered the same flaw. We were manipulating each other, and as long as we both knew it, the field would be even.

He and Jet arranged the details, and when she hung up, her hands shook so badly she hid them in her lap to avoid notice. I ground my teeth and said nothing. The meet wasn't until tonight, so she had time to rest before we set out.

"There we go," she said, the hardness in her tone belying her unsettled state. "All that's left is to armour up and wait. Make sure you get some sleep."

Zeke rose from the table, and the others followed his lead out of the room and upstairs to the bedrooms they'd assigned themselves. As naturally as if he'd always been Jet's second. A man the rest of the pack would follow as quickly as they did Jet. Seeing it made me appreciate how well she'd chosen her team. No power plays existed in her cream of the crop. No petty jealousies. They were a unified whole, each one valued for what they brought to the table.

I'd never been one for group efforts, preferring my solo missions, looking out for no one but myself, but for once I was proud to be one of many, one of the wolves in her pack.

"I'll go see to our preparations," Colm said, as though he understood we needed a minute. He kissed the top of Madison's head and left with the others.

Soon, the three of us were alone in the dining room, the original trio. Mugs and beer cans covered the table alongside the scattered plans and sketches and evidence. The room stank of people and fear, but I didn't want to open a window. We were better off closed in and secure, with no extra vulnerabilities added to the heap bearing down on us.

Jet rolled her neck, releasing a series of small pops, and sank deeper into her chair. "Why does it feel like I've agreed to walk into the pits of hell?"

"The country is already burning, Jet," Madison said. "There's nothing for it but to reach the heart of the fire and douse it."

"And pray we've brought a big enough fire extinguisher," I said.

Jet huffed out a laugh. "You're right. I know it. So here we go. Finally. Eight hours to wrap up any unfinished business, and then we fight for our country's freedom. With a big fucking fire extinguisher."

Chapter 27

Madison

S LEEP WOULD HAVE been smart.

Going against Michael would be so much harder if we didn't have every piston firing.

None of us, however, showed any sign that we wanted to leave the living room where we had settled after the dining room grew too close, too warm.

Colm had come back down to sit with me, but Zeke and the others stayed away. The floorboards creaked as Jet's team walked from one room to the next, growing quieter as they went to bed, louder as they readied their weapons. Occasionally the side door opened and closed as someone left to carry out last-minute business, but no one disturbed us.

At least the living room had the benefit of the bay window, filing the space with light and fresh air, and the afternoon sun warmed the chill in my blood.

Jet and Gideon sat on the floor on opposite sides of the coffee table, with Jet closest to the couch, her back to me as she hunched over the table. The trunk Meril had sent home with us lay open between them, revealing the weapons she'd offered as her gesture of support for the trials to come. Gideon played with the knives, readying the extra sedative cartridges in a pouch that he hooked on his belt. Three-inch blades, polished ebony handles. Remarkable craftsmanship that would hopefully keep a few people from dying.

"We have to assume Michael will set up reinforcements along every tunnel to box us in," he said. "Your team is prepared to split up to clear them out, which leaves me free to mist through the hub and make my stand by their primary access while you keep Michael busy. Once the team wraps up, they can join me, and we'll prevent the bulk of their reinforcements from reaching you."

"Their primary access?" I asked.

He pulled Jet's sketch towards him, ran his fingers over the quick labels she'd noted, and tapped the northwest tunnel. "The route that leads from their headquarters. If you compare the city map to this sketch, it's this one right here."

Colin frowned. "You think those basement tunnels you found under Main Street connect to this Labyrinth?"

"I do," Gideon said. "Nowhere close to the hub, but they would have been stupid not to choose their HQ with that sort of strategic trade route. They've been able to distribute ghost, troops, and who knows what else without anyone on the surface realizing it, and giving Jet no chance to cut them off. He'll probably have other units posted closer to the hub, but I suspect the main force will come straight from home base."

"If that's the case, how far do you think we should let them come down before you stop them?" Jet asked.

"All the way," he said.

Colm leaned forward. "You want to give them that much room to unite their fighters?"

Gideon shrugged. "Michael will want to learn if Jet's motivations are sincere. He'll hold his people back where she can't see them. If we stop them too soon, we'll give ourselves away. Let them come as close as he wants them, then we can draw our line. Zeke will coordinate our soldiers, but it'll be easy for me to mist in and out and put as many as I can to sleep."

"It's a solid plan," Jet said, and I caught her dash of relief. Relief that someone had come up with specific details to bolster her strategy? She had to feel frustrated the idea wasn't hers. I knew from experience how much she hated leaving tactical planning to anyone else, but I was glad she had people around her she trusted while she regained her strength. "While you do that, Zeke can get in place to take the rest of Michael's troops by surprise once they move. The hard part will be keeping everyone out of sight, but I'm hoping the shadows will help us."

"Just as Meril said they would." I was struck by how prophetic her words were turning out to be. The woman was nothing if not far-seeing. I wondered exactly how far. Did she know how tonight would end, or only the endless possibilities?

While they strategized, Jet busied herself with Meril's gun. It lay in pieces across the table, and she cleaned each part, her concentration so focused I doubted it would register if any of us left the room.

I wished I had a similar distraction to keep my mind off what the coming night might bring.

Scenarios ran through my head in a continuous loop, each one ending with at least a few of us dead. Only once in a rare while did we come out the victors.

It was times like these I resented my skills around the negotiating table. Experience gave me too great an understanding of our odds.

In my head, the clock ticked down, sometimes running through seconds like water, other times like a moth flying into a window trying to escape. My only anchor, my last cling to sanity, was Colm. He sat beside me on the couch, watching Jet work with fascinated interest. His fingers were looped around mine, his thumb stroking my palm whenever anxiety made my hands clammy or pushed me to tighten my hold on him.

Now and then, his attention shifted from the gun on the table to Jet's face or the shake in her hand, and I detected the puffs of concern, as short and pointed as popping corn, leaping off him.

"How are you holding up?" he asked when she dropped

her wire brush for the third time.

At his question, Gideon looked up from his knives, assessing her for himself, as if he hadn't done so a dozen times in the last half-hour.

"I'm fine," Jet said without turning away from her work. She flexed the fingers of her left hand and curled them in, repeating the gesture three times before resuming the intricate task of fitting the brush to the rod.

"Are you sure you don't want to—" Gideon started, cutting himself off at her brief, irritated scowl.

"I'm strong enough to do this," she said, and dropped her gaze again. "I can't afford not to be."

I wished she were wrong. If we could have wrangled her up to bed and knocked her out with a sedative to put her to sleep until this was over, I would have done it without hesitation. But she was our captain and, shaking hands or not, we needed her to lead us to Michael.

Colm chewed on the insides of his lips, his free hand picking at a fleck of invisible lint on his jeans. Goosebumps rose on my arms at his swirling apprehension, a stark change from the worry of a few moments ago. I eyed him curiously, but he didn't acknowledge my stare.

His apprehension morphed again, this time into an electric exhilaration, and my heartbeat jumped in response, so I was horrified but not unprepared when he said, "I want in."

Almost not unprepared.

The moment his words were out, my stomach dropped, and I sat stunned, speechless, as Gideon looked up and Jet turned around.

"Are you sure?" Gideon asked.

"This isn't the type of fight you trained for," said Jet.

What were they doing? Would neither of them push back? This was a supernatural matter, no place for a mundane, no matter how well trained.

"No," I said aloud, the fastest way I could think to make my point. "You can't."

"Madison…" Colm said, squeezing my hand.

I pulled my fingers free. "No. You have no idea what this fight will be on either side. Sara shoots lightning from her fingertips. Some people spew acid, stir up sandstorms, change into animals. Even armed, you would be helpless. I can't let you—I won't let you—" I couldn't finish. The thought terrified me too much to consider it. My chest tightened until breathing felt like sucking air through a narrow tube.

"I swore to fight for my country, and my country is in danger," he said, in no way deterred by my arguments. "It doesn't matter from what or from whom, I want to play my part and do what I can."

My panic grew in the face of his resolve. He would be obliterated. If the enemy discovered he didn't have any supernatural ability, they would target him and take him down just to get him out of the way. Just to spite us.

I wanted to crawl inside his head and force him to change his mind. Flood his system with terror, with sleepiness, with the desire to stay in bed with me until dawn—anything to keep him from leaving the house.

But even in the depth of my fear, I couldn't bring myself to manipulate him that way. His mind was safe from me, which meant I had to keep the rest of him safe from everyone else.

The others carried on as though I hadn't spoken, as though my worries counted for nothing in light of the coming battle. Maybe they were right, but as far as I was concerned, nothing mattered more than his life.

Jet handed him the gun. "I assume you know how to use one of these?"

"Point and shoot?"

"Pretty basic," she said. "The bullets are designed not to kill on first strike but to sap supernatural ability, so be strategic. Aim for the people whose abilities stand to do the most widespread damage. Dust Storm Guy being one of them. Carstairs. Michael."

He frowned. "How will I—"

"You'll know," Jet and Gideon said in unison.

They were right, of course. Michael would play it smart and only bring a few of his heaviest hitters with him. He'd want to keep some on standby for after he trounced us. The few he brought, though, would be his best. He'd need them to go against Jet, regardless of her weakened state.

And Colm would be in the middle of it, a man with a gun against a dozen soldiers with weapons so much more destructive than a bullet.

If I wanted to protect him, I had only one option.

I couldn't stay behind to wait again, especially not while a mundane fought our fight. If we were in this, we were in it together.

I drew in a deep breath, steeled my courage, and said, "I'm going as well."

Chapter 28

Jet

FORGET PINS. YOU could have heard a dust mote settle on the arm of the sofa in the silence that fell after Madison's announcement.

"Not a chance in hell," I said once the first shock wore off.

Anger sparked in her eyes. "You made no argument about a mundane joining your forces."

"Sure. A trained soldier. Someone who knows how to watch his back and use a weapon. He won't be defenceless in there, Madison. Against that many people, you will."

I'd seen what she could do to a person. Hell, she'd taken out Gagnon's goon with a touch of her hand, and I suspected that been a hint of her full ability. But this was war. That thug was one unconscious man. The hub would be loud, crowded, messy. She wouldn't have time to hold hands with all of them, and I would be too focused on Michael to watch out for her.

A red tint spread across her high cheekbones, soaked through the tanned hue of her skin, and I knew I'd pissed her off. I couldn't regret it. I couldn't lose her.

"You're dismissing me that easily?" she asked, her words sharp, pointed. "You of all people?"

I started at her tone. I'd always known she had backbone, but I'd seen more evidence of it in the past few days than I ever had before. The force of her stubbornness left me reeling.

"Come on, Madi," I said. "If this were a board meeting, there would be no one I'd rely on more to win the day, but you've never seen battle. People are going to die. I don't want you to be one of them."

My attempts to make her see sense backfired. She flushed a darker shade of red, and her eyes glinted.

"Is that gun loaded?" she asked, jerking her chin at the weapon in Colm's hand.

"No," I said.

"I hope you're right."

The words were barely out of her mouth when static filled my head and my pulse leapt. I had to run, get out of here, fight for my life. My mouth was dry as I braced myself against the floor, ready to move at the first sign of danger.

And it was here. I knew it.

My heart raced until I tasted blood, and sweat pooled in the small of my back even as a shiver rippled down my spine.

Across from me, Gideon's eyes had gone wide, wild, his

face pale. He was staring at me. About to come at me. Him or me. I had to be faster, stronger. Had to reach him first.

In a smooth roll, I snatched the gun out of Colm's hands and launched myself over the trunk on the table, tackling Gideon to the floor. The gun was light in my grip, as natural as if I'd been born with it, and it was no trouble to aim the barrel at his head.

Only to find the point of a green-edged blade at my throat.

Another shiver ran down my spine as my head cleared, taking with it all the static and confusion, the fear and hyper-awareness. No threat. Never had been. Just my lover beneath me, as ready to kill me as I'd been to kill him.

Gideon blinked, tensed, dropped the knife from his hand. It clattered against the hardwood.

My heart jackhammered against my ribs as I set the gun down and climbed off him, numb with shock. He stayed where he was on the floor, his hand on his chest, gulping deep gasps as he tried to shake off what had happened. Colm was on his feet, his hands outstretched as though prepared to pull the two of us apart.

The only person not shaken was Madison. A sheen of sweat covered her brow and the redness in her cheeks had faded to a faint pallor as though she were about to throw up, but otherwise she sat calmly and quietly, in total control of herself—and of the situation. Her hard eyes met mine, and she raised an eyebrow, a silent challenge.

I'd always known what she was capable of. She'd told me, and I'd seen it for myself. Experienced it for myself.

Except with me, she'd only ever soothed and calmed. Settling my stress, easing my sharp-edged emotions. Never had she done the opposite, spiking my adrenaline and cortisol levels, turning those sharp edges lethal.

We stared at each other across the room. I had just had my brain manipulated by my best friend. She had flooded my system with chemicals that had thrown me into a paranoid frenzy. It took me a moment to process the full extent of what might have happened if her control had slipped.

By the shine in her eyes, it had taken effort, but no time. No contact. If she could do that to prove a point, how far would she go to protect herself or Colm? Was it so far of a reach to think she could kill a person simply by suggesting to their brains they should die?

I looked at Colm, who'd dropped onto the sofa, stunned, then at Gideon, who met my eye with an expression laced with regret and apology. I reached for his hand, and he clung to me. His grip around my fingers decided me. If Madison could override our feelings until we saw each other as the enemy, she could take care of herself.

"Point taken," I said, my voice raspy, winded. "You're in."

She dropped her head in a nod of confirmation and rose to her feet. The tremble in her legs was subtle, but Colm stood beside her, his hand on the small of her back. I might have expected him to look afraid, or at least unnerved by Madison's show of power, but his expression hadn't changed. Had he known what to expect, or had he already accepted that on our side of the world anything was possible?

I hoped so, for his sake. That mindset would increase his odds of survival in the hours to come.

"We leave at ten o'clock," I said as I stood up. "Whatever business you have to take care of, whatever goodbyes you want to make, now's the time."

"And sleep," Gideon added from his place on the floor. "We still have a few hours left. We should take our own advice and make use of them."

Colm took Madison's hand, and she led him out of the room, leaving me and Gideon alone.

I knew he was right and I should close my eyes for a while, but a frantic energy buzzed through me, the same anticipatory rush I got before any mission. And this one… this was a mission unlike any I'd taken on before. Going against my own people. It was a special kind of nightmare.

Gideon stood and closed the distance between us, pressed himself against my back, and rested his chin on my shoulder, his hands on my hips, drawing me backwards so I fit snugly against him.

"That's not something I ever want to experience again," he said in a low rumble that made me ache with his love and remorse.

It echoed my own. Thank every god I'd ever heard of that I hadn't loaded the gun, that Madison had pulled back when she had. I understood why she'd done it, even respected the demonstration, but the thought of how it might have ended…

I had seen Gideon as my enemy. I'd spent the last two years saying I wanted to kill him, but had never meant it. Especially not now that I realized how much I loved him.

"You didn't know she could do that?" he asked.

"Not even a little bit."

"The world lucked out that she uses her powers for good. That kind of ability in someone like Gagnon—can you imagine?"

I shuddered at the thought. I could count on one hand the number of people I would trust with that level of mental control. For Madison's sake, I hoped she didn't have to delve too deeply with it tonight. I'd seen the look on her face once my mind was my own again—not only exhausted but sick. She'd made her point, but I wondered how disgusted she felt with herself for going so far. How would she cope if she needed to go even further?

"So, about that sleep?" Gideon said. His voice was soft now, a tickle in my ear as he pressed a gentle kiss against my neck. Goosebumps bubbled over my arms, and I leaned against him.

"Not quite what I had in mind," I murmured.

"No?" He chuckled, creating a vibration that ran all the way to my toes. "Less than twelve hours ago, you were unconscious in a hospital bed. You don't think some actual rest would do you more good?"

"I'm not saying we won't rest," I said, turning around in his hold to wrap my arms around his neck. "I'm just suggesting a little help to get me there."

On any other day, sex would have been the last thing on my mind before a mission. Usually, I made a point of directing that primal energy into planning, hoarding it up to let loose once we succeeded. But usually I carried the expectation of making it out the other end. This time, all bets were off, and if this was my last day on earth, I wanted to enjoy what was left.

***

My alarm went off at nine-thirty, and I came close to throwing my phone across the room. I didn't want to wake up, didn't want to unravel myself from the sheets and Gideon's arms. Although I'd been unconscious for the better part of the last couple days, I hadn't woken in the hospital feeling rested. After my few hours' nap, I was wide awake but too warm and comfortable to want to get up. Especially when this might be my last moment of peace.

But we had half an hour to get ready, and I had things to do.

Gideon didn't try to stop me as I rolled out of bed and slipped into the ensuite bathroom. I showered, dressed, and pulled myself into gear I hadn't worn since the day of the de

Lauer attack. None of it was my own issued kit, of course. Most of my stuff was in my locker at work, the rest at my apartment. But Ray, Katie, and Adam had thought ahead and brought some of their backup gear. Madison's explanations and their own suspicions had given them reason to think we might need the extra armour and weapons. Never had I been happier that I'd preached the wisdom of preparing for the unexpected.

I would have felt more secure in full gear, but if I walked in dressed for a fight, Michael would recognize immediately that I had no intention of talking, and I needed to make him doubt long enough for my troops to get into place.

So I pulled on my black jeans and a black T-shirt over my vest. It was bulky, but my jacket hid the most obvious lumps. On such a hot, muggy night, the extra layer was stifling, but the leather would offer some extra protection.

I'd armed Colm with Meril's gun, so I made do with my knives. My dad's hunting knife at the small of my back, two hooked blades strapped to my belt along with one of Meril's, and a third in my boot. Some line of defence if my abilities were slow to kick in or failed me completely. I hadn't had much chance to test out my air control since my surgery and could only hope desperation and the will to survive helped push me through the pain and fatigue left over from my parasitic guest.

Before I left the bathroom, I stared at my reflection. Typically this was when I gave myself a pep talk. Lead well, be smart, don't take chances. But I didn't have it in me tonight.

Instead, I took in the red line running along the top of my forehead where the surgeons had cut into my brain and the fading swelling around my third eye.

For the first time since leaving the hospital, I tried to open it and clung to the edge of the vanity in relief when no pain swept my legs out from under me. Gideon's recent movements on the other side of the door brushed faintly against my mind. If I hadn't known it was him, I wouldn't have recognized his shadowed form, but it was a start.

Hour by hour, parts of me were returning, but I had no idea how whole I would be by the time we entered the hub or how severely my blindness would hurt our defences.

Michael had caused this. My colonel, the man I'd looked up to more than anyone else in the department.

Even if I doubted my strength, I could rely on my anger to keep me going. He wanted me dead? He would have to work harder than firing a single shot to achieve it. By trying to give me such a horrifying, drawn-out end, he'd proved himself a coward, and I was eager to make him regret his mistake.

I uncurled my fingers from the edge of the vanity and closed my eyes. Three deep breaths to settle my mind, and then I was ready.

I returned to the bedroom, and Gideon pressed a kiss above my third eye before he took his turn in the shower. I paced the room, not ready to go downstairs but unable to sit still.

I had one last task to accomplish, and I'd been putting it

off. Hard to justify waiting any longer, though. Within the next fifteen minutes, I'd be on my way to the Labyrinth, my opportunity missed. Better to suck it up and get it over with.

I'm about to fight to save the country. How hard can a phone call be?

Somehow the comparison didn't make me feel any better.

My phone was on the bedside table where I'd left it, but it was no longer a lifeless piece of plastic and tech. It was a weapon, and I was about to wield it to cause at least two people no end of worry.

I picked it up and dialled one of two phone numbers forever programmed in my memory. Impossible to let go of the ten-digit sequence I'd used since childhood. The number I'd called only two or three times a year since I'd moved away.

After the third ring, my father answered, and I squeezed my free hand into a fist to find my courage.

"Hey, Dad."

"Jet? New phone?"

"Dropped the old one in the toilet."

"Hate when that happens. It's nice to hear from you, baby girl. How are you? You never returned my calls after..." He trailed off, and I cringed. All his voicemails after the de Lauer blast, and I'd never called him back, too caught up in covering my tracks to put my father at ease. *Selfish.*

"Yeah." I kicked at a pile of clothes heaped on the floor. "Sorry about that. Work's been busy."

"Bringing in the bad guys?" He let out a brief chuckle that

fizzled into nothing. "I've been watching the news. Three days of protests in Calgary and Edmonton, and the riots are getting worse. And then there was… I'm sure it's a misunderstanding, but Mom says she saw your face on TV last night in relation to the minister's death. Is everything okay?"

I appreciated his tact in not asking straight out why I was wanted for murder. That was a conversation I didn't have the energy or the time for right now.

"It will be," I said. "Me and my team, we're about to head in to clean things up. I just… wanted to call. Say hi. Let you know things are going down right now and to not believe everything you hear about me. How is everyone doing. How's Mom? Curtis?"

"They're good. Mom's out in the garden if you want to say hi."

Again, my heart squeezed when he didn't ask for explanations. If I survived, I'd take a trip out to Alberta and tell him everything over a few pints and a shared ice cream sundae. If we lost… the truth wouldn't matter.

"No point dragging her away from her zucchini bed." I didn't want what might be my last conversation with my family to devolve into a screaming match. "How's Grandma?"

"She's good. Wishes you'd call more often. She says you missed last weekend."

I laughed and tried to ignore the stab of guilt. "Yeah, I'm a horrible granddaughter. Pass along my love."

A stretch of silence on the line before he said, "You're sure everything is all right? You never call before you head out on a mission. You told me once you don't want to jinx it."

"Yeah, well…" What could I say that wouldn't make him panic? "This isn't exactly a standard operation. A lot of stakes riding on it. National security and all that. So just in case, I thought it would be best to tell you I love you, and that I hope to talk to you again soon."

"Jet… If it's that dangerous—no, never mind." Another chuckle, though I heard everything he wasn't saying. He was biting his tongue, doing his best to stay strong for me. My throat tightened. "I know my daughter well enough. You wouldn't sit this out if I strapped you to a chair. You'd drag the whole damned chair with you and use it as a weapon. You'll be careful?"

"As careful as I can be. I promise." I swallowed hard to clear the rock that had lodged in my throat. "We're ready to head out, so I should let you go."

"All right, sweetheart." A pause. More unsaid words. "Thanks for calling. I love you, too."

I hung up and tossed my phone on the bed. I wouldn't cry. I wouldn't lose hope that we would see tomorrow's sunrise. At the very least, I wouldn't give up until my dad and Grandma were safe from Gagnon's deal. I would fight for them as much as for myself.

The bathroom door opened behind me, and I wiped my

eyes before turning around. Gideon frowned, concerned, and I flashed him a smile to put him at ease. "Just called the fam. Getting that whole emotional nonsense out of the way. You have anyone you want to call?"

He shook his head, threw his towel on the chair in the corner, and wrapped his arms around my waist. "The only person who matters to me is right here, and I'm not about to say goodbye to her just yet."

I rested my cheek against his chest and soaked in his warmth, his steady heartbeat. Unlike me, dressed for battle, Gideon was in his standard outfit. White T-shirt, black vest, black jeans, army boots. All the better to mist away when the time came. All the easier for him to get hurt.

I couldn't let myself think like that. What purpose would it serve to consider all the ways tonight might go wrong? We were heading into the monster's cave. Its tentacles would entangle us the moment we stepped inside, ready to squeeze us out of existence. It would take strength, skill, and a shit-ton of luck to get us out in one piece, but I was determined to try.

For the sake of everyone who had pledged their loyalty to me, for the sake of the future I hoped to confront, I would do whatever it took to tear the monster apart, limb from limb.

Chapter 29

Madison

WE ARRIVED AT the entrance to the Labyrinth under the Somerset overpass near the University of Ottawa.

It had been a short walk here from the safe house. Too short. I'd hoped for more time to prepare for everything we might face. Though the chances of calming down were slim. I couldn't waste energy controlling my thoughts when I had to ready myself to tear apart someone else's. And if my nerves weren't about to settle by themselves, then I wanted this final game to begin.

When I checked out the faces of the people walking with me, I was amazed none of them looked nervous. I knew they were—their fear and apprehension oozed off them in a slimy aura that hovered over their heads like a cartoon smell—but there was enough exhilaration mixed in to mask their terror, and they hid both well. To watch them, I would have thought they were enjoying a late-night group stroll, on their way for a quick chat to request politely that Michael cease his preparations for a national feud, lower his weapons, and converse reasonably, please and thank you.

I wished that were the case. That was the sort of negotiation I was good at. After so many years of practice, I hoped so, anyway.

What we expected instead…

I drew in a breath, and Colm tightened his hand around mine, squeezing my fingers to reassure me he was with me. For now. Soon enough, he would have to let go, and we would both be on our own to fight for our freedom and survival.

Shadows crept towards us from the darkness. Jet's pack shifted into a defensive position, but I raised my hand to put them at ease. I sensed no anger, no fear—no threat.

"Madison?" a soft voice called, and I stepped away from the others.

"Good evening, Uncle."

Sercario came forward, his timeless face scrunched with displeasure. "You're sure this is the best plan? I don't like that you'll be so closed in and cut off."

"If we had any other options, we would do that instead. None of us want to be here."

"I know. What you told me about what they're doing…" He shook his head, his expression twisting with disgust. "The queen is aware, and she's furious. Kill them if you must, but if you're able, leave them alive to face her justice. I don't think any other outcome will satisfy her."

I hesitated for a moment, then pulled out the flash drive I'd brought with me filled with copies of the documents I'd saved and the photographs from Jet's and Gideon's phones of the papers they'd found in Lucien's headquarters, of the ghost lab, of the entire subterranean hideaway.

"I have more than my word for it," I said, handing it over. My heart raced against my rib cage, and I resisted the urge to yank it back once Serc closed his fingers around it. "If we don't—if for whatever reason we don't make it out of there, this is all the evidence we've collected against them. I suggest waiting to bring the drive to Meril until everything is finished. Once she sees everything, I don't know how she'll respond."

Serc nodded and scowled at the door that would take us underground. "Despicable. They hold a position of trust for our people. Frankly, they're lucky you found out before Her Majesty did. She wouldn't have hesitated to strike, no matter the repercussions."

"Then we're all lucky."

"Full disclosure, my presence here is not only at your request. I've stationed half my people near the headquarters in case anyone tries to escape. As soon as we have the all-clear, my orders from the queen are to burn down the house to remove access."

I voiced no argument. Considering the wear and tear on

the house, its loss wouldn't be a huge hit to the neighbourhood, and razing it to the ground would be the safest course of action. Later we could sort through the rubble and make sure no bombs waited underneath.

"You've heard from Lilith?" Serc asked.

"She's splitting her people between Wellington and Main Street, with a few scouts on hand near the other access points in case Michael thinks distance will protect them. If they try to run, she'll cut them off. One of Jet's team called in the local shifter pack, and they're in position to raid The Afterlife as soon as we send word we've handled the situation here. If all goes well, we'll take down Lucien, Michael, O'Malley, and Dougall in one sweep, giving them no chance to recover."

"Where do you want us?"

"At our backs," Jet said, coming up behind me. "My guys are good to go in first and take the initial hit, but the colonel's got numbers we can't match. If he brings everyone—if everything goes to shit—you might not get another opportunity to stop them before they sign the papers."

I held my breath. She was asking Serc to take direct action if we failed, something he was within his rights to refuse. Any application of force would be seen as acting on Meril's behalf, an official declaration of war. It would be the point of no return for the wall and for our secrecy.

After a shorter pause than I expected, Serc straightened his shoulders and nodded. "If it comes to that, we won't hesitate,

Captain. You're here with the queen's sanction, so an attack on you is an attack on the throne. We stand as reinforcements."

My vision blurred, and I blinked away my tears of gratitude.

Jet said nothing to acknowledge the support, but she pressed her lips together to compose herself before saying, "My people will remain in communication with you as best they can. With luck, you won't be needed beyond escorting the prisoners once we're finished."

"As the universe wills it," Serc said.

Jet walked away to issue her final orders, but Serc took my hand. "Your grandmother would kill me if she knew I was letting you go with them. She would also be very proud."

I smiled and wrapped his own pride around me like a cloak, wishing it would keep me safe in the chaos.

"Be careful, Madi," he said. "Your family—your *entire* family—wants to see you come out of this in one piece."

I was tempted to ask if Meril's concern was for my sake or hers, then decided I didn't want to know.

"Thank you, Uncle. Thank you for coming."

"Always."

He kissed my brow, then he and his guard stepped back and blended into the shadows, leaving the space around the entrance as empty as it had been when we'd arrived. They'd be somewhere nearby, observing everything that passed, but no one would see them until they wished to be seen. Although they weren't going in with us, their presence offered a vague sort of comfort. Like a parachute or a life jacket. We had help. It was possible none of us would make it out, but Meril could stop them—even if she brought the apocalypse with her.

"All right," Jet said when we'd gathered around her. She met each one of us with a hard stare. "We know what to expect inside, and you all know your roles. Gideon, you lead the way and take out the watch. Once we have wider access to the tunnels, Jason and Zeke, Sara and Ray, Adam, Katie, and Luvy, you keep to your teams and head towards the hub. Stick to the shadows, and if anyone spots you, silence them. However you need to. Madison and Colm, you stay behind me. Make sure no one comes up behind us, and keep out of sight." She drew back her shoulders and raised her chin. "If you see any familiar faces, you fight to incapacitate. If we don't need to take down another wolf, we won't. For everyone else… they killed our family. Trust your gut as much as I do. You are not only *my* pack, you are the *best* pack, and they made a mistake thinking they could fuck with us. Let's go prove it to them. Masks up."

She waited for us to draw our scarves, neckerchiefs, or simple cloth strips over our mouths and noses, readjusted her scarf around her neck, and signalled for us to move. Zeke opened the door, pulled a thin metal rod from his belt and held it in front of him. As I watched, the rod extended and widened until he carried a full shield in his grip. Gideon winked at Jet, so many unspoken words in the gesture, then misted away. I sensed him, though. His emotions were as fraught as everyone else's, if more scattered. He lingered near Jet, drifting at the front of the line.

Two by two, we made our way inside. There was a rustle of cloth, the sound of snapping bones, followed by a low growl, and a tuft of fur brushed against my palm as an enormous wolf, clad in modified tactical gear, pushed his way forward.

Colm gasped, barely audible in the echoing tunnels, and I squeezed his hand tighter. We'd stepped into the realm of the fantastical, and any remaining attachment he had for the perception filter would be severely tested.

Ahead of me, Jet closed her eyes. Her face pinched with pain as the traces of her third eye shimmered. After a few seconds, she opened her eyes and held up three fingers.

I detected Gideon's excitement as he zipped around the corner, and curiosity led me to follow him. Cautiously, I peered around the edge of the wall to where three sentries were posted in the tunnel. Without Jet, we wouldn't have known they were there until we'd stepped into view, but now they were the ones caught unaware. In a flash, a hand formed out of the mist and a blade lined with a streak of bright green took shape. The blade nicked the soldiers' necks—one, two, three—and they collapsed without a sound. Hand and knife disappeared, and in a heartbeat Gideon returned to us, an invisible cloud of sedation.

The way clear, Jet led us forward, every few paces stopping to scan our route. At every branch of the tunnels, one of the assigned teams followed it, reducing our numbers until only

Jason and Zeke remained with us.

Three more times Gideon left us to subdue the watch Michael had left in our path, and it didn't bode well to me that he wasn't trying to hide his doubts about Jet's intentions. What orders had he given? To take down anyone Jet brought with her? What if Jet *had* come on her own?

What if we'd raised another alarm by putting his people down? Maybe she should have gone in by herself with us watching behind. If their orders were to escort her to the hub and she showed up without them, Michael would know immediately that she'd lied.

It was too late to change our plan, so I resigned myself to the path we'd taken. Stringing him along might have bought us some time, but everyone here was prepared for the inevitable fight. There was something to be said for skipping the small talk and jumping right in. Everything would be over that much faster, and the butterflies in my stomach could stop fluttering.

Gideon returned to us again and materialized next to Jet. He replaced the cartridge in his blade for a fresh one and walked lightly, ready to disappear again at her signal.

Dread gurgled in my stomach, an oozing, festering pool of acid. The walls were too close, the light too dim. I drew in a deep breath to clear my head, but the mouldy air choked me, no cleaner than the last time I'd been down here.

Colm squeezed my hand, and I squeezed back. None of this felt right, but I had to stay calm. I'd shown Jet I was no defenceless damsel, but that much control over multiple people required a lot of concentration. If I distracted myself with fears of what might happen, how could I strike quickly enough when the need arose?

The deeper we journeyed into the Labyrinth, the more on edge our group became. Anticipation prickled my tongue like a lick of salt, and I wished I could block everyone out without limiting my ability. Yet the only confirmation I had that our team was nearby was the spiciness of their emotions. They moved silently. I heard their footfalls when I strained my ears to pick them up, but in the low light, they could have been shadows.

Somewhere farther ahead, the Minotaur waited, while we, Theseus on the hunt, prowled towards him.

What would we find along the way? What nightmare waited for us that we hadn't prepared for? I had to brace myself for the worst, because I hated being taken by surprise.

Despite my best efforts, my heart stopped and my legs grew rooted to the ground when we turned another corner to find four more soldiers, their weapons drawn and raised.

Jet stumbled to a halt and pressed her lips together. She hadn't known. A glitch in her third eye, or was one of these soldiers able to block her view?

A glance at Zeke's face reassured me these people weren't part of their pack, just mercenaries Michael had brought in, but even as I savoured a small sense of relief that we hadn't reached that hurdle yet, I caught Gideon's expression. He stood with his shoulders hunched, his hands clenched, and when I followed his gaze, I recognized the man in the middle. Carstairs. By the look in his eyes, he'd just received an unexpected gift.

"I'm starting to think you're trying to find me, Leigh," he said. "You act like you hate me, but admit it—you want to know how far I can take you." He stepped forward. "Maybe if you're lucky, we can find out when this is over."

The black emotions that burst out of Gideon pushed me back a step—terror and fury stronger than anything I'd ever experienced.

In that moment, the depravity Gideon had suffered in the darkened cell hit me like a punch to the head. All the blood and mangled flesh, the ceaseless trembling of his naked body, had come from this man's sick and twisted mind. My anger rose alongside his. Although it could never match his depth, it matched his heat, and I wanted nothing more than to wrap my hands around the sadist's neck and squeeze.

Without thinking, I slid my mental fingers into Carstairs's mind, but he slithered away from me, making it impossible for me to control him. The bastard was a snake through and through, but this was one fight I couldn't help win.

Jet's scowling features and simmering rage gave away her own desire to tear him apart, but she didn't move. Didn't even reach for the knife at her side.

"Foley, let the boss know they're here," Carstairs

commanded, and the soldier on the far right broke rank and disappeared down the tunnel.

I tensed along with Jet, sensed her need to go after Foley and stop her, but she remained frozen, her fiery glower locked on Carstairs.

He grinned at her and raised his hand. "Take down as many as you can," he ordered his two remaining troops. "These two here stay alive."

Gideon looked to Jet. "Stop her," he said. "She can't reach Michael."

"Gideon, you can't—"

"*Go!*"

She had no opportunity to argue further before the soldier on our left leapt forward. Jason lunged at him and took him down. A wet, slippery sound filled the tunnel as his teeth first sank in, then tore out the man's throat, but that was the last thing I saw. Jet grabbed my arm and pushed me and Colm through the narrow gap the dead soldier had left behind. The soldier on the right had fallen into combat with Zeke, but it took Jet's second-in-command all of thirty seconds to put him down and join us alongside Jason. What had Michael been thinking, leaving these people to stand guard? Had he honestly thought they would be a fair match?

He doesn't know about the pack, I remembered, and despite everything, I smiled. I did not want to miss the look on his face when he realized his error.

Jet looked over her shoulder, and fear flashed in her eyes, but she ground her teeth and pressed on. When I looked back, I spotted Gideon locked against Carstairs, the only two left in the tunnel. The soldier pulled his gun, but Gideon misted away and reappeared behind him, ready to pluck the weapon from his hand and hurl it into the darkness. The clatter of it hitting the ground echoed towards me, and then they disappeared from sight as we rounded the corner.

Foley was barely visible up ahead, and Jet upped her pace, leaving me and Colm behind as Jason and Zeke followed another branch of the tunnel. As soon as she was within reach, she launched off her feet and tackled the woman to the ground, clamping her hand over her mouth. The struggle was brief as Jet slipped the second green-tipped knife out of its sheath and sliced the blade across the back of the soldier's hand.

Foley fell still, and Jet rolled to her feet, her hair pasted to the side of her face with sweat. Colm helped her drag the unconscious woman against the wall, and Jet stared back the way we'd come.

Her desperation to return to the fight we'd left, to know what was happening behind us, spilled off her, but she squared her jaw, straightened her spine, and turned ahead.

I prayed Gideon would be all right. That he repaid Carstairs for every hurt, every nightmare. That Jet would see him again soon. But now that he was gone, we had no one to clear Michael's spies along our route. No one except me.

"You're sure?" Jet whispered as I took my place by her side.

"Trust me," I said, hoping I sounded more confident than I felt.

I knew I could do this, but my knowledge was more theoretical than practical. I would be pushing myself, testing myself more than I ever had, but I would do it. I refused to be the reason we failed.

"Another two up ahead," she whispered a few minutes later.

I closed my eyes, searched for their emotional energies, and found them. They were apprehensive but fighting hard to tamp down their anxiety. Behind us, someone cried out in pain—*let it be Carstairs*—and the soldiers ahead of us went on alert. I grabbed hold of their minds, flooded them with melatonin and serotonin, dragging them into a heavy doze.

As soon as they were unconscious, their minds emptied, all nervousness gone, any fatigue I suffered from the exertion vanished under my satisfaction. The fewer soldiers we had to kill, the better it would be for everyone. Many of these guys were SMOAC agents following orders. Some of them had no reason not to believe Michael's story that they were heroes fighting for the good of their people. We were the villains. To kill them for their foolishness would make us no better than Michael or Lucien. Better to knock them out and leave them in ignorance, to let the light of day and the revelation of their bad judgement greet them in the morning.

I raised my finger to my lips, and we shuffled past them.

New light poured into the tunnels, and Jet slowed to a halt. We'd reached the edge of the hub. Up ahead, Michael awaited her, and we would find out how thorough our planning had been.

Jet turned to me and raised her hand, palm facing me.

Wait here.

I nodded and leaned into Colm, who remained close by my side.

She gave me a smile, one so full of confidence and reassurance that I might have believed it was genuine if I hadn't picked up the weight of her doubt.

The team was divided; the first blow had been struck. Gideon had already begun his dance with the devil, and who knew how long it would be before the rest of us joined the performance. There was no going back. No time for second thoughts. Over the past week, Michael and Lucien had destroyed, ravaged, broken more than we could ever repair. Over the past week, we had planned, searched, gathered our team.

Now we made our stand.

I darted forward, pulled Jet into a tight, quick hug, and then she was gone, stepping into the light of the hub to face the Minotaur.

Chapter 30

Gideon

M Y HEART RACED as I threw myself at Carstairs.

Jet and the others had disappeared down the tunnel, but I didn't know if that had been thirty seconds or three hours ago. Here in the low light and solitude of the Labyrinth, time had no meaning. My only concern was that my hands were free to wrap around the fucker's neck and squeeze the life out of him.

If only he'd give me the opening.

Twice he'd fired his weapon. The first time he'd missed me, and I'd misted away to come up behind him. He'd escaped my hold before I locked on, and his second shot had grazed my thigh. Not enough to slow me down—just enough to keep him out of my reach.

And always, he taunted me with that laugh. That sneering, lecherous grin.

"You don't really think you can beat me, do you?" he asked,

sidestepping my punch and brushing his fingers over my cheek. Fire burned through the nerves in my face, blinding me on my right side, but the pain subsided as soon as I broke contact and misted away.

He had no collar to pin me down this time. Nothing to keep me in his company. I had control. I had power. It didn't matter what he said, I was no longer caged.

"You're weak, Leigh," he called to the air as he turned in a slow circle to watch for where I might reappear. "If you weren't, would you still be here? Would you feel this need to face me again?"

I bided my time, drawing myself together just enough to see him through the mist. The darkness helped me straddle both forms without being spotted, and I did my best to avoid the yellow pools of bug-spattered light from the metal sconces on the wall.

"I'm in your head, aren't I?" he continued, his voice like needles in my ears, piercing my brain, dragging me back to that cell where he had worked so hard to break me. I struggled to fight the sensation, block him out, but still he talked. "Have you been able to sleep since you left me? Have you been able to go an hour without thinking about me?"

He laughed again, and I held myself back from throwing a fist into his throat. I had to be sure of my move before I made it. It would be too easy for him to get the upper hand, otherwise.

But fuck, it was hard to stay in the shadows.

The man was a monster. He deserved to die, and I wanted to be the one to do it. To a point, he was right—he was in my head. He always would be. What he didn't understand was that my hatred for him gave me strength. I fought against every instinct by holding steady and not throwing him against the wall and driving my knife into his gut, but as long as I held on to the belief that I would be the one to draw his last breath, I could be patient.

I appeared at his side, jabbed my hand into his ribs, and disappeared again as he doubled over, the air forced out of his lungs. Appear—my boot to his crotch—disappear. Appear—a double-fisted blow to the back of his neck as he crouched down to catch his breath—disappear.

His chest heaved, but through his rasping, I heard another grating chuckle. "Not bad, Leigh, but how long can you keep up this game of whack-a-mole? Aren't you tired? Aren't you worried about your SMOAC captain and the trouble she might get into without you? Do you really want to waste your time in the dark with me when she might need you to save her again? How is she doing, by the way? She survived the parasite, but she looked a bit wobbly on her feet. Do you think she's up for what's waiting for her in the hub? Do you have any idea what you've walked into?"

I tried to tune him out. Jet wasn't alone. Soon enough, I would be with her to have her back, but until then, she had her team. Keeping Carstairs away from her and the others, destroying him—that would benefit her more. One less threat to face alongside everything else.

Ignore him. Ignore him.

I appeared again, but this time, he was ready for me. He grabbed my wrist, and my legs went out from under me, pain shooting through my back and hips, then numbness, as though he'd driven a blade into my spine. Ice-cold agony crept down my legs and up into the back of my head, and I couldn't move, couldn't draw breath.

He stood over me, his smug grin wide, twisted in the shadows.

"Hi there," he said, and the pain in my body flared like a sunburst, emptying my brain of thought, my nerve endings of any sensation other than being submerged in lava. Nausea twisted my guts, left me dizzy, and my vision filled with red-and-black spots, but somehow I clung to a glimmer of consciousness.

Enough to draw a serum-free knife and drive it into Carstairs's side. The son of a bitch didn't deserve a restful snooze. I wanted to watch him bleed out in front of me.

At his sharp intake of air, I hoped beyond hope my strike had been true.

He let me go, staggered back, and the grimy, dark tunnel returned to view. The knife was still in my hand, blade and skin blood-soaked, and Carstairs pressed his hands over his gut. From the location of his bleeding, I knew I'd failed to deliver a fatal blow, and disappointment crushed me. At least it had been enough to free me from his hold. I would have another chance, and next time, I wouldn't miss.

He hissed through his teeth as he pulled his hands away, and his palms and shirt were soaked red, but he only grinned at me again.

"If that's the kind of fight you want, Leigh, I think we would have more fun if everyone was involved, don't you?"

He turned to the tunnel, and for the first time since he'd appeared before us, my heart stopped.

By the lack of battle sounds coming from up ahead, he had to know by now that Jet had stopped Foley.

Which meant his next move would be to reach the hub and warn Michael she hadn't come alone.

If Carstairs reached the colonel, we'd lose our advantage.

His smile widened as he read my dawning awareness, and he took off at a run.

I tore after him, after Jet, praying I wasn't too late.

Chapter 31

Jet

MY HEART DRUMMED in my chest, a rapid percussion joined by the racing pulse in my ears and the rattle of my breath.

Time had slowed. Every step towards the hub took an eternity to land.

My scrambled brain did its best to register the scene that greeted me in the vast, pillared space, even as my imagination ran wild with the fresh hell where I'd abandoned Gideon.

How could I have left him alone with that evil? Was he up to fighting him on his own? Carstairs's ability, his enjoyment in messing with a person's nerves and skewing their physiological responses… What kind of damage could he cause when his victim wasn't strung up and at his mercy?

I clung to the hope that Gideon's speed and desire for revenge would keep him safe.

I had to believe in his abilities and let go of my fear. Couldn't stay focused on him when Michael stood in front of me.

A small smile touched the corner of my ex-commander's mouth as I stepped into view. He stood with his hands clasped behind his back, his grey eyes watching the tunnel behind me as I came forward alone. He'd dressed in full tactical gear with his stripes on display, as though the sight of them would remind me of his position, of the important role he played for his people and the governmental structure that defended them. All it did was enrage me. How dare he flaunt the symbols he'd turned his back on.

But I schooled my expression, dropped my gaze, and aimed for submissive. While my rage might motivate me, it wouldn't benefit me to let it show yet. First, I had to play my part, then I could unleash hell.

Did he buy that I'd come alone? Probably not, but as long as the others stayed out of sight, he wouldn't know how many of us lurked in the darkness.

I wished my friends—my family—could have stood beside me. Never in a million years would I have admitted to anyone that I wasn't up to seeing Michael again, but now that I was here, the sight of him clawed at my heart, my stomach, made me want to turn and run or throw myself at him and tear out his eyes. This man who had once been my teacher. My hero.

The man who had shot me in the face and left me to die in this underground cesspool in a more brutal way than I could have imagined possible.

Bile scalded the back of my throat, and I resisted the urge to throw up all over the concrete floor.

For a while we stood there, metres apart, measuring each other up in silence. Only part of my speechlessness was an act. Professional me wanted to give my team time to get into position. Emotional me had no idea what the hell to say.

"This is how it goes, is it?" he started at last. "All this trouble to meet with me, and you're not even going to say hello? Not even going to pretend to throw yourself at my feet and beg me to recruit you to our mission?"

"Would there be any point?" I asked, walking across from him in a wide arc to maintain the distance between us.

His smile vanished, his expression morphing into that same goddamned sincerity he'd shown the last time we'd met. "Always. If I thought you honestly wanted to hear me out and join me, I would open my arms to welcome you to our side of progress and security, away from your mad dash into insanity."

Red flags waved in my head. What was he doing? Did he really think I would fall for this pitch considering how our last conversation had ended? Or had shooting me been another step towards progress?

"Come on, Jet," he said. "Work with me." His smile returned. "Isn't one brain-eating parasite enough for a lifetime?"

There it was, his admission of guilt without the smallest hint of remorse. As though he were *amused* by what he'd done.

The picture of him and Gagnon laughing over his successful experiment flitted through my mind, turned the edges of my vision red, and I pressed my palms against my thighs to avoid clenching them. I wouldn't gain anything by throwing my fist into his face. Not yet.

"Apparently not," I said. "Why don't you have another go?"

His smile widened, goading me, and I realized too late I'd played into his hand. He'd been trying to get a rise out of me, turn me antagonistic, but I had to keep my cool. I knew what my plan was, but his remained murky. How many troops waited for us down the other six tunnels? Who else had he brought with him? If he expected to take only me out, I couldn't imagine it would be a large force, but with Michael, one never knew. He wasn't beyond doubling up his tactics to guarantee victory.

"I'd rather not," he said, to my disappointment. It would have been easier on me if he fired first. He probably knew it, which was why he stayed so calm. He would try to push me into taking the offensive, aware that I would struggle to attack him. I hated that this traitor was a weak spot for me. "I meant what I said, Jet. You called me to talk, didn't you? To hear more about our project? You may not be interested in hearing what I have to say, but maybe you'd be willing to listen to a friend."

He whistled a signal, one I recognized all too well, and I froze. A rock grew in the pit of my stomach. My already churning guts gave another wrench, and the air was sucked out of my body as Eric walked into the hub.

He looked… like Eric. While I stood here feeling as though I'd rolled through shit half a dozen times, he looked rested and healthy. No dark circles lined his eyes, and his uniform sat on him as well as it always had. His blond hair was neatly trimmed, his face freshly shaved. He was exactly where he was supposed to be, at his master's right hand. I was the letdown.

I was so focused on him, I vaguely registered the people who walked in behind him. It was only when he looked over his shoulder that I recognized the two soldiers standing at attention.

Marc-André, so recently released from hospital and already back at work and looking worlds better than he had, and Xander.

My soldiers, but no longer my pack.

So much so that Zeke and the others hadn't thought it worthwhile to bring them in when Madison had called. Whatever we'd once been, I'd lost them. Unless that changed when the truth came out. Maybe I still had a chance to open their eyes. Ideally before anyone fired a shot.

Eric leaned in to whisper something in Michael's ear, and the colonel frowned. What news had my lieutenant brought? That three of his troops hadn't reported for work today? Unfortunately for him, they had. Under their captain's command.

"Jet," Eric said, turning his attention to me with a stiff nod.

So cold after everything we'd been to each other.

"You see, Jet?" Michael said, gesturing to the group beside him. "Your troops are here. They need you to step up and take your place. To reclaim your pack. *I* need you."

His pleading note made me sick. A few days ago, I might have fallen for his sideshow, and my gullibility astounded me. He would have played on my heartstrings, led me into his story of progress, and I might have believed him. Too bad for him Madison was such an excellent public servant. So organized, so relentless and resourceful. If it hadn't been for her digging, I wouldn't be standing on this side of the fence, armed to the teeth against his lies.

"I see what you're doing," I said, keeping my attention on him. "It won't work."

His eyes widened, all innocence. "What am I doing?"

The corner of my mouth twitched. "You think I'm above making a scene in front of my guys? That I wouldn't want to embarrass myself? I'm way past that level of self-consciousness. You're the embarrassment, Michael. Everything you've done has been an embarrassment to your rank, your department, and your country."

"Jet," Eric said, begging me to stop.

I ignored him. I wasn't here to pat him on the head and make him feel better. I was here to stop Michael. Eric had chosen his side. Much as I didn't want to hurt him, I wouldn't hold back if he got in my way. We'd both made that clear after he'd shot Gideon. The last conversation we'd shared.

"I've made my choice," I said. "I won't stand by and allow you to turn us into a privatized commodity."

Michael chortled. "Is that what you think I'm doing?"

"Like I told you on the phone, I saw the papers, Michael. I know about your deal with FoSA."

"Then you know the Canadian supernatural community is about to get an upgrade. Better health care, better security." Gagnon's voice took me by surprise, and I looked up to see him standing in the shadows of the upper tunnel. He stepped into the light, and as he rested one hand on the railing, the other in his pants pocket, he might have been posing for a magazine article about his future in politics. His suit was neatly pressed, his tie straight, his shoes—though I couldn't see them—likely polished to a perfect shine.

Even here, even now, in this sewer, he was the quintessential politician.

Though what he was doing here was beyond me. Standing apart as he was, away from the soldiers on the ground, I took a stab that Michael hadn't wanted him to come. He was removed from any possible action, with Michael positioned between us. Had our acting minister wanted to watch the head of his personal security finally put down his greatest obstacle? No more disappointments, no more inconvenient Captain Dawson getting back up to disrupt his plans?

Whatever his reason, he'd made a mistake. He'd landed in *our* trap this time, no matter how high a perch he'd chosen.

"We would be owned by a foreign organization while you live the high life with three billion dollars in your pocket," I said, directing my accusation at him.

I watched Eric's expression out of my periphery, but he showed no reaction. Either he already knew or he didn't believe me. If the first was true, I'd lost him for good. If the second, then maybe—just maybe—I could push this conversation far enough to make him think for himself.

Gagnon laughed. "All great deals come with a price, Captain. In making this decision—in taking this step for my people—I'm trading myself out of a job. I think it's only fair to request some compensation, don't you?"

As if everything he'd done was legitimate, and *I* was the crazy one for seeing the dark side. For seeing that our people would lose more from this deal than we'd gain, needing to pay for services we currently received as part of our citizenship, not to mention pressed into military service and manual labour and who knew what else.

Once more I looked at Eric, silently pleading with him to take a chance on me. If he came to my side, both Marc-André and Xander would follow. But his blue eyes crackled with cold fire, and I understood I'd have to take a bigger step to get him to listen.

"I have the evidence to prove what I'm saying. You know we visited your base of operations, Gagnon. You know we found the ghost lab. You *know* I almost died because of that parasite you created."

Doubt, a brief enough flicker that I might have imagined it, passed over Eric's features, and I grabbed on to it.

"Everything we have is on its way to the queen. Turn your-selves in now and she might be merciful."

Gagnon laughed, and the sound echoed throughout the hub. "As if that woman scares me. The people have made their opinion clear—her time is over."

I turned to Eric. "Eric—"

He shook his head. "If what you're saying is true and you have evidence, then what are we doing down here, Jet?" He waved his hand at the tunnels surrounding us. "You don't push for an underground confrontation when your position is legit. You're standing on clouds and expecting me to follow you, and I won't. Not anymore."

Heat flared in my stomach as Gagnon's echoing laughter looped in my head, as loud as if it were real, and red danced in my vision. "You think I'm making this up? Lying? Give me a little credit. I wouldn't be risking everything if I had nothing to back me up, but I'm not about to let them lead this dance. They *want* a public confrontation." I looked at Gagnon. "You want me to scream my accusations where people will hear me so you can turn around and call it proof that Meril's lost her mind. But I have her sanction to be here. I'm acting as the court's representative, as the department's representative—as our *people's* representative—to make sure you don't cause any more damage than you already have."

If only I could get Michael or Gagnon to confess to some-thing damning. Something that would support my claim in my team's eyes. Already Marc-André looked uncertain, and Xander stood frowning, as though unhappy with the direction the conversation had taken. All I needed was a stiff breeze to blow them my way.

If I could get Michael to show his hand…

Shouts and the sound of bone crunching against bone reached us from the tunnel behind me. The sound of footsteps followed. My heart stopped when Carstairs tore into the hub. "Colonel, she brought reinforcements!"

Before I could worry that Gideon hadn't made it out, he flew from the tunnel and tackled the soldier to the ground.

Shit.

Any hope I'd had that I could push Michael into striking first evaporated, as did our plan for Gideon to move unseen towards their headquarters. I had no time to act before recognition—followed closely by anger—lit on Eric's face, and he shouted orders to take us down.

Madison and Colm stepped out of the tunnel, and the rest of my intentions for this meet vanished under the need to protect them. Through the chaos, Michael barked a series of commands, and within moments, at least fifty black-clad soldiers poured into the hub. They spilled out of the northwest tunnel like spiders, filling the space, blocking every escape.

The stone pillars helped me dodge and weave through the fight as I oriented myself, but there was no way we were getting out of here without casualties.

Gideon appeared by my side, partially healed wounds across his cheek and down his right arm, and we stood back to back, knives in hand. None of the soldiers surrounding me were mine, and while that freed me to use full force, I favoured Meril's blade as my primary weapon. We were better than Michael's mercenaries and O'Malley's thugs, here to save lives, not take them.

Fire spat towards us, and I raised my empty hand to control the air, sending the blast towards a group of mercs moving towards Colm. Gideon ducked at my side and sliced his blade along the cheek of a woman trying to take advantage of my open flank.

I swung my knife over Gideon's head to knock out a soldier with bat-like wings about to swoop down. As the sedative took hold, he lost control over his flight and steamrolled three of Michael's troops into the concrete wall.

Dust rose around us, obscuring my vision, filling my eyes with grit and tears, but a gunshot rang out, the dust cleared, and a grim Colm met my gaze across the hub before he scanned the enemy soldiers for the next big threat.

Gideon and I fought our way towards him and Madison, clearing the path with blade and air until we were close enough to keep the brunt of the battle away from them.

Somewhere in this mess was Michael, but I'd lost sight of him, and Gagnon had disappeared from his balcony view, no doubt cowering down the tunnel.

Blood stained my hands, the knife in my grip dark and slick. I'd already lost track of how many people I'd taken down, the bodies piling up across the hub.

Without thinking, I opened my third eye to take in my surroundings, wanting to get my bearings in the chaos, but pain slashed through my skull, and I dropped to my knees, just missing having my neck sliced open by a soldier who'd shot a blade out of his wrist.

Spots danced in my vision, nausea twisted my guts, but I spat blood and dirt out of my mouth and threw myself at the man with the blades. He bared another one, the sharp tip of a knife pressing through his skin as he bore down on me. I grabbed his elbow, snapped his arm, and twisted his wrist to bury the blade in his own chest. His eyes widened with shock, blood bubbled between his lips, and he collapsed at my feet just as my vision cleared and the last of my pain melted under the surge of adrenaline rushing through me.

Madison shrieked as a man ran at her, but when I jumped to help her, she'd already deflected the attack by sending the soldier after one of his own. The man's wide eyes were wild with terror but no less intense than the woman's confusion as her brother-in-arms drove his blade into her stomach. As soon as she dropped, he tore down the nearest tunnel, and Madison met my eye with a hard stare.

More shouts came from another tunnel, and my stomach clenched. The serum in my knife had run out. I had one cartridge left in my belt pouch, but no time to make the switch. If a second wave of reinforcements arrived, I had to accept that killing them might be my only option.

But when a wolf as tall as my hip barrelled out of the archway to my right and launched itself at two soldiers heading my way, I allowed myself a flicker of relief. Not their reinforcements—mine.

The horde opened under Jason's assault. I spotted Michael wheeling around in surprise as Zeke flew towards him with his metal rod now shaped into a club and revelled in my satisfaction. For all he'd anticipated my moves, he'd clearly not seen this coming.

The two men disappeared into the throng as the fight pushed me towards the middle of the hub. They outnumbered us, but I'd brought my best, and for now we were holding our own. Colm had taken out more than one of Michael's heavyweights—though I wished he'd get an opening to take down Michael himself—and Meril's blades had made quick work of at least a quarter of their forces.

"Get Gagnon out of here!" Michael shouted over the crowd.

My attention jumped to the landing, where the deputy minister had returned to watch the pandemonium with growing concern.

Eric gestured for two of his troops to follow Michael's order, but I couldn't let them leave via the upper tunnel. Serc's people waited at the door we'd come through. If Gagnon intended to walk out of here, we would control his direction.

I drew my hunting knife, swung it into the arm of one soldier, jerked it free, dodged a swing, and lodged it into the thigh of another, but too many people stood in my way. I would never reach him before he escaped.

I told myself it didn't matter. Lilith's people would be in position at the other exits.

But Gagnon wasn't a faceless soldier. He was the acting minister. If he reached the street, Lilith would be hard-pressed to nail him without drawing attention.

As I swirled a punch at the chin of an oncoming soldier, I caught Madison's eye. She and Colm were backed against a wall, both of them fighting hard to control their surroundings and keep the battlefield from slipping too far to our disadvantage. Blood dripped down Colm's side, but he moved easily, and I questioned whether the blood was his. Madison looked wild, her shirt and hair soaked with sweat, her eyes bloodshot. The effort of using her ability was draining her too quickly, but I needed her help.

I nodded my head towards the stairs. She followed my gaze towards the fleeing Gagnon and nodded, but a hand grabbed my arm and tore my attention away from her.

"You can still stop this," Eric said, his blue eyes pleading. "I know this isn't what you want. Call them off. Stand down. *Talk* to us."

I jerked my arm free. "You push so hard for me to listen, but you're the one refusing to hear. He's lying to you, Eric. What will it take to make you see it?"

Someone shoved me out of the way as a spray of acid flew towards me. The thick ooze struck the wall, burning into the concrete, but my rescuer was gone before I saw who it was. In the rush of the moment, Eric was drawn back into the fight, and I didn't waste time looking for him.

He was right about one thing: I had to end this. I had to get to Michael. Only when I stripped him of everything would we escape this underground hell.

Chapter 32

Gideon

I MISTED OUT of range of a soaring piece of concrete and reappeared behind the concrete-thrower, driving my knife into his hamstring and slicing upwards. He dropped with a scream, and I vanished again, leaving him to fight through the injury or retreat. In and out, I darted through the skirmish. Meril's blade was empty and my refills were gone, leaving only my own knives for defence.

The hub was madness. Dozens of people throwing magic as though we were in a stadium twice as large. Colm's eagle eye had so far saved us from the dust stormer, an earth shaker, and a man who'd appeared to be transforming into a crystalline behemoth. Our people were holding up, Michael's whittling down, and I pushed myself harder to even out our numbers. Somewhere in this chaos, Carstairs and Michael were hiding, waiting, letting others take the fall, but I would tear my way through to them and reveal them for the scum they were.

I dodged a flying axe, misted away, and wove through the crowd to another clear patch.

A form passed through me, and I brought myself back enough to distinguish friend from foe, but saw no one. The part of me that was still mist sensed someone there, but the air was empty. Invisible. Not one of ours. I swung out with my knife, and a screech pierced my ears as a woman collapsed to the ground out of nowhere, her hands pressed over the bloody gash across her eye.

In my periphery, I saw a mercenary with slick green skin draw back her shoulders and shoot a hunk of acid phlegm at a distracted Jet. I misted towards Jet and solidified my hand to knock her out of the way. The acid struck the wall and fizzed a dime-sized hole into the concrete.

If I'd been fast enough, I would have yanked Sampson into the spray instead of pushing Jet out of it. What did lover boy think he was doing, stopping to chat in the middle of a fight? Trying to get them both killed?

I hefted the knife in my hand to get a better grip on the handle, which was slick with sweat and blood. Navigating my way through the hub had grown increasingly difficult, the ground cluttered with the injured and unconscious. Unfortunately, not all of them were theirs. Luvy, though still alive, had dragged herself into a corner, leaving a trail of blood behind her mangled left leg. She fought on, throwing balls of fire at anyone who came close. More than one black-clad figure was forced to roll on the ground to put out the flames. Sara's corpse, her face slashed by what looked like multiple knives, sat propped against the wall, staring blankly at the scene in front of her.

The edges of my vision turned red, and anger burned through my fatigue, fuelling me to cut my way through the troops still fighting—and not half as gently as I had been. Jet wanted the SMOAC soldiers spared, but why should we show them mercy? They'd had a chance to prove their worth, but those loyal to her had made it clear: the rest weren't to be trusted. And if she couldn't rely on them to have her back, why should I have theirs?

I misted my way to Jet's side, not wanting to let her out of my sight any longer than necessary. This time I regretted I'd left her at all. Michael had found her.

She moved as though fighting against a tide, slow and heavy, but he kept stumbling backwards, pushed off balance by the force of the air currents she stirred up around him. Then, as though a switch had flipped, her movements smoothed, sped up, and every blow she struck, he matched, and each of his, she blocked. They were stuck in a state of attrition, both knowing the other too well not to take advantage of their weaknesses, but also anticipating each move, predicting each strike. Their only option would be to wear the other down, and with everything Jet had suffered, I didn't know if she could outlast him.

It would be such a simple thing to step in and put an end to their battle. Drive my blade between his ribs. No guilt on Jet's part, the confrontation over in an instant. I tightened my grip around the knife hilt. One single thrust was all it would take.

A rush of blinding pain took my knees out from under me, and I collapsed to the ground. My knife skittered away, lost under a heap of cotton and Kevlar, and I struggled to dissolve and escape. Breaking myself apart didn't help. The burning, stabbing pain followed me, caught now in every individual cell, concentrated, ten times worse, a fire raging in every atom, sharp and overpowering. I dragged my cells together and gagged over the floor as I writhed against the concrete, my vision filled with black spots, my breath short, the agony cutting through my skull, my skin, my insides.

A shadow fell over me, and I knew who would be there when I looked up.

My nightmare wore a wicked grin on his ugly face, his eyes full white, his uniform mussed, torn, and blood-spattered.

"You took me by surprise earlier," Carstairs said. "I needed a minute to get back into your head. But I'm there now, aren't I?"

He crouched down, and I flinched away from him. For a second, I was back in the reeking cell, surrounded by inescapable pain, no feeling, no sensation my own. At the mercy of this man who had none. My jaw screamed as I locked my teeth together, refusing to make a sound. He wouldn't claim that satisfaction from me, at least. Never again.

He chuckled and tucked his finger under my chin, drawing

my gaze to his. "I've missed this," he said. "You were such a good sport, resisting as hard as you did. Tell me, have you dreamed of me since then?"

Another surge of electric pain tore through me, and I curled in around my core, hating myself for being so weak. He was toying with me. He could kill me in an instant if he wanted to. Drive my pain receptors up so high my heart gave out. I had lost control, stripped even of the chance to end the agony on my terms.

Carstairs's imprint was all over me, inside and out, crawling through my veins, setting my nerves on fire, freezing them with a touch so cold it burned. The singing intensity of fresh bruises festered under my skin, and a throbbing bass beat its rhythm behind my left eye. Blood dripped to the ground beneath me, a steady flow from my nose.

Around me, the fight continued. Shouts and screams, punches thrown and returned, metal striking metal, gunshots. It was so close. I just had to lift my head to see it, but I didn't have the strength to do it. I was trapped in my mind—in my body—about to burst into a billion excruciating fragments. I had survived this man once, I'd survived Sampson's bullet, but there was no getting away from this. Not under my own power.

I longed to disappear, run, fight as I'd promised myself I would the next time Carstairs and I crossed paths, but I was tired of struggling against him. I didn't want to keep looking over my shoulder, haunted by his grin. I wanted to give in to the pillowy darkness waiting for me beyond the pain. Anything to make it stop.

"Giving up already?" Carstairs asked, his whisper in my ear a series of pinpricks down my neck. "You wouldn't do that to me, would you? Cut my fun short so soon? Come on, how about one more go?"

A scream pierced through my mental fog, the only sound that could have jerked me out of myself. I looked up, past the demon in front of me, and spotted Jet down on one knee. Blood soaked through her shirt and her right arm dangled, useless, at her side.

The heat of my rage beat against the fire of Carstairs's manipulations. I should have been there to watch out for her instead of getting held up by this monster. She needed me. I had to get to her. Which meant I had to get through him.

Carstairs followed my gaze, then turned back to me with a wider grin. "Do you want her to join us? Think about what I could do to you in front of her. Or what I could do to her in front of you."

Fury choked me, but still I couldn't move, my joints locked and my bones cooking.

Jet rose to her feet and switched her hunting knife to her left hand, fighting with as much strength and dexterity as she had with her right. Who was I kidding? She didn't need me. I needed her. She was my inspiration, my motivation. If she could keep fighting after all that had happened, I couldn't let this fucker be the one to take me down. He hadn't earned the privilege. He might be inside me now, but he wasn't the only one with that trick up his sleeve.

My pain increased as I focused on my body, diving deep into every screaming pinch, twist, and ache until I pulled myself apart. It had never been harder. With every limb that dissolved, the agony intensified, but I used it to strengthen my determination. Carstairs had torn me apart, so I would do the same to him. Make him feel my pain. Make him beg for me to stop.

Each piece of me passed through fire as I drifted towards him, each cell sizzling, charring. How much of me would be left by the time I was finished? I didn't care. Nothing mattered beyond wiping the smug grin off his face.

I brushed against him, searching for access points, needing only the smallest space. Cell by cell, particle by particle, I drifted into his nostrils, his eyeballs, his ears. I filled him the way his mind had filled me. I targeted his nerve centres as he'd targeted mine, swirling through his veins.

I sensed his rising pulse, the rush of blood as he realized what I'd done. The rapid movements of his lungs as his breath quickened, the flutter of his heartbeat. He fought back, ice and fire, torturing me with a stabbing, scorching, searing pain that dragged my separate pieces apart and made them dance with the need to escape his reach. But I latched on to him. All he'd done was arm me against him, driving my desire for revenge.

I burrowed inside him, stretched myself into every organ,

made myself comfortable.

And then I expanded. The individual particles of my make-up joined together, clumping into larger shapes, growing. Never in my life had I attempted anything like this, and the sensation was as satisfying as it was sickening, but I was too angry to stop. Bit by bit, I solidified in patches, choking him, cutting off his blood supply. I tasted his terror in the jerky movements of his body, in the echo of his screams that vibrated through me. His heart raced, and I gave it space, not wanting to snuff him out too soon, wanting to show the same generosity he'd shown in sparing me.

I expanded again, this time revelling in the snap of his bones. I clogged his arteries, filled his lungs.

His heart beat one last time, then fell still. The rush of blood slowed, his limbs went slack.

As he collapsed to the ground, I misted back the way I'd come, leaving his Gideon-choked corpse behind.

The pain in my cells eased but didn't disappear, and after I pulled myself together, the effort wild and confused, I couldn't lift myself off the ground, my arms wrapped around my middle, left to pray I would be overlooked long enough to catch my breath.

Carstairs lay on the ground staring at me as I gulped down air. Blood leaked out of his red-shot eyes, his nose, his mouth, his face bloated and purple. His expression, one of open-mouthed horror, imprinted itself on the back of my mind where it would stay with me forever. The man who had left the same expression on the faces of so many had been mine to kill, and I felt no regret, no remorse.

Only gratitude that he had pushed me as hard as he had.

What couldn't I survive after this? I had stared into the face of the devil and grown immune to his fire. What couldn't I endure?

I knew my answer, of course. Only one possible pain left me weak in the knees. Only one screamed at me to get to my feet.

But I was too exhausted to move. Too exhausted to hold myself together. I stared across the hub of the Labyrinth, and the last thing I saw before my body drifted apart was Jet fighting for her life.

Chapter 33

Madison

B ATTLE AND BODIES blocked our path to the stairs, and more than once, I tripped as I pushed my way through. A hand grabbed my arm from behind, and at the sudden contact, my mind defended itself with a burst of adrenaline. The soldier screamed, tore her hand away, her features petrified, as if she'd just watched my face melt off. She bolted across the room, and I led Colm forward.

So far, my ability had kept us safe, but without time to dig too deeply into their brains, the effects of their manipulated chemistry only lasted so long. Other emotions soon rose to override whatever I did to them, and the result was a bunch of pissed-off soldiers doubling down on their return to prove they weren't deserters.

Fortunately, no one seemed to have figured out I was the cause of their sudden, debilitating terror, or I suspected I would have become a critical target. As it was, most of them ignored us for what they saw as the greater threats in Jet's pack. For everyone else, Colm hadn't yet run out of ammunition. Each shot he fired sent his target reeling backwards as the bullet embedded in their flesh, and each time the same reactions followed: first shock, then confusion when they discovered they were still alive, a moment of smugness… and finally horror as it sank in they'd lost access to their abilities. They scrambled for their mundane weapons, but by then, we were out of range.

As we ran, I scanned the room for Jet and Gideon. I spotted Jet on the far side of the hub facing off with Michael, dodging projectiles that flew in from other parts of the fight. Her right arm was limp, bloody, but her jaw was set, her eyes narrow—an expression of fierce determination. Gideon was nowhere to be seen, though I saw Carstairs standing alone, his face red, his eyes wide, his hands tearing at his uniform.

I sent up a prayer for our people and pressed forward. We hadn't lost yet. We still had hope.

By the time I reached the stairs, my muscles ached as though I'd lifted my body weight a thousand times over, the effort of holding my thoughts so steady and focused taking its toll. My head pounded, my vision wavered, but I clenched my hands into fists and worked to gain control over myself. We weren't done yet. Lucien was ahead of me, hurrying towards the exit.

"Lucien!" I called.

He stumbled in his haste, but if he'd been tempted to turn

around and face me, the soldiers on either side of him kept him moving.

I reached the top of the stairs and concentrated on the woman to Lucien's left. Frustration and disappointment wafted off her, and I grabbed hold of her mental weakness. Stronger emotions were easier to manipulate. The chemicals already rushed through her grey matter, synapses firing, hormones pumping. It was the work of a moment to twist them to my advantage and send her into a berserker rage.

Her face flushed a deep red and her upper lip curled into a snarl. The fingers around Lucien's arm tightened, and she jerked him out of the way to gain access to the soldier on his right. Surprised and confused by his partner's sudden aggression, he raised his gun, but he was too late. She wrapped her hands around his throat and backed him against the railing before he fired a shot. The metal frame gave way beneath him, and the two of them crashed over the side into the battle below.

With his protectors gone, Lucien bolted into a sprint down the tunnel, throwing terrified glances over his shoulder as he ran.

"Lucien, stop!" I shouted, not for a moment expecting he would.

I reached for his mind, detected a trace of his fear, and wrapped myself around it, but somehow he shoved me out. In my surprise, I stumbled. Colm caught my arm to steady me, and I took off again.

It didn't make sense. Lucien didn't have the ability to block me out of his mind. I reached for him, searched for the barrier. There was none, but when I tried to wrap around him, a second shock wave threw me back.

I'd experienced that effect once before.

"Dougall," I breathed, and only then did I hear a fourth set of footsteps echoing against the ground. This one moving towards us.

Up ahead, the Ghostmaker rounded the corner.

His hair was pulled back, tidily contained in a ponytail, but the rest of him looked much the same as he always did. Baggy jeans, white T-shirt, plaid overshirt… and a wide grin that distracted me long enough that I missed the pouch in his hand. Lucien paused as Dougall hurled it, and I watched it sail over my head and strike Colm in the chest. Against the neckerchief that had slid down during the course of our fight. Colm fired his weapon as the plastic burst open and released a puff of white powder that clouded into his face.

"No!" I shouted.

Lucien fled, but I was too stunned to go after him.

My heart stopped as Colm's eyes widened, his pupils dilating to the full circle of his irises, and he collapsed onto his back with a wild stare at the ceiling. His breathing quickened with open-mouthed gasps and sweat beaded on his brow as the drug took hold.

Behind me, Dougall gurgled, and I glanced over my shoulder to find him clawing at his neck. The bullet had lodged in his throat. He scratched at it, trying to pull it free, but only succeeded in digging into his flesh. I made no move to help him.

Ghost drifted through my system, the few traces I'd inhaled when the bag had snapped dividing and spreading. It wormed its way into my mind, fighting for supremacy over my brain function, and it was so pure, so strong, it nearly broke through my defences. I wrestled my barriers into place, doubling the walls between the natural chemicals and the synthetic. I didn't have time to deal with the threat to myself. I had to stay in control. Had to decide what to do.

Colm had been hit with a full dose of the drug, Lucien was getting away, and I stood frozen between the two.

How could I save Colm when the threat to our country was about to escape?

How could I go after a man who meant nothing to me when the man I loved lay dying at my feet?

There was a chance I could save him. Not a big one, but it existed, and the longer I waited, the smaller the odds became. But if I tried, I would lose Lucien.

A scream built in my chest, and I didn't bother to hold it back. The depth of it filled the tunnel, bounced off the concrete walls, and echoed back at me.

No matter what I wanted, I had to think of the bigger picture. If Lucien got away, Meril would have no choice but to get involved. I loved Colm—couldn't imagine a life without him if I didn't make it back in time—but I couldn't abandon the world to the wrath that would rain down if I put him first.

Tears warmed my cheeks as I forced myself to storm around the corner. I expected Lucien to be gone, but he was still in view, stumbling forward, too focused on what chased him to pay attention to where he was going.

He was right to be afraid.

"Lucien!" I called after him, no longer pleading but commanding.

He tripped, caught himself, and upped his pace, but the tunnel stretched on without bend or turn, so I lengthened my stride. I refused to run after him—he'd led me down enough stray paths. This time, I was in control, and in another moment, he would know it.

Rage surged through me, and I pinpointed his terror, which had spiked when Dougall, his greatest asset, had fallen. With the Ghostmaker out of the picture, there was nothing to stop me from climbing into Lucien's mind, and I crept through his brain, inch by inch. I wound my mental fingers into the chemicals spilling through his veins, tightened my grip, pulled.

He cried out and clasped his hands to his head, and although he didn't stop running, he slowed. Step by step, I closed the gap between us. For the briefest moment, indecision held me bound. Not over what I was going to do, but how I was going to do it. Raise his terror levels to push him into a heart attack? Too easy, and the suffering too brief. This man had stripped me of my pride in my work, my confidence in my country, and my sense of self-worth, and with every crime, he'd run away from the consequences. Blaming Jean-Luc, Jet, me. I wanted him broken. I needed him to bear the weight of what he'd done.

So with a twist of his mind, I shifted the neurochemicals travelling along his synapses, reduced his terror, and flooded him with a guilt so intense he lurched to a halt and dropped to the ground with a wail that bounced off the walls and scattered down the tunnel, joining my earlier scream of grief.

Emotions were funny things. Everyone associated them with the heart—heart-stopping fear, warm-hearted love, broken-hearted agony—but in truth, the brain was everything. A bit of extra cortisol, a release of specific neurotransmitters, could bring a man to his knees as easily as a kick to the groin.

Until now, I'd gone easy on people—not for their sakes, but to conserve my strength. With Lucien, I let loose and allowed him to experience the full extent of my ability, urging more and more cortisol into his blood.

There was so much I wanted to say to him. I wanted to confront him about everything he'd taken from me. My family's legacy. My father's best friend—*my* friend. My throat closed as I thought of Jean-Luc lying on his office floor, killed by people he trusted. And I had doubted him.

Now Colm—but I couldn't let myself consider the idea that this bastard had taken him from me, too. It was bad enough that because of Lucien, I'd had to leave him dying in a dark and dirty corridor to get justice for a department that, at the moment, didn't deserve it.

I said none of it. This man at my feet wasn't worth my breath or the energy it would have taken to put my grief into words. And there would have been no point. Already, Lucien was too far gone to hear me, so deep in his despair he might never return from it, and I didn't care. He curled against the wall and released a moan loud enough that the sounds of fighting behind us subsided for a heartbeat as both sides of the battle absorbed his pain.

"You can stay here until we're ready for you," I said, pushing out the syllables through my clenched teeth. "Here in the sewers like the rat you are."

I spat at his feet as tears streamed down his cheeks and heavy sobs wracked his body, then I turned and left him. He wasn't going anywhere, and another man more deserving of my attention needed me.

From down the tunnel, the sound of limbs flailing against concrete caught my ear, and I hurried back the way I'd come.

On my way, I passed Dougall, who lay still against the wall, his blank eyes staring at nothing, but I barely spared him a glance as I dropped at Colm's side.

He'd lapsed into convulsions, foam spewing between his lips, and tears blurred my vision with a stinging heat.

"Hang on," I said as I rolled him onto his side. "Hang in there. Stay with me."

My hands shook so badly, I couldn't keep my grip on him,

and in the end had to shift my entire body to hold him steady, trying to protect him physically even as I scrambled to find my way into his head.

My thoughts were flurried, my focus too scattered with fears of what might happen, and I wanted to scream just to hear something other than the voice in my head telling me this was my fault. I should have tried harder to keep him at the safe house. I should have paid more attention to what Dougall was doing. Of course he'd come armed. We'd expected it, and still I hadn't noticed the ghost in time.

But there would be more than enough opportunity to beat myself up later. The rest of my life, as long as that might be. Right now, I held Colm's life in my hands. I had to concentrate.

I looped my fingers through his and squeezed them tightly as I picked apart the chemicals rushing through his body. The ghost had soaked into his bloodstream, and his brain was awash with serotonin and noradrenaline, too much for him to handle. I tried to tap into it, frantic, desperate to slow his brain before it burned out, but he resisted me. Every block I put up caused a leak somewhere else, and the seizures continued. I took off the blouse I wore over my tank top, slid it under his head, and stretched my awareness deeper into his mind.

"Listen to me, Colm," I said. "You're not allowed to die, is that understood? You told me you would look after yourself, that you were up for this. Prove it. Fight this. You beautiful, stubborn man."

I wouldn't give up on him. No matter how long it took, while he had breath in his body and any chance of coming back to me, I would fight as hard as he did.

Outside the tunnel, the battle waged on. Jet and Gideon were caught in the mire, her troops standing with her to whatever end. To win? To fall? It didn't matter. I couldn't spare a thought for any of them.

I was done with putting my country ahead of myself. The world was crumbling, but if I couldn't save Colm, what reason would I have to stop myself from crumbling with it?

Chapter 34

Jet

ALL AROUND ME the fighting continued, though the numbers had dwindled enough that the draft blowing down the tunnels cooled the sweat on the back of my neck.

Too many lay dead on the ground. Sara. Ray. Xander.

More of my own troops. More of the people who had sworn to follow me that would never rise again, and the weight of their loss lay heavy on me. No matter how I felt about him, Michael was right: I didn't deserve their loyalty.

Logic tried to tell me it was what we'd trained for. The nature of the job. It reminded me they'd known what the cost of this fight might be before they'd entered the Labyrinth.

But I'd made the call. My decision had brought us into this nightmare, and I wouldn't shrug off that burden.

We had done our best to show mercy knowing the other side wouldn't. We had planned for minimal loss of life, knowing Michael's goal would be to wipe us out.

He'd brought fifty people to stand against three.

Had he known about our backup, or had he finally stopped underestimating me?

Either way, the result was more blood on my hands, and my only option was to keep fighting until my soul was thick with it.

Pain pounded against my skull like a dribbling basketball, and I struggled to ignore it. With my third eye out of commission, I did my best to use my physical eyes to find my friends, but Madison and Colm were out of sight, and I'd lost track of Gideon, though I'd tripped over Carstairs's bloody corpse on my way across the hub.

Reaching for the air surrounding me, I wrapped it around my fists and delivered a punch to a soldier's gut that sent her flying across the room into the wall. Concrete crumbled at her back as she slumped to the floor, and when I turned around to check behind me, I came face to face with Michael.

It wasn't the first time we'd found each other in the chaos, but time and again, the battle had pulled us apart, and the most recent skirmish hadn't been gentle on him.

Blood smeared the creases of his brow, and an emerging bruise lined the edge of his cheek. I threw an air-wrapped punch at his face with my left hand, hoping to strike before he activated his ability, but a moment before it made contact, my fist slowed, as though I were pushing through sand. Using the momentum I'd gained, I released the air around my hand and launched it towards him. He stumbled backwards, hit his head on a stone pillar, and while he steadied himself, I drew more air around me.

He spat blood on the ground and wiped his mouth with the back of his hand. "Look at the hell you've wrought, Captain," he said, his voice hoarse with exertion. "None of this had to happen. None of these people had to die today."

I gritted my teeth and threw the air at him, but he side-stepped and avoided it.

"You're a weak leader," he said. "Selfish, arrogant."

I couldn't afford to listen to him. He was trying to get inside my head again, make me doubt. I used to hang off his every word. His praise had raised me to Olympus, his disappointment dragged me to Hades, and he knew it.

I summoned another blast of air, and again he dodged it.

"That's why your troops abandoned you. That's why you lost your authority. You stopped deserving it."

I had to block him out. I'd told myself he didn't have power over me anymore, yet here I was, absorbing his words into muscle and bone. I had to keep him out of my head, prove to him I was a stronger leader—stronger *person*—than he realized.

Step after step, I pushed him backwards until the wall under the upper access tunnel stopped him.

"With me, you could have been something," he said. "You could have stood above your peers and risen to greatness."

How was he still talking? He had nowhere to go, no way to

escape me.

"You owe me everything."

At that, my restraint, my temper, my patience snapped.

"I gave you all I had!" I shouted. I should have kept my mouth shut and let him talk. He wanted to goad me, distract me. But the idea that *I* had let *him* down was too much to bear. How dare he? "I gave you my loyalty, my trust, even my love, for fuck's sake. And you betrayed me. You betrayed all of us."

I raised my hand, ready to bring the wall down on his head, but Eric grabbed my arm and jerked it back.

"No, goddamn it—*you* did, Jet," he said. "You brought them here—troops *you* trained. Troops who would have followed you anywhere, and now look at them!" He wrenched me around and pointed to the scatter of dead bodies on the ground. So many. Some I knew, some I didn't. Some who'd followed Michael here with open eyes, but how many who'd had no idea what they were fighting for?

Thanks to Meril's gifts, a good number were asleep, others injured by the ability-sapping bullets and the damage of a solid clock to the jaw, but more than I would have liked to see would never reclaim their place in the ranks. Never raise a glass or laugh at the antics of their team. My throat swelled, my heart ached, but I couldn't break. Not yet. Not when I was so close to avenging my pack for everything we'd lost before this.

"You could have made things right, but you were so fucking determined to turn Michael into the villain," Eric said, drawing me out of my grief.

I turned to him and met the anger in his eyes. The disappointment. Maybe I deserved it, but not as much as the man he was protecting.

"You might be right," I said, and although I aimed for calm, the tremor in my voice was obvious. My self-control was slipping, and I didn't know how long I'd be able to hold on before I threw him across the room and finished what I'd come here to do. But if I didn't have to, I wouldn't. The chasm lay open before me, and I could either push Eric into it and lose him forever or guide him to take the leap with me. Here, at the end. "I don't know anymore. Maybe it would have been better to let some international organization take control of our people. At least FoSA would have some idea what to do with us, which is more than I can say for the current government."

But ask him who was responsible for the attack at the condo, Eric. Ask him who ordered Dougall to build the bomb. Ask him who gave the signal to set it off.

The words were on the tip of my tongue, just as I balanced on the tip of my anguish, but I clamped my jaw shut as the past dragged my memory deeper into the de Lauer subbasement. The claustrophobia of standing in the doorway holding back the flying white powder, working to keep the air still, to push back every last particle from finding its way out of the room and wreaking havoc on the bystanders outside. Watching my squad tear each other to pieces as the ghost set in before the drug burned through their brains and left nine of my troops dead on the floor.

Shaking, nauseated, fighting my desire to crush Michael under the weight of his crimes, I turned to the colonel, grounded myself in the justice my pack was due, and found stillness. Calling him out directly would achieve nothing. He would evade and he would twist the blame to point at me, but he'd revealed his true self the last time I'd met him here in this underground maze. I knew how deep his passions ran, how fully he believed in what he was doing.

He had to know how Eric and the rest of my team would take the news that he'd had a hand in their friends' deaths—he wouldn't have hid it from them, otherwise—but he'd made it clear to me that at no point did he think he'd made the wrong call.

I was beyond furious, beyond heartbroken, but I was a SMOAC task force captain. Tactics and strategy were as important as physical strength. Let Michael think he was safe, that his position was solid. Madison might have read him more clearly, but I knew this man. Which meant I knew how to break him.

If I was able to stay strong a little while longer, this battle could still end in our favour.

"Our people are at a point of crisis, Colonel. You know it. For so long, we have been trapped in a society that would never accept us for who we are. We have had to beg and fight for every scrap of respect, every resource, every community assistance that might keep us safe."

"What the hell do you think I've been telling you, Dawson?" Michael said. "You never stopped to listen."

"I was listening, and you were right. I may not agree with your methods, but I'm sure everyone here would agree something needs to change."

It made me sick to say it, but I caught the gleam in Michael's eyes. He was on alert, wavering between suspicion and hope. I had to tread carefully, or I would lose him. First disarm, then put down.

"And who knows, maybe you're right about FoSA being the solution," I said, flapping my uninjured arm in an exaggerated shrug. "I've got my opinions about it, but I'm just a soldier. Gagnon's people have done the research. I honestly don't know. What I do know is what Eric says is true. You wanted to help our people, and I was the one who led us here. To the deaths of my friends, my team, and the loyalty of anyone I had left."

My voice cracked at those last words, and I allowed my grief to show.

Michael narrowed his eyes. Did he see through me or was he so desperate to have me with him that he'd swallowed the bait?

I was too drained to keep going, and unless I offered to help him, which he would never believe, it was time to switch tactics.

"So what's next, Colonel? You've come this far. Done so much. How much more are you willing to do to finish what you started?"

"As much as it takes," he growled. "You have no idea how hard we have fought to reach this point. You have no idea how serious our situation is. Every forward move we've made in the last five years has been because of me, because of Lucien, because of the people who put in the actual *work* to make things better. Do you think we have Bastien to thank for the safety our people enjoy? That man earned over a hundred grand a year to pay lip service to the prime minister and act like everything was running smoothly. He didn't care that our people were going without health care or housing. As long as we stayed within budget and wore a good face for the PM's office."

"But you did so much more than that."

"Fucking right, I did."

"Because the minister was a useless politician who didn't deserve his power."

Michael scoffed. "The man was an imbecile. He was leading our people straight to the endangered species list, and he didn't have the decency to admit it."

"So you stood up for your people."

"Yes, I did."

"And got him out of the way."

"You're goddamn right."

He stopped, stunned.

Eric jerked back. "Colonel?"

I left Michael no room to backpedal. "It's what I've always

respected about you, Colonel. Something you've never given me reason to doubt, even through all of this. Your stand has always been for the good of our people. So what happened that night? Did you stab him? Or was it Gagnon? Dougall? Why did he have to die? Because he figured out what you were doing with the forged signatures?"

Michael scowled. "Lucien is a fool. He insisted on that fucking paperwork. I did what I had to do."

"What about Rourke? Mitchel Lafontaine? The other informants who trusted us to keep them safe, who supported the department, all winding up dead after I talked to them? You did what you had to do with them, too?"

"Snitches," he said. "Not worth your time or regret."

"*Our kind*," I shot back. "The people you claim to be fighting so hard to protect." Could he not see his hypocrisy? Was he so far gone—so delusional—that he was clueless to his inconsistency?

It didn't matter. The growing horror in Eric's eyes, his gradual shift away from Michael, was enough for me.

"They were nothing!" Michael roared. "Whining, gabbing little peons who got in the way. What benefit would they have added to our new world?"

"And my troops?" I had to bring it back to them. Eric needed to hear it from Michael. I wanted my lieutenant on my side. No matter what had come between us, he was my partner, my friend, and I needed him to be free of Michael's lies and manipulations. "Why keep your efforts a secret? The men and women who gave their lives doing what you believed would salvage our future—men and women that you helped train, that you helped lead? You won't give them credit for the sacrifice they made? I've believed a lot about you, but never that you were such an ungrateful bastard."

"*Ungrateful?*" he snapped, and stepped towards me. I held his glare, refusing to back down. Fury sparked in his eyes, and I needed to see it. I needed to watch his restraint slip so I could take advantage of it—my last chance to tear down the facade and expose the monster hiding behind his familiar face. "*You* are calling *me* ungrateful?"

"What are you ashamed of, Colonel? You said everything you did was for us. So why lie? Everyone here should know what you've done. You should be *proud* of the steps you've taken to lead us into a better tomorrow. Frankly, the people who died for your cause deserve your pride, don't they? They deserve the honour due to them as soldiers of SMOAC. Not to have died in a basement to spark a social revolution. Not to be seen as the victims of a maniacal chemist following the orders of a crime boss. Because that's not what you told me. Weren't they the tragedy you needed to throw the world off balance and set the gears of your plan in motion? A tragedy engineered by a coward who left them to kill each other and have their brains scrambled by a drug *you* commissioned?"

In the silence that followed, I realized the fighting had

lulled. My troops still defended themselves, keeping Michael's remaining mercenaries off them, but as I scanned the hub, I saw they were all listening. All waiting. Even those—*especially* those—who had remained loyal to the department and to this man who had led them astray.

"Where is Dougall, Michael?" I asked, raising my voice so everyone heard me. "Where is your errand boy? I'm sure he's lurking around here somewhere, no doubt with another ghostbomb waiting to go off. The easy solution as far as you're concerned, isn't it? *Dougall?*"

I projected my voice to fill the space of the hub, and Michael's terrified gaze flickered towards the tunnel where Madison and Colm had followed Gagnon. Fear wrapped around my heart—were they all right? Had they come back?— but I forced my attention to stay on him.

His terror at being found out had given him away, and I allowed myself a smile.

Eric fell in beside me, his lip curled into a snarl. "You son of a bitch."

Michael's expression morphed into rage, his face turning a deeper shade of red. "Fine. You want to hear it again? *Fine!*" He pushed himself away from the wall and closed the distance between us so we stood nose to nose. "I sent your team to die. I gave the order for the bomb to go off. I gave the order for the informants to be killed. Even killed a few of them myself. I did it all. Is that what you want to hear? What does it fucking matter? You've lost, Dawson. This is the end of the line for you. No more slow death. No more suffering. No more chasing me around like a goddamned *dog*."

He shoved me backwards and reached down to grab a discarded rifle. I raised my hands and grabbed hold of the air to thrust him backwards. He wasn't about to win. Not like this. Not now.

But he was faster than I'd expected, and before I could react, he'd aimed the gun at my face. No parasite this time. Just death.

As he fired, Eric slammed into my shoulder, knocking me sideways. For a too-brief moment, his gaze caught mine, and in the rich blue eyes I'd known, loved, for so long, I found so much depth it stole my breath. His regret. His apology. His loyalty at the last.

And then there was nothing. He hit the ground, a gaping hole where the round had torn through his body armour.

His silence, his emptiness, echoed through my shock. A scream squeezed my heart, choked me, but it wouldn't come out. It was stuck, and I bled on the inside, grief and horror spilling through me, tearing me part. The pain was too much. I had to unleash it.

I turned to Michael. His eyes widened, and his hesitation was his final mistake.

I threw myself at him and wrapped a band of air around his neck to pin him against the wall. His already red face turned purple as his windpipe closed off, but I didn't want him dead.

Not yet.

I grabbed the gun from his hand and tossed it well out of reach. He scratched at his neck, but his fingernails passed through the vise squeezing his throat.

Pulling my knife free, I reached for the colonel's stripes on his shoulder. So many honours, so much recognition for the work he'd done. For the crimes he'd committed.

I tucked my knife underneath them, tore them off, and flung them into the pool of blood spreading around Eric's body.

"You've caused so much pain. So much suffering." My own throat closed as my shock wore off. "No more. You've broken my heart for the last time. Give me the chance to return the favour."

He met my eye, and there was no fear in his gaze as, with my bleeding, aching arm, I drove my knife into his chest.

How could he not be afraid?

I was terrified.

Terrified of what it meant to lose him. Of what it meant that I was the one to take his life. Of what my future looked like without him. Without Eric. Without the structure and support that had been the last fourteen years of my life.

As Michael's blood poured over my hands, I realized how delusional I'd been. Throughout everything, in the back of my mind, I'd clung to the hope the world would return to normal if I brought Michael and Gagnon's plans to an end. That somehow everything would go back to the way it was.

Now, as Michael's eyes glazed over and he slumped against the wall, held in place by the band of air around his throat, reality slammed into me, hitting me harder than anything else had.

Shaking, I let go of my knife, and the first sobs filled my lungs. My blood-spattered hands trembled as I stumbled backwards and collapsed next to Eric's body. I reached for his limp fingers, desperate to feel the warmth and strength that had kept me going from our earliest days in the force. The laughs we'd shared at the most challenging moments, egging each other on, pushing each other to do better. To *be* better.

He'd lost faith in me, and I'd let him down, but at the end we'd found each other. One last time, he'd been my rock.

And now he was gone.

Michael was gone.

I bowed my head over Eric's chest and my tears fell.

All around me, the sounds of the fight faded as the last soldiers died or surrendered. With every loss, on our side and theirs, another fragment of my heart shattered into a million unrecognizable pieces, but it was done. The battle was over.

And somehow we had won.

Chapter 35

Madison

Four weeks later...

THE AFTERMATH OF the Labyrinth spread like ripples over the next couple of days.

Every night, my dreams were full of death—from the corpses scattered across the hub and through the tunnels to the empty eyes of the survivors as we'd shuffled, zombie-like, into the humid morning air.

It took no effort to close my eyes and bring myself back to that underpass.

Jet, covered in blood, clinging to Gideon's hand. Gideon, pale and gaunt, with a kaleidoscope of bruises covering his cheeks. Jason, in human form, walked beside me, cradling Colm in his arms. I'd refused to leave Colm in the filthy tunnel until the medics arrived to separate the injured from the dead, and

I couldn't stay behind with him. Not in the middle of all that blood and death and stink. Not with Peter Dougall's corpse staring at us from his slouch against the wall.

Even after four weeks, I hadn't fully recovered my strength from the effort it had taken to overpower the ghost in Colm's blood. Hours, or so it had felt, to slow his seizures. Finally, though, I'd calmed the deluge in his brain, and he'd fallen still. It had taken three days for him to wake up, five before he'd been able to speak to me, and six before Billy had agreed to release him from hospital.

And he'd been one of the lucky ones.

In my film of memory, Zeke walked behind me carrying Eric.

Jet had insisted. Gideon, Zeke, and Jason had all tried to convince her to leave him where he was, that a team would take care of him, but she hadn't moved until Zeke relented.

"I won't leave him with that demon," she'd said, gesturing to Michael, refusing to look at her fallen commander. Him, she'd left in a heap on the ground.

Following Zeke were Luvy and Marc-André, both of them looking ready to collapse themselves, dragging Lucien between them.

The former deputy minister blubbered, unable to muster a single intelligible word beyond, "Oh God, what have I done?" and I used my remaining strength to keep it that way. Soon enough, he'd be out of my reach, and until that time, I wanted him to suffer every drop of pain he'd inflicted on others.

Serc and Lilith met us outside with a small force gathered around them, more than one roughed up from having done their duty to prevent the mercenaries from escaping. The shifter packleader, Naomi, stood next to O'Malley, who her team had captured loading up his car behind The Afterlife. The crime boss was sullen, glowering at the world from under his dark brows, shooting murderous glares at Lucien.

A hush fell over us as the light at the end of the underpass shimmered and a woman appeared, flanked by a dozen guards in dark livery.

For the first time in countless centuries, the queen had crossed the wall.

She wore a dress made of the night sky, or at least that's how it looked to my scattered senses. Blue-black silk with diamonds woven into the skirt. I had to tear my gaze away to avoid losing myself in the stars and falling on my face.

Serc and Lilith bowed low as Meril passed, but no one else bothered. We were too exhausted. Too overcome with too many shocks in too little time.

She stopped in front of me and met my eye. "Well done, blood of my blood," she said, in a voice low enough for only me to hear. "I knew my faith in you was not misplaced. Rest now. There will be time later for us to speak."

While I appreciated her praise, not having expected it— not feeling as though I'd earned it—the weight of her meaning tugged at my already fragile psyche. My pending summons. For everyone else, tonight marked the end of the war, but for me, the true threat remained in my future.

After I'd fought so hard, there was still a chance I would lose everything.

I did my best to set my fears aside and focus on my responsibilities. The night wasn't over yet.

"I bring you two of the traitors, Your Majesty," I said. "The other two are dead."

Meril passed her gaze over the two men, her expression blank, her eyes cold. "Lucien Gagnon," she said, approaching him. "You and I will be spending a great deal of time together in the days to come."

He whimpered and closed in on himself, and O'Malley dropped his gaze to the ground, a wet patch spreading down his leg.

For a moment, I saw Meril as they did, a towering presence of power and wrath, a promise of future agony. When the vision passed, she was once again the queen I recognized, regal and stoic, untouchable and commanding.

Everything our people needed—even those who thought otherwise.

All my life, I'd believed her exclusive rule would be the worst thing for our people, but in that brief vision, in the face of the department's betrayal, I had reason to doubt. Not enough to change my mind about joining the Shadow Council or salvaging the department, but enough to make me understand how much better SMOAC would need to be going forward to make up for all the damage Lucien and Michael had done.

Serc and Lilith bowed again as Meril turned and walked back the way she'd come, her guard escorting Lucien and O'Malley behind her. Then she was gone, the traitors left to their fates.

Even now, a month later, I harboured no regret about sending them over the wall. Nothing the prime minister might have done to them would have been harsh enough. Justice had to be served, and only Meril, queen of our kind, could deliver the proper penalty for their crimes.

I didn't know what sentence she'd delivered. I'd chosen not to find out. Lucien had left me with enough sour feelings, self-doubt, and nightmarish memories, and I didn't need to add to them. I'd promised Serc that no matter how Meril responded, there would be no repercussions from the powers that be on our side of the wall.

Not that he had left me with entirely good news in return. The nature of our fight in the Labyrinth had shaken the structural integrity of the roads over the tunnels. Rideau Street had caved in, taking a city bus with it. Crowds of mundanes had gathered, and only Lilith's people stationed around the area had turned attention away from the lingering evidence of supernatural involvement.

The explanation our communications branch spread

across mundane news outlets was outdated sewer systems, and although questions had popped up through blogs and conspiracy theorists, no one found anything to suggest otherwise.

After he'd delivered his news, Serc had rested his hand on my shoulder. "And you, Madison? How are you doing?"

It had taken me a while to find an answer, but eventually I'd said, "Ask me again in a few days. For now, let it be enough that I'm alive and we won."

If only it were as straightforward as that. The next weeks were filled with paperwork, with laying out the evidence we'd gathered against Lucien and Michael. The correspondence Jet and Gideon had found in their headquarters, the kilos of ghost awaiting distribution in their subterranean lab.

Lucien's employees had been rounded up, made to talk, and brought to Meril for justice along with their leaders, and as far as I knew, none of them had made their way out from behind the wall.

The survivors of the battle, particularly the remaining members of Jet's pack, were brought forward as witnesses to Michael's confession. That evidence alone had been enough to condemn him posthumously, though tears had stained Jet's face throughout the entire examination.

I'd spent days locked behind closed doors with Jet, Jasmin Kaur—the new acting Minister of Supernatural, Magical and Occult Affairs—and the prime minister, detailing everything that had happened, justifying our actions, ensuring all accusations and blame landed where they should.

None of it had been easy, and it wasn't over yet. All of Lucien's and Michael's allies had to be tracked down, exposed, and dealt with, and the deal with FoSA had to be broken off. That, at least, was something everyone in the room had agreed on. The federation would continue, and no doubt thrive, but Canada would not include itself in its expanding union, and we could only hope our stance would serve as a signal to our neighbours across the pond and south of the border.

Most of what was left to do, however, would come later and be out of my and Jet's hands. For a blessed change, we didn't have to be in control of everything.

But with all our progress, the horrors of the battle and the memories of that night threatened to drag me into those tunnels far too often, and my words to Serc, my acknowledgement that I had survived and even come out on top, were all that carried me through the darkness.

Those words and the sunrise we'd walked into as we'd left the underpass. It had been a bright new dawn, and, finally, one we didn't need to fear.

Meril's warning had been our guide more than once, and I'd made a note to myself to send her a gift of gratitude in the weeks to come.

Not only for her aid in our cause, but for the other gift she'd given me. I had neither seen nor heard from her since we'd left the Labyrinth, but after one long, harrowing day of trials and cross-examination, I'd come home to find an Eye outside my condo building. She'd greeted me with a formal bow, but instead of the summons I dreaded, she'd stepped backwards in a gesture of peace.

"The queen sends word. As you accomplished what you promised to do, maintained the authority of the throne, and re-established the reputation of the realm, the Queen of Faerie, her Majesty the Divine Ruler of the Magical Order of Calibne, her Royal Highness Queen Meril has declared you ambassador of the land beyond the wall, tasked with upholding her author ity beyond the realm and serving as a reminder to all our kind that we have only one true queen."

She'd bowed again and disappeared into the shadows of the alley beside the building, and my shaking legs had given out as I'd burst into tears. She'd given me permission to stay, to maintain my position with SMOAC, and to carry on with my life.

And damned if I didn't intend to make the most of it.

"Madison?"

Colm's quiet voice broke into my thoughts, dragged me back to the present, and I shifted away from the kitchen window.

It took me a moment to register where I was. I'd been back in my condo for three weeks, yet I kept expecting to find myself in one safe house or another. Every time I opened my eyes, I was surprised to be at home and have it feel safe again.

Everything as it had been.

Nothing quite the same.

The greatest change, of course, was Colm's presence. He'd stayed with me ever since he'd left the hospital, and I knew deep in my bones he would never leave. Or maybe we would leave this place together and find a new home. Make a fresh start. One with a brighter outlook.

After all, there were no more secrets between us. Every part of my world was open for him to share. The ghost had guaranteed that. Though I'd succeeded in stopping the seizures and kept the overdose from killing him, the drug had erased every last scrap of the perception filter, preventing him from ever closing his eyes to reality. From the way he often zoned out, caught by what appeared to be nothing, I sometimes wondered if he saw more than I did.

A concern, but one I would monitor and assist with however I could.

So far, it hadn't hindered him. He'd taken a job as chief administrator at the expanded Peaview Hospital, a brand new undertaking under the supervision of the department's new minister. Billy and Rita would join him, having proved their usefulness when we'd transported over a dozen wounded supernaturals to Billy's home after leaving the Labyrinth. As soon as Colm recovered and was back on his feet, he would officially draw on his white coat for the first time in years. I'd known it was too perfect a fit for him not to wear one. Another victory in a stream of tragedies. Another anchor to hold on to when the grief threatened to sweep me away.

"Are you ready to go, Deputy Minister?" he asked, his smile as wide and as bright as I'd ever seen it. Love and happiness radiated off him, wiping away my own creeping emotions, and I wrapped myself in his arms, preferring his cheer to my shadows.

"Just about," I said, and reached for my purse and the bottle of Merlot.

Today wasn't a day to linger in the past. It was a day of celebration and recognition.

As I passed by Colm, he stopped me with an arm around my waist, pulling me against him. "You look beautiful," he said. "I couldn't be prouder of you."

I grinned. "Of me? For what?"

"For being you—wise, kind, a constant surprise."

"That's the drugs talking."

"Maybe," he said, but he took the bottle of wine from me, set it on the table, and pulled me closer, "but if that's the case, I can't hold it against them."

He kissed me, a gentle peck that deepened with a simmering, tantalizing heat.

With a moan of regret, I pulled away. "We'll be late."

"I got you a present," he said against my lips. "I planned on giving it to you later, but I don't think I want to wait. Do you?"

My gaze shifted involuntarily to the clock, but the ticking second hand didn't dampen my curiosity.

"What kind of present?"

He let me go and opened the kitchen cupboard. Persephone jumped onto the counter to see what he was up to, and he ran his fingers over her fur as he grabbed one of my grandmother's tea tins.

"For me?" I said when he brought it over. "You shouldn't have."

He grinned. "I thought it was a good choice. After all we've been through, a quiet moment and emotional reset is exactly what we need."

I raised an eyebrow, but my chuckle dried up as I pulled the lid off the tin.

The aroma of lavender and nostalgia wafted towards me, but lying on top, nestled in my grandmother's magical herbal medley, was a ring. Silver band, floral leaf design, with a round diamond flush in the centre.

"It was my grandmother's," he said. "If you like it."

An astonished laugh slipped out of me. "If?"

He reached into the tin to pull the ring out and held it up between us.

"Marry me?"

I took in the depths of his dark eyes, listening to everything they said that his two words implied. Though it didn't take much effort to interpret. With the skill he'd possessed from the beginning, he opened his soul to me, revealing the force of his emotions. They flowed over me, as though I were the sand and he the tide, and I closed my eyes to relish the sensation, the rare feeling of pure, passionate love.

A smile curled the corners of my lips, and I opened my eyes. "Yes," I said. "Of course."

He kissed me again, and I fell into his arms.

We were going to be late, but Jet would have to forgive me.

Chapter 36

Jet

Nervousness coiled through my stomach, a slimy, greasy feeling that left my palms clammy and my mouth dry.

I thought I'd finished with all these crappy emotional reactions. After everything I'd been through, how was I not hardened to a bit of public attention?

But today was an important day, for many reasons, and the pressure was on to make sure everything went smoothly. I owed perfection to so many people, and even if it made me sick, I would do whatever was necessary to deliver it.

I gave myself a last check in the mirror to make sure all my seams and edges were straight, then I grabbed my hat and marched out of the bathroom, heading left to the assembly hall.

It wasn't a room SMOAC used often. Located at the top of the office building, the theatre overlooked the Peace Tower, with the stage at the top of the room and hundreds of seats spread out to face it.

Every single one of those seats was full.

On the stage was a lectern. Behind that lectern was our new acting minister. Although I knew Jasmin to be a hard leader, strict in her values and determined to make changes, she had come with Madison's highest endorsement, and in the four weeks she'd held her position, she'd already made moves that laid the foundation for improvements in how we served our people.

An expansion to our hospital, a necessity following the events in the Labyrinth with so many injured supernaturals, had been the first change, but promises had been made for so much more, and if she followed through, we stood on the brink of a golden age.

"It is never easy," she was saying as I approached the edge of the stage, "to speak ill of the dead. Every person who walks this earth carries a dual list of heroics and villainy. How, when all is said and done, is that list to be balanced by those left behind? Michael Torrence, former colonel of the SMOAC special forces, served his country for thirty-seven years. He was, by all accounts, an outstanding leader, a sound commander, and over his years accrued many medals of honour for his efforts in maintaining the safety and security of Canada's supernatural community."

She frowned.

"Unfortunately, not even a life of good deeds can make

up for the crime of treason, not only against a government but against a population. As I stand before you today, I hereby revoke Colonel Torrence's rank and dishonourably discharge him from our special forces. His memory will serve as a lesson on the evils of ambition and as proof that the department will not stand aside to watch our principles be soiled for the sake of greed."

Even though she'd prepared me in advance for what was to come, I trembled at the announcement. Michael Torrence, dishonourably discharged. He had to be rolling in his grave.

Silence stretched across the room, and she gave her audience a full minute to soak in the news before a smile lit up her face.

"But that is not the only reason we're here today. We would not have known of Michael Torrence's or Lucien Gagnon's actions if not for a woman who stuck to her principles and, at great risk to herself, brought the truth to light and shut down a project that would have had dangerous and extensive repercussions for this country. She demonstrated strength in the face of great challenge, proved her unfailing loyalty to the department and, most importantly, to her people, and showed an extraordinary ability to gain the loyalty of those who follow her. It is with great honour," she said, "that I introduce SMOAC's new commander-in-chief. May I present Colonel Bridget Dawson."

The crowd erupted into applause as I stepped up to the lectern and shook the minister's hand. At the contact, our conversation when she first offered me the position came back to me.

"Congratulations, Jet. And thank you. So much. For everything. But you better not break rank under my watch, understand?"

She'd tightened her grip around my fingers to make her point clear, and I didn't hold it against her. I'd gone rogue. Instead of being punished for it, I'd earned a promotion, but I'd shown my true colours.

I hoped in time she realized she had nothing to worry about. As long as she remembered her priorities.

She stepped aside, her politician's smile firmly in place, and gave me the floor.

I stood behind the lectern, hands shaking, and stared across the room. There were so many familiar faces staring back at me, and so many that should have been there but weren't.

My gaze landed on Gideon where he stood against the back wall, and he winked at me. His being here helped me find my courage, and I raised my chin to stare down the crowd.

"It is *my* honour to stand before you today and accept this command. I served as captain for many years, and they were some of the best of my life. I served with the best, trained the best. And that is why—" my throat closed, and I swallowed hard to clear it "—I have a few other announcements to make. A few other acknowledgements to offer. In view of his courage, his quick thinking, his leadership, his kindness, and his compassion, I am proud and privileged to promote Ezekiel Evers to the rank of captain."

Applause as Zeke climbed the stage, his face flushed to the points of his ears and his handsome, scarred face split into a grin.

"And as a captain is only as strong as his lieutenant—or two—I announce the promotions of both Jason Hughes and Luvy Mirza."

One by one, I brought my surviving team to the stage with me, recognizing each of them for their services rendered and ensuring no one in the department remained ignorant of the sacrifices they'd made.

I curled my fingers around the sides of the lectern. "Before we leave, I have two final things to say. The first is to recognize William Rourke, a man who served this department from the shadows as long as I did in service. Our new information branch, headed by Sergeants Adam Masters and Katie Summers, will be named in his honour. Lastly—" I stopped and clung tighter to my anchor. I had to get this out. Had to stay strong. Just for a few more minutes. "Lastly, I would not be here to accept this promotion if it weren't for the support, loyalty, and friendship of an incredible human being. It's true I've been a soldier for this unit for a decade and a half, but I did not face those years alone. On my first day of training, a man by the name of Eric Sampson took great pleasure in kicking my ass at boot camp." A bubble of laughter rippled through the crowd, bolstering me. "He was the first person to encourage me to climb the ranks. When I made sergeant, he was my master corporal, and when I made captain, he was the only person I wanted by my side as lieutenant. He was loyal, determined, and thoroughly without ambition. He wanted to do the best job he could for the sake of his country and his squad. To the end, he proved himself my right-hand man, and it is with great honour and privilege that I posthumously award him the Medal of Arsheth, the highest honour that can be bestowed to one in service, for his great courage and sacrifice."

The applause rang out, even louder than before, and I closed my eyes as it washed over me. In that moment, he stood beside me, his eyes bright, his smile warm, and I remembered him for what he was: my friend, my lover, my enemy for a time, and, in the end, my saviour.

I wouldn't be here if it weren't for you, I said to him, and then he was gone and I stood alone to deliver his medal to his mother, who pulled me in for such a tight hug, I worried I'd never find the will to let her go.

We had won the day, but our victory hadn't come without a cost. I would never forget the fallen. I would carry their memory close to my heart, bringing them with me as I marched forward into future days.

Chapter 37

Gideon

I OPENED THE door to Jet's apartment, and she stumbled in after me with a stifled laugh. It had been a long day that had stretched into a longer night, with drinks with her squad at Mooney's to celebrate their promotions—and Madison and Colm's engagement. To the surprise of no one.

The buzz of one too many beers left me giddy as I turned on the light, and Jet was more than a little tipsy, though she did her best to hide it.

With a sigh, she leaned against the door to close it and peeled off her hat, throwing it like a Frisbee onto the nearest chair.

"I can't wait to get out of these clothes," she said, tackling the buttons on her uniform one at a time.

"I can help with that." I hooked my fingers around her lapel to draw her closer. With my lips pressed against hers, I undid the top button, freeing one after another until I was able to peel off her jacket. Carefully, not wanting to wrinkle it, I hung it on the coat rack and set to work undoing the buttons of her blouse.

As I went, I pressed a kiss into the crook between her neck and shoulder. Her skin was warm and soft, and I flicked my tongue along her pulse. A moan escaped her as she rolled her head back, giving me more space.

The white T-shirt under her blouse was damp after hiding for so many hours under so many layers, but I didn't remove it yet. She was exhausted and not a little drunk, and it had been an emotional day. Instead, I trailed my lips to hers, savouring the taste of her before I pulled away.

"What do you say to another drink?" she asked as she pulled her blouse off and tossed it over her hat. Her eyes were dark with want, making it so much harder for me to play the gentleman.

"I wouldn't say no," I said. "Allow me."

I went into the kitchen while she disappeared into the bedroom. A few minutes later, she came back in a pair of my boxer shorts and one of my T-shirts. Her hair was loose, her legs bare, and I wanted them around my waist more than I'd wanted anything in days.

She went to the open window to catch the evening breeze, and I met her there with a glass of water. She raised an eyebrow, and I grinned. "What can I say? I've turned into a responsible man."

"Oh really?" She sipped her drink. "Does that mean you're going to obey the minister's orders and go back to New York?"

Some of my cheer fizzled under the reminder. Jet had been lucky to dance under Minister Kaur's accolades for her role in taking down the conspiracy. I, on the other hand, had been pardoned for my involvement and encouraged, most heavily, to scurry posthaste across the border before I caused any more trouble.

Not that what awaited me at home would be all bad. Dark Wire had received my full report only a few days past my deadline and approved the minister's request for me to stay put during the investigation, and while they'd rattled off the expected bullshit about orders and expectations, I'd hung up with the satisfaction that, after helping to eliminate not only the ghost distribution threat but the producer of the damned stuff, I was back in SilverGuard's good books. For now.

"All right." I wrapped an arm around Jet's waist to fit her snugly against me. "So I'm not fully reformed. But I'm working on it."

"I can't imagine what that would look like," she said, her eyes dancing.

Gods, she was beautiful.

A new intensity touched her smile these days, a haunted expression that sometimes creased her brow, but all her cracks, all her fractures and breaks, only made her more spectacular. More perfect for me.

"It looks like a man who would do anything in his power to make you happy," I said, not aware I was going to say it until the words were out. "It looks like a man who will fight by your side whenever you need him, push you to fight harder, and catch you when you fall."

Her eyes softened, but the corner of her mouth curled. "What makes you think I need a man to help me with any of that?"

I swallowed hard as I passed my gaze over her face. "Because I'm asking you for the privilege of letting me."

Her lips parted, and she stared at me as though not believing she'd heard me correctly. She had, she absolutely had, and I wanted her to know it. I wanted her to know I would wait for her sign, and if she gave it, I would never leave her. Not until something stronger than an entire army came to tear us apart.

She carried her demons, but I had mine, too. Carstairs was dead, but he would never be gone. The darkness he'd created would always be there, which was why it was so important to seek out the light. She was my light. All I wanted was to be hers.

"So, you'd… what?" she asked. "Move here? Leave your job?"

Of course she would be practical at a moment like this. It made me love her all the more.

"No," I said with a smile. "I'm not going to throw my independence under a bus and plod after you like a longing pup. That would make both of us miserable. We'll figure it out. Step by step. All I'm saying is I'm not going anywhere. I love you, and I want to be with you."

She pressed her lips together, and although I didn't see refusal or rejection in her eyes, only a return of the love beating in my chest, my sign still waited.

"I've made so many mistakes," I said. "Acted like an idiot. But I promise you, Jet, I'm here. I'm yours. I'll never keep anything from you again."

Her chuckle surprised me, and her eyes grew brighter with a teasing smile. "You're such a goddamned liar."

My breath hitched as her fingers slid through my hair and pulled me in, and I sank into her kiss, taking that as my sign.

AUTHOR'S NOTE

Some people have comfort blankets, or an emotional support stuffed animal.

For four years, I have had this series.

You might think I'm exaggerating, but it's true. These characters have gotten me through some challenging times. They once even saved my life (okay, this is an exaggeration, but they most certainly saved my sanity).

In 2019, I went on my very first writer's retreat. Up in the gorgeous mountains of Gatlinburg, TN, with the lovely Writerly peeps. I was just starting the first draft of this final book, and for three days, I hit my goal of 10k words per day, bringing me well through the first act. It was invigorating. Thrilling, even.

Then came the sad parting and my excitement to get home and pick up where I'd left off on my draft. Maybe I'd be lucky and have the mental capacity to write some extra words on the plane.

Fate, however, had other plans.

The flight out of Nashville was delayed.

And delayed.

And delayed.

I finally made it to Toronto in the small hours of the morning, at which point I was given a voucher for the shuttle to take me to a hotel across town so I could spend the night comfortably until my 6:30a.m. flight to Ottawa.

Being exhausted and starving and stressed beyond belief, the last thing I wanted to do was trek across Toronto, close my eyes for five minutes, only to make my way back to the airport.

So instead, I found a comfortable chair, cracked open my last Coffee Crisp chocolate bar, and did what I could to stay awake.

Throughout this whole adventure (a total of 28 hours awake by the time I finally made it home and into the best shower I've ever had in my life), Jet, Madison, and Gideon kept me company. They were there to hold my hand and endure the final tortures I put them through as I distracted myself from my unpleasant reality. By 4:30 in the morning, Jet and Gideon were at the hospital, and my heart was breaking for Gideon more than for my own frustrations.

Whenever I think of this final book, I think of that night, how three fictional characters (and a curated series soundtrack) helped keep me calm, prevented me from breaking down into panic attacks, and generally made those 28 hours bearable.

Now I share them with you and hope they'll be able to help others the same way.

Thank You for Reading

Thank you so much for taking a chance on an independent author. We're living in a wonderful age where it's easy to upload a book to the internet, but that doesn't reflect the blood, sweat, and tears that go into making a book the best version it can be. It takes time, patience, perseverance, and to have the final result end up in a new reader's hands is the best reward. You are the reason we keep writing, so thank you.

If you enjoyed the read, please help support the author by leaving a review at the retailer where you purchased the book. Reviews make a world of difference for an author, helping us reach new audiences and bringing more people into the worlds you've spent time in.

For exclusive character content, announcements, promotions, and special offers, sign up for Krista's mailing list at https://www.kristawalshauthor.com/newsletter

ACKNOWLEDGEMENTS

So this is it.

The end.

Am I weeping like a little baby as I write this? Yes, yes, I am.

I always cry when I wrap up a series, but this one will be hard to let go. I'm looking forward to new adventures with new people (heck, I already have four projects on the go at the time of writing this), but it'll feel strange not to spend a portion of my day with these three.

I'm going to miss them.

But, as always, I wouldn't be here at all if not for all the people who helped me.

John Wenzel and Karolina Roussakis for revealing Madison's badass self.

Kate Sparkes for cheering me on, demanding more screentime for Colm, and making sure the Ghostmaker finale punched as hard as it could.

The Writerly peeps for giving me the time and space to get those first 30k words written during that amazing weekend in 2019.

Sadie Hall for helping me clean up, polish, and bring this last book to a shine.

Traci Otte and Wendy Smith, beta readers extraordinaire, for catching things everyone else missed and being my earliest, loudest cheerleaders.

My family for being there. It's been a hard year. Especially during the final months of this book's production, but your support allowed me to find the strength to push through and keep to deadlines.

Chris Reddie for being such a wonderful human being. My person, and all that entails.

My daughter, who at the time of writing this has just discovered the word "Yeah," which fills the house with sunny positivity.

My readers for coming with me to the end. I hope you enjoyed the twists and turns, the jumps and scares, the emotional punches and hurdles. I'm grateful for your time, your support, and your encouragement. I look forward to continuing this adventure with you.

About the Author

Known for witty, vivid characters, Krista Walsh never has more fun than getting them into trouble and taking her time getting them out.

When not writing, she can be found reading, gaming, or watching a film – anything to get lost in a good story.

She currently lives in Ottawa, Ontario with her husband, toddler, and epileptic blue heeler.

You can find her at www.kristawalshauthor.com or at the local Second Cup coffee shop... but only if you come bearing a Vanilla Bean Latte, half-sweet.

Other Works by Krista Walsh

The Meratis Trilogy

Evensong

Eventide

Evenlight

The Cadis Trilogy

Bloodlore

Blightlore

Bladelore

The Nayis Trilogy

Veilfire

Dreamfire

Cairnfire (coming soon)

The Dark Descendants

The Invisible Entente prequel novella

Death at Peony House

Song of Wishrock Harbor

Shadows in the Garden Hotel

Howl of the Fettered Wolf

Light of the Stygian Orb

Gods of the Stone Oracle

The Ghostmaker Trilogy

Obscure

Oblivious

Obsolete